Migration to Mars

Migration *to* Mars

It All Started with a Flock of Seagulls

Barry Brown

Supracity
Publishing

Cover art and design by Trevor K. Brown

Supracity Publishing, LLC
www.supracity.com

ISBN 978-0-9830908-3-0
10 9 8 7 6 5 4 3 2 1

Introduction

Isaac Newton's third law of motion states "for every action there is an equal and opposite reaction." Ignorance of this law creates another law called "the Law of Unintended Consequences."

Our earth has provided her children with everything they needed to survive. Since the dawn of time very little has gone unchanged. The animals, who have roamed this beautiful planet for years, enjoyed everything she offered. Man later appeared on the scene and he also worked in harmony with nature for many lifetimes. Then one day, man became dissatisfied with his lot in life. He wanted more. As he gained knowledge in the arts of mathematics, biology, physics and chemistry, he learned that he could mold and shape this world to his liking. Did he have the wisdom to accompany his newfound knowledge? Could he improve upon nature in just a few years what it took centuries to create? Since man decided to take on this monumental task of changing his world, one has to wonder which road did he take? The one where we work in concert with Mother Nature or the one in which we favored chaining Mother Nature to our endless wants and needless whims regardless of the long-term consequences?

Today, our world is full of new and improved technology. We learned to split an atom creating massive amounts of energy, which led to creating nuclear bombs and nuclear waste. Man learned how to manipulate his crops to be able to withstand poisons that kill everything else they touch, and subsequently we are seeing a precipitating rise in certain diseases. We learned how to turn fossil fuels into energy creating enormous amounts of air pollution that we now must breathe. Manufacturing companies found a cheap and easy way to dump their waste products, using our lakes and oceans, causing some of our beaches to be declared unsafe in which to swim. Today, more and more people turn to drinking water out of plastic bottles rather than sipping from a nearby stream. Like a chess master, if we don't take time to figure out our opponent's response to our next move, we will more than likely be put in a losing position.

Migration to Mars is a story of man's short term thinking and how it affected the world in which he lived. His reckless actions culminated to a point where Mother Earth could no longer sustain him. That was when the Law of Unintended Consequences raised its ugly head and forced man from Earth in search of somewhere else to live.

Man fled from Earth to settle on Mars. He thought he could run away and leave his problems back on Earth, but to his dismay the unintended consequences followed him to the Red Planet. There, he was forced to face his own shortcomings and to figure out a way to right the many wrongs his ego and pride had done, not only to the world he inhabited, but also to himself.

Chapter 1

MARS

Month: Gemini
Week: Sol Saturday
Day of Month: 7
Year: 0012

Thornton Residence
Domette 64
Dao Vallis, Hellas Planitia
Hellas Quadrangle, Mars
1900 hours

A streak of fire burned through the Martian atmosphere illuminating the nighttime sky over a kilometer wide as it passed the Gale Crater where Ken and Tima Thornton lived. The blazing inferno was on a mission of destruction as it traveled low across the Martian skyline. The fire trailed a huge burning ball of ocean blue plasma half a kilometer wide and two kilometers long with its tail extending out from the depths of hell itself. The flaming orb arced in a strange, unnerving way as it covered the entire sky and demanded its rightful place supreme over all other night sky objects. It soon found its destination and slammed into the Martian's main military base located on top of Aeolis Mons. The tremors rumbled through the Martian soil in all directions creating clouds of red dust a kilometer wide billowing up into the outer Martian atmosphere.

The domette homes located around the blast radius cracked under the intense gyrations created by the explosion. Many people died that night as the toxic Martian atmosphere invaded and destroyed any living thing it found. The atmospheric temperature shot up to over a thousand degrees Celsius as the sparks and flickering lights shot out from ground zero in every direction, melting any domettes within its reach. The yellowish white inferno was brighter than the sun itself. The flames continued to engulf the Martian sky to such a degree that it could be seen for kilometers.

Tonight would be a display of raw power never seen before on the Red Planet. Only seconds before impact, the deadly plasma fireball from Hell passed directly over the Thornton's domicile sending out its death rays in every direction. Fortunately for Ken and Tima it ignored their little home and surrounding village as it continued its death swirl. The Thornton's residence however, fought off the intense heat as best as it could, but the damage sustained was enough to question its lasting integrity. The rays emitting from this low flying comet of death passed through the skylight illuminating the entire living room. The flash hit Tima's eyes with intensity brighter than a welder's torch. Tima had been resting in her lazypod sipping tea watching the meteor showers when she encountered the blistering white light. The sudden pain caused her head to turn but it was too late. The unwelcome intruder found her and dug deep into her retinas as it quickly invaded and burned every nerve ending it encountered. The swelling and the pain that followed were excruciating.

"Oh my god!" Tima screamed.

Ken had been busy fighting with a defective Elotec actuator in his lab when the bright light lit up his office followed by a loud explosion shaking Mars to a point where he thought it was a marsquake. The house rumbled in complaint as his lab instruments fell all around him. He dropped the actuator to the floor and headed toward the screams. The domette was still shaking as Ken ran out of the lab and was soon stopped by an overturned dining room table blocking his way to the living room.

"Tima? Are you okay?" he asked as he moved the table away from him.

"The power's out!" she yelled to her husband.

"No it's not," Ken replied. He stopped short, noticing drops of a silvery-looking liquid substance splattered across the floor. "What in the world is..." and then he looked at the skylight. "Oh no!"

The window to the stars had been partially melted from the intense heat thrown from the passing ball of fire. He feared the compromised skylight would not be able to hold back the hostile Martian atmosphere for much longer. His gaze quickly centered on Tima. He saw her in the recliner with her hands holding her head as she rocked back and forth. As the rumblings continued, Ken's coffee cup sitting back in his lab decided to leave the safety of the table and crashed to the metal floor below. Tima jumped from the noise and turned toward the direction of the lab. Ken's body went limp as he looked on in horror when he saw the stillness in Tima's eyes. They stared at him, wide open, unblinking. They were as motionless as a summer pond.

"It's my cup in the other room. I think my coffee is probably all over the lab floor now," he said absent-mindedly as he was trying to make some sense of what was happening.

Tima's fingers gripped the arm of her red lazypod chair and she turned her head to the side. She reminded Ken of what his dog, Sparkle, used to do when she heard something moving in the yard back on Earth. "Do you feel something?"

Ken stood as still as a cornered mouse and seconds later he knew exactly what was coming. "Aftershocks!" he yelled.

The Martian residences were built mostly underground with a Plexiglas dome as a roof to let in the sun's warming rays. A tremor could easily cause an entire Martian home to collapse but no one ever had considered the possibility since Mars, unlike Earth, has no tectonic plates. Today had become the worse nightmare to the new Martian colonists. The domettes lying within ten kilometers of the impact zone collapsed killing thousands of unsuspecting Martians.

"Ken, where are you?" Tima asked and reached out in front of her with arms and fingers spread wide as they groped for a nearby table. Ken couldn't find his voice. He was usually the take-charge kind of guy, but when he saw her so helpless, it took his breath away.

"Ken?" Tima's words shook him back to reality. He felt the floor once again shake as the dishes complained about the disturbance. He rushed over to Tima and held her tight.

"What are you doing?"

"Be still," he said as the whole domicile rattled. They felt the floor rumble all around them. The pictures soon gave up their places on the wall and fell with a resounding crash.

"What's going on?" Tima demanded.

"We need to get to Sanctuary."

"Are we being attacked?"

"I don't know." Another rumble shook the house as their lamps now joined the pictures as they crashed to the floor.

"It's the Terra Bulls isn't it?" Tima screamed. "They killed my parents and now they're after me!"

"Calm down! We left them on Earth, remember?" Ken stroked her hair and whispered in her ear. "Don't lose your head, I need you."

"Where's Togo and Tiga?"

"In their room playing last time I saw them," Ken said and looked down the hallway. "I don't know how long the skylight is going to last so we gotta go." He helped Tima off the floor gently lifting her to her feet. "This way." Ken grabbed her hand and pulled her toward the bedrooms.

Tima and Ken quickly, but cautiously, navigated their way through the living room's wreckage of scattered broken glass, overturned tables, and chairs creating multiple barriers between the parents and their children. Holding on to Ken's hand Tima did her best to keep up but her feet and legs kept tripping over picture frames and lamps angered for being pushed around and knocked over. Tima's foot caught an overturned chair leg near the hallway throwing her face down to the floor. Ken stopped in his tracks when he felt her hand leave his with a jerk.

"Go! I'll catch up!" she yelled.

Ken knelt down beside Tima. "We gotta keep moving," he whispered in her ear and waited for her to regain her senses.

"I'm okay," she said as she struggled to regain her balance.

Ken grabbed her with both hands and quickly pulled her to her feet. "Come on!" The adrenaline pushed through his veins as he hurried toward the bedrooms with Tima in tow.

"You have to slow down some!" she yelled out as her bruised and beaten feet, legs and toes complained.

BANG!

"Ouch!" Tima's foot caught something slippery on the floor sending her head and shoulder into the wall. She fell to the ground losing Ken's grip once again.

"We're almost there!" Ken said.

"Just go!" Tima screamed in frustration and with one hand motioned Ken to continue. He stubbornly waited and looked down the hallway to where the kids' bedroom lay. With both hands pressed against the cold hard metal floor Tima picked herself up and gripped the wall using it as an aid to help her to her feet. Once up, she took a couple of steps and noticed her gait was unstable as dizziness overtook her. Ken quickly grabbed her left hand and pulled her as they both stumbled toward the back bedrooms. The pounding in her head had now reached epic proportions as she instinctively felt the top of her head only to find a nice sized lump.

"Ouch!" she said as she quickly removed her fingers from the injury.

"What's wrong?" Ken asked.

"Nothing," Tima sighed. "We need to get our babies."

As soon as they reached the children's bedroom, Ken saw the house light up with the same evil fire and unholy brimstone brightness as before.

Another blue plasma ball of hellfire passed by the Thornton household on its way to the Martian Government Center located in Syrtis Major. The blast destroyed the entire government facility bringing the new Martian colonists to their knees. No government to lead them and no military to protect them anymore.

"GET DOWN!" Ken screamed as he felt another tremor begin beneath his feet. He placed his arms around Tima and pulled her to the floor and covered her body with his. A few seconds later, a distant boom resonated throughout the house followed by the now familiar rumblings. More pictures and lamps smashed to the ground. Hearing the distant noise Ken peeked down the hallway and saw the chandelier as it swung back and forth like an angry scythe. He hoped it was secure enough to withstand this mighty onslaught. But as fast as Satan's demons came for a visit, they left as quickly. *But for how long?* He looked around the house and felt an eerie stillness. It was like being caught in the eye of a hurricane and having to suffer once more the uncontrolled fury of wind and rain as it punishes you one last time before it makes its way toward some other unsuspecting victim.

"Kenny? I'm scared."

"It'll be okay," Ken reassured her as they lay huddled together waiting for the room to calm itself. The Thornton's house was finally quiet except for the ticking of the cuckoo clock as it defiantly stood its ground.

"Kenny?"

"Okay, I think it is safe now." Ken cautiously helped Tima to her feet. He looked around the room and wondered what kind of horror had happened to them, their neighborhood, and Mars.

"What was that?" Tima asked.

"I don't know but we gotta keep moving," Ken said and walked briskly to the bedrooms with Tima in tow.

"Kenny! What could be so bright to blind me? Kenny?"

Ken pulled her along with him as they turned the corner leading to the bedrooms.

"Kenny? Are you listening to me?"

"What?"

"Why are we getting these shockwaves?"

"We're almost there," Ken said and pulled out his PeeP, shook it, and seconds later a bright light emanated. "That's better."

"Tell me!" Tima yelled.

"Tell you what?"

"The shockwaves."

"What about the shockwaves?"

"Why are we...?"

"I don't know!...Togo! Tiga! Are you in there?" Ken yelled outside the kids' bedroom door. He placed his hand on the scanner. "Damn it!" With both hands he pushed against their door.

"What's wrong?" Tima asked.

"It's blinking red. The door's stuck. The tremors must have shorted the pad."

"Use the override switch."

"I tried, but the hinges are damaged and unless I can somehow release the pressure, the override switch won't work. We've got to release some of the stress or this door isn't going anywhere."

"But Togo and Tiga are in there. What are we going to do?"

"If I could somehow break those hinges, it should take enough pressure off the door and allow the override switch to work." He took a step back and threw his shoulder against the bent metal, but nothing happened except for the searing pain that radiated from the impact. "Ouch!" He rubbed his arm.

"What's wrong?"

"Nothing." He took another step back and again slammed his body against the door. A short blast of pain reminded him that his body wasn't as young as it used to be. He knew time was short and something had to be done quickly, but what?

"Hurry!"

"Tima, I can't get it open."

"What do we do?"

Ken stared at the mangled door and watched the scanner blinking red. *Think man. You've gotten yourself out of worse messes than this.*

"Kenny?"

"What?"

"What are you doing?"

"Nothing!"

"You can't do nothing? You gotta do something."

Ken turned to Tima. "Like what?"

"I don't know but we can't just stand here and…"

"Shhh…I'm trying to think." *The hinges are forcing the door against the frame and that's causing the override switch to fail. The hinges are bent and if I could remove just one hinge, it should be enough to reduce enough stress to open the door. But I can't think of anything to break the hinge. This new alloy was made to be pliable in order to prevent this exact thing from happening. A hammer is no good. The hinges will just take the impact and bounce back. A crowbar won't work because the hinges would stretch and simply return. I just can't think of…*

"The hinges, they need to come off," Ken said.

"How about burning them off?"

"With wha…? That's it! Tima, go get my spot laser."

"Spot laser?"

"Yeah, it should be able to melt the hinges enough for me to break down the door. You've got to get to the lab and bring me my spot laser."

"I can't see anything, why don't you…?"

"That last tremor took out the power grid and all I have is my PeeP. The emergency generator should be on by now, but it's not and I need to find out why."

"But."

"Look, I wouldn't ask you if it wasn't important. I need to make sure the generator hasn't blown a fuse. Like I said, it should have kicked in by now. Go! I'll be back by the time you return."

"It's starting to get cold in here," Tima remarked.

"It's going to get a lot colder if I don't fix that generator," Ken said in a worried tone. "Now go!" Ken gave her a gentle shove toward the lab. "We need to free this door and get the kids. Time is our enemy. I don't know how long that skylight can last. Now go get my spot laser. It's in my jacket by the lab door. Hurry!" Ken noticed Tima still hadn't moved. He gave her another little push in the direction of the lab. Tima stumbled down the hall feeling her way through the living room and then past the dining room as she felt her way to the lab. She walked in with arms stretched feeling for the coat rack, but it wasn't there.

"This doesn't feel right," she said aloud. *Ken's lab always has this funny smell to it* she thought to herself as her hands now moved along the countertops until she felt some knobs.

"Damn it! I'm in the kitchen!" Tima felt her way back out into the dining room and finally into the lab. She was so focused on not falling she forgot what he had said. She unconsciously flipped on the light switch, but nothing happened and even if it had, she wouldn't have known. She moved cautiously over to the work desk and waved her hands back and forth as she made her way slowly down the counter. *Now where did he say that laser thingy was?* Her hands started to shake as she pulled on the drawer. The desk drawer now twisted by all the commotion hesitated and then quickly opened causing her foot to slip on Ken's spilt coffee. Her other foot gave way as she reached out to catch her fall but it was too late. Her body hit the floor hard and she heard glass break underneath her as something sharp impaled her skin cutting deep into her thigh.

"Ouch!" she cried out. In the darkness, she grabbed the countertop and pulled herself to her feet only to feel some blood as it found its way down her leg and soaked her shoe. She cut her little finger on the shard of glass deeply embedded in her leg as she carefully pulled it out. "Oh my god! What else could go wrong?" she said to the ceiling above as her voice began to shake.

I've got to calm down and find that stupid laser, she thought to herself. She continued her search as a few renegade tears crawled down her cheek. *Time is our enemy* she remembered Ken saying. "I know. I know," she said to herself as she felt her way through the desk's drawers.

"Ken!" she called out, but she knew he couldn't hear her. *Okay, relax now and think. Now what did he say? Exactly?* She could feel her heart pounding and she started to feel a little light headed as the blood continued down her leg pooling on the lab's floor. She knew that the lives of her little ones hung in the balance as she continued her search for Ken's spot laser.

"Togo, Tiga," she said aloud and that unnerved her to a point she started to shake again. *I can't help them if I don't stop and concentrate.* With that resolve she slowly thought back to the conversation. *I can't break the door free and it needs to be burned off with the spot laser. I don't have enough time... the spot laser is... where...where did he say it was?* She felt some more of the aftershocks as they rumbled through the house. *The spot laser is, is, it's in my...my...coat? No! My jacket near the door!* She felt her way back to the lab's entrance, grabbed the first jacket she found and rifled through the pockets. She pulled out the spot laser and stumbled back through the house.

Halfway through the dining room she tripped over a table chair causing her to fumble the spot laser as she fell to the ground. She raised her head and heard the laser as it effortlessly bounced down the hallway.

Ken stood, looking at the silent generator. He noticed the fuse switch was turned to off. Ken flipped it back on and nothing happened.

"Damn it!" Ken checked the connections for the usual problems but nothing was afoul. He grabbed the handle and did a few emergency pulls when finally the generator kicked in. The lights came on all around the house, but as soon as Ken turned to go, the lights went out again. "I don't have time for you!" Ken shouted at the fickle machine and ran back to the bedroom door with a hammer he found sitting next to the silent metal beast.

"Togo? Tiga? Are you two alright in there?" Ken yelled from the other side of the door. Nothing. *What is taking her so long?* "Tima?" he yelled down the hall as he continued to wrestle with the door. He hit the hinge with the hammer and watched as the hinge effortlessly bounced back. "I knew it!" he said aloud in frustration. "I need that spot laser. Where in the hell is Tima?"

A few minutes later, Ken heard some noise in the hallway. *I've got a bad feeling about this* he thought to himself and turned to walk down the corridor in the semi-darkness guided only by the light coming from his

PeeP. His foot kicked something and sent it railing towards the other end of the hallway. *What was that?* He moved his PeeP slowly to where he heard the noise. The light soon uncovered his faithful spot laser leaning against a broken lamp.

"Tima?" he shouted.

"I'm okay!" she yelled back as the pain in her thigh worsened. She put her hand on the injury and then said in a much-lowered voice, "Well, maybe not that okay."

With laser in hand, Ken ran back to the bedroom. Just like an old friend, he pressed and held the switch knowing it wouldn't let him down. He waited. As the seconds passed he could feel the power gathering until all at once the familiar blue flame burst into life. He cautiously placed the tip of the flame on the first hinge. He could see the hinge begin to glow bright red and he felt its heat. A small thin line began to form on the metal and he knew it would soon give way. Ken slammed once again upon the now weakened and compromised door and he watched the top hinge release, but the door stood firm.

"Open!" he cried out in desperation. He moved the spot laser to the bottom hinge and watched the blue fire find its victim. Minutes, which seemed like hours, passed when he finally saw the familiar cut line appear on the hinge.

"Togo! Tiga! If you can hear me move to the back wall!" Ken readied himself. He slammed his body against the door and this time the door admitted defeat as it creaked and came down hard on the floor with Ken on top. Bits of hot metal exploded into Togo and Tiga's bedroom lighting up the room like an Independence Day sparkler. The generator groaned and finally kicked in as a faint light crawled across the domette.

Ken picked himself off the door and looked around the empty bedroom. "Togo! Tiga! You guys in here?" Ken tried to control the fear in his voice. *If they're not here? Where could they be?* Something grabbed him from behind. "What the...?" he jumped and turned around and there was Tima holding onto him. He looked down and saw a red puddle on the floor. He noticed his shirtsleeve had turned the same shade.

"You're bleeding." Ken pulled a couple of rags he had been using to clean his equipment out of his pocket and wrapped them around Tima's leg. "That should stop the bleeding for now." He tightened the cloth as much as he dared.

"Ouch!"

"Sorry."

"Are they clean?"

Ken looked down at the rags with streaks of grease and spots of red dirt falling off her leg. "Of course, dear."

"Uh huh."

"What happened?"

"Long story. Do you have the kids?"

"They're not here," The pain in Ken's shoulder escalated. He wondered for a minute if something was broken.

"No? Where could they be?" Tima moved her hands in front of her.

"Togo! Tiga! Where in heaven's name are you?" Ken called out.

All of a sudden, two little pillows popped up from behind the bed. Togo and Tiga had covered their heads with their pillows pulled down on both ends. They looked like two big marshmallows with faces.

Tiga was the first to answer. "Mommy! Daddy! My toys fell off the shelf and…"

"It's okay!" Ken could see the fear in their eyes as they danced back and forth. They wanted to run, but their little feet wouldn't budge and they stood like they were caught in quicksand.

"Come here you two, we've got to get to the DTs!" Ken reached over the bed for Tiga's arm. Tima put both hands on the bed and felt for Togo. With Togo's help, she found his hand and they both ran from the bedrooms down the hallway. Ken, leading the pack, stopped at the end of the hallway and waited for the rest of his family to pass as he reached up and pressed the half-dollar-sized flashing red emergency button located on the wall next to him. Ken watched as the security door slammed shut sealing off the bedrooms from the rest of the house.

"Pressure lock secured"

came the computerized voice.

No going back now, Ken thought to himself.

As the loss of blood started to affect Tima's sense of balance she could hear another rumble knowing that seconds later, the living room would be in danger of collapsing under the force of the tremors. Ken saw the room light up with that same eerie glow as before. He could see the cracks forming on the walls as they desperately tried to hold back the Martian atmosphere but the evidence was unmistakable. They were losing the battle.

"Not again!" Ken said as the floor began to shake. Tima squeezed Togo's little hand.

"Ouch, that hurts!"

"GET DOWN!" Ken yelled. "NOW!"

The entire family hit the floor as another flash lit up the sky followed by more explosions. The shockwaves shook the entire house down to its foundation. Togo looked up and saw multiple cracks lining the kitchen wall and it reminded him of little tributaries he had studied back in school.

"Mommy, the walls are leaking!"

"This can't be happening!" Tima screamed.

"The DTs are just ahead. Let's go!" Ken rose to his feet.

The little entourage found their way toward the kitchen as the dishes leaped off the counters and crashed to the stone floor below. The rumblings continued shaking the house as the dining room chandelier swung violently back and forth throwing shards of broken glass in all directions.

Before Ken knew it, another rumbling shook the walls followed by more sounds of angry dishes as they joined their friends on the hard floor.

"Oh no! That sounded like my grandmother's…." A tear fell from Tima's cheek. She could hear the cascade of glassware and china as they continued their onslaught against the kitchen surface. Soon the pots and pans came out to join the chorus. "We've got to get out of here before that skylight cracks," Tima said holding both Togo and Tiga. "Kenny?"

"I'm going as fast as I can. Just a few more minutes."

Ken opened the closet door, bent down on one knee and pushed the spacesuits to the side revealing a small hatch on the wall sitting on the floor with a metal handle and he smiled. Soon his family would be on their way to Sanctuary. He'd never used the Down Tubes before and had hoped he would never have to. He looked around their house one last time and saw Tima next to him on the floor with his children in her embrace.

"Time to go," Ken reached down, but before he could grab the hatch, the lights went out again. *What else can go wrong?* he mumbled to himself as he felt for the handle.

Tiga started to cry and Togo clutched even harder to Tima making her even more lightheaded than she already was. Tima pulled her little ones to her breast and started to sing, "Hush little baby don't say a word, Momma's gonna buy you a mocking bird." She noticed that Tiga's crying slowed to a whimper, but she still held her tight as she continued, "and if that mocking bird don't sing, Momma's gonna buy you a ...," she stopped in mid-sentence as a loud creak echoed from the living room. Seconds later, the cuckoo clock jumped off the wall and joined its friends scattered across the hard metal floor. Tima tried her best not to cry as her favorite little clock she brought from Earth was no more. She was going to miss hearing that little cuckoo bird sing its song during the day. As the tears made their way down her cheeks, she valiantly continued her little song, the one that her mother sang to her when she was scared. "...Momma's going buy you a diamond ring..."

"Aarrggh!" Ken yelled out.

"Kenny. What's taking so...?"

"It's stuck!" He pulled and twisted with all his might, but the escape hatch wasn't going to budge.

"Kenny?"

"NO!" The night sky lit up once again. Ken looked around at his little family huddled close together and felt a deep pain inside his soul, because he knew that there was nowhere else to run.

Chapter 2

MARS

Thornton Residence
Domette 64
Gemini - Sol Friday 6, 0012
1600 hours

(One Day Earlier)

"When will Bedipida and Grandma be coming over? I'm hungry," Togo asked as he wandered around the kitchen. "Are we having something special?"

"Yes, we are, honey. As a matter of fact, I've been experimenting with some exotic spices lately. We have been growing chives and I want to try them out tonight. You guys will be the first to have Martian chives!" Tima replied excitedly.

"How do they taste?" Ken asked.

"I don't know."

"So we're your test subjects now?" Ken smiled.

Vegetables were the staples in the Thornton household like all other Martian homes. Livestock demanded too much food and gave back too little to be a viable option on the Red Planet. Cows returned only one pound of meat for every sixteen pounds of grain and soy they ate. The other fifteen pounds were used by the animal or excreted. Ten years ago, the World Cattlemen's Association screamed of discrimination and demanded that their BuffaPrimes be allowed transportation to Mars. The Ministry of Agriculture refused; even a chicken's average ratio was seven pounds of grain and soy per one pound of edible food. After careful deliberation, a decision of four to three was handed down that no animals were to be allowed on Mars. Martian real estate was too valuable to have animals roam the planet for the mere purpose of enjoying a steak and egg every now and then.

"They should be here by now," Ken replied. "Any later and it will be too cold. It's already forty below."

"I think I hear them!" little Tiga said. A big grin appeared on her face.

Togo jumped off his blue metal chair and ran to the pneumatic door. The metal behemoth towered over Togo as he waited patiently for compression.

"It's starting!" Togo said as he watched the compression numbers climb.

The digital readout beside the door began –

50 millibars... 200...600...800...1000

The readout stopped.

Ding!

rang the bell.

"Can't we get another ding?" Tima asked.

"It is annoying, isn't it?" Ken smiled. "It reminds me of those old stove timers when dinner was ready."

"Air Pressure – 1015 Millibars – Please Stand Back."

stated the computerized voice.

Ding! Dong!

"Togo! Get away from the door!" Tima yelled. No sooner did the familiar hiss sound along with a puff of exhaust smoke eke out as the door slid into the wall.

"It's about time!" Yeri said as he walked into the room with his wife, Beth, at his side.

"Bedipida!" Togo barreled toward his grandpa with arms stretched, full speed and burrowed into his stomach.

"Whoa there, partner!" Grandpa Yeri said. He put his arms around Togo. "You're getting too big for this. One day you're going to knock me back outside!"

"Oh, Grandpa," Togo held on tightly.

Grandpa Yeri Thornton was pushing seven feet in height, balding early with gray hair around the temples, which gave him a wise scholarly look. He had graduated with top honors in medical school and followed after his father's footsteps in the science of genetics.

Ken greeted his father. "Hey Dad! Dinner will be ready in about an hour."

"I never thought we would ever get here. Your lift is awfully slow. I've seen rock climbers climb faster than this thing. Is it broken?"

"No," Ken said.

"Are you still using the old G-2000?"

Ken nodded.

"Don't you think it's about time for an upgrade? I just had the G-4000 installed last month and it compresses in half the time, not to mention..."

"Dad! You told me all about it last week, remember? I told you we're waiting for the prices to come down a bit. It's too expensive right now."

"They're still making the G-3000. It's not as fast as the four, but certainly a lot faster..."

"Dad!" Ken interrupted in frustration.

"You don't know what you're missing, Son." Yeri unzipped his suit and stepped on to the copper metal floor. "Tima, this floor was silver last time I was here. New?"

"Yeah. The kids put so many dents in the old one that we decided to upgrade to the Ziliar plus. It's a centimeter thicker and that should take care of most of the dents. It's guaranteed or they'll replace it for free."

"They better for the price you paid," Grandpa interjected.

"Do you like it?" Tima asked.

"We don't need new flooring for the two of us. Is the floor always this cold?" Grandpa Yeri removed his other shoe.

"It's the compression exhaust from the lift. They piped it directly underneath us. It'll warm up in a few minutes."

Yeri shook his head. "You should have gone with the Triple-A dome instead of the... what plan did you choose?"

"A plus," Ken said. "Can we talk about something other than upgrades?"

"What did you bring me?" Togo butted in.

"Let's see what I got here," Yeri reached in his pocket and jingled it for a few minutes. He made a face and stuck his tongue out the side of his mouth.

"Come on, Bedipida."

"I think I brought it with me," Yeri looked at his wife. "Beth? Did I forget his birthday present again?"

Beth shook her head and returned to the conversation with Tima. "Isn't copper in short supply?" Beth moved her foot back and forth on the floor.

"It's actually iron even though it looks like copper. Mars is rich in iron you know and it went on sale a few weeks ago so we said what the heck. Anything to replace all those dents."

"Did you have to go somewhere while they installed it?"

"They put it in while we were at work and the kids at school."

"You know iron rusts, don't you?" Yeri interjected.

"It comes with a sealant," Tima turned to Beth. "Is he always this bad?"

"Sometimes he's worse, but for the red dust on me I can't remember when."

Tima shook her head and went to the kitchen. "I think the timer is beeping."

"Is dinner ready yet?" Yeri sang out in harmony with timer.

"Almost! I have a surprise for you guys tonight! We are having chives with dinner."

"I don't like chives," Yeri said, "and I don't like being a guinea pig either."

"You have become one old ornery coot in your old age. You know that?" Tima said with a smile. She and Beth walked toward the kitchen.

"Drinks?" Ken asked as he followed the girls.

"Sure," Yeri answered. He waited until Ken was out of sight and turned to Togo. "Now that we're alone, I have a secret present just for you!" Yeri said in a hushed voice to Togo.

Togo watched as Grandpa Yeri continued fishing around in his pocket until he could no longer stand it. "Bedipida!" Togo shouted.

"Okay, okay. I think I got it." He pulled his hand out of his pocket and placed the strange object in Togo's right hand. "Do you like it?"

"What is it?" Togo turned over the metallic contraption.

"It's called a jimmy, it's a universal key."

"It looks like a pencil. What do you do with a jimmy?"

"Open locks."

"Can it lock things too?"

"Yes it can."

"Cool. How does it work?" Togo stared at the pencil looking device.

"You insert it in a lock or place it against a keypad and then wait. It will tell you when it's ready. This key was built long ago from nano technology."

"Nano what?"

"Subatomic technology. A jimmy uses particles so small we can't see them. Our scientists back on Earth found a way to harness them. They built these keys using quantum physics. Dr. Baxter used a particle accelerator sending tetraquarks and baryons into a ..."

"What?" Togo interrupted.

Yeri could see the confused look on his grandson's face. "Um. Let's just say the jimmy here scans any lock it encounters and then it figures out how to open it. It can mimic retina scans, hand scans, and thumb prints. It can even open up a combination lock. It is very versatile."

"How come I've never seen one?" Togo asked.

"There were only seven made. The Companions used them mostly when they needed to uncover a Terra Bull plot. Before we colonized Mars the Sevens told everyone they had destroyed the keys, but in reality they just sent their jimmies to Mars so we could finish the buildings before they arrived. Of course the Sevens never made it."

"Did anyone ever figure out what happened?" Togo asked

Yeri shook his head.

"Why didn't we just use retina scans like on Earth?" Togo asked.

"The problem was the retina scans couldn't be used to enter Martian buildings because the faceplates on our suits would distort the scans. It wasn't until we installed airlocks were we able to remove our helmets, which made having the keys basically obsolete. They told us that the keys were destroyed but some people here on Mars decided they wanted them for their own, um personal uses."

"Who?"

"Some really bad people. They wanted them so they could do mean things."

"How did you get this one?" Togo asked

"A friend gave it to me and told me to hide it and now I am giving it to you to hide. Okay?" Yeri whispered in his ear.

"What's going on between you two?" Ken asked as he walked back into the living room with a couple of potato vodka shots. He handed one to Yeri and turned on the holovision.

"Is the game on tonight?" Yeri asked.

"The 1962 NBA Championship. It should be a good one," Ken replied. "The Boston Celtics are taking on the L. A. Lakers."

"Do you know who is going to win?"

"Ha! I wish. No one knows the outcome of Earth's sports history. If they ever released the scores early it would kill advertiser money. I mean, who would want to watch a game knowing the outcome?" Ken asked.

"Some people know," Yeri responded. "Last year I threw the 1961 NBA Championship sports party and a friend of mine brought her new boyfriend, Curtis. He knew all the stats and games and kept interrupting everyone telling us the outcomes. He ruined the whole night."

"I don't remember you ever talking about Curtis."

"No one talks about Curtis." Yeri smiled. "Not even his ex-girlfriend."

Ken laughed. "I went to a movie with a friend of mine who had seen it before and halfway through it he told me how they did it. That's an hour of my life I'll never get back."

"Some people just can't keep their big mouths shut," Yeri shook his head and took a sip of his povka. "You know, this would make four in a row if the Celtics win this one."

"I didn't know you were such a big NBA fan."

"Not really, but it's something to pass the time."

"So, who do you think is going to win?" Ken asked.

"I know who is going to win."

"Curtis?"

Yeri nodded.

"So, what were you and Togo talking about earlier?" Ken asked.

"Oh, nothing much. Togo was telling me about school," Yeri said and gave Togo a wink.

"Uh huh."

Yeri took another sip of his potato vodka. "This is some pretty good povka."

"I picked some up on my way home last night. They were out of Jacks so I splurged and bought a bottle of Antoniadi."

"That's what I drink."

"It's a little pricey for us but I said what the heck."

"How's work?"

"We had a couple of ReDS go down last week," Ken remarked.

"ReDS?" Yeri asked.

"Sorry. Relay energy Distribution Station. It's how we get power from the generators to your homes."

"Oh. So why are they going down?"

"We switched to a new company called Elotec," Ken paused. "I've had to replace three faulty Elotec actuators this month. They tell us there is no difference between the old Martex ones and these new ones. Humph!"

"You don't think so?"

"This morning I had a meeting with Caroline, my boss. She has been screaming at me on a daily basis about all the overtime my men are using. I argued that if a ReDS goes down it causes power outages and without power people can die."

"Why did they change manufacturers?"

"I heard the Minister of Defense was behind it all."

"What does he care?"

"He wants more Krugers to fight the Halks."

"The Halks?"

"That's the story, but word on the street is he has a partial interest in Elotec."

"Really?"

"Yeah, they make space gloves, suits and these crappy actuators we are forced to use now," Ken said and took a big swallow of his potato vodka drink. "Are you ready for another povka?"

Yeri nodded.

"I'll be back with the bottle."

"Sounds like a really rough day for you," Yeri said.

As Ken headed for the kitchen Togo elbowed Granddad and whispered, "Where did you get the key?"

Yeri downed his remaining povka. "That's some really good stuff."

"Bedipida!"

"Okay, okay. I got it from an old Earth friend. Earlier this morning your grandma sent me to Frankie's Clothiers. She said I needed a new dinner jacket. I was rummaging through the discount bin at the Mall when…"

Hellas Chaos Mall
Hellas Chaos, Mars
6 hours earlier

"Hallo Yeri. Lange nicht gesehen."

"Hi." Yeri turned to see a man wearing a black leathertex jacket with a hood pulled low, covering most of his face. His collar was up and he wore a pair of dark glasses.

"Maltido. Danny Maltido. Remember me?" Danny whispered in a British sounding voice.

"Maltido?" Yeri shook his head. "Sorry."

"The German bar back on Earth?"

"Danny Maltido? I thought your name was… oh never mind. I can't remember what I had for breakfast this morning. It has been a long time. It's good to see you too!" Yeri said and was quiet for a minute. He stared at the white metal ceiling above Frankie's. "Yes, yes yes! I do remember you," Yeri returned Danny's gaze. "You were talking about working with some advanced theories in quantum factorizations? Crypto-something or another? Did you ever figure out those algorithms?"

"Yes! With some help," Danny said and smiled. "Actually with a lot of help."

Yeri returned his grin. "I bet! That was a late night wasn't it? Do you remember the name of that place? I think it was called…Some Song or something like that?"

"Nussbaum?" Danny corrected. "Zum Nussbaum. It means 'to the walnut.'"

"So that's why they had all those paintings of trees and squirrels. I do remember it had an inn above it."

"Good thing because I don't think we could have made it very far that night," Danny said.

"You're telling me. Man! Those Krauts sure know how to brew a strong beer. You never told me what you were doing in Germany."

"Military stuff. You know."

"Still won't tell me, eh? I don't think it matters now," Yeri paused and noticed Danny's eyes skirting from left to right, "or does it?"

Danny gave a quick nod.

"Hey I know a little German Bistro at the end of the mall next to Dusty's. It's not real German, but close enough for a Martian I guess. They have some pretty good German povkas I hear."

"Not today. There's a lot going on around here and I gotta leave before I'm seen with you."

"Are you in some kind of trouble?" Yeri asked.

"I need a favor and you're someone… I can trust."

"What do you need?"

Danny moved behind the clothes rack away from the store's cameras and slowly unzipped his top suit pocket. He reached in and pulled out a small metal device and placed it in Yeri's hand closing Yeri's fingers with his hand. "Don't show this to anyone!"

"What is this?" Yeri snuck a peek at the shiny golden little contraption resting between his fingers.

"It's a jimmy. My team was entrusted with three jimmies when constructing the new qubit computer algorithm systems for the villages."

"I thought only a Companion could have a jimmy."

"That was on Earth. Anyway someone leaked that I had an extra one. You see, I found the original design online."

"I thought that stuff was highly encrypted and only available for the top officials."

"Yes, but I created a qubit encryption code breaker and I copied the files."

"So, this is what a jimmy looks like."

"That was what I was working on when we were drinking ales back on Earth."

"What do you want me to do with this one?" Yeri said as he casually picked up a sweater off of the rack.

"You gotta keep it hidden. You see, we created a security system that no one could break unless they had a jimmy. The code constantly changed at random intervals and the only way you could keep up was by inserting the jimmy. It would adapt to each new change in the code. To work on the system the code must always equal zero or the computer would shut down. The jimmy would match the code allowing us access to the root directory. So you see these keys are very important. The Minister's concern was that the keys also allow access through any type of lock. It can open anything. We weren't allowed retina scan authorizations to the building because they were afraid we could work without supervision and create a backdoor access to the system. They always watched us when we had the jimmies."

"Well then, why are you giving one to me?"

"Yesterday, I found out that the Minister of Defense has ordered the confiscation of all jimmies. I don't think he trusts us."

"I don't think he trusts anyone."

"He's been looking for me. He wants mine."

"A personal jimmy is against the law, isn't it?"

"Only if you can prove it. Earlier this morning T-Minus walked into the office and took all our jimmies. They roughed me up a bit and broke into my domette looking for mine."

"They can't just search your homes," Yeri said.

"The Minister invoked the Martian Patriot Act."

"The I-can-do-what-I-want-without-due-process act?" Yeri shook his head. "I remember a similar act was created on Earth back in the early twenty-first century. It happened right after a group of terrorists led by a man named Benjamin…?"

"Bin… Bin Laden," Danny answered.

"Oh yeah, I remember now. He was responsible for the attack on the World Trade Center using our own airplanes. It brought America to its knees. We never realized how vulnerable we were until that day."

Danny nodded. "In the aftermath the United States government passed the Patriot Act. That enabled the military to carry out covert operations of collecting metadata in attempts to uncover any terrorist activities. The problem arose when some government agencies drifted to using torture, search, and seizure without due process totally ignoring the Constitution. They hid behind the Patriot Act when confronted. I don't think that was the intent."

"Torture? You mean enhanced interrogation, don't you?"

"You could call it that. Kind of like calling a nuclear bomb an enhanced firecracker."

Yeri laughed. "I think that religious nut who orchestrated the attack back then didn't do as much to America as we did to ourselves out of the fear he generated."

"America was never the same after that. We closed our borders, spent millions building silly walls all because of one man and I'm afraid Mars is following in the same footsteps. I can't even be trusted and I'm the guy who helped design the whole system!"

"What if there is a system failure?" Yeri asked.

"We were informed that the Minister's guards would be in charge of the jimmies. They would be the only ones with access to the main building. So they would basically lead us around like good little children."

"T-Minus now has all the jimmies?"

"There are still a couple of them floating around, but not many. T-Minus wants to be the only ones who can access the information for what good it will do them. I guess the Minister of Defense thinks it's better if we are watched while we fix their problems."

"How did the Minister of Defense gain so much power?"

"The Halks. They created a lot of fear as you know and there was a big demand to rid our villages of them."

"They have done their share of damage," Yeri agreed. "So what do you want me to do with it?"

"Keep it safe and out of sight. They have been watching me, but I managed to give them the slip a couple of hours ago. I don't want you to be caught with me if you know what I mean."

Yeri nodded and slowly placed the key in his lower pants pocket and secured it with his zipper.

"Can I help you?" asked the salesman.

"Do you have a dinner jacket in extra large?" Yeri asked and when he turned around Danny was gone...

*****

"Time to eat!" Beth yelled from the dining room.

"Everything looks great," Yeri said as he grabbed a big helping of potatoes.

"Now don't hog the potatoes." Beth looked at Yeri.

"I'm hungry."

"So is everyone else," Beth said.

As Tima and Beth cleared the table, Ken walked back into the living room and turned on the holovision.

Togo moved his chair next to Yeri and watched him finish his drink. He looked at the jimmy lying in his hands under the dining room table. "Wait till I show Apollo and Felix!"

"The game is on! Can you two be a little quieter?" Ken yelled out from the living room as he moved side to side in his chair mimicking the basketball player's moves.

"You can't do that, Togo. If the Minister of Defense finds out you have this key, he will come and take it," Yeri whispered in his ear.

"You said it wasn't useful anymore. Why does he care?"

"Don't shoot!... No no no!... Another miss?... Foul?... No way!" Ken yelled at the HV.

Yeri leaned close to Togo's ear. "He wants it because we have it and he's jealous. Do you have a special place to put things you want to keep where no one knows?"

"Yes."

"Where?"

"I can't tell you and I'm not going to let him in."

"Good! Let's just keep this our little secret. Okay?"

"Roger."

"That's my boy! Happy birthday, Togo." Yeri said as he got up from the table and joined Ken in the living room.

"Dad, what did you give Togo?" Ken asked during a commercial break.

"Oh, something I brought from Earth," Yeri said and turned away. Ken frowned at Yeri. He knew his dad wasn't going to tell him what it was, but he would find out later. "Any more surprises in your garden of delights?" Yeri asked Tima as she walked into the room with another bottle of povka.

"Not watching the game?"

"Already know the outcome."

"Oh… Oh? No one knows the outcomes I heard they kept it…"

"It seems some do," Ken interrupted as another ad for Elotec's new and improved domette security system droned on.

Tima shrugged her shoulders and walked over to Yeri. "Great news, Dad! We're growing spinach."

"I never liked spinach," Yeri told Tima.

"Liar." Tima refilled Yeri and Ken's glasses. "You've been the one hanging around the department pushing us to grow some."

"Oh yeah. Well, what do you expect from a man of my advanced age. I can't remember what I did yesterday." Yeri laughed.

"We just received a new shipment of fertilizer yesterday and I am excited to see what else we can grow!"

"How about some corn. Rye maybe?"

"I'm a horticulturist, not a waitress!"

"I guess we're stuck with povkas then," Yeri sighed.

"Hasn't it been tried?" Ken asked.

"Yeah. The only problem with growing corn is it takes eight months here on Mars instead of the usual three and because of space limitations we decided it would be better to concentrate our efforts in other areas. Sorry."

"What about rye?"

"You just want to drink it."

"What else is it good for?" Yeri smiled.

"Bedipida!" Tiga burst into the room. "What happened to Great Granddad? Daddy won't tell us anything." Yeri looked at Ken.

"Just keep it down so I can watch the game."

"Well, it was around five or so years after the One Day War when my father, Dr. Oystein Thornton, working at the Center for Disease Control, was approached by a company called Humanochore. They were attempting to genetically reengineer deadly diseases to make them harmless to humans. There came an opening working with the Yersinia Pestis germ, better known as the bubonic plague. He joined this select group of scientists and they came up with a working model. Unfortunately, his experiments uncovered that his mutated pathogens hadn't stopped metamorphosing."

"Meta-what?" Tiga asked.

"Changing, evolving."

"Oh," Tiga said.

"Dad wanted to do more testing before they used live subjects, but the higher ups wanted results. So Dad, against his own reservations, acquiesced and two weeks later, on a Wednesday, they injected two hundred seagulls with the experimental mutated virus. The birds were exposed to salmonella, trichomoniasis, aspergillosis, and avian pox. By Friday, those pathogens had severely sickened all of the seagulls. Many were on the brink of death, but come Monday morning when everyone was expecting the worse, they found all of the seagulls had returned to perfect health. Dad saw this as success, but upper management, however, wanted to see if the birds could withstand even more stringent testing. They wanted to see if the seagulls could withstand situations that would normally kill other birds but Dad refused saying they had done enough. The following day he was called upstairs to explain his reasons. While he was gone his fellow scientists shot, stabbed, and choked half the birds to death and poisoned the rest."

"They killed the seagulls?"

"They tried, but the new seagull DNA recoded itself and only after a few hours, a bunch of supposedly dead birds suddenly woke up in perfect health."

"Wow!" Tiga exclaimed.

"When Dad returned to the lab he was furious and said there would be no more new seagull trials without his signed authorization."

"I bet that made his bosses mad."

"It sure did."

"Did they just fire Granddad?"

"No. You see he was hired as a contractor and not an actual employee. So he could sue them if they broke his contract and took his findings to another company. He was also the only one with the blueprints on out how to make the DNA recoding sequences work. So the company had to abide by his rules which really put a thorn in their side."

"I bet they didn't like that."

"No, they saw a huge market for this and wanted to exploit it."

"So they had to sit around and wait?"

"They would have but then a terrible accident happened the following week."

"What was that?" Togo shouted from across the room as he slammed the living room closet door.

"Don't slam the doors, Togo!" Ken shouted.

"Sorry."

"By the way, what were you doing in the closet?" Ken turned toward Togo.

"Nothing," Togo said sporting an innocent smile. Just then the crowd shouted from the HV redirecting Ken's attention.

"Foul?... No way!...Someone give the ref back his glasses!" Ken yelled as he watched the replay of the call.

"Daddy is sure getting mad," Tiga said

"He's just having fun," Yeri said.

A confused look appeared on Tiga's face. She pulled on Bedipida's sleeve. "What?"

"Tell me more." Togo pulled up a chair.

"Okay, okay I'll get back to the story. My dad and the rest of his crew were finishing up one afternoon when someone released isopropyl methylphosphonofluoridate into the ventilation system."

"What's that?"

"Sarin gas."

"What's sarin gas?" Togo asked.

"It's a chemical when released into the atmosphere blocks an enzyme in your body called acetylcholinesterase which controls your muscles. Your muscles have... um switches. To raise your hand or breathe certain muscles must activate, switch on so to speak, while others muscles have to turn off. Sarin gas causes all your muscles to...turn on all at once making it impossible to breathe."

"Did they catch who ever did this?" Togo asked.

"No. The police were called and some people were questioned, but no arrests. It just didn't make sense," Yeri said.

"What didn't make sense?" Ken turned away from the HV as another commercial droned on.

"The building was owned by Humanochore and the security was the best available. The cameras weren't operating at the time because the security system was going through an upgrade. Usually that would be done on a weekend when they would bring in the equivalent of an entire police force because the building would be compromised. But this was done on a Monday and there were only a handful of armed guards at the entrance."

"So?"

"Usually it was a big deal to do upgrades, but this time it wasn't."

"You suspect something other than upgrades was going on I presume Dr. Watson?" Ken asked in his best Sherlock Holmes impression.

"I'm just saying the seagulls got another dose of testing again without Dad's consent."

"What did Great Granddad do?" Tima asked.

"Dad, like the rest, was killed in the..." Yeri raised two hands making quotation marks with his fingers. "...accident... along with everything and everyone else except for those two hundred seagulls."

"With Granddad gone I guess it stopped all of the experiments then."

"Actually no. Earlier that morning his house had been broken into and ransacked. Nothing was left untouched. His computer drives had all been cleaned, not just erased. Someone had to really know what they were doing. I told this to the authorities time and time again, but they told me there was nothing they could do and kept asking me if I knew if the drives had anything on them anyway." Yeri lowered his head and stared at the oval throw rug lying on the floor in front of him. "I lost a good friend that day. He was my dad, but he was a lot more. Mankind lost even more because of what happened."

"Why?" Togo asked.

"With Dad's genetic blueprints on DNA recoding now in the hands of Humanochore, they would be able to recode the DNA of other species including people. This terrible accident was the beginning of the end for us."

"Not for the seagulls. They lived," Togo said.

"Yes, because those seagulls were the only ones with the modified version of a deadly level four virus called the Yersinia Pestis."

"Level Four?"

"Yes. The Center of Disease Control refers to a level four virus as one that has a high fatality rate and no known cures."

"The Yersi...What?" Tiga asked.

"The Yersinia Pestis virus. It goes by other names. Some called it the Bubonic Plague while others referred to it as the Black Death."

"Black Death sounds scary," Togo said as he moved his chair closer to Yeri.

"Think about it." Yeri took another sip of povka. He put the shot glass down on the table and turned to both kids as his face took on a serious note. "If man could recode his DNA like the seagulls, we could be shot, overdosed, or exposed to highly toxic chemicals and be fine. You think there would be a market for that?"

"Definitely, but it sounds too good to be true," Ken said. "If you know what I mean."

"Tell us more about the Black Death, Bedipida. When did it start?" Togo asked.

"It all began long ago back in the fourteenth century on Earth. The Black Death started with twelve merchant ships. Rats had boarded these ships at one of the ports in the Black Sea. These rats were infested with fleas that were carrying the deadly virus. The fleas began to bite the sailors transferring the virus to the men as they travelled home to

Sicily. Once the ships docked, the Sicilian dockworkers boarded the infected ships to unload the cargo but to their horror they saw most of the sailors were dead and the ones alive had black boils that oozed blood and pus. The workers quickly left the ships and forced the boats back out to sea but it was too late. Some of the fleas had already bitten some of the workers. The Black Death had officially landed in Europe and all through the coming summer months it destroyed over fifty percent of the European population. Estimates range from 30 to 50 million deaths depending on who you ask."

"Wow! All that from one little flea bite?" Togo asked.

"Not just one. The fleas were all over the ships by the time they made port. When the innocent dock workers boarded the boats the fleas attached themselves to their clothing."

"Why didn't they just shake them off?"

"Because fleas are so small it's hard to see them and even if they did, they didn't know something that small could carry something so deadly. People were dying within days of getting bit."

"Oh my gosh! That's horrible!"

"It created widespread panic because no one understood what was happening to them."

"What did they do?"

"People were dying left and right. The ones unaffected scattered like the wind. They left the cities and moved to more rural locations. Fear swept the countrysides. Some believed it was God's vengeance on the non-believers and those who sinned. This disease was so deadly it could, and most times would, kill you overnight. You could be in perfect health one day, get bit, and end up dead the next morning."

"Did it kill everyone?"

"No. Like I said this happened during the summer and fall. When the cold winter weather hit, it killed off the fleas. At least that's the theory. The record keeping was lax during the medieval times so most of this is conjecture at best."

"Is that why we moved to Mars?"

"To get away from the fleas?" Yeri questioned.

"Uh huh."

"No. Stupidity got us here."

"What?"

"It all started when some very arrogant and near-sighted leaders drunk with power and a sick desire for world domination decided one day to launch a nuclear attack. The problem was, we all lived on a round planet. They didn't think that the radiation and fallout would affect them, but it did."

"What happened?"

"If not for one lone renegade private we may have ended our existence..."

Chapter 3

EARTH

North American Aerospace Defense Command
Cheyenne Mountain, Colorado U.S.A.
0800 hours

"Launch the goddamn missiles Private or you'll be scrubbing latrines with a toothbrush for the rest of your pathetic life!" General Weissburg screamed into Overman's ear.

"No sir! I will not launch these missiles. It's suicide!"

"Guards! Remove Private Overman and cuff him for treason! Get this traitor out of my sight!"

The guards grabbed the Private and jerked him out of his seat. They smacked him around a couple of times until Weissburg spoke. "Enough already! I don't have time for a show. Get him outta here!"

Weissburg turned back to the screen and sat down in Overman's chair as the guards roughed up the belligerent Private a little bit more and hauled him out the door.

"I'll launch the goddamn things myself! Think he can defy my orders does he? Well, we'll see about that? Now where's the goddamn codebook!?" Weissburg yelled out to anyone who was listening.

A young Private named Sanchez handed him a piece of paper. Carlos Sanchez had grown up in a touch neighborhood and being of short stature did not help at all. Feeling picked on early in life caused him to work out everyday with weights. He learned how to street fight to a point where he finally gained the respect he longed for from the neighborhood bullies. Carlos found he enjoyed watching the other neighborhood kids shy away when they saw him. Now he was in the military with new challenges to overcome.

The General looked at his name badge. "Sanchez?"

"Yes sir."

The General arose from his seat. "Private, launch my babies."

"YES SIR!" Sanchez said with a big grin. He turned to Private Rice at the other end of the room. "Keys to turn."

"Ready, sir!"

"Insert now."

"Keys inserted and ready."

"Count and turn after three. You know this has to be at exactly the same time. Right?" Sanchez asked.

"Copy"

"One…Two…Three…Turn."

The entire console turned a bright yellow. Sanchez had never realized it sported a light constant green before. In fact, he looked around and the console wasn't the only thing yellow. The entire room took on this messenger of caution.

- Missiles armed -

flashed on the overhead screen.

"Numbers to enter on my mark.

6…6…6…1…7…7…6"

How ironic, Sanchez thought. *Those numbers are the sign of the devil followed by the year of our independence. I guess we're gonna have to go through hell to be free.*

"Sir?" Sanchez looked away from the console to the General. Weissburg sported a big grin and nodded. Sanchez turned back to the console which flashed

- Launch countdown commencing -

Everyone held their breath as they stared at the screen on the wall. The computerize voice blared overhead,

**"Ten…Nine…Eight…Seven…Six…Five…Four…Three…
Two…One…"**

A hand scanner appeared to Sanchez's left. It was also yellow and began blinking.

"Damn safeguards!" Weissburg yelled. "Let's go, Sanchez!"

Sanchez pressed his left hand on the scanner. It went from yellow to red and the console on the right side of him slowly flipped over showing a new set of buttons, a new screen, and another scanner. Both the screens on his panel and the one overhead moved from displaying the world map to showing the rockets resting in their silo. There was one last scanner to press. Sanchez glanced at the General for final confirmation.

"Launch the goddamn things!" the General ordered.

Sanchez took a deep breath and placed his right hand on the blinking red scanner flashing

- Launch -

He felt a slight tremor where his hands were resting. "Birds away!" he screamed aloud.

Seconds passed with all eyes on the big overhead.

"Well?" Weissburg asked.

Everyone continued to stare at the monitor.

"I don't know sir. I felt a tremor on the console and I thought that was from the engines."

"That was the air conditioner. Those rockets are in a silo in Texas. Look at the screen you idiot!" Sanchez's face turned bright red at being shown a fool by the General in front of everybody. "What's wrong?" Weissburg yelled. "Those birds are still in the nest! We have allies waiting for us! Do you have proper clearance? Did you enter the codes correctly? Don't screw with me Private or you'll end up cellmates at Leavenworth with your buddy Overman!"

"Sir, yes sir!" Sanchez said nervously. "Overman must have changed the launch codes."

"Goddamn it! Somebody, get that son of a bitch back up here. NOW!"

"Yes sir!" replied Private Smithson as he pressed the intercom.

"Ackerman here."

"Bring Private Overman to the launch room."

"What?"

"Yeah, he changed the launch codes."

"Jesus! You want me to beat the codes out of him?"

"No, just get that son of a bitch up here STAT."

"Roger."

Private Mendez walked into the room where the General was standing. "General Weissburg you have a telephone call and I..."

"Take a message! Can't you see I'm busy defending the goddamned country?"

"Yes sir, but I don't think the President is going to..."

"The President? Why didn't you say so in the first place?"

"Sorry sir!"

"Shut up and get out of my way!" The General pushed the Private to the side and walked into his office and picked up the receiver. "Madam President, what can I do for you?"

"NORAD just informed me the skies are clear. There is nothing on their radar. I want to know why those missiles have not been launched."

"I am sorry sir, uh ma'am, but one of my privates refused a direct order to launch. He also changed the goddamned...um, sorry ma'am. He changed the launch codes and I can assure you Madam President he will give us those launch codes and then he will be summarily shot for treason!"

"Do not launch those birds, General."

"What?"

"Satellite tracking has picked up a massive cloud of fallout and radiation moving eastward at an alarming pace right toward the countries occupied by the People's Coalition. It should hit them within the week. There is no stopping it and they have surrendered. They need to evacuate and want our help. This radioactive dust cloud is so thick it is blocking the sun. Eighty percent of the radiation has moved off our lands and is heading directly back to...its home. If we launch it will probably be the end of mankind."

"We can't just sit around and let those bastards get away with this."

"They are not getting away with anything. They will pay for their arrogance, but now we need to fight for our own survival more than simple revenge."

"But sir! Er, I mean ma'am!"

"No buts. Cancel the launch."

"Yes Madam President," Weissburg hung up the telephone. "God...DAMN IT!" he screamed out so loud Sanchez, along with the rest of the crew in the other room, jumped when they heard the General screaming.

As he walked back into the launch room, he looked at everyone and said in resignation, "Cancel the launch." He turned and walked away. "Those godless Communist bastards got away with it," he said under his breath in frustration.

*****

The People's Coalition was founded by a group of extremely wealthy individuals who were bored with acquisitions and decided they wanted something bigger. They slowly infiltrated Middle Eastern countries by creating media unrest and then, with teams of well-placed mercenaries wearing police outfits, attacked and killed thousands of their citizens. When the people began to revolt, they swooped in with their private armies and overtook country by country. They tortured the leaders into admitting wrong doings and subsequently hung them for crimes against the people and then installed their own handpicked puppet leaders. This continued for years until their empire became a force strong enough to threaten the free world. As discussions increased between the leaders of the free world and the People's Coalition they realized something needed to be done to remove the mounting tensions. The People's Coalition had been secretly purchasing the news outlets of the free world for years and now it was time to put it to good use. The Coalition's announcers reassured the free world these acts of violence were to free the people from tyrannical governments throughout the world. They assured the world their actions were necessary to end the communistic and socialistic scourge. The world believed the newsmen and everyone went back to business as usual. Then one day the People's Coalition launched a nuclear attack against America, her allies, and the rest of the free world.

The new Allies agreed to counter and set up an attack of their own. Within a matter of days they began their own launch countdown against the Coalition. The generals of the other countries quickly created a scenario where each country would launch in ten-minute intervals from different sites in order to confuse and destroy their common enemy. If not for one man, Private Dennis Overman, who refused to launch the missiles, life on Earth may not have continued. Life continued, but it was never the same. That one day entered the world into a new form of terrors to be faced. The world, already beaten down from man's continuing greed, ignorance, and disrespect, had to endure another one of man's atrocities. He took everything the world had to offer and gave nothing of value back. Little did he know, the chessboard had been set with Mankind on one side of the board and Mother Nature on the other. How was she going to respond to these repeated attacks? No one knew, but then no one really cared, at least not until they saw the moves Mother Nature was about to play.

The war was over the same day it began. Thousands of square miles were quarantined indefinitely due to the massive amounts of radiation.

Cities had been destroyed and the entire world needed healing. The Coalition was dismantled and the puppet leaders were tried and hung just like they had done to others. It was seen as poetic justice by the world, however the wealthy individuals who started it all simply disappeared. The New Allies took a hard line on the countries occupied by the People's Coalition and abolished all military and destroyed all their weapons and Intel. No one now had a military advantage or much of a military since the first strike was aimed at the military bases throughout the world.

After five years of rebuilding, the world moved from a war torn planet to one of growth and survival. The attacking countries were tasked with the majority of the rebuilding and they, to a certain extent, did a good job.

In order to prevent another nuclear holocaust the leaders from all over the world held a world summit in Huuk, Greenland. They were in complete agreement that they desperately needed to live together. One of the leaders, representing a new country recently founded in the northern Asian blocs, suggested a computer pick the new world leaders. He recommended they should form a council with seven members - each one of them representing one of the seven continents. He told the council the leaders of their respective countries still had control, but they would all agree to serve the Sevens. This way if things went south the Sevens would take the blame which was a big hit among the other leaders. Four weeks later the seven names provided by ENIAC2 was approved.

On the day the Ana Asea Sevens (an acronym representing the seven continents of the world) took office, the inauguration address was televised throughout the entire world.

World Inaugural Address
Times Square
New York, New York U.S.A.
2330 hours

"Greetings to all. I am Ana Asea One and behind me are the other six Ana Aseas." The television cameras moved in for a closer shot at the other leaders of the New World Order. "We are humbled to have received the highest office in the world. We will work together to bring about a new hope for our planet," he paused as the sign flashed

CHEER...CHEER...CHEER

and the crowd obediently clapped and cheered.

"With the advent of new technology in animal and plant genetics along with our enhanced power sources we will turn this war-torn planet into a paradise that even God in Heaven Himself would be jealous."

More claps and cheers erupted from the carefully selected crowds.

"Together we will achieve what no man has achieved before. The New Age has dawned and with it a New World Order." He waved his hand in the air with one finger pointing toward the skyline. "Today will be our new beginning! No child will go hungry. No family shall live in poverty and how will we achieve this you ask? From now on your money will no longer serve as a unit of wealth."

There was a collective groan among the crowds, but Ana Asea One quickly raised his hand. "Hear me out," Ana Asea One shouted to the crowd. "All of your wealth has not disappeared, it has only changed to a more modern and convenient method of exchange." Ana Asea One took a breath and waited for his words to sink in. Suddenly the screen behind him revealed a golden looking credit card with a person's picture on the front of it displaying a big smile. "These cards of gold are being sent to every individual across the entire planet."

The crowd still uncertain shuffled uneasily as they tried to understand what was happening to their money.

"You have worked hard for your money and you will all be reimbursed dollar for dollar. Plus, to make the transfer easier we are increasing everyone's credit wealth by fifty percent. That's right! You are going to be much richer with the 'My Card.' The poorest among you will no longer live in poverty, but not to worry. They cannot use their 'My Cards' to buy liquor, drugs or anything deemed unhealthy."

The crowd erupted with smiles, claps, and excitement about the thoughts of expanding their wealth.

"We will refer to the currency on the 'My Cards' as Krugers derived from the golden coin from South Africa called the Krugerrand. Of course all silver, gold, and Kruger coins you hold will be turned in and you will receive fair value." Ana Asea One paused as the signs told the crowd to clap and cheer which they did as instructed.

Once the noise died down Ana Asea One continued. "To mark this occasion our first order of business is communication. English will be our world language. In time people will be able to come together from all over the world and be able to speak together without having to have a translator. This will eliminate another barrier that separates us. To commemorate this special occasion, the worldwide calendar that everyone will reference has now been reset to January 1, 0001. Today will usher in a new foundation of a new era for mankind's ultimate advancement!"

The countdown clock with only a minute left slowly ticked down behind Ana Asea One. He waited until it reached zero when all at once a banner behind the Sevens lit up showing the new date as fireworks exploded in the background.

Sunday, January 1, 0001

The signs to the sides of the stage flashed cheer and applaud as Ana Asea One smiled and nodded as he looked across the crowds of onlookers. He waited, enjoying his time on stage, reveling in the adoration heaped upon him.

They seem easy enough to rule, Ana Asea One thought to himself. *I think I'm going to like this job.*

The lights on top of the cameras blinked yellow telling the leaders it was time to wrap it up.

"Thank you. Now go in peace and watch the unfoldment of our new plans before your very eyes," Ana Asea One said and turned away from the cameras. The televisions across the world instantly switched over to the news as a slim young lady with strikingly beautiful blue eyes and silky long blonde hair in her mid-twenties appeared on the screen.

"Hello everyone! I am Courtney Hughes on *The Wolf*. And now the news. Deadly radioactive winds have appeared near Dallas, Texas registering approximately 1000 MilliSieverts. Stay tuned to see if it is heading your way."

Fade out - Fade in.

"Hi I'm Doctor Christopher Imes and I am please to announce our new and improved radiation detector the Sievert Healthwatch Plus. As you know a brief exposure to 1000 MilliSieverts can make you very, very sick. The longer the exposure the worse it can be. The original Sievert Healthwatch picked up harmful radiation down to 750 MilliSieverts, but you told us that wasn't enough. Now we have the Plus which detects down to 500 MilliSieverts allowing you additional time to protect yourself and your loved ones from harm. If you want to assure your safety from dangerous radiation you can order the Sievert Healthwatch Ultimate which will detect radiation down to 250 MilliSieverts. The Ultimate will give you plenty of extra time to evacuate the area before it gets too toxic. When ordering, remember to ask for your ten percent discount and mention my name, Dr. Imes. Thank you."

Fade out - Fade in.

"Courtney Hughes here." She held up her watch to the camera. "If you live in or around Dallas or anywhere in Texas for that matter I recommend you buy this wonderful life saving watch. The Sievert Healthwatch Ultimate also keeps time and works with your pursal!"

The pursal was a combination of a smartphone and wallet. It was created from nano technology, which allowed it to change shapes depending on the owner's needs.

Chapter 4

World Inaugural Address
Times Square
New York, New York U.S.A.
Sunday, January 4, 0010
1000 hours

(Ten Years Later)

The Ana Aseas had ruled the planet for ten years and the planet was still dealing with deadly radiation along with increased toxic waste spills and pollution. The rulers needed a win to appease the masses if they wanted to stay in power. Rumors of dissolving the leaders were becoming more evident each passing year. The leaders needed a solution and they needed one fast. Every year the Sevens continued to increase the financial incentives to anyone who could provide a workable solution to clean up the environment. Company after company tried and failed to eradicate the ever-floating radiation resulting from the One Day War. No one felt safe or knew which direction the wind would move the deadly radioactive particles. Then a company called Humanochore did something no one had thought of before. Instead of changing the environment to suit man, they turned to what happened to those seagulls from years ago. Could man's DNA be altered like the seagulls' DNA? That was what they wanted to find out. The Yersinia Pestis virus worked well on transforming bird DNA but failed miserably in animal trials. So they reengineered the DNA of other level four viruses with no success and then they found the Ebola virus. Dr. David Smitherman had replaced Humanochore's lead scientist Dr. Oystein Thornton who had died years ago from sarin gas exposure. With the help of Dr. Thornton's algorithms on recoding the

Yersinia Pestis virus Dr. Smitherman was able to neutralize the Ebola virus' deadly effects. The new Ebola virus recoded all the animal test subjects with ease and with very little side effects. Humanochore decided to run tests on human subjects and it worked. The test group became stronger and the sick ones returned to perfect health.

The Ana Asea Sevens upon hearing this major breakthrough decided to unveil this new procedure to the world.

Today was going to be a big day for Humanochore's CEO, Dr. Angie Hoffstander-Steward. Dr. Hoffstander-Steward was from German decent and was considered a genius in the field of bioengineering. She wore brown-rimmed glasses and had trimmed nails and silky blonde hair cut just below her ears.

At twelve o'clock she would unveil the results of their work. The only issue was on how to sell it. The price tag would be substantial and it would make Humanochore one of the top industrial powerhouses on the planet, not to mention getting huge payouts from the Sevens. Dr. Hoffstander-Steward would even have an opportunity for a seat during the Ana Asea meetings regarding new biomedical treatment standards.

"What if someone wants to see the studies?" asked Dr. Smitherman.

"Smitty, just show them the data." Angie handed him the papers. He looked at the results.

"There are only three trials here."

"Very perceptive of you. I want you to notice how clean they look."

"That's not an accurate representation!"

"Of course they are. They all showed hybridization as a safe and effective method for humans."

"What about all the other trials we ran that didn't? You've seen the side effects! Angie, aren't they going to want to review all of them?"

"Don't worry Smitty. Back when I worked in pharmaceuticals we ran our own trials and then submitted the results we liked to the FDA."

"The FDA doesn't require all the trials?"

"Nope. Those poor suckers are so understaffed they don't have enough money to run their own trials much less review all of ours,"

Angie laughed. "Why do you think we spent so much money running so many trials?"

"I don't know. What I do know is we spent a fortune running so many of them. Have you seen our stock price lately?"

"Smitty, it's all a matter of time and money. If you have enough time and money you can make the most dangerous drug in the world look like it's as pure as Rocky Mountain spring water."

"What are you going to say if they ask why only three trials?"

"First of all, they won't and if they do we'll tell them we had to change the parameters of the study and the other trials didn't fit the new requirements."

"But doesn't that prejudice our findings?"

Angie laughed, "Of course it does! That's the way we do business. Remember those cholesterol-lowering pills back in the twentieth century?"

"Yes."

"Do you really think it lowered the incidences of heart attacks?"

"That's what the doctors told us."

"That is what we told the doctors to tell us. Are you really that gullible?"

"But isn't all of this misleading the public's trust?"

"Capitalism at its finest!" Angie smiled.

Dr. Smitherman took another look at the human hybrid data before him. "Don't you remember what this type of procedure did to those seagulls?"

"It saved them from the sarin gas incident," Angie said as she slowly thumbed through her speech. "Besides, we're using a different virus."

"We are still seeing side-effects with this one too. I don't think we should sweep all this under the carpet. I mean this doesn't sound very ethical." Dr. Smitherman looked up from the studies.

"Do you have a problem with making a profit?" Angie stared at him. All of a sudden there was a knock on the door.

"Are you ready?" George Stables, Angie's public relations man, peeked his head around the door.

"Yes! Dr. Smitherman was just leaving. He isn't feeling well today." She continued to stare at Smitty.

"I feel fine!"

"So...are you with me?" Angie paused. "In fact, if I were you, I would buy our stock before we go out there." Angie turned and walked toward the door.

"That's insider trading," Dr. Smitherman muttered under his breath.

"Smitty? Did you say something?" Angie looked back at him.

Dr. Smitherman paused and then looked at Angie. "You're right. I'm not feeling well, if you'll excuse me."

"Of course." She turned to George. "By the way, Dr. Smitherman will not be accompanying us today. He's still feeling some side effects of a new germ he's been working on." She looked at Dr. Smitherman. "Smitty, it looks like I'll have to keep my eye on you from now on," she said threateningly and then nonchalantly waved him out of the room.

"Is he contagious?"

"We're not sure, but I wouldn't get too close to him, if you know what I mean."

"Everyone's here, Dr. Steward," George said. "By the way I like your new white and gold-trimmed glasses."

Angie put a finger to her mouth. Once she was sure Dr. Smitherman was out of earshot she continued, "Are you sure this will work?" She looked at him with a tone of doubt in her voice. "Not everyone is of a religious bent you know."

"Angie," George Stables reminded her, "eight out of ten people believe in God. That's a whopping eighty percent! Not to mention these are desperate and trying times. People are also looking for a Savior. We just need to give them one. Trust me," he grinned. "The rest will take care of itself."

"What about the non-believers?"

"No problem. The crowd has been vetted. There will be no negative reactions."

"Are the trumpeters ready?"

"Yes, but we won't need them."

"Well, keep them on alert just in case."

"Everything will be fine as long as you don't stray from the plan," George said.

"If you're wrong it's going to cost you your job!" Angie flared.

"No worries. It may have cost us a lot of Krugers in the beginning, but in the end it will be worth it. All the major news reporters have been briefed on what to report and what to...overlook." George winked at her. "And remember, the audience is 100% composed with people of faith. Just stick to the script and you won't have any problems."

*****

"Good evening and Happy New Year! I am Courtney Hughes with *The Wolf*. The Ana Aseas are about to address the world describing a new way for us to extend our lives and return to perfect health. I know we all want to see this."

The cameras faded out for their commercial runs and returned to show the Ana Asea Sevens as they walked on stage. The crowd erupted as they saw the six men milling around as the One approached the podium.

"My fellow humans," Ana Asea One said into the microphone, "it has been a struggle living on such a war torn planet. Mother Earth has suffered greatly from the fools that placed pride and ego above everything else. There are still many areas in which we cannot live due to the long-term effects of the One Day War. People today are still dying from diseases like cancer resulting from the intense and..." Ana Asea One lowered his head, "low levels of continued radiation exposure," the Ana Asea paused for effect. "We have suffered for years and years, but not any longer because today is a day to be remembered for all time." The Ana Asea looked to his left as a woman approached the podium. She was dressed in a pristine white dress with a small golden rope tied around her waist. The dress sported a collar that thinly stretched halfway across her on each side giving the appearance of two white wings peeking over both shoulders. Around her neck was a golden chain with a large golden Christian cross attached. "I want you to give a warm welcome to Humanochore's CEO, Dr. Angie Hoffstander-Steward."

The crowd clapped and shouted as Angie Hoffstander-Steward approached the podium.

"Thank you all. We at Humanochore are here today to tell you we now have the ability to eradicate cancer and extend your lives almost indefinitely!" she screamed out with her hands raised fueling the enthusiasm of the shocked crowd. "You didn't hear this wrong. A miracle! A miracle that came from God Himself. Our Savior has once again saved mankind from his past sins. HE... has reached down from Heaven and used Humanochore as HIS holy hands."

Just then a choir appeared from behind the stage dressed in white robes began humming and singing in the background like one would hear in church.

The crowd went silent. Angie, not to be dissuaded, turned up the heat.

"A gift from HIM on most high who has heard your prayers and how did HE answer them?"

No one moved.

"By sending HIS angels with information from HIS unlimited knowledge. Why? It is because HE loves you and wants to help you and how?" She gripped the podium and looked across the crowds as they stood and stared. "Was it a dream?" she asked, paused, and lowered her head for effect. "I don't know."

The singing and humming grew louder.

"Oh no, here she goes," George sighed. "I told her to keep to the script."

All at once her eyes shot skyward along with her outstretched hands. "But what I do know is late one night while in bed I felt my body move. It floated up and up. I moved past the moon, the stars and then all of a sudden I came to a stop. I opened my eyes and lo and behold I was standing at a gate towering into the heavens made of pure gold. The majestic golden entrance sat upon a cloud of white, which slowly opened in front of me, and there stood a majestic white horse. I had to shield my eyes from the Holy Radiant glow emanating from this magnificent beast. There was an Angel dressed in white sitting upon this horse and his name was Faithful. I saw a beautiful golden trumpet draped across his magnificent chest. To his right was another Angel holding a raised golden sword in her right hand also dressed in white sitting upon a white horse and her name was True. I saw many white horses and riders behind the two and I fell to my knees. I bowed my head before them and as the first Angel spoke the Heavens began to rumble beneath me! 'My name is Faithful! In HIS righteousness we have been called to tend to our flock!'" She paused and looked to the crowds. "His voice boomed throughout the Heavens. His words pounded me with such intensity I began to cry. It felt like the Second Coming was upon me! As I wept He said to me," she drew a big breath and shouted, "'You have been given the secret to immortality as promised by HIM. The devil's curse has been lifted.'

He then blew God's mighty Trumpet and shouted out to me, 'Satan's curse upon mankind is no more!'"

In the distance the crowd heard the blasting of a chorus of trumpets intoned with the choir singing at full volume followed by a pause of silence. She stared at the crowd before continuing.

"Then I awoke with a formula etched into my mind! That is when I realized this Holy formula was the key to immortality given to me by one of HIS Angels! God's prophecy for everlasting life has been fulfilled! As it was written it now has become!" She paused waiting for her words to sink in. She took a sip of water and then continued. "HE has chosen me to pass on HIS will through Humanochore," she paused once again. "I want you to know that we at Humanochore are nothing more than HIS humble servants and through all of our prayers HE has chosen us to be the bestower of HIS gifts." She turned toward the men standing behind her with microphone in hand. "Do you see these men standing beside our beloved leaders? These men and women you see at the side of each of the Ana Aseas are called their Companions. They have gone through HIS new procedure called hybridization. Hybridization is a method where the body's DNA has been altered to make one faster and stronger. Their senses are more acutely aware of what is going on around them than us normal mortals. They will always be cancer free and their lifespan teeters on that of immortality. You too will never have to worry about radiation or its effects. Old age will become a thing of the past. One day we all may have an opportunity to become saved through God's compassion just like the Companions!"

The choir again began their singing and humming slowing raising the volume.

Angie yelled out to the crowd throwing both her arms high looking toward the Heavens. "THY...WILL...BE...DONE!" she shouted at the top of her lungs as the speakers behind her blared out the sound of a thunder strike along with the trumpeters sounding off in the distance.

The crowd exploded upon hearing the news. Many clasped their hands in prayer and looked to the sky while others took to the ground on bended knee performing ancient rituals passed down to them on how to worship their god.

Fade out - Fade in.

"This is Courtney Hughes from *The Wolf*." Her eyes opened wide. "My god! Have we just witnessed a miracle?" In the background, the camera showed the people crying and praying to the stage of the Ana Asea Sevens. "Let's go back and see what else they have to say." Courtney turned her head to the background as it filled the holovision screens throughout the planet.

Fade out - Fade in.

Ana Asea One's Companion, Erica Bloom, walked to the microphone and waited for the crowd to settle down before she spoke.

"A new day has come unto us! I once was battling my own demons. I fought cancer and muscle weakness from being exposed to floating radiation. It seemed to be everywhere. I thought I was going to die, but now I am going to live a very long and healthy life. Why? Because I have undergone hybridization and I am healthier and stronger than ever. I know how exciting all of this is. Heaven on Earth has been realized!" she screamed into the microphone. "A new world of hope has arrived. God has blessed our planet!" Erica, with a lower tone, continued. "All the Ana Aseas ask for is your patience as we continue to clean up our world and soon you will be saved from sickness and death thanks to Humanochore and the One who made it all possible." Erica lowered her head, made a sign of the cross, and bowed with her hands clasped together as she slowly backed away from the podium.

Ana Asea One walked across the stage and grabbed the lonely microphone. "I am sure you all have questions, like when will God fulfill His promise to me of everlasting life? All I can say is soon. As you may surmise the treatment is very expensive. Those who have the resources will be the first to receive God's favor. I promise that everyone will have their turn." Ana Asea One clasped his hands in a position of prayer. "His will be done. Amen! And thank you all for coming." The Ana Asea turned off the microphone as the Companions escorted the Ana Asea Sevens off the platform and to their vehicles.

"How did I do?" Angie asked George.

"From the reaction of the crowd I would say you knocked it out of the park. Our site is down right now from all the hits. People are bidding on the procedure. We are going to make a killing!" George replied.

"Good."

"Yes, but didn't you go a little too far out there?"

"What do you mean?"

"The script. There was nothing about you being in Heaven."

"I didn't think the crowd was buying it so I figured I had to juice it up a bit and it worked!" Angie giggled.

"I don't think I've ever heard you giggle before."

"I've never been this rich before. Hey! See if Bruce in accounting can get us a church tax exempt status." Angie stared at George for a brief second. "Now!"

"Okay." George pulled out his pursal and walked across the floor. He turned and looked over at Angie while he waited for someone to pick up.

"Hey George. What can I do for you?" Bruce asked.

"Angie wants you to look into something."

Silence. "What was all that about her being in heaven?" Bruce asked.

"Marketing," George said with a sigh. "She wants a tax exemption."

"Ahh, of course. We may have to change the company name."

"How about the Church of Yours to Ours?" George laughed.

"Hold on," Bruce said as George watched Angie talking to a couple of the Ana Aseas and strained to hear their conversations but to no avail. "George? Are you still there?"

"Yeah. What have you got?"

"I've got preliminaries on Angie's request."

"Thanks Bruce," George said as he hung up and returned his pursal to his belt. He walked back over to Angie and waited for her to finish her discussion with Ana Asea One.

"Of course Ana Asea One, we have already signed agreements with other manufacturing facilities throughout the rest of world," Angie said noticing George staring at her. "Excuse me, I must tend to matters at hand." Angie turned her back to the Ana Aseas and walked over to where George was standing.

"Aren't you supposed to wait until our leaders dismiss you?" George asked nervously.

"They need me," Angie laughed. "Any news?"

"He doesn't see any problems. Possibly a name change."

"Good," Angie said and pulled out her pursal. "Excuse me."

"Yes ma'am." George quickly turned and walked away.

"Richard here."

"I need a favor."

"Anything for my girl."

A slight grin appeared on Angie's face.

Richard continued, "By the way congrats on your earlier performance. You almost had me believing in Angels. So what do you need?"

"I want you to keep a close eye on Smitty."

"Can I ask why?"

"He knows too much."

"I have a couple of men I can assign to the job."

"Good. Just to make sure he doesn't …er…rock the boat, so to speak."

"And if he does?"

"I don't want to hear about it. Understand?"

"I won't let you down."

"Good." Angie hung up and turned her pursal to HV mode.

"Courtney Hughes back with *The Wolf* and you heard it here first! Now I have been instructed to inform the citizens of the world to respect and obey the Companions should you ever have the privilege to meet a modern day… Angel. As you know their job is to protect the Sevens from harm. Now here's a message from our local sponsor."

"They didn't hear it here first from us. This was announced on every station across the world," the cameraman said.

"I know, but what they don't know won't hurt them. Anyway it's good for the ratings," Courtney replied.

The camera's red light turned on as Courtney reappeared on the screen. "Thank you for staying with us. I believe we should take some time and thank God for sending us our modern day Saviors of the World, Humanochore and The Ana Asea Sevens!"

Fade out - Fade in.

"Have you been feeling lonely lately? Victimized by our war torn planet? Rest assured that we have the answer to all those nagging problems. Have your doctor prescribe Biochore's new multi-genetic nerve enhancement drug, Smilenol. Smilenol has been recommended by 4 out of 5 physicians to turn you from depression to being your old happy self again. Ask your doctor for more information.

"Happy me! Happy you! Happy happy family too! Feeling down? Feeling low? Not sure which way to go? One pill a day, troubles go away. Smile.an.all you'll feel is happy when life is gray!" sang a chorus to some cheery music while dancing in the background.

Fade out - Fade in.

"Welcome back! I am Courtney Hughes with *The Wolf*. I am glad you are still with us and I also want you to know the reason I am happy is because I take Smilenol every morning when I get up. It just puts a *smile on all* my face all day long! Now back to this momentous meeting taped earlier of the Ana Asea Sevens tenth year world address."

The camera cut from Courtney back to a replay of the video of the speech from Dr. Hoffstander-Steward and the Ana Asea Sevens standing with their bodyguards standing beside them.

"Do you really take that stuff?" the cameraman asked Courtney off-camera.

"Are you kidding me?" Courtney replied. She turned toward the camera and waited for another commercial to end.

Chapter 5

EARTH

Federal Building
Suite 303
New York, New York U.S.A.
Monday, February 16, 0015
0900 hours

(Five years later)

Colonel Carlos Sanchez had just turned forty-three and he had faithfully served Ana Asea One for the last fifteen years. When Number One wanted someone silenced or removed, he knew he could always count on Carlos. Colonel Sanchez was very good at what he did. Carlos had a very impressive history in his dealing with neutralizing those who were deemed a problem. In fact, he was a little too good and that sometimes concerned Ana Asea One.

Colonel Sanchez was previewing the events of the day to come when he received a call he would long remember.

"Colonel Sanchez?" Kim buzzed in. "You have a call on line one. It's the Secretary of Defense."

"What does he want?"

"To talk to you."

"Watch it Kim! You can be easily replaced, you know?"

Kim had run away from home when she was sixteen. Her father was a sergeant in the army and as hard as he was on his men, he was even harder on his three children. Kim was the oldest and took the brunt of her dad's abuse especially when he came home drunk, which he had done more and more after his wife left him for a marine. Now, nine years later, she found herself working for a dictatorial and cruel boss. There were times when she felt like she had never left home. She came from oriental descent, petite with jet-black hair and eyes to match. She always dressed professionally and worked hard at her job.

However, a week didn't go by without Sanchez trying to grab her when no one was around.

"Hello Mr. Secretary. It is an honor! What can I do for you?"

"The President wants you to train a lieutenant we have high hopes for in the future. Perhaps you may know him. You two served together years ago as privates under General Weissburg."

"Chris Rice?"

"No. Overman. Dennis Overman."

"What?"

"He's your man. Now keep us posted on his development. The President has big plans for him." The Colonel hung up the telephone and seconds later there was a knock on his door.

"Lieutenant Overman is here to see you." Kim poked her head through the door.

"Can this day get any worse?"

"Sir?"

"Let him in."

Knock knock!

"Enter!" Colonel Sanchez said.

Dennis Overman, now twenty-five years older, was still in tiptop shape weighing a muscular 165 pounds and sporting a thin mustache. He entered the room in full military garb.

"Overman! We meet again!"

"Excuse me sir?" Lieutenant Overman said with a slight British accent.

"The coward that failed to follow orders of his Commander."

"We were only teenagers back then and with all due respect, it saved our planet. I received the World Medal of Honor for my actions."

"You can't change a leopard's spots but I guess giving it a medal makes everything fine," Sanchez said under his breath, but loud enough for the Lieutenant to hear. Sanchez stood up from behind his desk and leaned in toward his new recruit. "Look Overman. I don't like cowards and do you know what I dislike even more?"

"Sir?"

"Cowards with medals."

"Perhaps I should have asked for a different assignment sir."

"No. As a favor to our President I have been tasked to take you under my wing. But let me tell you something," Sanchez placed both hands on his desk and leaned in even closer within inches from Overman's face. "If you screw up again Son, there won't be any more medals hanging on your chest, just one thick rope around your neck. Do you understand?"

"Perfectly, sir."

Sanchez relaxed and sat down behind his desk. "I have a task for you." Sanchez gathered up a pile of papers lying neatly on the side of the mahogany desk. He handed the papers to Overman. "Review these and get back to me when you have some intel."

"Yes sir, but what is the assignment if I might be so bold?"

"Terra Bulls."

"What's terrible?"

"Terra…Bulls, Overman," Sanchez said in disdain. "You are to pick a team and gather intel on their whereabouts and any future plans if possible." Sanchez sat in his chair and stared at Overman. "Don't come back until you have something of value. Understand?"

"Yes sir." Lieutenant Overman walked to the door. He put his hand on the knob then turned back to the Colonel. "By the way sir, may I ask what is a Terrible?"

"They are called Terra… Bulls, not Terribles. They are a group of insurgents who have been causing a lot of problems for the Ana Aseas lately. You have your orders, now get out of my office!"

Overman closed the door, paused, and turned to Kim. He looked at her until she raised her head. "Can I help you?"

"How do you work for a man like that?"

"Um, the pay is good?"

"Not good enough I'd wager." Overman looked down to see an unadorned left hand. "Perhaps we could meet for coffee. How about 0600 Wednesday?"

"I think I would like that," she smiled.

"Akela's on Lafayette Street?"

"I know the place."

"It's a date." He smiled back with a wink as he closed the door behind him.

A few seconds later Kim heard the intercom beep. "Kim!"

"Sir?"

"Get me the President...Yes, the guy in the White House!"

"Yes sir."

"No, wait, never mind," he said and hung up. He turned his chair back to the window. "I have a better idea for you, Lieutenant Coward," Colonel Sanchez smiled.

Akela's Café
Lafayette Street
New York, New York U.S.A.
Wednesday, February 18, 0015
0600 hours

(Two Days Later)

It was six o'clock in the morning as Dennis Overman waited for Kim to navigate her way between the tables and chairs to where he was sitting in the back of the room. "It's good to see you," he said.

"You too!"

"What made you decide to join me?"

"I have a thing for British accents I guess," she chuckled. "Besides you seemed nice."

Dennis smiled. "So where are you from?" He blew over the top of his coffee mug hoping to cool it down a bit. "Oh, I ordered you a cup of java. Hope you don't mind."

"Thank you," she said as she put her purse to her side. "All over. I'm what some people call an army brat." Kim took a careful sip of coffee. "Ouch! They always serve this stuff too hot."

"They have iced coffee."

"Yuck."

"Have you ever tried it?"

Kim shook her head. "How did your meeting go with Mr. Sanchez?" she asked in a disrespectful tone holding her coffee cup with both hands carefully balanced under her nose.

"He wants me to uncover a plot concerning a group of terrorists."

"The Terra Bulls?"

"That's them. I'll be gone for about six weeks doing some recon." Dennis leaned toward Kim. "I'm not supposed to tell anyone but I guess you already know."

"Just be careful," Kim whispered in his ear. "Sanchez cannot be trusted."

"I guess you heard our conversation back at the office?"

Kim nodded.

"What do you know about them? The Terra Bulls."

"They're Crossers."

"Crossers!" Dennis' eyes went wide. "Wow! Sanchez didn't mention that! They must be pretty well off to afford hybridization. I heard it's guaranteed to cure cancer and extend your life." Dennis dropped a couple of brown sugar cubes into his black elixir.

"Is that actually sugar?" Kim whispered in his ear and looked around the café.

"Brought some home when I was assigned to South America for a couple of months last year. I had a friend who grows it near the border of Brazil and Bolivia."

"But they are naturally grown, aren't they? I mean they aren't artificial or have been genetically altered, right?" Kim kept her voice low as she scanned to see if anyone was listening in.

"Yes and they taste really good."

"Don't you know it is illegal to eat anything that hasn't been processed?"

"Yes, I know they tell us it's for our own good," Dennis whispered back and shook his head. "So, aren't you the least bit interested in having the procedure?"

"Hybridization? It just sounds too good to be true if you know what I mean."

"I don't thinks so."

"Well, there are some drawbacks."

"I said it is very expensive."

"That's not the problem."

"The side effects?"

"Yes."

"So the virus turns you into a carnivore. Not having to eat any more broccoli sounds pretty enticing don't you think? I mean, hey I think being in perfect health is worth the trade off."

"Not everybody shares your enthusiasm." Kim slowly sipped her coffee.

"There was a pilot program where a selected group of our police officers received hybridization."

"Becoming a Crosser is not a good idea if you ask me."

"You would if you saw those guys. I gotta tell you, it's amazing! They have twice the strength and agility of what they once had. The women are equally impressive," Dennis said with a wink. "If you know what I mean."

"Forget it," Kim sighed shaking her head.

"Oh come on. You're not listening to those liberal tree hugging welfareons are you? Everyone knows their complaints about unintended consequences are a bunch of hype. I think they're just jealous because they can't afford it."

"How do you know?"

"I just know. Don't you ever watch *The Wolf*?"

"No."

"Well, I do and *The Sports* on *The Wolf* is showing men who are stronger and faster than I've ever seen! Crossers have taken sports to a whole new level! As soon as people saw how well this new breed of man has performed there has been a huge increase in demand."

"I don't think we should be messing with our DNA like this. Don't you think we should respect the way nature has handled our planet so far?"

"Nature's done a good job, but that doesn't mean we can't do better. You don't want to go back to living in caves now do you?"

"Does it have to be one extreme or the other with you?"

"Well, no. I just think if there was a problem it would have been reported by now, don't you think? I mean who in their right mind would pay attention to those idiot liberal welfareons anyway?" Dennis signaled the waiter. "A chance to never have cancer, heart disease, diabetes, and to hit a golf ball over five hundred yards. Wow, I think I'll take my chances."

Kim frowned.

"What is that for?"

"The other side effect."

"What other one?"

"The one no one is talking about."

"Would you like a refill?" the waiter asked.

Chapter 6

Federal Building
Suite 303
New York, New York U.S.A.
Tuesday, March 31, 0015
0900 hours

(Six weeks later)

"Colonel Sanchez?" Kim beeped in.

"What?"

"Lieutenant Overman is here."

"Good. Send him in."

"Do you have good news for me?" Sanchez asked as he moved his plate to the right side of the mahogany desk as he stealthily placed his left hand beneath it to turn on his recorder for his secretary to hear.

Overman walked over to Sanchez and stood with his hands clasped behind him, chest out.

"At ease, Soldier."

"Yes sir," Overman replied noticing what looked to be steak tartar resting beside Sanchez. "I am sorry if I interrupted your breakfast, sir."

"It can keep. So what do you have for me?"

"I think we may have narrowed the location of the next attack to three cities."

"And?"

"Nuuk Greenland, Moscow, and Washington."

"Nuuk? That is where the Ana Asea Seven members are located."

"Yes sir. I believe the Terra Bulls' intention is to disrupt our planet's government in order to establish their own." Overman pulled out a transmission sheet. "I've been monitoring these transmissions for the past week and an attack is near."

"How near?"

"Word on the street has it that there is a meeting scheduled in the warehouse district located in London." Overman placed a map with a red circle outlining a warehouse district in England, the East Thames mead area. Overman had placed a small X on a warehouse near Hailey Road. He had scribbled a note on the side of the map *Terra Bull possible meeting scheduled Saturday April 22ⁿᵈ at 0700 hours.*

"Centrally located to all attack locations. Sounds plausible."

"Yes sir. We have information on where the insurgents are living and where their weapons are located. In the next couple of weeks I should be able to verify the validity of what my sources are telling me. This mission is very important to the Sevens I suspect?"

"You are quite right. They grow weary of dealing with these insurgents and their terrorist activities."

"Yes, I would think so. I would like to send a notice to the Ana Asea Sevens and a copy to the Secretary about this new information that we've uncovered." Overman looked up from the map to the Colonel. "With your permission of course."

Sanchez picked up the map. "Hand all of this to Kim and I'll see to it that she sends it along with what you've told me. When you return in two weeks from Europe I trust you will have confirmation, correct?"

"Yes sir. I will be leaving in the morning."

"Good work... Captain!" Colonel Sanchez stood and offered his hand.

"Captain? Thank you, sir." Overman shook hands, saluted, and turned toward the door.

"Overman!"

"Sir?" Dennis turned back as Carlos pulled his breakfast toward him.

"If word gets out what you are doing it could jeopardize the entire project. Do you understand?"

"Yes sir."

"Good. You're dismissed."

"Congratulations Captain!" Kim winked as Dennis walked over to her.

"Thanks." He handed Kim the papers as a big smile crossed his face. "How about a little celebration dinner when I get back?"

"You know my number," Kim said as her eyes brightened. "Be careful."

"You know me."

"I'm getting to," Kim said and smiled.

As soon as Sanchez heard the outer office door close he called in his secretary. "Kim, bring me the map and the notes Overman left you."

Kim walked in holding the sheets of paper Overman had given her.

"Just put them here." Sanchez pointed to the center of his desk. "I am going to make some revisions and then I want you to retype it all and insert my name instead, understand?"

"Yes sir," Kim replied, "but won't Overman get suspicious?"

"You just leave that to me," Sanchez said. "Now get busy. I don't have all day."

Later that day Kim handed the typed revisions to Sanchez who looked over the information, signed his name, and handed the report back to her with a nod of approval.

It was five o'clock when Kim's intercom buzzed. "Sir?"

"I want to see you for a second."

Kim poked her head through the door.

"Well?" Sanchez inquired.

"I sent it a half an hour ago," Kim said and held up her pursal in *texpanded* mode for him to see. Kim snapped her pursal on her connector as it returned to *traveling* mode.

"Good girl," Sanchez said with a wink. "You've earned a little reward pat on the back. Why don't you shut the door and come on over here?"

"No reward necessary, sir. Just doing my job," Kim said and paused, "but I will shut the door as you asked." She turned, walked out of the office, and closed the outer door. She continued down the corridor with a grin on her face.

Sanchez looked at the closed door for a minute. He went over to his personal bar and poured himself a drink. "One day I am going to make that girl pay for her insolence." He picked up his pursal and dialed.

"Colonel Rice's office. Can I help you?"

"Colonel Rice please."

"May I ask who is calling?"

"Sanchez. Carlos Sanchez."

"Thank you. Let me see if he is still here. Just a minute..."

"Rice here."

"Hello Chris! I haven't seen you since you screwed up that missile launch. How have you been?"

"Sanchez? Me? Ha. I guess you're not scrubbing latrines with Overman, unless you're calling from Leavenworth. Good thing Weissburg doesn't make good on his threats, eh?" Rice chuckled into the phone.

"Guess who is working under me?"

"No way!"

"Yep."

"You're kidding? Working under you has got to be his worse nightmare no doubt."

"Oh I haven't even started," Sanchez laughed. "Overman just left for London and when he returns he'll have the confirmation on the Terra Bull Europe location."

"Nice. So I am to assume this isn't a social call?"

"I want you to help me coordinate an attack."

Pause.

"Are you there?"

"Why me?"

"Because I can count on you. By the way how is Julie?"

"Umm... Not too good."

"I heard."

"Yeah, well nothing's working. The doctors said it's just a matter of time unless..."

"She undergoes hybridization?"

"Yep."

"How do you feel about your wife becoming a Crosser?"

"Better than how I would feel if she was dead! I'm not sure I can take any long assignments right now. I want to stay home with her."

"I'm surprised you can afford the procedure on a Colonel's salary."

"If I could she would have had it already."

"Right, right. Listen," Sanchez paused, "it's only for a week, ten days at the most. Think of this, you will get a lot of credit for helping stomp out a Terra Bull cell and this could go a long way to get Julie crossed over to becoming a human hybrid."

"I don't need credit. I need cash."

"Yes and I could put in a request for some hazardous duty pay. It should be enough for a down payment if all goes well."

"When do you need an answer?"

"Right now."

Silence.

"Chris? Are you still there?"

Silence.

"I need to know if you're with me. Chris. This could be the lifeboat you and Julie have been praying for." Sanchez put his glass of brandy to his lips and took a small sip.

"I want to clear this with Julie," Chris said pensively.

"It can't wait. I need an answer now. Sorry, but plans are already in the works. I have a couple other officers who I know will jump at the chance to shine for the Ana Aseas. I guess I'll have to..."

"Wait!" Chris interrupted.

"Yes?"

"Okay. What do you want me to do?"

"You made the right decision. Now clear your calendar because we have got a lot of work to do. I'll see you in my office tomorrow at eleven hundred hours."

"Roger."

"Don't be late." Sanchez hung up his pursal as a big smile crossed his face.

Chapter 7

EARTH

(Three Weeks Later)

Ring…Ring…Ring…

"Hello?" Dennis groggily answered his pursal as it popped into *celling* mode.

"Did I wake you?"

"No…YES! Who is this?"

"It's been over three weeks since I've heard from you and I got worried."

"Kim?" The eagerness in Dennis's voice made her smile. "I've been across the pond doing recon." He looked at the clock on the table. "It's twenty-three hundred hours. You woke me up you know?"

"I thought you were supposed to be out for only two weeks."

"I was scheduled for only two weeks, but Sanchez wanted me to check out some additional Terra Bull activity his sources had said was going on over there."

"Really?"

"Yeah, I don't know who his sources were, but there was nothing unusual to report. I had a feeling he sent me on a wild goose chase."

"He had a reason, I fear," Kim stated.

"What was it?"

"I'll tell you later."

"Why not now?" Silence. "Kim?"

"Can you meet me at Akela's?"

"Akela's?" Dennis searched for his slippers. "Now?"

"No, silly. How about Friday morning, say sixish?"

"Great!" Dennis crawled back in bed. "I am looking forward to seeing you. By the way I have a meeting with Sanchez at nine that day. I don't think it's far from the café."

"I know. I have his schedule." Kim hung up her pursal and a nice feeling came over her.

Akela's Café
Friday, April 24, 0015
0600 hours

It was a few minutes before six on an unusually cool Friday morning as the sun slowly opened its sleepy eyes over the small shops along the street. Dennis liked this time of day especially when it was cool and there was a slight breeze blowing in his direction. He hesitated for a minute to feel the wind against his face then turned and walked into the café. He spotted Kim sitting in the very back as she slowly sipped her coffee. She gave him a quick wave as a smile crossed her face. He could hear the café's air conditioning humming in the background as he walked over to her. She pulled out a chair and motioned him to sit beside her.

"Is this seat taken?" Dennis asked with a grin.

"As a matter of fact I am waiting for a good looking officer."

Dennis looked around the café. "Well, I don't see anyone who fits that description."

"Look in the mirror."

Dennis grinned as he sat down next to her. "I thought you might want to sit up front to watch the day unfold."

"It's better back here for now."

"I'm hungry! What's good here?" Dennis asked as he took a sip of his coffee. "Thanks for ordering me some."

"Do you have any sugar left?" she whispered and gave him a wink. Dennis reached into his pocket and pulled out two brown cubes. "Thanks."

He dropped a couple of them in her cup and pulled the coffee stained menu to his face. "So… what do you recommend?"

"They have freshly made whole wheat raisin bagels."

"Sounds yummy," Dennis said as he rubbed his thumb on the menu stains.

The waiter brought a full carafe to the table. "Care for a refill?"

"Thank you," Dennis said as he watched the waiter fill his cup. "This is by far the best coffee I've ever had."

"Thank you sir. The beans are grown in Hawaii. We have fresh bagels today or you can order from our new menu." The waiter handed Dennis a brand new menu showing different cuts of raw beef, chicken and pork.

"I'll stick with the whole wheat raisin bagel."

"An excellent choice! And you ma'am?" the waiter asked.

"I'll have the same."

Dennis gazed at the new menu and then looked over the dining room as some of the other patrons stuffed themselves with slabs of raw beef and pork. He watched as the blood from the meat dripped from their mouths onto their plates.

"Hybrids?"

"Yes. I am seeing more and more these days." Kim waved another pesky fly away. "Have you noticed there are a lot more flies swarming these days?"

"Not to mention mosquitos. They're making it hard to go out at nigh…"

"Hide!" Kim interrupted.

"What?" Dennis asked as he put the Akela's menu in front of his face mimicking Kim.

She peeked over her menu and noticed Carlos had already passed by. "My boss just walked by, but I don't think he saw us."

"Carlo..?"

"Shhh...," Kim interrupted. "Yes. Sometimes he comes this way to work."

"Isn't it a little out of the way?"

"He never takes the same path twice in a row to work."

"From my experience dealing with him I can see why. Do you think you were followed?"

"Nah. He doesn't view women, especially me, as much of a threat. A weakness if you know what I mean."

"Especially when it comes to a girl like you I bet."

Kim smiled and nodded slightly. "I have something I need to tell you." Kim placed her hand on his leg and moved closer to him.

"Sounds like something I am going to want to hear."

"Not really," Kim's voice lowered to a whisper. She reached over and grabbed Dennis' pursal attached to his belt.

"Hey! What are you...?"

Kim turned her face to Dennis and placed an upright finger to her lips. Dennis nodded and kept silent. His pursal was still only the size of a quarter being in *traveler* mode. Kim pulled out a small container and placed it in her lap. She opened it and placed both her pursal and his in the box and slowly closed it.

"We can talk freely now," Kim said in a hushed tone.

"We can?" Dennis asked as confusion appeared on his face.

"Sanchez plans on double crossing you on the Terra Bull attack. He had me send the Secretary of Defense a letter describing your incompetence."

"You're kidding!" Dennis' voice raised an octave.

"Shhh...I wish I was."

"Why did you take my pursal?"

"Ears."

"Mine is bugged?"

"They all are. Don't worry. The box is sound proof so now we can talk without anyone listening in," Kim assured him.

"I had no idea I was being spied on."

"No one does." Kim shook her head.

"You mean we're being tracked and recorded without our knowledge?"

"You got it. The system is wired to pick up certain groups of people, words and phrases. You and I are," Kim looked to the ceiling for the right word, "relational to Carlos Sanchez. The Colonel is high profile and Big Ben puts him in a constant priority mode."

"What do you mean?"

"I'm his secretary and now you are having meetings with him. It's like each of us are on a separate point on the same triangle. At least this is how Big Ben sees it and that is why Big Ben probably knows we are here together now. No problem, right? So far it's just a coincidence. Big Ben hears us conversing, still no problem, but now it has moved from level green to yellow."

"Who is Big Ben?"

"It's not a who it is a what. Big Ben is a super computer like ENIAC2 except Ben's sole function is gathering intel from our pursals. Every time you use it to buy, record, or talk, Big Ben is always listening."

"What does yellow mean?"

"It starts a low level recording of our conversation looking for any illegal activity."

"Like my sugar cubes?"

"Yep."

"Then what?"

"If you say certain words Big Ben will decide if you are a threat or a non-threat. If you are considered a non-threat the recording erases. If you are a threat then you move to level Orange or Prime Status."

"What is Prime Status? I don't think I am going to like it."

"You're not. It means you are a person of interest. That's when Big Ben starts collecting information on you through not just your pursal, but also all channels available to it and uses complex algorithms to create a profile. If your profile remains positive it moves to level Red. Once that is done the authorities are alerted and they review the information and decide if you are a threat to the greater society."

"Wow! All of that is going on in the background when I call someone?"

"Or talk to someone."

"Oh my god! You're right. As long as I have my pursal or the person I'm talking to has theirs we are being recorded."

Kim nodded. "Any type of communication traveling through the air is fair game to those who know how to capture it. They got the idea years ago when people put these little black box looking devices in their homes that could play music, turn on your television, or switch your lights on and off. You could even purchase products from them online and all you had to do was ask."

"All this new technology everyone thought was so cool because it could do so much for us. No one ever considered that it could do just as much against us."

"Yep. Those companies would listen in on your conversations at home. Then they would target certain commercials to what they had heard you say."

"That's illegal. Isn't it?"

"You paid them to put their microphones in your bedrooms." Kim shrugged her shoulders. "Espionage or eavesdropping has been going on since the beginning of man. Those who hunger for power, once they achieve it, fear that others may take it away from them."

"Got to be one step ahead I guess," Dennis paused. "I never thought about how much control I have been giving up for the sake of modern conveniences."

"It's not just you. We've all fallen from grace. Haven't you wondered why there are so many more arrests these days?"

"I thought it was just a lot of people forgetting to take their anti-depression, anti-anxiety, or one of those other types of strange medications that are always coming out with on the market these days. At least that is what the news channels are saying."

"It can be profitable too. The commercials are telling you if you are feeling angry or have thoughts of doing something harmful or illegal to contact your family doctor."

Dennis nodded. "So they can take your money and drug you into subservience."

"The doctors are only following orders and the media is only telling us what they are instructed. There is no freedom of news anymore."

"Why do you say that?"

"When the news companies were allowed to be bought by big corporations, they lost their right to report the news. They just report what they are told."

"And let me guess. The government controls the big corporations?"

"No. The big corporations control our government!"

"Sounds like you are being a little bit paranoid to me," Dennis remarked.

"Perhaps, but it's better to be a little overly cautious these days." Kim looked around the café and then back at Dennis. "I guess I have seen too much."

"Sounds like you have been doing your own recon."

"How do you think I know all this? Sometimes I work late after Sanchez leaves and I know where his jimmy is located."

"You mean you can access his database?"

"I learned some very useful skills while doing time," Kim smiled.

"Sounds like time well spent!" Dennis laughed.

"Remember the raid on Summerhill Ranch in New Mexico last week?"

"Of course. It was all over the news. *The Wolf* televised the raid. Our soldiers attacked and burned down the ranch. It was reported to be a Terra Bull headquarters. Some of the help were killed in that raid. The ranch turned out to be owned by a Senator Richards, I believe was his name. His son had been shot and was in intensive care. He still is, if I recall correctly. It was a huge mistake with the media crying out for justice. I heard there is going to be an internal investigation and charges will be brought within the next few weeks."

"Sanchez was behind it all and he told the Secretary it was you who set it up and authorized the invasion without his consent," Kim informed Dennis.

"What! I was in Germany that day and I can prove it. I stayed in this little inn right above this German bar called Zum Ness-something or another. I met this scientist from Atlanta. Yeri was his name I believe. He was working with the CDC and we ended up swapping stories while drinking lagers. I didn't get much sleep that night."

"Hangover?"

"Noise. The more those Germans downstairs drank the louder they got. They sang songs until the bar closed around 0300. God it was a long day the next day."

"Poor baby," Kim said, "but having a little morning sickness is nothing compared to what Carlos has in store for you."

"But I have an alibi."

"Doesn't matter. You didn't have to be there. Remember the information you left with Sanchez about the Terra Bull suspected cell location in London?"

"The letter I gave you to send to the Secretary?"

Kim nodded. "After you left, Sanchez rewrote the entire letter. He changed the location to the Summerhill Ranch. I read it before I forwarded it on and I wanted to give you a heads-up, but I couldn't find a way to contact you. Sanchez usually has me listen in on all his conversations."

"Isn't he taking a chance that you may," Dennis gave Kim a frown, "do what you are doing right now?"

"He has something on me."

"Blackmail?"

"Remember when I told you I ran away from my abusive father?"

Dennis nodded.

"I got as far away as my savings could take me. Then I was really on my own. No one would hire me because of my age and I didn't have a permanent address, so I ended up running with the wrong crowd. We got caught holding up a Mini Mart. I was the driver because I was the only one who hadn't lost her license. They told me to keep the motor running because they would only be in the shop for a minute or two and it was really hot outside. I never thought they would actually rob a store. They would do a little shoplifting, run out of a restaurant without paying, but nothing as serious as this. I didn't even know Joey had a gun. All four of them got out and Joey stuck his pistol right into the clerk's face and pulled back the trigger. I freaked and backed up right into another car getting gas. The gas spilled on to the pavement and before you knew it both cars were on fire."

"Oops," Dennis said.

"Yeah, a big oops and the next thing I knew I was telling my side to the judge, but he was the hard-on-crime type and ignored my story."

"Didn't your friends say something?"

"They blamed me for spoiling their getaway and made a deal with the prosecutor. If we all pled guilty, we would all be charged with a lesser crime and spend less time in jail." Kim sipped her coffee. "I just got flushed down the drain with the rest of the scum."

"How did Sanchez come across you?"

"Actually he frequented the prisons quite often. He saw me and said he could get me out."

"As long as you do his bidding?"

Kim nodded. "Carlos finds out who is getting close to parole and he has a reputation with some of the members on the parole board. Play his game and you get out. If you refuse, you better count on serving your whole sentence."

"Why is he doing this?"

"Sometimes he has to circumvent the law and who better to do that than a former con? So he interviews them in prison and offers them a job when they get out. Or he gets them released early depending on what he needs them to do."

"You could go back to jail if your boss sees us or finds out you're seeing me."

Kim nodded. "I knew something bad was about to happen and I had to contact you."

"Now I know why Sanchez wanted me to go dark these past few weeks. No contact made it easier to make me the fall guy."

"I think the whole purpose of the raid was in order to frame you." Kim sipped her coffee and moved a little closer to Dennis.

"I've got to do something about this." Dennis started to get up, but Kim grabbed his leg and squeezed.

"There is more," she whispered in his ear. "Yesterday he had me send another letter to the Ana Asea Sevens and the President with a copy to the Secretary about the London Terra Bulls information you gave him. He left you totally out of the equation. He said he has been out of contact with you for weeks now." Kim carefully looked around the café. "He told them he thinks you're on the run."

"Jesus!"

"That is why I called you so late. I thought you might want to know what has happened before you meet with him today."

Dennis sat in silence for a long time staring out the window. Kim knew he needed some time to process everything he had heard. "So he wants himself to shine at my expense, eh? Do you think I'll be arrested when I show up today?"

"No. He still needs confirmation before he raids the Terra Bull headquarters. After that I don't know."

"Okay."

"Why does he hate you so much?"

"We were both privates under General Weissburg. I was the one who wouldn't launch our missiles during the One Day War."

"That was you?" Kim exclaimed. "You're a hero."

"Not in Sanchez's eyes. Weissburg threw me in the stockade and Carlos took my place. He tried to launch the rockets but I had changed the codes."

"That wasn't Sanchez's fault."

"No, but since then I guess he has been looking for revenge. When the Secretary of Defense asked me if I would work under Sanchez, I figured that little incident was forgotten. Apparently not."

"What are you going to do?"

"I think it is time for a little payback."

"Be careful dear." Kim opened the box and handed him back his pursal still in *traveler* mode.

Dennis turned his pursal into *celling* and showed it to her. "I'll call you later." Dennis bent over and gave her a kiss goodbye.

Federal Building
Suite 303
New York, New York U.S.A.
Friday, April 24, 0015
0900 hours

"Good Morning Captain," Sanchez greeted Dennis Overton with a smile. "I trust you have good news for me?"

"Yes sir! I have confirmation on the Terra Bulls location. They will be packing up next Friday and moving from their secret headquarters the East Thames mead area in London to an undisclosed location. Word is out they will be moving to a new location on Saturday May 1ˢᵗ and I am planning to invade their camp the day before on Friday, April 30ᵗʰ."

"Hmm... that sounds like a good plan. Okay Overman I am giving you a go on the raid. Be careful because I've heard they can be quite aggressive."

"Thank you, sir. If anything changes I will let you know."

Chapter 8

EARTH

Topographie Des Terrors
Niederkisrchner - Strasse 3 Berlin, Germany
Thursday, April 30, 0015
0530 hours

It was daybreak Thursday, one day before Dennis Overman's planned raid when Colonel Sanchez, along with Christopher Rice, ordered a strike on the London warehouse. The strike yielded no results except for a lot of finger pointing.

That same day Captain Overman gathered his squad and raided the Terra Bull headquarter cell in Berlin, Germany. The Bulls had been meeting in the basement of the Topographie Des Terrors on Niederkisrchner Strasse 3. The building was a landmark site once headquarters to the Schutzstaffel (SS) and the Gestapo. The basement was where the Nazis tortured their victims. It was closed to the public because it had recently undergone reconstruction. The Terra Bulls had landed a contract to do the work making it a perfect place for the Bulls to conduct their business.

Sanchez's warehouse held nothing more than crates of used machine parts infested with cockroaches and a few rats. While Sanchez's men were going through crates looking for weapons of any kind, Captain Overman's team was busy interrogating their prisoners.

Chris was looking through another crate of machine parts when he felt his pursal clipped to his belt in *traveler* mode expand into *celling* and rang. He pulled the pursal off his belt. "Chris Rice here."

"Hi honey! I just saw on the news about your success in raiding the Terra Bulls."

"Julie?"

"Yes. I've always wanted to go to Germany."

"We're not...."

"Oh that's okay. I know it was all top secret, but you can tell me now. Everyone's talking about it."

"Damn! I gotta go," Chris said.

"But I thought we could..." Chris hung up the pursal, watched it return to *traveler* mode snapped it back on his belt and walked into the adjacent room where Sanchez was barking orders to some privates.

"Colonel?" Chris shouted over the noise and walked over to where Carlos was standing and whispered in his ear.

"Not again!" yelled Carlos. "I am going to make that son of a bitch pay if it's the last thing I do. This is the last time Overman is going to make me look like a fool!" Sanchez snorted.

"What do you want me to do?" Chris asked.

"Round up the men. We're through here."

As the men vacated the rat infested building Sanchez picked up his pursal.

"Wolf News London."

"Carlos Sanchez here. I need to speak to Courtney Hughes, right away."

"Just a minute."

Three hours later the cameramen were on the set as Courtney's assistant walked over and pinned the microphone on Sanchez's lapel.

"Hi. I am Courtney Hughes with *The Wolf* and today we are here with Colonel Sanchez." Courtney turned to the Colonel. "I understand you are the driving force behind the capture of some of the most ruthless terrorists in the world."

"Thank you, Courtney. As we speak my men are interrogating the prisoners and we have found that there are other Terra Bull cells still in operation and I personally will not rest until all of them have been brought to justice."

"How did you find this one?"

Sanchez smiled. "Courtney, if I told my secrets then I doubt I would be able to find the others."

"Of course. Anyway thank you for your service to mankind, Colonel Sanchez." Courtney turned to the camera. "And there you have it. Colonel Sanchez, the one who brought down one of the biggest terrorist cells in the world. This is Courtney Hughes with *The Wolf*. If it's news it's with us."

Fade out - Fade in.

The scene showed a doctor's office lined with diplomas and bookcases. "And now a message from your friendly doctor on combating depression," the off-camera announcer said.

"Hello," said a soft-spoken man in a white coat with a stethoscope slung around his neck as the camera panned to a large desk where he was sitting. "I'm Doctor Imes and I get worried when a patient tells me he is having angry thoughts." The doctor clasped his hands and gingerly placed them on the desk as the camera moved in for a close-up shot. "As you know, we are friends and we care about you," the doctor's voice softened even more, "and since we are friends you can tell me if you are having angry thoughts now and again." The doctor showed a picture of a frown. "I know you want to be happy and I want you to be happy, but I can't help you unless you see me." The doctor turned the picture upside down showing a smile.

"Together let's turn that frown upside down. Okay?" He returned the picture to the desk and sported a big grin. "For your own safety, please pick up your pursal and give your local friendly neighborhood physician a call. The doctor showed the camera a prescription pad with 'Smilenol Extra Strength' written in bold letters. "And tell him you want the new Extra Stren…"

Click. "We're going to make a lot of money advertising that one," Courtney said as she watched the monitor fade to black and turned back to the Colonel. "Thank you for allowing me an exclusive." Courtney extended her hand.

Carlos grabbed her left hand instead and pulled her closer to him. "I don't see a ring?"

Courtney gently but firmly pulled away. "I'm married, but the producer thinks that showing me young and single will attract more viewers."

"If you want more exclusive interviews perhaps you can play the single part off-camera too?" Sanchez raised one eyebrow.

Courtney shook her head, turned and walked away.

"I'm going to make that girl pay for her insolence one day." Carlos pulled out his pursal.

"Overman here."

"Congratulations on bringing down the Terra Bull cell in Germany. Why didn't you tell me?" Sanchez asked.

"I wasn't sure if my sources were valid, sir. I felt it better for me to take a squad of men in and if we found nothing it would not look bad on you. So I guess there is no need to check out London tomorrow."

"I would agree. Well, smart thinking but I need you to keep me in the loop next time. There will be a prisoner van in your area in two hours."

"Yes sir."

"Next I want your team to meet me at my London headquarters."

"Which base are we flying out of?"

"We don't have the resources at this point to fly you."

"We'll have to drive?"

"Do you have a problem with that, Captain?" Carlos snarled into this pursal.

"I guess not," Overman sighed into his pursal. "It's just that England is going to take us over thirteen hours traveling by jeep and my men are already showing signs of fatigue."

"They can sleep in the Humvees. This is urgent and that is all I can say at the moment. I will see you later tonight."

Captain Overman turned to his men. "Okay ladies, we will be driving to England in a couple of hours."

"England?" Sergeant Louis exclaimed. "With all due respect sir, but my men are tired and need a break."

"They can sleep in the Humvee," Captain Overman replied as he tried to keep his disappointment from his men.

RAF Lakenheath Air Force Base
Suite 2110
London, England
Friday, May 1, 0015
0100 hours

It was one in the morning when Overman's squad arrived. He watched his men stumble into the Colonel's office. Many were yawning while others were having trouble keeping their eyes open.

"I wanted to personally congratulate each and everyone of you in your efforts to protect the New World Order! The terrorists have now been transferred to a more secure area for interrogations. A fine job!" The Colonel smiled at each man. "I can appreciate your eagerness to be reunited with your family and friends..." the Colonel bowed his head and paused, "unfortunately, your loved ones will have to wait just a little while longer." He could see the looks of disappointment cross the men's faces.

Sanchez continued, "It's due to your excellent work in the field that the Ana Asea Sevens have rewarded you with one more top secret mission before a well deserved little R & R," Sanchez smiled. "Yes, when you get home you all will be rewarded for your hard work in this matter. Two weeks additional paid vacation time this year to begin immediately after this last assignment." The men were still shuffling back and forth. "When you return you will all see a very nice big bonus along with your pay. Call it hazardous duty pay." A few grins came to a couple of the soldiers. "That's the spirit. The plane is on the tarmac as we speak. Grab your gear and let's get going."

No one moved.

"You're dismissed. If there are no more questions we need to move. Now!" Sanchez ordered with a forced smile waving his fingers to the door.

Overman thought that odd. He had been on covert missions before, but he was always briefed beforehand about the mission. He was left in the dark on this one and that concerned him especially when it came from Sanchez.

Sanchez was packing his briefcase when Overman grabbed his arm. Sanchez swung it wildly and stared at Overman. "Watch it!" he yelled with a look Overman would not soon forget.

"Excuse me Colonel, but who has the M.O?"

"The Mission Objective?" Sanchez paused. "You don't need to concern yourself with the Mission Objective," he replied with a snarl. He then calmly said, "Oh sorry, I've had a very long day and I apologize if I came across a little bit hostile toward you." Sanchez smiled and patted Overman on the back with a gentle push slowly escorting him out of the office. "The Mission Objective is with Jenkins. Lieutenant Arthur Jenkins will be waiting for you when you land in Nuuk. There you and your team will be briefed on what to expect and where you will be heading. That is all I am allowed to say at the moment. I am sorry, but this is coming from the top."

"I understand," Captain Overman replied, then turned away.

"Good luck! I am looking forward to hearing another big success from you and your team!"

Dennis Overman was not happy straying from the normal protocol when going on a covert assignment. *There is something fishy going on,* he thought to himself as he remembered the look Sanchez gave him concerning the M.O.

Overman's men were still gathering their equipment while some walked toward the airplane with backpacks stuffed and ready for another mission. Sergeant Louis stopped the Captain in his tracks.

"Excuse me sir, but these men need a break. We haven't been home in over a week not to mention the lack of sleep."

"Military life at its finest," Overman smiled.

"Isn't there anybody else who can take this one? That basement in Berlin gave me the creeps and I know some of the men are still shaken by the experience."

"I know. I could almost feel the pain and misery calling out from those walls."

"Yeah well, what are we getting ourselves into now and where are we going?"

"Sanchez didn't say," Overman replied as he watched his men gather near the transport.

"You haven't been briefed? Don't you think that odd? I mean where are we going? Do you at least know that?"

"Greenland."

The Sergeant stared quizzically. "Greenland?"

"Yeah, Nuuk. That is where we will meet our contact to give us more information about the mission location and objectives." Overman smiled at the man he had fought side by side for so many years. "And no I don't know why Sanchez couldn't give us the M.O. here, but I assure you I'm going to find out."

Captain Overman motioned his friend to board the military transport while he stood on the tarmac with his hands on the clipboard counting the remaining soldiers.

"Let's go ladies! I am not going until everyone else is on board!" he yelled over the engine noise. The soldiers picked up the pace and twenty minutes later the flames fired out from under each wing. Sanchez's office shook from the raw power being generated from the metal beast.

Sanchez looked out his office window and watched the plane taxi down the runway. He turned to face the picture of Fidel Castro hanging above his beloved humidor and pulled out a Cohiba cigar along with his double-blade cutter. He then gently pulled out a bottle of Baron De Sigongnac and slowly poured it into his brandy sniffer. He raised the glass to his chin and waved it side to side allowing the aroma to fill his nostrils. "To you Captain." He saluted with a laugh and downed the magic elixir in one fatal swoop. He then lit his cigar, sat down with his feet resting on his desk and waited.

KA-BOOM!

It was a little past three in the morning when the holovisions throughout the entire world were ablaze with the explosion just off the coast of Ireland. The citizens of Dublin were being interviewed remarking about the flash in the skies above them. The plane carrying the soldiers simply blew up and fell into the sea never to be recovered.

Chapter 9

MARS

"What do you have in your hands, Dad?" Ken asked.

Yeri raised his right hand holding a wad of papers. "These?" Ken nodded. Yeri handed them to Ken.

"Bubonic Plague Saves Seagulls!"
- The Big Apple

"Humanochore Cures Cancer!"
- The Chicago Elitist

"We have Been Saved!"
- The Western Gospel Today

"Humanochore Scientist Warns Side Effects Too Dangerous!"
- The Journal Of Global Health

"The Journal of Global Health? What about it?"

"It was written by your grandfather."

"What does it say?"

"Why don't you read it?" Yeri asked.

"Because you're here and you can just give me the Cliff Notes version."

"It was this last article my dad wrote that no one wanted to know about." Yeri shook his head. "Dad knew Dr. Hoffstander-Steward was intelligent and the people needed to know what was going on behind the closed doors of Humanochore. Dad's article about the seagulls was met with skepticism and was eventually dismissed. *Wolf News* said it was all made up because Dad's work failed and he blamed Humanochore for firing him."

"I thought he died from sarin gas exposure at work?"

"He did."

"I guess that was kind of left out," Ken said.

"He was replaced by another scientist, Dr. Smitherman was his name. He went on the air and told everyone that it wasn't God or angels who came up with this cure. He told them the procedure was the direct result from Dr. Thornton's work. He talked about the adverse side effects and how they were conveniently removed from the trials. He said he was going to expose Humanochore's CEO Dr. Hoffstander-Steward for the liar and crook she was."

"I bet that created some repercussions."

"You bet. She got wind of what he was doing and made a few calls. The interview never aired and the next day Dr. Smitherman was killed from a hit and run. When he died, it struck fear in the other scientists so they all kept their mouths shut. They allowed the lies about God and the angels to continue," Yeri frowned and continued his story, "Remember when I told you someone poisoned the lab with sarin gas and everyone died but those seagulls?"

"Yes," Ken replied as Togo walked into the room and hopped on Yeri's leg not being used by his sister.

"Humanochore tried injecting people with the same virus. Unfortunately it killed them."

"Hmmm...It could save the seagulls, but killed humans?"

"It seemed to only work on birds, but the barn door was now open. They tried mutating other level four germs' DNA. They continued to recode and recode until finally they found one that worked. The Ebola virus didn't work very well on the birds, but the animals were a huge success. It wasn't long before they started phase four trials."

"Phase four?"

"Using human test subjects."

"Why would someone agree to being a guinea pig? Especially when the viruses killed the others?" Togo asked.

"Because they used desperate people. People with end stage cancer and the like. They had nothing to lose."

"Oh."

"The Ebola virus cured everybody, but there were unintended consequences."

"Side effects?" Ken asked.

"Yep. The virus mutated at first according to what we wanted. It not only healed the test subjects but it also made their bodies a lot stronger."

"Wow! I bet they liked that!" Togo exclaimed.

"Oh yes. But Dad wouldn't have."

"Why not?" Togo asked.

"Because it was a new side effect that hadn't appeared in the animal test subjects. He didn't like surprises. He told me you have to be very careful dealing with the life force. He said it was better to err on the side of caution when delving into the unknown."

"But he wasn't around anymore was he?" Togo asked.

"No, he wasn't and no one would dare stand up to the corporate CEOs. They became too powerful, they infiltrated our government and they put their people in government positions in order to gain favorable rulings for them against the public interest."

"So everyone just sat around and did nothing?"

"The ones that tried just couldn't compete with corporate money. They used commercials to convince us this was a good thing. Management simply ignored the unforeseen side effects and worked on gaining FDA approval. It didn't take long before we were recoding thousands of people a day."

"Did they grow a tail?" Togo asked.

"A tail? No."

"I want to grow a tail. If I got the treatment could I get a tail?"

"No. DNA recoding is outlawed on Mars."

"Shucks. Then why did we leave?"

"We saw dangerous trends developing. Anywhere from three to six months after recoding, the Crossers caught what we thought was a nasty cold. The illness lasted from ten days to about two weeks and afterwards they couldn't stand the sight of vegetables. They only wanted to eat meat and raw meat at that."

"What made them sick?"

"We think it was the virus mutating. Just like Dad was afraid of. We were losing control of how to manage the virus. That's if we ever had any control."

"Did they stop it?"

"Hardly, It quickly became the company's cash cow. Humanochore with the help of some well paid politicians turned this problem into a benefit."

"And people believed them?"

"Absolutely! Millions of dollars were spent on advertising the New Man. They showed films of the New Man's superior athletic ability. They showed people who were sick and dying before the procedure and how healthy they had become after the procedure. 'Crosser only' restaurants opened up making it a status symbol. They downplayed the aggressiveness that was showing up in people who underwent hybridization. They hid the facts about the dramatic increase in missing pets. Dogs and cats were being killed and eaten by the New Man."

"Wasn't this reported?"

"There were only a few independent news stations left and they reported their concerns but it was met by the major news feeds calling them fake news."

"I don't think I would want to be a New Kid."

"No you wouldn't. But the corporations continued blanketing our controlled news media with perceived advantages of being a Crosser. They showed people in Tokyo wearing masks to protect themselves from the intense smog while the Crossers walked around taking big breaths of polluted air acting like it was no big deal."

"They didn't get sick?"

"No, they didn't and this delighted the corporate bosses. They petitioned the courts to remove all smog-related devices to show that pollution was no longer a threat."

"It was to animals."

"They didn't care about other creatures that lived on Earth. They only cared about one thing."

"What was that?"

"Money. They even altered our plants' DNA. They manipulated the DNA in our corn and wheat to secrete deadly toxins if a bug tried to eat them."

"Why?"

"So we could eat them."

"That doesn't sound right."

"It wasn't. Those who didn't undergo hybridization got sicker and sicker. A small group of scientists sued the corporations for altering the DNA in our plants. They showed study after study of healthy people getting sick from eating their GMO trash."

"What happened?"

"Nothing. The courts ruled there was nothing different in regular versus genetically modified DNA food."

"But that's not true!" Togo said.

"It is when big business owns the government."

"So they forced us to eat something that secretes poisons?"

"Yes and after the suit they got the courts to agree that GMO tainted foods need not be on the labels. Their argument was, 'since nature does it, why shouldn't we?'"

"That's true! I mean, what was wrong with altering plants? I read nature does it all the time. It's called a higher bird?"

"A hybrid."

"Yeah. You just put two plants together and they form a different one. Isn't that what we were doing on Earth?"

"Yes, but not according to the rules of nature."

"Nature has rules?"

"Our bodies are very complex organisms. When you eat, the cells in your body know exactly what to do with the food. It sends a protein to your eyelid and another to your heart muscle, one to your finger nail and some to your brain."

"How does it know where everything goes?"

"It just does and we don't have a clue. That is why we shouldn't force plants to become something that nature would never do."

"Because breaking the Law of Nature would be bad. Right?"

"If you drink something like poison that kills your cells what do you think would happen?"

"You would die I guess?"

"Exactly."

"Then why didn't people die when they ate the new food?"

"If they died right away then no one would eat it, but the GMO toxins had to build up in the body before it could make you really sick. It took years before we could convince people that smoking cigarettes was harmful and a major factor in lung cancer deaths. Even then people continued to smoke knowing it could prematurely end their lives."

"Why?"

"Because they don't think it will happen to them."

"Like eating bad food and breathing toxic air?"

Yeri nodded. "Now off my legs so I can go get a drink."

Togo and Tiga hopped off his legs and sat down cross-legged on the floor.

"They are getting too big to sit on my knees," Yeri said as he hobbled into the kitchen.

"Perhaps you should sit on the floor with them," Ken said.

"Funny man." Yeri opened the kitchen cabinet. "For that I'm going to make me a double."

"Well it's getting late and you two need to get into your pjs," Tima said to the kids.

"I want to hear more about Earth," Togo said.

"Me too," Tiga chimed in.

"No more tonight," Ken replied. "I have a busy schedule tomorrow and I have to check out an MMU."

"I thought you had a rover?" Tiga asked.

"I did."

"Why don't we have *Spirit* anymore Daddy?" Togo asked. "I thought you could keep anything you found on Mars, right?"

"Yeah, well the Minister of Defense decided that all rovers like the MMUs should not become privately owned. He passed a new law called The Rover Search and Seizure Act. Anyone who found a rover would be required to report his findings to eGAD."

"What is that?" Tiga asked.

"Oh sorry, it's the elected Government Acquisitions Department. They basically refit the rovers for passenger use and we have to fill out some stupid forms if we need one. What I found interesting is thirty something rovers have been reported and I know Earth never sent that many, but then I really didn't have privy to the payload sent to Mars each time," Ken paused. "It just seemed like a lot of rovers to me."

"But don't we have Pat?" Togo asked.

"Yes."

"Why do we call it Pat?"

"That was the name on it when I found it. Pat was the only thing I could make out. The rest of the letters had been erased from all of the Martian dust storms. Now don't tell anyone okay?"

"You guys sure like to keep a lot of secrets!" Togo said as he fiddled with the jimmy in his pocket. "Won't the Minister of Defense find out?"

"I hope not," Tima said. "Your dad and Grandpa totally rebuilt this one and built an engine that runs on...?"

"Dioxathane," Ken answered.

"Dioxathane. Yes that's it. Your dad developed it in his lab. It's a process of turning carbon dioxide into an enhanced liquid methane fuel using an electric field?" Tima looked questionably at Ken.

"Yes," Ken nodded. "It is highly explosive."

"Like Togo's farts!" Tiga interrupted and started laughing along with Togo. Even Yeri from the kitchen cracked a grin.

"Tiga!" Tima turned a bright red. "You apologize right now."

"Sorry Grandma. Sorry Bedipida."

"Good. Now if you or Togo see a canister lying around here do not touch it. Understand?"

"Yes ma'am," Togo said as they both continued giggling.

"Did someone mention my name?" Yeri asked from the kitchen.

"The kids are acting goofy as usual. We're just trying to explain to them about Pat," Ken said and turned back to Togo. "Since Mars is primarily made up of CO2 we'll have virtually an unlimited supply of fuel and we can cruise around at night and no one will ever see us."

"Except maybe a Halk or two," Tima interjected with concern on her face.

Togo said, "I think it should have a better name than Pat."

"What do you want to call it?" Yeri walked in with a tray of four povka shots. "This one's mine," he said pointing to the tallest glass on the tray.

"Friday."

"Friday?" Yeri questioned. "From the book *Robinson Crusoe?*"

"Yes, kinda."

"Because Friday helped out a lot?"

"Sorta. Yeah and Friday means the day of Frigg."

"The day of what?"

"Frigg was the Queen of Asgard and a prophet like Odin. He was the King."

"That sounds a lot like Norse Mythology," Yeri said.

"It is! I read about it in school." Togo turned to his dad. "I think we should call that mean old Minister of Defense, Loki."

"Loki?"

"Yes. Because he takes things that doesn't belong to him."

"Like taking our Rovers?"

Togo nodded. "Is Loki going to take Friday too?"

"Can we call it Frigg instead?" Ken asked. "Friday sounds too confusing and first of all, the Minister has to find it before he can take it."

"Where is it?"

"Grandpa and I hid it."

"Where?"

"In the bat cave," Ken smiled.

"Bat cave?" Togo's eyes went wide.

Tima burst out laughing. "I didn't know I was married to Batman."

"You're not. I'm Batman," Yeri said and then glanced at Ken, "and I guess that makes you?"

"Holy mistaken identity!" Ken replied, "So if you're the Cape Crusader then where's your cape?" Ken asked and looked at Yeri.

"Today is wash day."

"Then where's your mask?" Ken asked.

"Dad!" Togo said a little irritated, "where did you find *Friggy*?"

"It was a year ago around this time, as a matter of fact. Grandma and Grandpa were over here having a few drinks with us when my pursal rang," Ken said remembering.

*****

Ring...Ring

"Ken Thornton."

"Ken, Melissa here. We have a problem."

"A ReDS?"

"You know it. Just went offline a couple of hours ago. We need you out there STAT. I'll have an MMU checked out when you get here."

"Which one has the problem?"

"865."

"The one in Hellas Planitia? That's in Nocachis Quad. I don't even cover that area."

"Sorry. Heather's team is out doing upgrades in Terby."

"But they are closer than I am."

"You know they can't leave until all the upgrades are completed. We need this one back online immediately. This one powers the portal grids and if not back online soon it will cause a chain fail."

"A chain fail?"

"Like a bunch of dominos."

"I'm on my way." Ken hung up his pursal and clipped it to his belt as it returned to *traveling* mode and ran into his office and grabbed his equipment.

"Where are you going, honey?" Tima asked.

"Big power failure, 865 is offline. Possible chain fail."

"Isn't that…?"

"Yes, but she and her team are busy doing upgrades and they can't leave until they're finished."

"Why you?"

"Because they know the best when they see him!" Ken winked at her as he walked to the door.

"Aren't you forgetting something?" Tima asked. Ken reached over and gave her a kiss. "Your spacesuit?"

"Oh yeah," Ken said and grabbed the first one in the closet and as he suited up. Yeri handed him his gloves.

"How many of those povkas have you had, Son?" Yeri asked.

"Not now," Ken said with some irritation and locked his helmet down.

Relay Distribution Station #865
Schaeberle, Hellas Planitia
Noachis Quadrangle, Mars
Taurus - Sol Tuesday 10, 0011
2000 hours

The repair at ReDS #865 was worse than Ken thought. It was getting late when he arrived and he had to manually open the entrance. Once inside the dome he looked at the panels lining the station.

"Nothing!" Ken said to himself and pressed the reset button. "Damn! Why no battery back-up?" he wondered aloud.

He had to get this station online and he knew he had a good twelve hours in his suit. That should be plenty of time to fix the problem. He first checked the battery connection and found a charred connector.

"What could have caused that?" He frowned and replaced it with a fresh connector. He pushed the reset switch and nothing. "Come on! What's wrong with you?"

He opened the reset switch panel and found some of the circuit breakers were fried. "What is going on here?" He fumbled through his pack pulling out additional circuit breakers. Once all of them were in place he pushed the main reset button.

Click! The lights came on and the control panels blinked.

"There you go. Just a bad relay switch. It must have caused some arcing in the battery connections. I'll write up a work-and-replace order for the team when I get home."

Ken removed his helmet and gloves and started a system recovery check when he heard some banging against the hull of the station. He turned on the outer monitor as the floodlights lit up the perimeter. The monitor was showing a windstorm coming from the north. Two hours had already passed and the sky had turned dark, as the sun had quietly disappeared from the horizon leaving a small orange yellowish light fading into the night. The storm continued to gather more speed and power as pebbles and sand pelted the relay center. His little rover would never make it through such a devastation of wind and rocks and it was going to be a cold night with the north wind bringing the temperature down into the triple digits.

"I don't remember the weather calling for a windstorm tonight," he said as he watched the swirling mass as it gathered steam. Soon there was a cascade of rocks and debris pounding against the outer hull. One hour later he heard the breaker trip leaving him in total darkness. The battery backup lights blinked twice and powered on.

"WARNING!"

came the mechanical female voice over the intercom.

- Relay Station Power Failure -

appeared on the screen accompanied by a long and high-pitched tone. Ken reached over and turned the sound off while the main screen rebooted flashing a countdown:

8:00:00...7:59:59...7:59:58...7:59:57...

"What! Only eight hours of juice left?" Ken exclaimed in disbelief. "These batteries are built to last for twenty-five!"

He hadn't fixed the main problem and he surely didn't relish the thought of sleeping in his suit all night in case he couldn't restore power to the station. He only had a few more circuit breakers left and he couldn't risk having them fry just to keep the station temporarily running. With his PeeP in hand he started painstakingly checking each circuit in all the indoor panels. He was finishing panel #3 when he again heard the voice of doom.

"WARNING!"

came the mechanical female voice over the intercom once again.

- Total Relay Station Power Failure in Five Hours -

flashed on the screen. It was midnight with only four panels left. He was averaging one panel per hour and that was too slow. The howling of the wind along with constant hammering of the Martian rocks against the hull was unnerving at best. While finishing up power conductor panel #7 he realized he was probably going to have to stay over night. He unsnapped his *traveler* to call his family and Melissa but the *traveler* wouldn't change into *cellular*.

"Damn! This storm is blocking the signal," Ken sighed.

- WARNING! -
- POWER FAILURE IN ONE HOUR -
- COUNTDOWN ON THE TENS -

flashed on the screen. Seven hours had passed and everything inside was clean. But every time he would power on, nothing. In one hour the station would go completely dormant.

"The problem isn't in here," he said to himself. He would have to check the outside panels. He put on his Martex helmet and gloves. He reached over and pressed the power button on his left sleeve the mechanical voice echoed in his earpiece along with information streaming across his helmet view screen.

"Pressurization test – 100%

Tank capacity – 15%

Primary Seal - 100%

Secondary Seal - 100%

Tertiary Seal - 100%

Sealing...Completed

Containment... 100%

Caution!... Caution!...Caution!...

Low Power level detected."

On hearing that bit of bad news he immediately looked down at the suit's power levels resting just below his left gloved hand.

"Damn!" He thumped his suit's power level indicator hoping for a change. The power level lights were at the edge of yellow moving toward the red zone. He was in such a hurry he had picked up the wrong suit. This one was due for a recharge. How stupid he thought to himself, but he had done this before and he usually just did a suit recharge at the station. It was never a big deal until now where it had become a huge deal.

Well, I'm going to freeze to death in an hour if I don't fix the station he thought to himself as he stepped into the airlock. Fortunately the battery back-up was strong enough to move the doors and commence the compartment pressurization procedure.

"Pressurization Complete"

came the mechanical voice as the outside door opened. The wind was blowing so strong it made it hard for him to see anything. He felt his way around the dome to the panels. He quickly worked through the first outside panel hoping he wouldn't overlook anything when he heard

"WARNING!"

came the mechanical female voice over his headset.

"STATION POWER FAILURE IN TWENTY MINUTES"

"What!" Ken exclaimed. "I've only been out here five minutes at the most. I should have at least forty left." Then he thought about it. "Crap! It took a lot of power to operate the airlock not to mention those heavy metal doors. I should have done it mechanically. Now by the time I get back inside there will be no power at all. In fact I may not even be able to enter the station!"

He opened the second of the four smaller outside panels and had barely started when he saw something out of the corner of his eye. "What the hell?" There was a cord swinging wildly on the lee side of the dome.

"That's it!" he said hopefully, fighting the hostile Martian atmosphere along with the attacking rocks. "The power actuator must have snapped! This shouldn't have happened!" There was going to be hell to pay when he found out who replaced it and didn't fasten it down properly. Actuators had to be secured and replaced every three months to prevent this type of problem because they are partially exposed to the Martian atmosphere. Each one is marked and dated. He removed the actuator and examined it with his PeeP.

"WARNING!
TEN MINUTES UNTIL TOTAL RELAY STATION FAILURE!
ALERT!
COUNTDOWN ON THE ONES"

barked the computer within his spacesuit.

"I'm going as fast as I can!" Ken yelled back at the computer. He turned the actuator and read the inscription: Manufactured by Elotec. "Elotec! They're not built to handle this type of load." He pulled out a heavy duty Martex actuator and quickly replaced and secured it to the building. He crossed his fingers hoping that was the issue. He looked up but it was too late. The station's light dimmed to black leaving him in total darkness to fight an angry storm all by himself. His suit showed only fifteen minutes of power left.

"The station's gone dormant! I gotta do something," Ken said to himself as he noticed his rapid breathing. "Just relax yourself and head to the entrance." He hoped the new actuator would save him. He shuffled to the entrance as fast as his suit would allow. He knew it was going to be close. He opened the panel and pressed the unlit entrance button, but the outer door didn't budge. Everything appeared dead and as a last ditch effort he grabbed the handle with all his might and pulled, but it was just too heavy.

"Damn! I gotta crank this out manually? I don't have enough time! I spent five minutes just getting here!" He kicked the door out of frustration. He tried the outer reset switch and nothing. He waited and counted to five and then opened the protective plate and pressed the unlit switch once more. He was running out of time and air. The storm was increasing at an alarming rate and all he could do was just stand and wait.

Chapter 10

Kangerlussuaq World Office
Nuuk, Greenland
Friday, May 29, 0015
0700 hours

As more and more people underwent hybridization, the demand for meat skyrocketed. Prices went through the roof causing a significant amount of unrest among the people. The Ana Asea Sevens held a special meeting where they decided to use the continent of Africa as a cow pasture...not for just any old cow, but a newly modified BuffaPrime type - one whose DNA had been genetically modified to grow three times as big in only half the time. Once these beasts reached maturity their legs would break under the intense weight, but it was felt to be a small price to pay for progress.

The Landhelpers were built to help turn Africa into one giant feeding lot. They were nothing more than oversized bulldozers topping twenty feet tall and as wide as an eighteen-wheel tractor-trailer. One of these great metal beasts could level one hundred acres of forest in a day.

Carlos Sanchez recently had been promoted to General due to his effort in the Terra Bull captures in Germany. He pushed to have himself assigned as the liaison to the African people. Sanchez's job was to inform the people of Africa about becoming the new middle class, along with the new imminent domain laws, and how they would be handsomely paid for their land and relocated to a less environmentally hostile area. When the General found out how much the World Development Group (WDG) intended to offer the African people, he had a change of plan...

General Sanchez patiently waited in the Ana Asea's office as he watched the secretary field the Ana Asea's calls. The General was dressed in pressed army fatigues, spit shined black-laced boots, a tan and brown camouflage shirt, pants and hat to match. He had to leave his revolver at the guard's office, but kept the holster. He continued to stand erect with hands clasped behind his back almost like he was at attention. He would now and again drift over toward the secretary in hopes of getting a glimpse of the Ana Asea's activities. The Ana Asea screened his help carefully and she was well aware of what the General was trying to do.

"Can I help you?" she asked as she quickly placed her hand over the memo pad.

"Oh, I'm sorry. I was just looking at that beautiful painting behind you. Is that the original portrait of Nicholas ll?"

The secretary nodded and pointed to the wooden chair sitting across the room.

"He was the last Russian Emperor. Russia was never the same after Nicholas." General Sanchez turned to see Ana Asea One hang his overcoat.

"Good morning Ana Asea One." General Sanchez saluted.

"At ease, Son."

The Ana Aseas were given a number from one to seven. Identifying them by number verses name served two purposes. The first was to create an air of mystery about them. No one really knew who they were and where they came from. Once they took the position all past records were erased, along with any individuals who refused to sign the non-disclosure contract. This stopped any reporter of the controlled media from acting in a rogue manner especially if she happened to uncover malfeasants about one of the leaders. The second reason was based on the early kings of England. The masses knew King George and it would be easy to add second to his son's name and the third to his son. This made it easy for the masses to know who was in charge and kept a sort of consistency in the kingdom. But the elected ones were not chosen due to lineage but from ENIAC2 should one die.

"Yes, morning," the Ana Asea replied. "1896. Painted by Repin. Ilya Repin died in 1930." He walked behind his secretary and gazed at the painting like it was the first time. "A masterpiece!"

"I can see it holds great significance."

Ana Asea One turned away from the mural. "The painting is to remind us that the era of local governments and their leaders are a thing of the past. The Ana Aseas will lead mankind into an era of great wealth and contentment," Ana Asea One said and opened the door. His office was composed of a majestic hand-carved walnut desk facing the entryway.

No sneaking up on this man the General thought. *So this is what real power looks like.* He took a step and stopped at once.

"Is that a Meshkabad!?" The General hesitated to step on such a beautiful work of art. He noticed the Ana Asea had removed his shoes and placed them near the door. Sanchez followed suit.

"An original. One can tell by the floral patterns and intricate geometric designs. This one took over five years to weave. It comes from the finest baby lamb's wool available. The work was completed somewhere around 1918 and was owned by Sharif Hussein bin Ali."

"Owned by the man that started the Arab Revolt of 1916?" General Sanchez bent down on one knee and carefully brushed his hand over the Persian. The reds and greens around the rim of the rug led the eye toward the circular tan colored patterns in the center. The colors were created from a vegetable dye. He stood and turned toward the Ana Asea. "I suspect you don't own much without an underlying reason?"

The Ana Asea smiled. "Hussein's main purpose for the revolt was to free his people from the reigning Ottoman Empire. He alone was responsible for creating a single Arab unified state. We are doing the same today, except on a much larger scale." The Ana Asea sat down behind the ornamental desk and clasped his hands. "I'm a busy man."

General Sanchez gave out a deep sigh and placed his hands gingerly on top of the luxurious desk. "Sir, we have a problem."

"I am sorry to hear about your men dying in that airplane explosion last month," Ana Asea One said. "By the way, where were they headed?"

Taken aback concerning the question Carlos stuttered for a second. "The...the transport?"

"Yes," Ana Asea One raised his voice. "Where... were... they... headed?"

"Greenland."

"Greenland? Why?"

"I received a report about some terrorist activities near Nuuk."

"Really? Why weren't we informed?" The Ana Asea rose from his seat. "Who sent you this information?"

"Overman, sir. Dennis Overman. He was doing some recon for me and stumbled across a planned invasion by the Terra Bulls. It wasn't confirmed but I didn't want to take any chances on any of you getting hurt."

"Hmmm..." Ana Asea One sat back down and stroked his chin. "I don't like being kept in the dark when it comes to my safety. Do you understand?"

"Yes sir!"

"I want to speak to this Overman."

"He was killed in the transport explosion." Sanchez lowered his head. "A good friend and a great loss. He uncovered the plans and wanted to lead the charge."

"Overman...Overman..." the Ana Asea pondered. "Wasn't he the one who orchestrated the raid on the Richards' ranch?"

"Charges were pending, but no arrests had been made yet, sir," Carlos said nervously. "He showed up at my office and wanted to pay for what he had done."

"Why didn't you arrest him on the spot?"

Carlos hesitated and looked to the ceiling in order to gather his thoughts being caught unprepared for the slicing questions Number One was firing at him.

"I asked you a question and I won't ask it again!" Ana Asea One stood up from his desk.

"Forgive me, sir. I considered Overman a friend and remembering what happened…"

"Guards!" The Ana Asea pressed a button on the intercom.

"Sir, please!" Carlos cleared his throat. "Captain Overman begged me to allow him a chance to prove his innocence. He did a lot of work in order to uncover a suspected Terra Bull attack on Nuuk. He gave me the intel concerning the safety of the Ana Aseas kind of like an olive branch."

"There was no attack," the Ana Asea said as two men entered his office fully armed. The Ana Asea waved them away and relaxed back into his chair.

"No. At least we can say they lost their lives to protect you and the other Ana Aseas. I think the Terra Bulls got wind of what we were doing and blew up the airplane and aborted their raid."

"Most unfortunate," Ana Asea One paused and stared at Carlos for a good fifteen seconds before proceeding. "What do you want?"

"Ana Asea One, there is a growing problem in the African nations."

"Does this need an audience?" the Ana Asea asked.

"That is only for the Ana Asea to decide," General Sanchez replied and looked down at the desk in a submissive gesture all the while he hoped to catch a glimpse of the documents that rested to the Ana Asea's left.

"Go on," the Ana Asea said as he placed a hand on the documents.

"Ahem…" Sanchez straightened and pulled his shirt taunt. "A group of militants are protesting *Clear-Vision*."

"Protesting?…*Clear-Vision*?"

The General nodded his head. "They've ignored your divine plan, sir. I've told them of your generosity and they spit on your efforts. They want to stay in Africa. If we can't relocate them then we won't have enough grazing land for the cows."

"They are not simply cattle General Sanchez!" Ana Asea One arose once again from his chair. "We have spent years genetically engineering this perfect beast from a cow as you called it. This animal will be invaluable in feeding the world."

"I deeply apologize Ana Asea One. Um...I meant to say we will not have the necessary acreage for our new BuffaPrimes to graze." Sanchez waited for all this to sink in. He knew how controlling a man Ana Asea One was and which buttons to push, but he had to be careful or he might find himself serving the rest of his military life with leg irons in a dungeon. The Ana Asea turned toward the videoconference screen when the General spoke. "Your highness, I don't think there is a need to call the others as of yet. Perhaps we could resolve this issue without an audience."

"How so?" The Ana Asea turned back toward the General.

"I think the African people just need to be... um... educated. I have some ideas on how to... uh... peacefully resolve this issue."

General Sanchez knew that it wouldn't be long before the WDG under Ana Asea Six made a visit to the African people. He needed a way to stall them from showing up until he could figure out a way to buy their land and sell it to the WDG without anyone being the wiser. He first sent out fliers to the residents that told them that their homes were worthless and would be torn down by the World Development Group in a matter of months. The fliers explained that the WDG would force them off their land under the rules of imminent domain and they would get nothing in return. The fliers told them he might be able to offer them something for their property if they sold now. But the people of Africa refused to sell.

He told them they could continue to work the land until middle class housing became available, but they still refused. He tried verbal threats and violence. He poisoned their water supply, which sickened their children and livestock and still the African people held their ground. General Sanchez knew he was overstepping his bounds, but the money was worth the risk. He couldn't get the idea of amassing such tremendous wealth in such a short time out of his mind. If this village would fall, then others would also. He even upped his offer, but they still refused. He needed a victory before the WDG made their appearance.

"Are you returning to Luanshya?" the Ana Asea asked.

"Yes. Hopefully this time I will, with the Ana Asea's permission, persuade the African villagers to agree to your generous offers."

"Then go and report back as soon as you have word. This is of the utmost importance and needs to be resolved at once. Don't fail me again!"

"I assure you, Most High, that this humble servant will accomplish your desires."

Luanshya
Luanshya District, Copperbelt Province
Zambia, Africa
Monday, June 1, 0015
0900 hours

It had been another week of record-breaking temperatures and the announcer said it was going to get even hotter in the coming week. Carlos turned off the radio and absentmindedly turned up the AC as he tried to relax while the transport headed for Africa. General Sanchez turned to Colonel Christopher Rice sitting next to him. "I'm glad you came on board with my plans."

"After the London fiasco I had decided not to go through with any of this but Julie has taken a turn for the worse. She doesn't have much longer to live without the operation."

"You'll have the money this time. I guarantee it."

"Isn't there a long waiting list?"

"Trust me. She'll get the operation as soon as we are finished with these Africans."

"I can't let this drag on you know."

"I have it all worked out. Once the villagers see what they are up against they will come around."

"Are you sure we are doing the right thing?"

Sanchez just glared at the Colonel.

"She needs help and time is running out!" Chris shouted out at Carlos before he recomposed himself. "I guess I just don't want anyone to get hurt."

"I promise that everyone will get what they deserve." Carlos turned to face Chris directly. "Look Colonel, these people have never had money and they wouldn't know what to do with it once they got it. We are going to help them move to a much cooler climate and for that I think we should be paid."

"Why Africa? Shouldn't we turn the northern parts of Russia into farmland instead of relocating the Africans there?"

"The Sevens need more workers for their camps, I mean their gated community is just about finished. It's just way too hot down here for them to work all day."

"It's getting too hot everywhere," Chris retorted.

"Are you concerned about global warming?"

"I don't know, but the world has been getting hotter and hotter every year."

"That's just talk from a bunch know-nothing liberal welfareon scientists. If there was a problem, don't you think our leaders would have done something by now?"

"Maybe, but the vegetation in Africa is slowly dying. I think instead of relocating the African people and taking the lion's share of their payouts we should..."

"I thought you needed money for the operation."

"She's dying."

"Well then, I suggest you do what I tell you and you'll have plenty of money to not only pay for the procedure but also you'll have plenty left over for you and your healthy wife to enjoy the rest of your lives. Heck, you can give what you don't need back to some of them. It'll be your money, you know."

"I still can't get comfortable with treating those people like this."

"Think of it this way," Sanchez replied. "The money will now go to saving a life, your wife's, instead of going to a bunch of ignorant Africans who will probably just blow it all on alcohol and drugs."

"How can they afford to relocate if their money is gone?" Colonel Rice asked.

"Look! The transports will escort them to their new homes. Anyway we're not taking all their money! Just our cut for helping them. I'm sure they'll have no problem finding their way to Russia. If not, I'm sure the Sevens will figure out a way to get them to camp."

"And no one gets hurt?"

"Trust me."

Luanshya
Thursday, June 4, 0015
0700 hours

The village elders were gathered in the meeting hall in the center of the village. The Meeting Hall of the Elders was the location used by the king and his leaders when discussing matters of the state.

The General, wearing his battle fatigues, strolled into the meeting carrying a loaded pistol for all to see, along with Colonel Rice.

"This is your last chance to walk away with some money in your pocket. I have also decided to double my previous offer which I have to tell you I think it is more than fair," General Sanchez said.

Kenya, the Luanshyan leader, rose to meet the General. Kenya was in his sixties, dressed in a suit known to have had more years than most. There were stitches starting to unravel and areas of it patched as close to the original color as possible. Kenya, like his father, was loved by the people and was very concerned about the climate, his world, and what those across the waters were doing to it.

"Our land is not for sale. Even if it was, your offer is not enough for us to find someplace else to live. My people are poor and life is hard. It is difficult for us to feed our families with what we have now. You offer us less than what we can survive on. I am sorry," Kenya said.

"You don't understand, if you don't take my offer now, then the Ana Asea Sevens are going to take that as defiance and you don't want to incur their wrath. I'm just trying to stop you from hurting yourselves. You need to think of the safety of your people."

"Mr. Sanchez..."

"General."

"Excuse me...General Sanchez, we have no anger toward you or your people and we wish to live in peace. Africa is a big country and I believe that your Ana Aseas can find an area more suitable to your liking than Luanshya," Kenya said.

"All of you listen," Colonel Rice said. "This is your last chance. Neither the General nor I can be held responsible for what will happen if you turn us down again."

"We have listened to what you have said, but the money is not enough and we don't want to leave our land. The matter is settled," Kenya said. "I am sorry."

"I'm beginning to believe the Valley of Death is an appropriate name for this place," Sanchez grinned. "Wouldn't you agree?" The elders said nothing. "Aren't you the least bit afraid of the return of the River Snake?" Sanchez asked.

"Those are old myths," Elder Narmien said.

"Perhaps. But this is your last offer."

The elders shook their heads in unison and with that the General and the Colonel left the meeting.

*****

A raw burst of power exploded from the jet engines as the military transport traveled down the runway preparing for her time in the sky.

Both Carlos and Chris were quiet as the military transport noisily flew them back to Greenland.

"That went well," Colonel Rice shook his head in frustration.

"We aren't done with them yet." General Sanchez looked up from his pursal now in *texpanded* mode. "In fact, I was kind of hoping they would refuse."

"What do you have in mind?"

"A day when I will go down in history!"

"Really?"

The General winked at Colonel Rice as a big smile covered his face.

"What was all that about the Valley of Death?"

"Oh that? The African term for Valley of Death is Luanshya. Black water fever struck the Luanshyans years ago during their earlier mining days. So many people died back then they still refer to a Luanshya as a place or valley of death. Who said God doesn't have a sense of humor?" Sanchez laughed out loud.

"What is the River Snake?"

"An old story about a deadly river snake who carried the black water to the Luanshyans. I just wanted them to know the snake is about to return."

"I thought we were there to just scare them."

"We are."

"Okay. What's next? I don't know how much longer Julie can go without the procedure!"

"I told you she'll be the first on the list. When we get the money I will deposit it into your account so you can send your cut immediately to your wife and then we'll transfer out the rest. Okay? Now excuse me while I have some calls to make," the General said as his pursal recessed into *celling* mode.

"Okay." Colonel Rice got up and took another seat at the rear of the plane.

Sanchez continued with his call. "Mr. Donager, this is Sanchez."

"Sanchez? I can barely hear you. How are you and your African relocation plans doing?"

"I've just finished a sit-rep on the Luanshya issue in Africa."

"What's going on?"

"It's all in the situation report. I'll send it to you once we land."

"Good. Volga Russia has been cleared and camp construction has been completed and ready for promotion to middle class for the African refuges. I will be in Zambia next week to finalize the offers."

"That is what I called about. Like I said, I have just departed Africa and I suggest that you may find it preferable to push your visit to Africa back a few more weeks."

"Why on earth would I do that? I thought you were finished explaining to the African people on what to expect?"

"Oh I have done that. I can guarantee you," Sanchez said trying to hold back a giggle.

"What's so funny?"

"You're just hearing cabin noise. The military cares more about speed than comfort and quiet."

"True…true…now what can I do for you?"

"The reason I called is that there is a problem in…" Sanchez paused, "in closing the deal."

"What?"

"Yes, there are some terrorists we will have to deal with before we can resume negotiations. I would hate for you to find yourself in a hostage situation."

"Agreed! What do you want me to do?"

"Don't you still have some work in Australia?"

"My team can handle the rest, mostly paperwork and such."

"I'm sure they can, but it may be of benefit if you stick around Down Under for another few weeks at least if you know what I mean."

"I see. I'll inform Ana Asea Six about the change of plans. He's not going to like it. The factories are ready and we are going to need those workers."

"Let's just say it would be safer for everyone involved if you spent a little more time lying on a beach down there."

"This goes directly against the timeline!"

"Nothing we can do about that!" Sanchez changed his tone that demanded attention. "This African situation is starting to get out of hand if it hasn't blown up already."

"I didn't realize…"

"You have no idea what is going on here," Carlos interrupted forcefully. "Look," Carlos said in a more relaxed tone, "there are terrorists holding the village hostage. I'm planning a first strike to free these poor villagers."

"My god!"

"Exactly. So sit tight until the smoke clears."

"Roger on that. When I get the sit-rep I will update Six on what to expect. Thanks."

"Just looking out for you."

"Good luck and don't do anything foolish."

"Oh no, not me. I am however going to see those terrorists get their due."

"Hear, hear my good man. Take care."

Three hours later the plane finally touched down in Greenland and the General headed to his hotel room. He knew tomorrow was going to be a busy day and he was not about to screw it up.

Kangerlussuaq World Office
Nuuk, Greenland
Monday, June 8, 0015
0630 hours

General Sanchez stood by the door waiting patiently for the Ana Asea One's arrival. The armed guards had been busy checking the building for security reasons as they did everywhere the Ana Asea Sevens went.

"Good morning Sanchez. I am a busy man. Isn't our meeting scheduled for this afternoon?"

"Ana Asea One, the problem is with the African relocation program," Sanchez lowered his head, "and it has to do with terrorism."

"Terrorism? What on earth are you talking about?" The Ana Asea walked into the waiting room leaving Sanchez in the hallway by the door. "Don't just stand there! Come into my office and tell me what is going on!"

Ana Asea One escorted the General into his office and carefully shut the door. He went to his refrigerator and pulled out the head of a raw pig and placed it on a plate.

"Care for a bite?" he asked as he pulled off one of the pig's ears and offered it to him.

"No thank you."

The Ana Asea sat down and started eating. He waved his hand for Sanchez to continue.

"Insurgents are controlling the village of Luanshya. That is why the elders have been so hostile. They fear for their families. I'm afraid that stronger methods may be needed in order to assure a successful implementation of *Clear-Vision*. Therefore, I urge you to consider requesting an audience."

The Ana Asea pushed the half empty plate to his side. He leaned back in his chair and crossed his arms. "What does Mr. Donager say about these terrorists? I haven't heard any problems from World Development."

Sanchez saw the Ana Asea's eyebrows rise slightly and he knew that he better make it sound good if this was going to work.

"I am sorry to say that the WDG has been delayed by at least two weeks in coming to Africa."

"I was unaware of this delay!" Ana Asea One rose from his desk and put his fist on top of some papers awaiting his signatures.

"Forgive me Ana Asea One. It was my fault. I asked for an extension from the WDG in order to rid the African people of the terrorists that now occupy their village. The elders are unable to accept our generous offerings for fear of their lives. These hostiles need to be neutralized before any type of peaceful negotiations can be achieved. I fear this is going to be an uphill battle all the way..." he paused. "According to World Development, Australia's nuclear waste disposal site is at the top of their list but we first have to deal with these hostiles if we are to move forward in Africa. I believe we will be able to resolve this African issue within a few weeks, but I need your permission to move forward on this."

"Okay, if there is no other way then do what is necessary to help those people relocate. I don't want this African thing to drag on, Sanchez. We are ready and need the Volga factory up and running. I have a timeline to consider you know," Ana Asea One replied in a gruff voice. "You have my vote."

And with that remark General Sanchez smiled. He had only to win three more votes.

General Sanchez met with council and explained the need to use force in order to free the Luanshyan people from the terrorists holding them hostage. He explained that there were at least thirty to forty insurgents, possibly more, and they found out about the WDG's offer. They were demanding the money for themselves and had threatened to kill everyone in the village if their offers were not met. He told them the village leaders were being tortured and beaten by a select group of mercenaries in order to instill fear in the people and it was working. He had intel that they had plans for other villages in Africa once they were paid off.

"I recommend we neutralize the terrorists. In my humble opinion it's the only way to defend Luanshya and protect the rest of the surrounding African villages," General Sanchez said.

"That is kidnapping!" Ana Asea Three was the first to speak.

"We do not pay ransoms to terrorists!" Ana Asea Four intoned.

"Where did you get this information?" Ana Asea Seven asked.

"During my last visit, Kenya, the leader of Luanshya, had been severely beaten. Beside him was a General sloppily dressed in a military uniform I had not seen before. This General Guerrero explained the situation and what would happen if we did not comply."

"What do you intend to do?" Ana Asea Seven asked.

"I do not think he is a man of his word. I saw the horror he inflicted on the villagers with my own eyes and it made me want to vomit. Women and children were beaten and executed while we stood there helpless."

"And you didn't try and stop them?" Ana Asea Seven asked.

"Colonel Rice and I felt it was better to bring you the news instead of the two of us trying to free the whole village from so many armed soldiers," Sanchez said.

"I see," Ana Asea One said and arose from his desk. He walked over to the window and stared at the sky as if deep in thought. Sanchez noticed the Ana Asea's hands tightly clasped behind his back and wondered if that was a good thing or not.

A couple minutes later, Ana Asea One turned back from the window and noticed sweat lines crawling down the face of a very nervous General. Ana Asea One stared at the General a little while longer as he enjoyed the General's unease before he spoke.

"That will be all," Ana Asea One said with a half smile. "We will inform you of our decision."

The weekend slowly passed as General Sanchez eagerly waited for the Ana Aseas' response.

Federal Office Building
Suite 303
New York, New York
Friday, June 12, 0015
0900 hours

(Four Days Later)

"How did the vote go?" Chris Rice asked.

"Won by one vote," Sanchez replied. "I told them I had sent word to the terrorists telling them it will take some time to gather the funds and to be patient. This will allow us time to plan our invasion."

"Invasion? You said no one would get hurt."

"When the people of Luanshya see an army at their doorsteps, they will happily agree to our terms. I mean wouldn't you?"

"I would figure I had no choice."

"Exactly."

"So when is our little show going to take place?"

"A month out at the latest. We also need to make a few trips to Africa in the mean time acting like we are trying to negotiate a peaceful settlement. It would seem odd that a bunch of terrorists would just wait around that long twiddling their thumbs without a word from us."

"I didn't think about that."

"That's why I'm the one in charge."

"You're the boss."

"Yes I am and don't forget it."

Winning by one vote was always the case when dealing with the Ana Asea Sevens. This reduced the opposition's anger should the ruling have gone against him. No matter how strongly in favor the Ana Asea Sevens were for or against a popular proposal it always came down to one vote. The votes were in secret, so anyone who was upset with the outcome would never know who was for it or against.

The General's strategy was now in play. He referred to his plans as PERKs [Persuasive Enhanced Relocation for Kraals.] He used the term kraal because he liked its definition - an enclosure for domestic animals in southern Africa - and since he was going to treat them like animals, it seemed only fitting. He liked the PERK acronym since he was going to enjoy many perks after this little adventure was over.

Chapter 11

MARS

Relay Distribution Station #865
Taurus - Sol Wednesday 11, 0011
0600 hours

Ken stood by the relay station's door as he watched the storm continue its mighty onslaught.

Time of death 0615. He resigned the thought to himself and then he stood up straight.

"No! I can survive! I'll figure out a way!" he shouted to the storm.

He then looked over to where his MMU was nestled comfortably inside the rock shelter as the Martian squall gathered intensity throwing a flurry of rocks and debris in every direction. Ken turned away from the entrance and started moving slowly toward the vehicle. He knew he had to get out of harm's way but the MMU would not be able to support him for very long. These storms had been known to last for weeks at a time and he only had enough life support for a few days inside the MMU. He took three steps toward the MMU and turned back toward the relay station. "Come on! Open!" he yelled. Nothing. He shook his head and looked back at his vehicle. *If I can make it inside the MMU, I could possibly make it home as long as it isn't damaged and I don't get hit by a rock or anything and the wind isn't strong enough to flip me.*

But the wind speed suddenly picked up, from a mere ten kilometers to a dangerous thirty kilometers per hour. Ken knew his suit wouldn't be able to withstand the onslaught much longer. He resigned himself to the fact that he had no choice. With low visibility he pressed a button on his arm turning the MMU light location beacon on. It sprayed a blue light in every direction as he slowly trudged toward the light on top of the MMU. He knew it was now impossible for him to move his little car anywhere at present but it was either that or stand in the middle of a Martian squall in hopes that the station's door would decide to open for him before he ran out of air.

The MMU finally came into sight as Ken stood beside his vehicle. He sighed and pressed the entrance button on the side of the MMU and waited for the mechanical door to open. *I've got to get inside before I run out of oxygen* he thought to himself as he watched pebbles and rocks fly by him like angry bullets. Ken looked back toward the station, which could be out for weeks if he didn't fix it now. He knew that if people lost their power for that long many would suffer a fate worse than he was dealing with now. The vehicle door slowly opened as Ken crawled inside and pressed the auto-shut button.

I have no choice but to sit it out in this MMU and wait. He sighed and noticed his suit's air pressure gauge slowly faded from red to black. "DAMN!" he said. *Now my suit doesn't even have enough oxygen for me to get out of the MMU and make it into the relay station even if the weather clears.* Ken remembered a Star Trek movie when part of Captain Kirk's command training placed him and his ship in a no-win position. Earlier Kirk had cheated because he rewrote the program so he didn't have to lose. "Well Captain? Any ideas how to cheat death once again?" Ken asked aloud. He was in his very own Kobayashi Maru damned-if-you-do and damned-if-you-don't scenario. He thought about when he was a boy playing chess with his dad and he kept losing. His dad told him the reason he lost was because he limited himself to the tactics he knew.

"Sometimes Son, you have to look at the game from a different perspective," he remembered Yeri telling him. He didn't understand it then and it didn't seem to help now. As he struggled to breathe the remaining oxygen left in his suit, he nervously waited for the MMU to begin re-pressurization. Ken felt his lungs all of a sudden gasp for air. There was nothing left in his suit. He quickly unsnapped the latches and removed his helmet. He felt his lungs scream as they gasped for what little oxygen had been released into the vehicle. Feeling lightheaded as his body began to go limp Ken forced himself to remain lucid. He leaned forward toward the front console and put his mouth on the air vent. He took short controlled breaths as the oxygen slowly trickled out into the cabin. The storm continued unabated and Ken knew he would not be able to get home or even go outside. All of a sudden he heard a beeping from the MMU console. It had found a wireless connection and Redtoothed the relay station enabling him to turn on the remote cameras. The interior was showing lights and working consoles while the outer cameras were showing the outer door fully open waiting for its next visitor.

"Aarrggh! If only I had waited I would be inside now." Then he thought about it a little longer. "Well, I would have run out of oxygen and I don't think I could have held my breath that long."

He sat in his MMU and wondered if he could survive the raging storm or would he run out of oxygen first? He could see the station only ten meters away up and running and he watched as the outer door slowly closed.

"At least my death will have saved some people." He thought about his family, knowing they were probably concerned about him. He was required to check in twice a day and since he was stuck inside this rock he couldn't radio them. If they sent a rescue MMU it would have to wait until the storm had cleared.

Six more hours passed and the storm continued its deadly onslaught throwing rocks and red dust slamming against the relay station and the MMU to a point where he couldn't even see out the MMU's window.

"I can't wait any longer," he said aloud. "I have to come up with a solution. This isn't a chess game where you shake your opponent's hand when you lose. I could die out here." That's when it occurred to him. "Dad said I lost because I always did the same moves. I was afraid if I tried something new I would lose," Ken laughed in spite of himself. "And so I played it safe, the way it was comfortable and I still lost."

BANG!

All of a sudden a rock the size of a baseball slammed into the MMU. Ken watched in horror as a crack appeared on his windshield. "What else can go wrong?"

Ken looked around the MMU and the gauges showed he had only nineteen hours of air left. He knew if that crack started to spread it could compromise his vehicle and vent the rest of his much needed air. He reached in the back and grabbed the emergency toolkit snapped to the side of the MMU. He pulled out some duct tape and carefully taped the crack. "There. That should hold for a while," he said and then an idea came to him. *Like the windshield I can use duct tape for my suit. Then I can transfer oxygen from the MMU tank into my air canisters. I can also charge my suit with the MMU and with enough air in my tank I could get into the station!* He had to calm down his excitement that this idea just might save his life. He looked over his shoulder and saw the open toolbox and the med kit sitting on the opposite side. He grabbed the med kit and pulled out some stockinette, padding and plaster along with some gauze and tape. "Well Captain Kirk, what do you think of my solution?" he said with fear, along with emerging confidence that at least he wasn't giving up. He pulled his left arm out of the suit and layered it with stockinette and padding. He wrapped the plaster around his arm and turned the heater on high to quickly dry the plaster. Once the case was mostly hardened, he slowly wiggled his hand out of the cast and closed all the air vents. The MMU was still humming along with the air now pushing on the closed vents.

"ATMOSPHERIC PRESSURE WARNING!"

Ken turned off the audio and placed his homemade air hose on the front vent of the MMU and connected it with duct tape. He shaped the other end to fit his suit, but the suit connector was a lock and click.

"Damn," he said as he looked at his homemade oxygen transfer unit. "All I need is about five maybe ten minutes of air to get in the station." Ken grabbed his spot laser and carefully burnt off the metal lock and click seal to his suit. He let it cool and then attached the other end of the cast to his suit. He turned on the vent and watched his suit's oxygen power level bars turn from red to yellow level one. He didn't want to use all the MMU's life support so when it reached the second yellow bar he removed the cast from his suit and that is when he felt a rush of air hit his hand. He placed strips of duct tape over his suits intake value, but the air simply rushed around the tape. He pressed one hand on the tape hoping to slow the escape as the hissing sound filled his ears.

"Oh my god! I forgot to vent the carbon dioxide! The oxygen has nowhere to go!" he screamed out in frustration. *Don't panic.* He vented some of the CO2 out of his air canisters into the cabin and grabbed some gauze. Ken snatched his toolbox and cut the gauze into strips and hung it all around the dashboard. *I only have one more shot* he thought to himself as he reconnected his homemade arm cast to the vent and his suit. He turned the vent back on filling the MMU's oxygen tank into his suit. He checked his suit's tank levels as they stubbornly pushed their way to level green. He then pulled his homemade cast away and the air once again quickly rushed back out of his burned out air intake vent. He stuffed it with gauze and then placed the duct tape over the hole but the seal still didn't hold.

"What?" The tanks were still showing over ninety percent CO2. He removed the gauze letting more carbon dioxide along with his much needed oxygen vent into the cabin. He watched as the CO2 levels normalized to seventy percent. "That should be enough."

He reattached the hose from the MMU to his lock and click. He turned the air vent back on and carefully watched as his suit's gauge went from red to yellow and finally when it touched green he removed the hose and quickly grabbed some gauze and duct tape. As he worked in securing his suit, he noticed the air was not forcing itself out as hard as it was earlier, but this was in the MMU. Leaving a climate-controlled environment might be a different matter.

While holding the gauze and duct tape against the intake valve with one hand he grabbed the burnt lock and click with the other. It was in pretty bad shape, but it just might still fit. He pulled the duct tape to one side and pushed the lock and click against the gauze and replaced the duct tape slowing the escaping air to a crawl. When everything was secure he looked down to see his oxygen levels had faded back into the lower yellow region. He had limited oxygen and a homemade patch along with a Martian storm to contend with and he didn't even know how long it would all last walking through a Martian storm, but it was a workable plan and Ken smiled in spite of himself.

The MMU screen lit up along with another audio.

"WARNING
OXYGEN TANK LEVEL 20%."

flashed on the screen along with the mechanical female voice.

Ken powered down the MMU and reattached his helmet. He opened the door and slowly walked to the station. He could barely see a meter in front of him as the dust angrily swirled in an attempt to block his path to safety. He tried to keep his bearings hoping he wouldn't miss the door or even the dome for that matter. He kept his head down and walked heel to toe in an effort to travel in a straight line, but the wind blew away his footprints as quickly as he made them. Minutes slowly passed by as he began to wonder if he had walked right past the station until his helmet hit something hard and metallic. He felt his way around the dome until he came to the door. He pressed the control switch as the ground below him started to shake as the door slowly opened. He walked into the airlock as the outer door closed behind him and he waited.

"Air Pressure – 1015 Millibars – Please Stand Back."

came the female voice as the inner door opened. He walked back into the station and yelled at the computer, "That was just too damn close! When I find out who has been replacing our Martex actuators with this Elotec trash, he is going to find himself working at ReDS #7880 at the North Pole overlooking the Herschel prison yard!"

The prisons were few and a prisoner's punishment was to dig for ice crystals located underneath the Martian soil. Some would die due to the demands of living and working at Herschel, but then every now and again one or two of the prisoners would simply disappear. There were no guards at the dig sites at Herschel because nobody could survive the trek to the safety of a nearby village. After all, the only tunnel the prisoners had to reach civilization was heavily guarded. So if they escaped, there was nowhere to go. If they didn't meet their ice quotas then their rations were cut along with the temperature in their cells. It was thought that some walked away into the cold Martian desert preferring to die than to continue working and living in such pain and despair.

Ken saw the lights in the dome flash as the screen above his head appeared.

- RELAY STATION POWER LEVEL -

25%

When a station goes red and recovers it stays in dormancy mode along with minimal life support until someone can check it out and affect repairs. Ken kept his suit on noticing the power levels had returned to red once again. He walked to the console and began a total system reboot.

"SYSTEM RECOVERY CHECK ACTIVATED
STANDBY
ALL SYSTEMS FUNCTIONING WITHIN NORMAL
PARAMETERS
RELAY STATION POWER LEVEL

75%"

came the loveliest voice on Mars.

"Now I know why they made it a female voice," he said as a big smile crossed his face. All systems finally showed green. He took off his helmet and did another full system check. After all he had plenty of time until the storm passed. When the power levels hit one hundred percent Ken relaxed and fell into a deep sleep.

It was five days until he could see the Martian sun as it slowly appeared on the horizon. Ken had finished repairing his suit. He grabbed a new lock and click from storage and attached one to his suit with some epoxy. His MMU appeared undamaged except for the duct-taped window. He fixed the crack well enough to make it back home. With his suit showing a full charge he decided it was time he headed for home. As the MMU bounced toward home he thought about how lucky he was to be alive. The faulty actuary overloaded the capacitor and caused it to misfire shorting the batteries, which in turn blew the circuits. He would have to send a technician to replace all of them and then find out who changed that actuator. He made a note to always take a spare "fully charged" suit, battery pack, and definitely a spare actuator.

It was a beautiful Martian morning as the little MMU shook and bounced him around the cabin. He used to hate traveling in these things, but this one just saved his life. He had some time before his site ReDS #4658 visit and inspection and decided on a whim to take a different route home. Well, it wasn't quite on the way home, but he had some time. He turned southward toward Noachis Terra thinking back on Earth where he had read in a book in the Galactic library that a rover was thought to be lost in these canyons during one of the earlier attempts in discovering the mysteries of Mars. His part-time passion was searching for rovers. So far, the Spirit was the only one he had ever found. He slowly rode dangerously close to one of the many crevices found on Mars hoping to see something. He figured that would be where a missing rover would have to be. If on the surface it would have been found and recovered by now. He was about to give up since his eyes were getting tired of staring down into nothing but dark red Martian clay lining the crevices when he saw a shiny object. "What's this?" Ken said aloud as he saw some metal dancing off the mid afternoon rays. *The storm must have uncovered something down there.* He walked over to the canyon and peered into the darkened crater for a better look but there wasn't much to see. There was definitely something down there, but it was mostly covered with Martian dust.

Chapter 12

EARTH

John Washington lived his entire life on Dewey Street. He started his life with little, but he was a man with a dream. Orphaned at an early age due to the death of his mom and dad, he became his extended family's "hot potato." No one wanted another mouth to feed. Things were hard growing up and he learned that getting ahead in this world meant holding on tight to what you have. When you don't have much, the few things that you do own mean a lot. John kept himself neatly groomed with short hair and always had a clean-shaven face. He wore a suit when he went out. He felt it was important to present oneself in a professional manner. His kids wanted to wear the hoodies and such, like all the other kids, but John was strict on them because he knew the importance of first impressions. He had survived the streets and now owned a small grocery store on the corner of Dewey and Palladian Avenue. The business didn't bring in much, but it was enough for him to put a roof over his head and take care of his wife, Carol, and their three kids. He wanted to pass on his values to his children, Suma, James, and Ket. He would tell them stories about when he was a child in an effort to teach them morals and values. He always stressed the importance of getting a good education and the power of positive thinking. He would at times say how true the old saying was, "Birds of a feather, flock together." He told them even if they do the right things that hanging around friends who cheat and steal could cause them to eventually get pulled in the same direction.

"I don't think I would let someone tell me to do something I wouldn't want to do," Suma said.

"That's what I thought," John said.

"What changed your mind?" Suma asked.

"One afternoon I was hanging around with some guys outside of Uncle Ben's Diner. They were older than me and I looked up to them. Ben told me to be careful because he said they were troublemakers. I wasn't listening to him because they were cool and one had a motorcycle. I thought it would be neat to be seen hanging around the tough kids. I thought it would make everyone think I was a tough kid too," John sighed. "It was a cloudy Saturday afternoon when we all met at the diner. Nicky had borrowed his dad's car and so we drove to the mountains. When we got to the entrance of Henry Hudson Drive it was closed for repairs, but Nicky just drove around the barricades. I was a little concerned, but it was fun because I had never broken the law before. Nicky stopped the car and we all got out and hiked one of the trails. At the top you could see the roads below as the cars passed by. Tashia leaned against one of the bigger rocks as Nicky pulled out another beer. The rock started to move as some pebbles trickled down the side of the mountain. Tashia along with the rest of the gang thought it would be fun to see if they could loosen this gigantic rock even more. They started to push and push. The rock started to move and so they pushed even harder. I didn't have a good feeling about this and suggested maybe we should stop. They just ignored me and then all at once this huge boulder broke free and started rolling down the mountainside. They were all laughing, drinking, and kidding around until Cindy noticed it was heading right toward the highway. We could see cars traveling up and down the roads below and there was nothing anyone could do but watch. This massive rock picked up speed as it barreled down its death path toward those unsuspecting people. I could only stand there and watch as innocent men, women, and children were coming into the crosshairs of this moving mass of destruction totally unaware of what was about to happen to them. All of us just stared as the boulder crashed into two cars sending them sprawling across the lane into on-coming traffic. There was a huge pile up of cars and trucks strewn along the highway with smoke and fire billowing out of the wrecked cars. People were running frantically pulling people out of the smashed cars all caused by our recklessness. I almost fainted at the sight and then I felt someone grab me.

'Come on! We gotta go!' Tashia yelled. So I, along with my so-called friends, ran down the path to Nicky's car. We jumped in and Nicky drove some back roads towards home. I told Nicky that we should turn around and help them, but he, along with the rest, threatened me and said if I ever told anyone they would make sure I and my friend Ben would pay."

"Did you ever say anything?" Ket asked.

"No I didn't. I was young and afraid. I should have listened to Ben. Even though I didn't push the rock or have anything to do with what happened, I was hanging around trouble makers and that pulled me into a situation I would rather have not been in," John said and shook his head. "I saw the tragedy on the evening news. I saw the names and faces of the people who had died and the ones lying in the hospital fighting for their lives. The police found the beer cans where we were but no arrests were ever made. I felt really, really bad about the whole thing."

Carol could tell from John's expression how bad he felt. "But you tried to stop them and then you tried to help. You were young and couldn't have…"

"Stupid!" John interrupted Carol before she could finish her sentence. "I knew they were trouble makers, Ben even told me but no no no! I wanted to be a big shot and that incident has haunted me ever since." John turned to his kids. "That is why I want you to be careful of who you hang around with, because you never know what might happen if you choose the wrong crowd."

"How do we know who is good and who is bad?" Suma asked.

"You have to listen to your feelings. We all instinctively know what is right and wrong. I knew those guys were trouble by the way they acted and the way they treated others but I ignored my feelings." John stared at the holovision. "Spend your time with people who are positive and helpful. Stay away from those who are always negative and complaining all the time."

"Is that why you rarely let us watch the news?"

"Yes. They only talk about bad stuff. I call them spiders."

The holovision was on when the sound suddenly increased along with a flashing – Breaking News – appeared in the middle of the screen.

"VIDEO OFF…"

"Wait a second John," Carol interrupted. "Let's see what this is all about."

--- BREAKING NEWS! ---

streamed across the bottom of the screen while men in white physician coats were walking hurriedly around the hospital halls. An announcer in the background began, "A new strain of the Tiberan Flu has been reported in Cancun, Mexico. Ten people have died so far and one hundred others are reported sick. This new strain is the deadliest one so far and could enter the United States as early as next week!" The film showed people in hospital beds and others wheeled in by attendants donned with protective masks and gloves. "The CDC has issued a level five alert."

LEVEL FIVE ALERT!... LEVEL FIVE ALERT!... LEVEL FIVE ALERT

replaced the "Breaking News" scroll as it constantly moved across the bottom of the screen.

The lady announcer reappeared with a motherly concern on her face. "Please wash your hands often, cough into your sleeve, and if you have any flu symptoms," the camera went in close, "go immediately to the hospital. Don't take chances with your life or your loved ones'." The camera slowly faded back and revealed both newscasters.

"Thank you DeeDee… Runny nose and feeling a little weak? Don't wait! Stock up on Flu-Away recommended by nine out of…"

"MUTE!" yelled John.

"…ten physicians. So don't wait and pick up some…"

"MUTE!" yelled Carol.

"Muted," the voice inside the unit replied.

"Do you want it off?"

"No, but thank you for muting those spiders," John said.

"It takes a female voice to control that thing," Carol smiled.

"Uh huh."

"Daddy why do you call them spiders?" Suma asked sitting beside Ket on the floor.

"If you listen to them, you'll hear them weaving their *negativity web*," John Washington replied.

"I don't see them weaving anything," Ket said.

"It's just an expression, little guy." John turned away from the TV. "Did you see those folks in the hospital?"

Ket turned toward his dad and nodded.

"Did it scare you?"

Ket nodded again and turned toward the blank screen. John bent down closer to his son and whispered in his ear, "Do you want to watch more?"

"Uh huh," Ket replied, eyes focused on the holovision. He turned his head and tried to hear what the announcer said but the mute button flashed on the screen to let him know it was of no use.

John saw the announcers had faded into the background as the cameras were now focused on the hospital patients. They looked sad and defeated as they walked using their IV pole to steady them while others with their heads hanging low were being pushed around in wheelchairs, by the staff. All of them had tubes running from their IV poles into their arms concealed by the dirty looking smocks they wore.

"They look sad," Ket said.

"Those people are very old aren't they?" John said.

"Old and sad," Ket stated.

"Does it scare you?"

"Being old and sad sure does," Ket said.

"The people they are showing you are most likely immunocompromised. See how their bodies are so frail?"

"They should eat more."

"Eating isn't going to help, Son," John said as he put his arm around Ket. "They are approaching the end of their lives and that is why their bodies look the way they do, but the news media wants you to think this will happen to you if you catch a cold or the flu."

"I don't want to get sick."

"No one does, but if you do your body is strong enough to fight it and you will get better."

"I don't want to go to the hospital." Ket held his brown ragged one-eyed teddy bear a little tighter.

"Oh, I doubt it will come to that. You'll feel bad for about a week and then your body will be rid of that little bug. Then you'll feel like going back out and playing again."

"How do you know?"

"Because I've gotten sick many times when I was a child. I still do at times but I'm not scared." John leaned down and put his hand gently on Ket's little shoulder. "Because I know something very important."

"What?" Ket turned away from the holovision and now focused on his dad.

"I'm not scared because I know that only a small minority of folks will find this little bug life threatening, and those people already have a medical problem. I don't have any medical problems and you don't either. So that little bug is probably going to make you feel bad for a few days and then it will go away. I bet you didn't know that, now did you?"

"Why don't they say that?"

"Because they want to scare you. Are you scared?"

"I was, but not anymore. That mean old bug can't scare me," Ket said with a big smile on his face. "Why do they want to scare little kids?"

"Fear is a strong motivator. It gets people to do things that they normally wouldn't do. The news media wants you to be afraid of losing your life. They show you all these sick people in the hospital. They know if you are scared then you will watch their program. If you watch their program, they can charge their advertisers more money."

"But they're not telling the truth," Ket said.

"The *negativity web* only works when ignorance trumps knowledge," John turned the channel looking for something a little more uplifting. "Isn't it about time to go to bed?"

"Can't we stay up for thirty more minutes, Dad?"

"No."

"Twenty?"

"No."

"Can we read in bed?"

John looked toward his wife as he watched her enjoy him being the one to order the kids to bed. She shrugged her shoulders and smiled. "Ten minutes and then lights out," Carol said.

"Thanks Mom," the three intoned as they hustled off to bed.

The following morning around 6:00 AM, John Washington had just settled down in his favorite recliner. He noticed the arms were starting to tear, but it was still comfortable. His shop was always closed on Sundays to give him time to be with his family. The store had turned a nice little profit this month and he was feeling happy.

"A few more months like this and I'm going to see Jamie at the Dewey Depot and get myself a new recliner," he said aloud as Ket and Suma walked in.

"Who are you talking to?" Suma asked.

"No one," John replied.

"Are you talking to yourself again?" Ket asked and turned to Suma. "I think Dad's going nuts again." Suma pointed her finger to her temple and made circling motions sending both kids into a laughing fit.

"News ON!" John shouted to the holovision and smiled at his kids having fun at his expense. Instantly the wall screen brightened with a picture of General Sanchez speaking to a reporter.

"... and the rumors are right," Sanchez replied with a grim face. "We have a major problem in Africa. *Clear-Vision* has come to a halt due to a group of terrorists who have captured a small African village.

The Ana Aseas received a ransom note and it said if we don't adhere to their demands the beatings and killings will continue."

"Are we going to pay them?" the reporter asked.

"Our wise and benevolent leaders, the Ana Asea Sevens are keeping with our stance. We do not negotiate with terrorists." Sanchez looked directly into the camera. "We neutralize them." He then turned back to the reporter "I have been ordered to bring down those terrorists who are holding our African brothers hostage."

"How dangerous could this situation become?"

"Very. There could be bloodshed I fear, but we will be victorious even if I have to lead the charge myself."

Courtney turned to the camera. "Hero or fool? To fight and die for one's country sure, but to fight the wrongs done to his fellow man, in my book, is a hero."

"That's right Courtney," her co-announcer responded as they switched to an old tape of people milling around in some remote African village.

"A renegade group of insurgents have taken control of a small and peaceful African village located in the town of Luanshya. General Sanchez will be taking his troops into Luanshya in an attempt to free this terrorist controlled village in the next few days. So stay tuned to *The Wolf* for all your fast breaking news. If it's news, it's with us. And now a word from our sponso..."

"MUTE!" John yelled out. The news anchor returned with films showing old pictures of tanks and armored personal marching in a field.

"Why are those mean people hurting that poor African village?" Ket asked.

"We don't know anything about the village of Luanshya. We don't really know why this General Sanchez is attacking the village."

"He's not attacking the village, he's trying to free them from some bad men," Ket replied.

"We don't know that for sure now do we?"

"We do too. Didn't you hear the announcer?"

"Yes I did."

"You don't believe him?" Ket asked.

"I don't believe him and I don't disbelieve him. I don't know what is going on down there. What concerns me is if the villagers are really in danger then why don't they fight back? In fact, they haven't even shown the actual village or the villagers, just this army."

"They did too!" Ket said exasperated.

"They showed a village, but I don't think it was the village. Even if it was it sure looked peaceful enough."

"What's the diff?"

"I would expect to see homes destroyed, people dead or dying from being attacked, but all I see are a lot of men in uniform marching. I mean, wouldn't you fight back if someone tried to take your toys?"

"You bet, I would," Ket said as Suma grabbed his teddy bear. "Give it back!" Ket yelled.

"That's enough. You made your point."

Suma handed the ragged teddy bear back to her little brother. "Here you go," Suma said with a smile.

"Haven't you wondered why there was no word about any villagers being injured or dying in their struggle against these supposed invaders?"

"No," Ket said.

"Well I do, because I know people. No one is going to just lie down and let someone take everything they've worked hard for all their life without fighting back. When the announcers tell me things that don't make sense is when I start to question the accuracy of their statements. I'm not there and I can't pass judgment on what's going on in Luanshya, but what I do know is what is reported is often changed to appease the masses. The conquerors are the ones who write the history books. Don't ever forget that."

"Video OFF!" John yelled at the screen as the pictures still continued showing the military along with some Sergeant barking orders and pointing. "The holovision is getting a little hard of hearing." John shook his head.

"It's just getting old dear, like the rest of us," John's wife chuckled as a commercial spot appeared.

"Clear-Vision helping mankind! Clear-Vision just in time!" flashed on the screen as a voice over of men and women singing the words. The camera switched to a man standing beside a desk with rows of bookshelves behind him with his name Ana Asea One on a big bold sign sitting beside him. "My fellow neighbors of the world. As one of your leaders I am proud to tell you that our goal to elevate everyone in the world to middle class standards is coming true!" The Ana Asea grinned as the camera moved from him to a white chart with black arrows heading in an upward path. "As you can see, we have a long way to go, but we are winning in our victory over poverty, crime, and..." Ana Asea One paused, "over disease. No more medical bills to contend with, no more fear of being burglarized or not having enough to eat. A new and better world is at hand." The scene faded as the singers resumed. *"Clear-Vision helping mankind. No more burdens. No more pain. Clear-Vision that's the name!"*

John got out of his chair, walked over to the wall and manually jerked the cord out of the socket as the holovision screen went blank. "I am getting sick and tired of everyone trying to tell me what I should and shouldn't do."

Clear-Vision was favorably received by John's neighbors and friends. He kept his mouth shut as he listened to them talk about all the things they were going to get from Clear-Vision. John wasn't so sure this was a good thing or not. John was a proud man and never freely accepted a handout. If someone helped him during times in need he would always find a way to repay the debt. He knew from his dealings in business and from growing up on the street, that whenever you get something from another, there is always a price to be paid. The Ana Asea Sevens concerned John on how they were running the planet, enacting Clear-Vision, the genetic manipulation of the crops, and the increasing amounts of air and land pollution. No one seemed to care and John knew that eventually someone was going to have to pay for all of this. It took him a long time to get to sleep that night thinking about where all of this was heading.

Monday morning found John behind the counter looking out the window of his Mini Mart as the weatherman talked about another record high. John noticed his store's air conditioner seemed to never cut off these days.

"Now we can get what we deserve!" Chondra pushed one of John's tiny shopping carts around the store. Chondra was nearing forty and her clothes looked to be a little tighter than they should. Her hair was braided down to her shoulders. She always wore heavy red eyeliner which she put on pretty thick, according to most people's opinions.

"Huh?" John woke from his self-induced fog. He turned away from the window where he watched a couple fight over who was first to get on the bus. He put down his coffee mug and watched the steam as it slowly faded into the musty air.

"Clear-Vision John. What else?" Chondra pushed the cart to the register. She opened her pocketbook that had given her many years of faithful service and was ready to retire, except there wasn't one to take its place. She fished around until she found what she wanted.

"I wouldn't be so eager to take gifts from strangers." John pulled a box of cereal out of her cart.

"Why not? We've been put down all our lives and never given a chance." Chondra held out a cigarette. "Do you have a light?"

"Sorry, no smoking in the store," John replied as her smile turn to a frown. "Do you think that this is your big chance?" He scanned a carton of cigarettes.

"Yeah. The time has come where we can finally lift ourselves out of this rat hole."

John continued to ring up more groceries. John paused when he heard the term rat hole. He had heard it before from other customers and neighbors. The streets were relatively safe and the little community was thriving. Sure, it didn't measure up to the holovision's Beverly Hills crowd, but he wasn't interested in living a Hollywood lifestyle. He liked his friends and neighbors. They always pitched in if someone needed help. They watched out for one another, which is something he seriously doubted the rich and famous ever did, not with all their alarm systems, security fences, and neighborhood rent-a-cops patrolling all the time.

"We're not lifting ourselves out of this." John shook his head at Chondra. "What you call a rat hole, I call home."

"Well, I'm tired of living like a gutter rat." Chondra opened her pursal and punched in her code as John checked his.

"You're about twenty short," John said.

"I'm a little stretched this month."

"You can't buy the smokes and the bottles." John pulled the two bottles of wine out of the bag.

"What are you talking about?"

"Your card has been restricted by order of the Ana Aseas. It seems you've been spending too much of your Krugers on unhealthy items."

"They can't do that!"

"They just did. You can file a grievance, but I can tell you it rarely works."

"I have a couple of silvers," Chondra whispered as she pulled out a silver coin.

"Chondra! You're back up to your limit! You're going to have to pay down some of this bill, you know." John showed her the total of what she owed.

"Two hundred Krugers! Are you sure this is right? I can't possibly owe that much."

"You do and I can't let you go over two. You know the rules."

"Oh honey, I'm doing the best I can. Times are tight right now. That bottle of wine is for some guests," she said stroking his hand affectionately.

John quickly moved his hand away. "And who would these important guests might be?"

"My new boss is coming over tonight and it could mean a raise. I could pay you back then. Okay?"

"Your boss?" John asked. "Times are the times. I'm afraid I'm going to let you have only one bottle." John picked up the silver coin from the counter. "And from now on I am deducting ten Krugers to pay down your debt each time you come here. Just think. In twenty visits you will be debt free." John placed the other bottle of wine behind the counter along with the carton of cigarettes.

"Hey! My smokes?"

John pulled two packs from the shelf behind him. "There you go. See? Now you only owe one hundred and ninety Krugers as he handed her the bag full of cereal, cigarettes, wine, and soda pop."

"That silver coin is worth at least two bottles of wine," Chondra said putting on sad face.

"Okay." John grabbed the other bottle of wine and placed it in her sack. "Where did you get the silvers?"

"None of your business."

"You know they are illegal now. I just don't want you to get in trouble."

"Yeah, sure you don't. You're just like everyone else. Only thinking about yourself. Don't worry. If I get caught, I won't turn you in," Chondra said and grabbed her bag of groceries." She stopped at the door and turned back to where John was standing. "When I get promoted to middle class, World Development will give me thousands of Krugers for leaving this dump." She threw her head back. "Then I'll be as rich as you, richer in fact." She opened the door and stormed out of the shop. As the door slammed behind her, he shook his head. He knew Chondra like a sister and she had never talked like that before. She had managed to eke out a pretty good life on Dewey and she seemed quite happy until she had heard about Clear-Vision. Now she thought she deserved to live like a queen without paying her way. He had never had a problem with her paying for groceries until recently. She was marking time until she got her new middle class house and she just didn't care about the neighborhood anymore. He knew that kind of thinking could and often did ruin a person's life and even a neighborhood if it grew.

The weeks slowly passed as neighbor after neighbor came into the store and repeatedly told John how great it was going to be living in a gated community. John just nodded and rang up the groceries. It was a late Saturday night when he got home and he saw a letter tacked on the fridge. *"John, Mary is sick. The kids and I went over to fix her something to eat – Love you, be back soon."*

Great, John thought. He hunted around the bare fridge shelves and found some leftover hotdogs from last week. "No thanks," he said to himself out loud. He donned his overcoat and headed down to Uncle Ben's Diner. He looked through the dirty windows and sure enough, there were plenty of seats available. He didn't know how much longer Ol' Ben could make it, but at least Ben would earn some revenue tonight. He opened the door to the diner and smelled the familiar odor of fried foods floating through the air. *This diner needs some work,* John thought to himself. The red bench seats were wobbly from many years of use and the tables were covered with old plastic tablecloths. Ben Harper had been running Uncle Ben's Diner as long as John could remember. John even remembered the first time he met Ben. John asked him if he was the guy on the rice box in the stores. Even today whenever he rang up a box of Uncle Ben's Converted Rice it always reminded him of Ben.

Ben came over to the table with a crinkled and faded menu that had been in too many hands. "Hello John. Good to see you."

"Why is a millionaire like you still hanging around this place?" John smiled.

Ben gave John a slap on the back with a resounding laugh. "I had you going back when you were younger."

John nodded as he perused the special of the day.

Back when John was ten, Old Ben had told him that he made millions being the guy on the rice package and now he ran the diner just for fun. John told him he was crazy to do that when he had all that money. He remembered how Ben would laugh and turn back to the grill. Uncle Ben's Diner was a landmark here on Dewey Street and John was going to miss him.

A while later, with a full stomach of burger and greasy fries, John headed home. It was around eight when he walked by Chondra's house. He saw a bunch of his friends gathered on the front porch. He slowed down but didn't stop.

"John!" Sands shouted. "Come on over."

John slowed, turned, and ambled up the stairs. He grabbed a seat on the top brick and accepted a cold beer. He knew the routine quite well. He would listen to his friends as they gathered on their front porches and complained about life on the street. John would tell them that instead of complaining, maybe they should take all that energy and focus it on cleaning the street and taking care of it.

"Why should we clean up around here?" Sands asked. "We didn't make this mess."

"Doesn't matter who made it," John said. "It's our neighborhood and if we aren't responsible for the way it looks then..."

"Yeah, well, who says that someone isn't going to come around and just trash it again?" Steve interrupted.

"That's just an excuse Steve and you know it."

"We deserve better," Steve said.

"What we deserve is the right to make our own choices on how we want to live. We aren't entitled to anything other than the right to pursue our happiness in whatever way we choose. That's all and when someone comes in and tells us he is going to *give* us all these things for free, I just become a little concerned," John's voice raised a few octaves.

"You're wrong. Nobody wants to give us a chance around here and you know it," Chondra interjected. "We're finally getting what we deserve and you're not going to take it away!"

"Where's your new boss, Chondra?"

"Uh, he couldn't make it tonight."

"Right, so... how long have you been out of work?"

"Why all these questions?" Chondra lit up another cigarette.

"Ever since you heard about Clear-Vision, you haven't even looked for work, have you?" John asked.

Chondra picked up her pocketbook and placed it in her lap. "I don't have to answer that. Folks don't want our kind around them."

"That's a cop out and you know it. Hell, I've had a *Help Wanted* sign sitting in my front window for six months now. Do you know how many people around here have applied?"

"You don't pay enough," Chondra countered and took a long drag then exhaled it in John's direction.

"How do you know?" John waved the smoke from his face.

"You're just lucky," Chondra replied. "You got it made with your little shop and all. You don't have to worry about making the rent every month. When Clear-Vision is enacted you won't be any better than the rest of us."

"Better? If working long hours and doing what it takes to provide for your family is better, then I've got to ask you Chondra. Better than what?"

Chondra grabbed her coat and left the little group without saying goodbye. John watched as she walked home.

"She just doesn't get it," he sighed.

"What are you talking about? We're all going to get it," Sands said with a big smile sporting a newly missing tooth from a drunken fight he had with a neighbor the other night.

"We're going to get it alright." John shook his head. He left his friends and walked back to check on the store. He could hear them gleefully talk about all the things they are going to buy when they become the new middle class.

Everyone on Dewey thought the same way. They all believed that they were somehow entitled to what they thought of as *the good life*. When it was offered, no one objected to what price tag came with it. No one even thought about it, except John Washington.

Chapter 13

MARS

Thornton Residence
Domette 64
Gemini - Sol Friday 6, 0012
1800 hours

"What was down in the crater?" Togo asked.

"I wasn't sure so I stepped on the wench hook from the MMU and lowered myself down for a closer look. I attached the hook to the metal object and had the MMU pull me and the rover to the surface."

"It was a rover?"

"Sure was. That was the one your grandpa and I have been working on for so long."

"The one in the bat cave?"

Ken smiled. "Yes, the one in the bat cave."

"Hey Robin! Tell your son how you got the rover back here," Yeri said.

"Very funny, Batman," Ken replied. "I hitched it to the tow line on the MMU and took a round-a-bout way home."

"Tell how you ran out of fuel and I had to come get you," Yeri said.

"I was getting to that."

"Uh huh."

"It was nighttime and my solar panels quit working. The backup battery was exhausted and without sunlight I ended up stranded near Reull Vallis where Mr. Bruce Wayne here came out and gave me a tow into town."

"That's southeast of here?" Tima interjected, "Hellas Planitia is southwest."

"The military base is between Dao Vallis and Hellas Planitia and I didn't want anyone to see me bringing in a rover."

"Because they would take it wouldn't they?" Togo asked.

Ken nodded.

The Martian temperature was dropping quickly as the sun faded into the night sky when suddenly the lights in the domette began to flicker.

"Is it getting cold in here?" Tima turned to Ken.

"The generator should have kicked in by now." Ken pushed his chair away.

"Are you going to have to go to work?"

"Depends on the ReDS."

"Don't Halks come out around this time?" Tima asked.

"Have you ever seen a Halk?" Tiga asked.

"Once. Three years ago I was working a ReDS on our northern quadrant in Hadriacus Mons. It was a little after midnight when I heard some banging coming from the signaling tower."

"Were you scared?" Togo asked.

"Let's just say I like to keep a respectful distance between them and me. Say fifty kilometers or so."

"Well, what happened?"

"It was night when a second windstorm turned and headed directly for the crater. ReDS #8310 got hit pretty hard by the first storm. That's when I got the call…"

*****

"Hello?"

"Ken. This is Melissa and we have an outage report. ReDS #8310. Mariner One is fueled and ready in bay one."

"Who is on call with me tonight?"

"Peter Johnson. He is already here. Our weather satellite has spotted a dust storm brewing from the south and it is heading for Aonia Terra but if you hurry you shouldn't have any trouble beating the storm."

"Okay. I will be there in thirty."

It took Ken and Peter a little over two hours to reach the station. The storm hit them faster than expected. They had to stop a few times as the sand pebbles ricocheted off their windshield as the wind gathered speed.

Relay Distribution Center #8310
Hadriacus Mons
Hellas Quadrangle, Mars
Pisces – Sol Sunday 1, 0009
2100 hours

"There it is!" Peter yelled over the gushing wind.

"I see it." Ken maneuvered the Mariner One into the docking bay which was nothing more than a hollowed out rock near the station. A few minutes later the two slowly made their way to the entrance. Ken pressed the switch and they both waited as the door to the airlock opened. Once inside, Ken checked the oxygen levels and then took off his helmet. When he heard…

"WARNING!"

came the mechanical female voice over the intercom.

"RELAY STATION POWER FAILURE"

The message was accompanied by a long and high-pitched tone.

"Turn that damn thing off!" Ken yelled.

"Aye aye, sir." Peter walked over to the console.

They both looked up in silence as the screen on the monitor changed and showed the number of hours flashing red against a white background.

- 21 HOURS -

Ten minutes had passed when a muted buzzer went off again and the flashing sign changed followed by the familiar female mechanical voice,

"WARNING
RELAY STATION POWER FAILURE
20 HOURS"

"Okay. She's been down for five and we have twenty left."

"The communication modules looked good and I'm running checks on the power grids," Peter said.

"Let me know if you see anything."

BANG!

"Did you hear something?"

"Yeah."

"What did it sound like?" Peter asked as he rechecked the signal meter. "There are some wild fluctuations going on around here."

"Probably some rocks hitting the domette. Nothing to be concerned about," Ken replied. "It's pretty nasty outside."

BANG! BANG! BANG!

"There it goes again. It doesn't sound like a few pebbles hitting the surface. It sounds like something's banging on the hull," Peter said.

"Nothing can survive this Martian atmosphere. You're letting your imagination get the best of you." Ken walked over to the view monitor.

"Halks can," Peter countered.

"Have you ever seen a Halk?" Ken replied.

"No."

"Well, me neither and to tell you the truth I think this Halk stuff is all made up in order to scare us."

"I dunno, Ken. There are a lot of people reporting break-ins at night and such."

"Yeah, well let's stick to the problem at hand. The forecast tonight is high velocity winds and you know that always creates trouble. This storm is worse than I thought. Hopefully this time we can find out why this station is always the first to go offline during these storms," Ken replied.

This particular recharging station in Hellas Quadrangle had been a problem child from day one. No one could figure out why it kept failing. Every time a storm would pass, it would knock out the whole station. ReDS #8310 was crucial to keeping communication and travel open throughout the Crater. It was one of the bigger stations and continuously monitored.

"There's that banging again. We need to do a sweep and beep," Peter said.

"Alright, as soon as I finish with these diagnostics, we'll suit up."

"How are the circuit panels looking?"

"Checking on the last one now. I don't think the problem is in here."

"You know, we're not going to get a bit of sleep around here if someone doesn't fix whatever it is out there making all that racket. It's been over four hours. We should have already done that sweep and beep," Peter said.

"Sounds like the actuator has come loose. That's probably causing the power drop," Ken said. "As soon as I close these panels and do a restart we should be…"

"Do you have the spot laser?"

"Right here. Ten Krugers says it's a faulty actuator that is causing these power failures," Ken said.

"You're on," Peter replied…

…"Ken?" Tima interrupted.

Ken abruptly turned his head toward his wife. "I was telling a story."

"The lights?"

The lights in their domicile had turned completely off only to be replaced by small emergency red ones lining the walls. Grandpa took note of the change. "Forget to pay your light bill again, Son?"

Ken smiled and turned to his dad. "Holy lack of funds, Batman. I think I only sent them a partial payment this time."

"Very funny," Tima shook her head.

The main lights blinked twice and then returned to normal.

"Does that happen very often?" Yeri asked.

"No."

"You know Ken, unlike your A-Plus, the Double and Triple A domes never blink like this."

"And why is that?" Ken asked in exasperation.

"They're double wired."

"Oh."

"What happened next?" Togo asked.

"Well Son, things quickly took a turn for the worse," Ken said. "With only fifteen hours left we decided to do a sweep and beep."

"What is that?" Togo asked.

"A perimeter walk around with the ELink scanning for energy leakage. Peter decided to stay inside while I with more experience suited up."

"Then what happened?" Togo asked.

"Well, I locked my helmet in place and waited for the spacesuit to go through the usual diagnostic checks..."

*****

"Pressurization test – 90%

Tank capacity – 85%

Secondary Seal defective...

Leak detected, please repair or replace."

flashed across his faceplate along with the computerized voice.

"Damn this thing," Ken said through his microphone.

"Problem?" Peter asked.

"I tested this suit before I left. Last year they changed manufacturers. Everything is going to Elotec these days and it's been nothing but a headache." Ken pulled off both gloves and replaced them with his spare.

"Secondary Seal defective.

Leak detected, please repair or replace."

Ken threw the new gloves against the wall. "Someone's going to hear about this when I get back tomorrow. I don't care how cost effective this piece of Martian dung is."

"Here." Peter threw his gloves to Ken. "I know they're smaller than what you like, but hey they're the old Martex ones."

Ken struggled to put on Peter's gloves and retested the suit one more time.

"Pressurization test - 100%
Tank capacity - 85%
Primary Seal - 100%
Secondary Seal - 100%
Tertiary Seal - 100%
Sealing...Completed
Containment...100%"

"It's about time." Ken entered the airlock. As the airlock equalized the pressure to the Martian atmosphere he thought about how sometimes rocks thrown by the high winds could knock loose the actuator. When that happened, it would usually just swing around and make an awful lot of racket tripping the circuit breakers. Ken thought they should have enough juice in battery backup to protect them through the night.

"Spot laser is on," Ken spoke into the mike.

"Are you out there already?" Peter asked.

"No. I just don't want to be out here any longer than I have to."

Ken saw the laser turn from red to a dark blue as the outer door opened. He smiled knowing the spot laser had reached operating temperature. He exited the chamber with laser in one hand and the ELink in the other. He walked to the other side of the dome and placed the ELink's micro detector which looked amazingly like a microphone connected to a cord next to each panel while the ELink data streamed across his faceplate.

"No beeps or sign of power panel leakage," Ken radioed.

"There is still a lot of banging going on."

"Roger," Ken said and with only a few meters to the power coupler he turned the corner only to see a seven-foot tall lizard with scales and fur banging on the hull. It was covered with matting that resembled some type of thick hairy like substance. He dropped the ELink and slowly backed away only to find that it was too late. The thing was on him before he knew it. The Halkomelem grabbed him by the neck and lifted him off the ground and smashed his head into Ken's helmet. Ken panicked and shoved the spot laser right into its throat and he watched as the sparks flashed from the glow of the radiant heat emanating from the knife. The Halkomelem jerked his head back in pain and dropped him to the ground. Ken sat on the red dirt and watched the creature disappear into the night…

*****

"…AND THAT was as my first and hopefully last encounter with one of those beasts," Ken said to Togo.

"Wow. Good thing you had the knife," Togo said.

"Yes it was. The Halkomelem had apparently ripped the power coupling off the domette and he was hitting the actuator with a rock when I stumbled upon him. I think he was trying to break in to avoid the storm. Fortunately, I startled him enough that he dropped the rock or I doubt I would be here today."

"I didn't think Mars had any life on it before we came," Togo said.

"There wasn't any and it has been a mystery."

"You told me Mars couldn't sustain life."

"Not as we know it. But this creature seemed to have adapted to the planet's harsh environment rather well."

"Uh oh," Togo said and looked around at the darkness. "The power just went out again."

"Tima, you better get the back-up ready." Ken turned to his mom and dad. "I guess you guys are stuck with us tonight."

"Doesn't your lift have a battery backup?" Yeri asked.

"No."

"The new G-4000s do."

"My old G-2000 only has a hand crank," Ken turned to Yeri, "if you're in such a hurry."

"No thanks," Yeri said.

Ken went to his lab while Tima walked over to the control panel.

"Got any candles?" Yeri asked.

"The PeePs are in the closet next to the front door."

"Finally moving with the times I see."

"What's a PeeP?" asked Togo.

"It replaced the LEDs years ago. It's short for Photo Thermal Nano Particles. It was constructed using a new type of nano-particles which allows it to be molded and it can stick like Silly Putty if you want. You can place it along corridors or just about anywhere. We took one at the lab a few years and molded it into a football and threw it around. That was a lot of..."

"Bedipida! Why do you call it a PeeP?" Togo interrupted.

"Togo, I was talking."

"Sorry."

"They first called it PTNPs but that was too long and confusing. Then we dropped the N and called it PTPs and if you say it fast enough it sounded a little like peep, so that is what it is called these days."

"How does it work?" Togo asked.

"You are full of questions aren't you?" Yeri asked as he continued to search in the closet. "Like your dad said, it is a polymer containing nano-materials that glow when stimulated with an electric charge."

Cuckoo - Cuckoo....

"Okay, kids you know what that means."

"What?" Tiga asked.

"Time for bed."

"Okay, goodnight."

"How did you get that cuckoo clock past Martian security?" Beth asked.

"I took it all apart and hid the pieces in my suitcase and such," Tima replied.

"Clever."

Ken walked back into the room holding a PeeP. "I'm going to start the generator," he told Tima as she watched him walk down the hall, the light from his PeeP bouncing rhythmically from wall to wall.

"What shape is it in?" Yeri yelled out from halfway inside the closet as his tone took on a hint of frustration.

"What shape is what in?" Tima asked.

"Grandpa," Togo said and grinned. "I think he's getting a little out of shape if you ask me." He started to laugh.

"That's enough young man! Didn't I tell you two to go to bed?" Tima said trying to stifle herself from laughing.

"The PeeP?" Yeri said in an even louder reply.

"It's in the shape of a flashlight on the top shelf. It has a big round crystal on top. Actually more like a big lollipop... Pop." Tima giggled as she yelled across the room.

"Found it!" Yeri said.

BANG!

"What's that?" Tima asked.

"My HEAD! I don't know what you guys have on the top shelf in this closet, but it nearly killed me!" Yeri felt a knot starting to form on the top of his scalp. "That's gonna leave a mark. At least I'm not bleeding."

"Hey old man, you need any help?" Beth asked.

Yeri closed the closet door. "I don't need anyone's... Tima? Your PeeP isn't working."

"Just shake them," Tima said.

"Shake them?"

"Yes. Move them up and down rapidly."

"I know what shaking means," Grandpa replied as he shook them harder this time and watched as the particles lit up the living room.

"Where's Ken?"

"He's gone to start the generator," Tima replied.

"He should have been back by now," Yeri said and placed the PeeP on the coffee table. "Why do you keep one in the closet?"

"Ken wants to have one near the DTs."

"Oh."

Fifteen minutes ticked by as the group sat in a worried silence. The only noise in the room was coming from the sound of the cuckoo clock.

"KEN!" Yeri yelled from the living room.

"He can't hear you," Tima said, "and you're going to wake up the children screaming like that."

"They just went to bed. I think it should have started by now. I'll go find out if he needs some help." Yeri headed down the hall.

"It's starting to get a little cool in here, don't you think?" Beth asked as her body shivered slightly.

"I've got something that will warm you up," Tima said with a devilish smile.

"What might that be?"

"I've been fermenting a new strain of rice."

"I thought rice needs a lot of water."

"This new strain can grow in less water than the ones on Earth. We've been working on this for a while and the first batch showed up a few months ago." Tima walked into the kitchen and returned with two full glasses of a bluish liquid.

"Blue?"

"I added some coloring so I don't mistake it for potato vodka."

Beth took a sip.

"Do you like it?"

Beth nodded and took another sip. "Yum!" She sat her glass on the coffee table.

"It's fermented rice. I guess you could call it rice wine."

"Martian sake!" Beth said. "Better than that potato vodka stuff."

"I agree. I think I'll leave the povkas for the boys."

"What does Ken think about having his own personal home brewer?"

Tima shrugged her shoulders as the generator kicked in. Tima and Beth watched as the lights flickered on and off for a couple of seconds and then brightened.

"You haven't told him?"

"You know how those two can put away those povkas," Tima replied, "Rice is going to be a big staple in the Martian community and there are those who frown on using it as a drink."

"Same ones about the povkas?"

"Yes and I don't want Ken and Dad telling everyone." Tima and Beth together laughed as they sipped on their homemade sake.

"Here they come," Beth said. She quickly swallowed the last of her drink as the men walked into the living room.

"What is that?" Ken asked, noticing two empty glasses sitting on the coffee table.

"Oh nothing," Tima said.

"Have you been drinking your new rice wine?" Ken headed for the kitchen.

"How did you know?"

Yeri laughed. "Tima, you know you can't keep alcohol a secret around here!"

"I guess you're right. Would you guys care for some?" Tima asked in resignation.

"I didn't think we could grow rice," Yeri said.

"Normally no, but this is a hybrid. It can survive in this Martian soil and it doesn't use nearly as much water or time to grow. This is the first batch."

"Opening up a Martian tavern are we?" Yeri smiled.

"No, the sake is something I cooked up in the lab. The rice will be an additional food source as soon as we can figure out how to grow it in bulk. But for now we can only harvest small portions at a time. Would you like a glass?" Tima asked.

"I think you're too late," Yeri said as Ken walked out of the kitchen with two full glasses. He put one on the table next to himself and handed the other one to Yeri.

"As a matter of fact it's very good. I ran out of povka the other day and this made an excellent substitute," Ken said.

"Substitute?…Oh no!" Tima said and ran to the kitchen and opened what she thought was her secret hiding place. She looked around and nothing.

"Ken? Where are the other two bottles?" she inquired walking back into the living room.

"In my stomach. Why?" Ken asked.

"You drank it all? I'm supposed to do a presentation Monday and those bottles were for the board members."

"Tell them you lost it."

"I'm about to lose it all on you! What were you thinking? That wasn't yours!" Tima's voice raised an octave.

"Now how was I to know?" Ken innocently asked.

"I don't go drinking things you've concocted in your lab," Tima said as anger welled up in her eyes.

"No. But then I'm not brewing liquor in there either. If you had told me I wouldn't have drunk it," Ken said sporting a righteous smile.

Chapter 14

EARTH

Mobile Military Outpost Bravo Alpha Delta
(ten kilometers east of Luanshya)
Monday, June 15, 0015
0600 hours

The townspeople of Luanshya awoke to the sounds of metal squeaking against metal as the array of military machines slowly made their way toward them. The rumbling of tank tracks echoed throughout the valley forcing the wildlife to quickly vacate the area for safer pastures. The soldiers dressed in full battle gear marched in time stirring up clouds of dust as the early morning sun peeked over the peaceful town. The Shyans gathered at the front entrance to watch the tanks and armed soldiers as they continued their march toward them. The townspeople were frightened as the tank tracks plowed their way forward destroying the small dirt roads that led to the little village. In front of the troops was General Sanchez in his finest outfit with his personal sword at his side. The lights danced off the highly polished steel as the sword generously reflected the sun's early morning rays. Sanchez had asked the media to set-up the cameras fifty meters from Luanshya, Zambia. He wanted his majestic entrance to be viewed throughout the world.

The cameras transmitted pictures of the plumes of smoke and dust kicked up by the troops and armament as it all headed toward the sleepy little town. The audio technician cued a marching tune as he readied for the main event. The villagers stood in awe as the distant noises wafted through the town as the ground beneath them rumbled. More and more townspeople had gathered at the entrance and gasped as the thousands of foot soldiers and tanks slowly crept toward them. Courtney placed her back toward the village and shouted, "Roll it!"

The camera's red light came on and it was focused on General Sanchez with his troops behind him. They moved toward the village and the announcer began her rehearsed speech.

"The troops are closing in on the Luanshyan terrorists located in the heart of the city." The camera moved away from the troops and focused back on Courtney with the villagers gathered in the far background. "As you can see the insurgents are using the villagers as a human wall. There are no depths low enough these terrorists will not go in order to oppress these poor people."

"What's going on Dad?" Kenyan asked.

"I'm not sure, Son. It looks like a lot of people and vehicles stirring up a lot of dust out there."

"They're coming toward us!" Kenyan yelled to his father over the noise.

Kenya noticed what seemed to be half the town standing at the front entrance. He pushed his way to the very front and turned to face them. "Listen to me. No one knows what is going on out there, but we do know they are coming this way. You need to go back to your homes and wait. I will tell you everything once I know their purpose."

"They want to take our village!" screamed a man in the back.

"Let's not be hasty. We are a peaceful people. We have no weapons to match their tanks and army. I don't think they have come here to attack us." Kenya turned his head to the soldiers and then back to his people. "But to be on the safe side I want you all to remain calm and go back home. Please."

The General turned on his mouthpiece and ordered his troops to stop. The length of a football field stood between the citizens of Luanshya and a full regiment of General Sanchez's military with Carlos standing ten yards all by himself right in front. The townspeople slowly started to leave. Sanchez watched as the townsfolk turned their backs on him.

Sanchez raised a flag sporting the emblem of a large menacing black snake a little higher for all to see. He began to wave it back and forth when all at once a shot rang out catching Kenya in the shoulder. Before he could move another and then another hit the leader until he fell to the ground soaking the dirt with his blood.

BANG!

Blood spewed out from the chest of another man who was standing right next to Kenya. He dropped his young son and crumpled to the ground.

BANG!

This time a child screamed out grabbing her shoulder as the red blood oozed down her little white dress. "Mommy, Mommy!" she screamed in pain.

BANG! BANG! BANG!

Three and then four more bullets found their mark. Blood and screams sifted through the crowd as the townspeople collapsed to the ground. The wounded tried to hobble away from the cacophony, but ended up being easy prey for the snipers' deadly bullets. The rest of the villagers scattered. Many were shot multiple times as they tried in vain to find refuge.

"The terrorists are attacking the hostages! They've killed Kenya!" Courtney turned to her co-host and screamed into the microphone.

"A respected and peaceful leader of Luanshya, Kenya ruled for over forty years. He will surely be missed," Patriot Pat said and turned back to Courtney.

"It's a blood bath out here. Thank God that General Sanchez has arrived in time to free these people," Courtney continued. The cameras moved off the villagers back to the soldiers.

The General's men watched in horror as the village pavements turned from a dark gray to a bright red caused by the vicious slaughter by the unknown assailants.

"It's the terrorists!" shouted the General into his microphone and he radioed his men to move in.

Just then, a shot rang out and hit the General in his left arm which caused him to drop the flag as he fell to his knees. Two soldiers came to his aid but before they could reach him, the enemy's bullets cut them down within seconds. Three more soldiers ran to help their fallen leader, but they suffered the same fate as the other two. By now the entire regiment was only a yard behind Sanchez. Sanchez bent over one of the soldiers and turned him on his back and looked at the camera. He slowly, painfully pulled himself to his feet and shoved his fist in the air showing his defiance and anger. "Defend the villagers!" Sanchez screamed into his microphone and fell back to the ground.

The platoon opened fire on the town, killing even more innocent villagers. The media was caught in the stampede as they scattered to a nearby hill. All the while, they continued to video the soldiers as they advanced upon the town and fired at anything that moved. The villagers ran helter-skelter as more bullets continued to impale the advancing army. The men continued their march onward as their brothers in arms fell to the ground. Hand grenades were tossed from somewhere in the village toward the oncoming army. They exploded and killed dozens more of the General's men.

Tank operators, who saw their comrades lying helpless on the ground, opened fire into the village with their 80-millimeter Howitzer scatter shells. Those weapons of destruction annihilated anything they contacted within a twenty-meter radius. Buildings exploded sending glass and bricks raining down on the Shyans.

The Shyans that were still alive ran for cover, but the Howitzer's death shells made it no easy task. Like a bird with a broken wing, the villagers were helpless as they watched their family and friends die all around them. The noise and violence of the General's army settled upon them like a raging storm.

General Sanchez finally lifted himself off the blood soaked ground and radioed Colonel Rice. "Send in the Hueys."

"Sanchez! What are you doing?" responded Chris.

"Saving the villagers!"

"You said there wouldn't be…"

"Colonel! If you do not follow my orders and send in those choppers I will have you shot for treason."

Five minutes later, two gigantic black birds of prey hovered over the village and fired her rockets into the city's business district and killed hundreds more in milliseconds. The black smoke of death rose above the town as the cameras continued to roll. Courtney continued her blow-by-blow description of the invasion.

Sanchez stumbled mightily toward the village only to fall once again to the ground.

"Our fallen hero, General Sanchez, is badly wounded," Courtney remarked.

Courtney's co-announcer Patriot Pat interrupted. "He's getting up again! He is shouting to his men to continue the fight for freedom against those evil terrorists." The camera turned from Courtney to the General now kneeling down in the grass.

A medic rushed over to the General. "You're lucky General. It's only a flesh wound." He reassured the General as he field-dressed the area.

"Are you finished yet?" the General shouted as he suddenly noticed the camera. "Hold on a minute, act like it's life-threatening."

"But General?"

"DO IT! Take that bandage off my arm and wrap it around my head."

"But General, your head is fine. Here let me get you a fresh banda..." The General collapsed to the ground. The medic fell to one knee, "General, are you okay?"

"Bandage my head with the bloody one or I'll bloody your goddamn nose. Do you understand?"

"Yes sir," the medic said with his back to the camera and hurriedly unwrapped the bandage soaked with the General's blood and placed it around his head.

"Now help me up."

"Certainly sir. Easy now."

"It looks like the General has sustained a head injury too. His head is bleeding and it looks like he's staggering. The medic is helping him to his feet," Courtney said as the camera turned to her co-host.

Patriot Pat put his microphone close to his mouth. "He's sustained multiple wounds and I doubt he'll be able to...."

"Wait!" Courtney interjected, "He's drawn his sword and holding it with both hands. He has it pointed toward the village. It looks like...like he's arguing with the medic."

"What do you think they're saying Courtney?" Patriot Pat asked.

"He's pushing forward. He wants to continue to fight even though he's been shot! Twice!" Courtney shouted.

"They don't make 'em like him anymore."

Courtney turned to the audio tech. "Play a marching tune or something." The tech nodded and cued up the Battle Hymn of the Republic. *"Mine eyes have seen the coming of the glory of the Lord..."* played on as the camera's eye watched the General as he stumbled toward the village with his sword raised high.

It was a few hours past sunset when the fighting ceased. There wasn't much left untouched by Sanchez's army. The village looked like a category-five tornado had spent the entire day there destroying everything it could find. There were still some stores and buildings untouched by the fury of the attack, but not many. Only a handful of townspeople remained while the rest had scattered to the outskirts of town. Cries and wails from those shot and dying rose in an eerie tone throughout the night. Even the hospitals had taken fire as the nurses and doctors frantically tried to douse the burning wards along with moving their patients to safer floors.

"This is Courtney Hughes bringing you an exclusive on..."
- Operation Free the Luanshyans -
flashed on the HV screens around the world.

"I am here with General Carlos Sanchez. He is the man solely responsible for freeing the people of Luanshya from the terrorists who had beaten and tortured these poor souls for weeks now." Courtney turned to the General.

"We have freed the villagers from the terrorists' iron grip," Sanchez said to the camera as the blinding lights revealed his bloody face and clothes.

"You've been shot...twice..." she paused for effect, "and are in dire need of medical attention. Are you sure you want to be interviewed tonight?" The camera turned to Sanchez.

Sanchez looked directly into the camera. "Before I go I want to let the world know that we are there for you. And as long as I can stand," Sanchez grimaced in pain and stumbled a bit as the camera rolled, "I will be there to fight for peace and the freedom to be safe from those who might otherwise do us harm."

The camera's red light went off as they rolled footage of Sanchez during the attack when he was bandaged and pointing his sword marching toward the village.

"Here we have a picture of true hero," Courtney remarked with awe.

The light on top of the camera returned its bright red glow letting them know they were back on air.

Courtney turned to Sanchez and leaned in. "General, you were bleeding, shot multiple times and you still marched forward. Can you tell us why?" she moved the microphone to his mouth as the camera zoomed in for a close-up.

"I would have been happy to give my life to save any one of those fallen villagers." Sanchez turned away from the camera, gathered himself, and continued, "Some will call this a victory, but in my heart it is a loss." Sanchez's eyes welled up as single tear made its way down his face. "The loss of one hostage is a sacrifice I had hoped not to make. If only we had gotten here sooner." Sanchez lowered his eyes and shook his head. The camera turned back to the reporter.

"Now stay tuned for the six o'clock news. I am Courtney Hughes and we were talking to not just a man, but a real hero who fought the good fight to make our world a better and safer place to live. With heroes like General Sanchez I know I will sleep better tonight knowing he is out there protecting us."

More footage of Sanchez's army recorded earlier appeared on screen as the credits rolled. The faceless announcer's voice echoed throughout the world. "Stay tuned for more news and sports just after these messages…"

Carlos turned toward a jeep waiting for him, but Courtney caught his sleeve and he turned back to her.

"Thank you for the interview General. Do you need a lift to the hospital or anything?"

"I have to visit the Luanshyans to make sure we have ridden them of those terrorists."

"But you are wounded!"

"It is small price compared to those who have lost their lives and to those who have lost their limbs and loved ones."

"Good luck, sir!" Courtney said as she beamed with pride. *We should have gotten that statement on air,* she thought to herself. She tried to do a salute to him as he returned her homemade gesture and turned away.

Patriot Pat walked over to Courtney. "I got your last conversation on film!"

Courtney smiled. "Good work, Pat! If we hurry back to the hotel we can get it on the late news as a little bonus!" she said then turned to her crew. "Okay folks. The show is over and it is time to pack it up."

The camera crew had their footage for the day, so they loaded the trucks and headed back to their hotels in Kitwe Zambia located thirty kilometers away.

Carlos walked over to the jeep where his private was waiting for him. "I overheard your conversation with Courtney Hughes. Are we going to Luanshya now?"

"Hell no! Can't you see I've been shot?" the General reached in his knapsack and pulled out a bottle of Sea Dog Whisky. "Take me to the infirmary back at camp."

"Sorry sir. I thought you wanted to…"

"Shut up and drive Private," Sanchez interrupted. "I don't have time to wet nurse those fools," Sanchez paused as they hit a bump on the road torn up by the tanks. "And drive slow, please!" he said with a hint of sarcasm.

"Yes sir," the Private said as he slowed the jeep to a crawl.

"That's better," Sanchez said as he put the whisky bottle to his lips.

Chapter 15

EARTH

**Roan Forest Reserve
Zambia, Africa
Tuesday June 16, 0015
0500 hours**

Morning came early for the General. His left arm was a little sore and sported a nice sized bruise. He rolled out of bed and donned a freshly pressed uniform. He had a very important appointment that could not be missed. He quietly crawled into his jeep and headed northeast toward the Roan Forest Reserve located directly north of Luanshya. An hour later the General's jeep turned onto an old abandoned dirt road. The jeep argued with the potholes as the General more than once had to duck his head in order miss a branch or two. The sun's first rays flowed through the low hanging African clouds as small openings allowed the orange and yellows to light up the once dark jungles of the land.

"He is near," the man said as he lit his cigar. "I want you to... disappear for now," he said to his friend, "and keep your sights on him."

Carlos pulled the jeep to the back of a row of tents and turned off the motor.

"Good morning General," the dark haired man said and took a drag from his Cuban cigar and blew the smoke up into the air.

"Qué pasa amigo?" Sanchez said sporting a big grin as he sat relaxed behind the wheel.

"Do you have my money?" the dark haired man asked taking another puff on his cigar.

Sanchez watched the end of the cigar glow and nodded as he shoved the door open with his bruised shoulder. "Ouch!" he grimaced.

"Lo siento," the man said.

"It's alright. It had to be done. I'm just glad your men were as good as you said. Where are they?"

"They are fine, General. They are here." The man looked around the thick brush of limbs and trees surrounding them like he was searching for something. "Do you have my Krugers?"

"Sí," the General replied and grabbed a knapsack from the backseat.

"In the sack?"

"Don't be silly."

"Don not play games with me Mr. Sanchez. I took big chance yesterday."

"And you will be well paid when I decide."

"Decide? My men are getting… what do you say, um…anxious?"

"I said when I decide," Sanchez smiled.

"You are testing my patience, Señor," the man said in a deep Cuban accent denoting a hint of anger.

"Ricco, you need to relax a little more." Sanchez pulled out one of his own Cuban cigars, clipped off both ends and pointed it towards the man. "Tienes el fuego?" he asked.

"My men took a big chance yesterday." Ricco lit up Sanchez's cigar.

"Gracias, Ricco," Sanchez said and took a deep drag from his cigar.

"You say my name one time more and you might not make it back. Mr. Sanchez."

The General blew out a puff of smoke and watched as it slowly disappeared into the calm morning air then looked Ricco in the eyes. "General!" Sanchez barked. "Did anyone get caught?" Sanchez took another drag on his cigar. He blew out another puff of smoke and watched the cigar's tip as it glowed red in the predawn shadows.

"No. They escaped unharmed. Everything went as planned."

"Do you still have the capsules and the sniper rifles?"

"We have disposed of all the cyanide and all of the weapons have been dismantled."

"Good. I thought the hand grenade launchers added a special touch, don't you think?" Sanchez pulled out his pursal, turned it to *texpanded* mode and after the retina scan he entered a combination of numbers and letters. He then waited as Ricco checked his own pursal *texpanded*.

"This is only half Señor!"

"Ricco. You didn't expect me to transfer all the funds we agreed on at once did you? If so, then who's to say I wouldn't find a bullet in my back when I leave?"

"If the rest is not in my account by tomorrow at this time you just may find a bullet looking for you, maybe worse. So either pay me what you owe or save a poison pill for yourself," Ricco grinned. "Because it would be an easier death than I would give you."

Sanchez grunted and threw the knapsack at Ricco's feet. "Here are some items I borrowed from the Shyans. They are yours to do what you wish along with six bottles of Sea Dog Whisky for your men that I picked up on my last visit to Durban," he stepped back and looked at his watch. "I hate to break up our little party but I have more important things to do than trade empty threats with someone like you." He turned and mounted his jeep for town.

Ricco watched as the dust kicked up from the fading jeep as the sun was slowly gaining mastery once more over the grassy meadows in the distance.

"Don disappoint me Mr. Sanchez," Ricco smirked.

Just then his friend appeared from out of the deep underbrush with a rifle slung over his shoulder. He walked over to Ricco. "Why did you tell him we destroyed everything after we attacked the village and shot some of his troops?" Raul asked.

"A man like that I no trust," Ricco said and picked up the sack then walked away.

Later that morning, Sanchez was back in his tent resting on his cot when he heard a vehicle just outside. "Good morning, General Sanchez," the medic popped his head through the tent. "I looked in on you earlier but you were gone."

"Morning. I had to....What do you want?" the General shot back at the medic.

"Just checking on your wounds. You're a hero you know. The holovisions have been broadcasting Operation Free the Shyans all morning long. I heard that the Ana Aseas are planning to award you with the World Medal of Honor for bravery above and beyond that expected."

"Humph," the General grunted as he rummaged around for his sword. "Where's my sword?"

"I took the liberty of having it polished while you were out."

"Don't you ever touch anything of mine again or I'll have your head!"

"Yes sir, sorry sir." The medic disappeared and then returned through the entrance with sword in hand. He proudly held it with both hands similar to a ceremonial offering. "Here is your sword."

Sanchez snapped it quickly out of his hands. "Good. Be gone then and don't come back. I'm fine."

"Yes sir!" the medic quickly exited the tent as the General holstered his sword and followed close behind. He watched the medic drive off and waited outside his tent. He glanced at his watch. "0701? He's late!" Sanchez said to himself just as another jeep came into view.

"Good morning Mr. Rice," Sanchez said as he crawled into the back of the jeep. "You're late."

"Sorry sir. The jeep needed some gas."

"I don't want excuses, I want results now let's go."

"Yes sir!"

When they arrived at the war torn city of Luanshya, Sanchez smiled as he looked around to see the massive amounts of destruction his army had inflicted on the Luanshyan people. Sanchez headed for the Elders' Hall and when he arrived he walked over to their flagpole and lowered the Luanshyan flag and replaced it with that of a black snake he had carried with him yesterday. He smirked as he saw the snake waving in the wind for all to see. He then entered the Elders' Hall.

"Good morning, Kenyan, son of Kenya, and Narmien, son of a..." the General paused and smiled enjoying himself as he and Colonel Rice entered the room uninvited. "I see you have realized the futility of resistance against the Ana Aseas' wishes?" the General smiled.

Kenyan, the now high elder of the village spoke, "You have made your point. We will sign over our land to you at your last offer."

"Well," Sanchez said as he stroked his chin and placed his right hand on his newly polished sword, "that was when your land was in pristine condition." He walked over to the window and looked out. All he could see were smoldering buildings and damaged crops along with the massive holes in the ground created from the mortar fire of yesterday.

"My army can sure make a mess of things when they want to," Sanchez turned to Kenyan and smiled. "Don't you agree?" He waited but got no response. "Ah yes, I can see you are impressed with my power. Tell me, what did you think of yesterday?"

"Can we just get this done?" Kenyan asked.

"What? This is time for celebration! You get a fair offer for your land and I get to help a town that by the way looks desperately in need of some." Sanchez punched in a figure on his pursal *texpanded* mode and handed it to Kenyan.

"This is not the price we agreed on!"

"Oh! You must be talking about the time I was here before when my kindness was met with hate and anger from your father."

"He treated you well. He just knew we couldn't live on your offer."

"Not all of us can live like kings you know. I guess your father didn't think about that. Anyway, your land is hardly of pristine value wouldn't you agree? In fact it's only a fraction of what it once was, but I'm not an unkind man." He turned to stare at each of them. "I will give you my original offer." He knew he had them over a barrel and he loved to see them squirm. "Kraals," he said under his breath and smiled.

Kenyan motioned the others to assemble and after a few minutes they agreed to accept his original offer. The General sent Chris outside the Meeting Hall of the Elders to inform the rest of the town's people on their agreement.

"You are to sign and date your contracts. We need two retina scans for your safety and security."

As the people formed a line Colonel Rice ushered them into the Elders' Chamber one by one. The General had the forms and contracts neatly placed along with the two retina eye scanners each mounted on the wall. As they entered one would stare into the first scanner, sign away his property and then stare into the second scanner. When the last signature was captured Sanchez arose from the table, put the papers in his pouch, and turned to Kenyan. "Any questions?"

"Why two retina scans?"

"You want your people to get to their money, right?"

"Yes, but the other one?"

"That is um, well to make sure they are um, who they say they are."

Kenyan didn't like that answer, but he felt much like a caged dog who being constantly poked with a stick from a cruel owner would eventually end up just sitting there taking it. He didn't know what the second scanner was for but he knew whatever Sanchez was up to would not be good for him or his people.

"When will we get our money?"

"There is only one task I have for you and your precious Krugers will be in your accounts as soon as it's completed."

"What do you want us to do?" Kenyan looked at the General with a deep sadness in his eyes.

"Before I graciously buy this worthless swamp you call home I want you to send representatives to your surrounding neighbors in Mpatanomatu and Venture." Sanchez turned and smiled at Chris. "Oh, and don't forget Fisenge. I want them to tell the story."

"The story?"

"Yes. How your greedy old and now dead father refused my generous offers and the results of his actions on his people. Tell them how many of your people have died because of his foolish pride. Tell them so that they won't make the same horrible mistake Daddy made," Sanchez snickered in Kenyan's face. "Look, if you, like your father, don't care about your people at least let the elders in the other towns and villages know what can happen if they choose pride over good sense. Maybe they *care* about their people. I want this done immediately! Do you understand?"

Kenyan rose with anger in his eyes, but Narmien placed a hand on his shoulder and spoke in his stead, "We will honor your wishes, Mr. Sanchez."

"GENERAL... Sanchez! After yesterday I would have expected you to treat me with a little more respect."

"Of course...GENERAL," replied Narmien.

This was a day long remembered. He was now a hero in the eyes of the world and about to be rewarded the infamous World Medal of Honor along with selling Luanshya to the WDG for a tidy profit. As he and Chris left the village they both knew that Africa was going to make them rich, very rich indeed.

The following morning General Sanchez and Colonel Rice flew to Durban and checked into the Sea Point Hotel. The rooms were not ready, so they took a seat by the bar overlooking the ocean.

"A bottle of Sea Dog Whisky please," Sanchez said. "A few days of rest and relaxation for all the good work you did in Luanshya, Colonel."

"What happened back there?"

"Terrorists."

"I didn't see any terrorists."

The bartender returned with a bottle and two sniffers. "You have made an excellent choice! The distillery is not far from here. You can take a tour if you want."

"Yes, yes. Florida Road Distillery makes a fine whisky."

"Will there be anything else? I am going on break."

"No thanks, just bill it to my room."

"As you wish."

Carlos slowly poured himself a drink. "What was I supposed to do? We had to defend ourselves, right? I was almost killed! We couldn't just sit there and let them massacre all of those innocent people. Could we?"

"I don't know, but you said no one was going to get hurt."

"Now Chris, how was I to know we were going to actually run into a real battle? I figured anyone in his right mind would run after seeing what they were going to be up against."

"It still seems strange."

"I wouldn't give it a second thought. What's done is done. I will have the money in your account by next week, so why don't you call your wife and tell her to schedule that surgery. You have just saved her life! Now we have a few days to relax and enjoy ourselves. I hope you take full advantage of it."

"Thank you, General. How many days?"

"We'll be here three days before we head back home. Like I said, go enjoy yourself. In fact I'll even pick up the tab." He unsnapped his pursal from his belt and punched in a code. "Everything you buy in the next three days will be charged to my account."

"You're too generous."

"You've earned it, now go have some well deserved fun. By the way, I will need you back here at twenty hundred hours sharp tonight."

"Can't we meet tomorrow maybe? I'm a bit tired."

"Oh I think what I have for you will perk you right up."

"Sir?"

"We have a lot of things to go over. Tonight is a call for a celebration, don't you think? Now go out and have some fun and don't forget about tonight."

Chris sighed, "Okay, where do you want to meet?"

"I'll call your room. After that the rest of the time here is yours. I promise." Sanchez put his pursal *celling* mode to his ear. "Excuse me," he said and turned slightly away.

Colonel Rice nodded and pushed the stool out from underneath him. He walked out the door, stopped and looked back at Sanchez. "I need a stiff drink," he mumbled to himself. "Man, this wasn't what I bargained for."

Sanchez with his ear to the phone waved Chris goodbye. "Busy. Damn!" He hung up his pursal. He downed his drink and went over to the hotel's concierge.

"Can I help you?"

"Yes, I want you to send a lady to Room 415 at eight o'clock tonight."

"Sir, with all due respect, we do not participate in such matters."

Sanchez walked around the concierge's desk and discreetly placed three gold Kruger coins in the concierge's hands. "I understand, but I am sure your hotel can make exceptions when necessary. I want her young and pretty, the man's name is Chris. Christopher Rice."

"I will see what we can do."

"Remember, eight o'clock tonight."

The General unsnapped his phone as he walked back to the bar and poured himself another drink.

"Donager here."

"Brian. This is Carlos."

"How's the African evac going?"

"Almost done!"

"I caught a glimpse of you on holovision yesterday, quite an impressive show old boy."

"No more terrorists and the people of Luanshya have agreed to relocate. They're packing and preparing to move as soon as they get paid," General Sanchez said.

"Excellent. We are finished with Australia and Sergio can be there in the next few days with the contracts."

"I thought I could save you some time."

"Really?"

"Yes. The people of Luanshya were so thankful that I ridded the village of those terrorists that they asked me to act as their liaison. The contracts have all been signed, retina scanned and I should have their bank accounts online, um, tomorrow evening if all goes well. All you have to do is deposit the money in the accounts. Easy for you, easy for them."

"Thanks Carlos, but this is Sergie's job. I don't think he'll be too happy about this not to mention that's a lot of work on your part. Are you sure you don't need our help?"

"These poor people are so ignorant. My heart went out to them and I felt a sort of...duty to make sure these people get what they so truly deserve."

"A big reward from the Sevens when you get home I bet. You're a good man Carlos."

"My reward is Africa. I need no others."

"I am proud to call you my friend."

"Just doing my part to better the world, like yourself," Carlos replied. "I will be sending you the Luanshya account numbers to deposit the Krugers and I will send you the signed contracts tomorrow. Deal?"

"Are you sure you can do or should do this all by yourself? Protocol states we have to be working in teams to ... well you know. To keep everything..."

"No worries, Brian. That is why I had Colonel Rice with me the whole time. We worked together side-by-side setting up these accounts in the name of the people of Luanshya. I watched him and vice versa. I can have him call you if you want. Second of all, if you look you will see those accounts can only be accessed through retina scans. I took one scan of each person and sent it in. As you know those retina scanners we used to set up accounts automatically erase the imprint when the account is activated. When they are finally relocated all they have to do is stare into the monitor for their money. It's pretty foolproof, don't you think? In fact, you can monitor the accounts if you want. It is your call," Sanchez said and grimaced hoping Brian would bite. A few minutes passed as the General held his breath.

"I think that should be adequate. You're the big hero and as long as Colonel Rice was there that should be enough. I am sure you wouldn't make any... um... mistakes. It's just a lot of money and I don't like going against protocol." Another long pause. "But I guess we can bend the rules this time."

"Well the good news is since we processed everybody on Luanshya you can tell Six we are ahead of schedule."

"I didn't think about that."

"Yes. It kind of makes you look like a hero too."

"Hmmm....Six will surely be happy to hear the good news!"

"Trust me on this one, Brian. Everything is working out fine."

"Send me the information and Sergie will wire the money."

"You should get the account numbers within forty-eight hours depending on how clean the transmissions are down here. I just want you to know it feels good to see how Clear-Vision will benefit so many." General Sanchez paused as if in thought.

"General? Are you still there?"

"I have one more thing to ask. I don't know if it's possible, but these people have suffered greatly from the terrorists and sadly they've lost family and friends from the hostiles... and from..." General Sanchez paused again, "friendly fire."

"What is it you want me to do?"

"Maybe. I don't know. If there is any spare change laying around that no one has claimed, it would help soothe the enormous wounds suffered by these poor people."

"I think I can find some additional funds to help. Carlos, you've made such a difference in these people's lives. I don't know how they could ever thank you enough."

"Just doing my job. Thanks again, Brian," Sanchez paused. "Oh, and by the way, since I am already here in Africa would you like me to contact Luanshya's neighbors and help explain what they should expect from us?"

Chapter 16

MARS

Thornton Residence
Domette 64
Gemini - Sol Friday 6, 0012
1900 hours

"It's getting awfully cold in here," Tima stated.

"The generator's running now. It'll warm up in a few minutes." Ken took another sip of his drink. "You should market this as Martian sake."

"Don't push it mister. I'm still mad at you for…"

BANG! BANG!

"What's that?" Tima asked.

"I don't know, but it sounds like it's coming from the far bedroom. I've been having trouble with that generator lately," Ken said.

"How long have you had that thing?" Yeri asked.

"It came with the dome."

"Maybe it's time for an upgrade? They have a big sale going on this week at TerraMars. I bought the new Rabbit last year and haven't had a bit of trouble," Yeri said.

"I'll think about it," Ken said.

"Aren't you going to check it out?" Tima asked.

"I said I would think about it."

"No. The generator is making a lot more noise than usual."

"After I finish my sake," Ken replied. "I'm sure it's fine, but I'll take another look."

"The sale ends on Sunday you know," Yeri stated.

"I'm cold!" Togo said as he walked into the living room followed by Tiga.

"You should be sleeping," Tima said.

"Grandpa woke us up yelling."

"Uh huh? Alright you can stay up, but just for a little while."

Togo and Tiga grabbed a blanket and sat next to Tima shivering.

BANG!...BANG!...BANG!

"There it goes again." Tima turned to Ken. "You need to find out what's going on."

Ken walked back to the bedroom area and returned a few minutes later. "It's not the generator."

"Then what is it?" Tima asked.

"It's coming from outside," Ken said. "Dad, want to take a stroll?"

"Do I have a choice?" Yeri said with a smile as the two suited up.

"Don't forget your laser knife, Daddy. There might be a Halk or two out there," Tiga said.

"I don't think there's anything..." Ken hesitated. "Maybe you're right."

Armed with a PeeP and laser knife, Ken and Yeri prepared for the cold Martian night air. They entered the lift and took turns cranking the lever as the lift slowly rose to the surface. It stopped with a sudden jerk. Yeri looked at Ken.

"No, I'm not getting a new lift." Ken returned the stare and shook his head.

"Depressurizing, please check your suit."

came the automated voice. A few minutes later...

"Depressurization completed."

Ken grabbed the door handle and pushed it open as a burst of subzero freezing air attacked their pressure suits.

"I gotta turn the heat up some more on this thing, it's fricken cold out here!" Ken shouted.

"Mine's on high and I'm still freezing. Hurry up so we can get back inside."

"The bedroom is over there." Ken pointed to the south end of the building. He turned on his laser knife and watched its red tip heat to a soft blue. The unique color reminded him of the encounter he had with the Halkomelem years ago. His father was ahead of him and turned the corner and quickly disappeared from sight.

He must really be cold, Ken thought.

All of a sudden he heard his father scream and watched as his dad flew head over heels like a rag doll. Yeri landed on his back on the red Martian clay as his helmet slammed hard against a nearby Martian rock.

"What the hell?" Ken ran over and knelt down to check on Yeri. He then turned his head and looked up only to see his dad's attacker.

Chapter 17

EARTH

Dewey Street
Saturday, July 4, 0015
0700 hours

It was an early Saturday morning when John Washington unlocked the back door to Dewey's Market. It was still dark and since he always closed on holidays he decided today would be a good one to finish the inventory. He remembered the discussion he had with Chondra and how she had quit shopping with him ever since he told her about paying down her bill. He figured she had found another market where she could run up more debt until she got the call to move to middle class status.

As the sun slowly chased the moon away and reclaimed its rightful place in the sky, John decided it was time for a break. He soon found himself fixated at the window once again with a cup of coffee held loosely in his grasp. He leisurely watched as a crowd of people slowly began to form a circle in the middle of the street. First it was ten, then twenty and more came down the street. John unlocked the front door and stood on the sidewalk holding his half empty cup. He heard his friend, Sands, shout from across the road.

"John! John! Come here quick!"

John looked around to make sure no one had entered the store and walked across the street. "What's going on?" John asked as more people gathered around them.

"Clear-Vision, John! We're moving! I am middle class bound. No more struggling to survive. Glorious, it's going to be glorious. It's like winning the lottery." John looked around and saw Chondra in the distance with her three kids. She looked right at him, but pretended she didn't see him. He turned away from her amid all the noise and confusion as the others grinned and chatted with each other. "John?" Sands asked. "Are you okay?"

"Why is everyone on the street?" John asked.

"Didn't you hear this morning on the news? Dewey Street has been the first neighborhood to be approved for promotion and they are sending the transports as we speak."

"Promotion? What are you talking about?" John asked.

"Jesus, John don't you ever watch the news? We're the first to be promoted to middle class," Sands replied. "On the fourth of July for god sakes." He threw his hands up and looked to the sky. "It's Independence Day!"

"It is, huh?" John asked with caution in his voice. "Where are…*we*…going? Don't…*we*…have a choice in all this?"

"It's Independence Day! I mean who cares? We're headed to the Promise Land! The Landhelpers are on their way and should be here sometime tomorrow. We don't have to take any of our belongings. The Ana Asea Sevens promised us that they would provide us with lots of money, new homes, fine clothes, free medical care, food, and plenty of recreational activities. Hey, maybe one of those new hologram holovisions."

"You don't need a hologram HV. You don't need any of that stuff. Think about it. Why are they going to give you all this for free?" John asked.

"Independence Day, John! Come on man get with the program! In fact you better get in line for the transports. Those Landhelpers will flatten this rat hole in less than a day."

"Rat hole huh?"

"Middle class living. They've got everything you could ever want."

"Yeah… well, good luck, Sands."

"You're not coming with us?"

"I've got some unfinished business before I leave."

"No you don't. Just leave everything here. Heaven, I tell you, I've died and gone to Heaven." Just then Sands saw the media crew pulling up. "I'm gonna be on HV! Come on, John. There's Chondra and we can all be on the big screen!"

John turned and walked back to the store.

"John? Where're you going?"

John turned around only to see that Sands had left. He saw Chondra and a couple of other people being interviewed as they waited for their promotion to middle class. John went into his store, gathered some supplies and stuffed them all in the company van out in the back parking lot. He watched the transports as they landed. One after another pulled over to the side across from Dewey's Market and picked up the people waiting. The transports were named TJ One and so on. John thought about that for a minute as he watched more and more people run to get in line to catch their once in a lifetime ride to Heaven. The waiting lines were long. John sighed as he watched the nervous excitement pass through the crowds.

It was a little after 2:00 PM when TJ Four landed. John had finished loading the van and called his wife to pack and bring the kids. He walked out the front door and saw Ben Harper waiting for the next transport. Ben looked over his shoulder and saw John in the middle of the street staring at the crowds. He walked over to John with outstretched hand.

"John? Why aren't you in line?" Ben asked.

"I don't know Ben, why are you?"

"Didn't you hear?" Ben asked. He looked down the street to his diner. "I think I'm going to miss this place." Ben sighed.

"Don't you think all this is a little too surreal? You've been here longer than I have. Ben, don't you find it odd that they're going to raise our standard of living just like that?" John released their handshake and snapped his fingers.

"I don't know, John I'm an old man." Ben shrugged his shoulders. "I try not to think about it. Why don't you come with me and we'll board the next transport together? We can talk then. Your family is just over there near my diner." Ben waved them over, but before they took the first step, John held his hand toward them palm out.

"They don't need suitcases, John," Ben said. "Everything will be provided. Everyone is leaving, John. You can't stay here you know. This place is going to be nothing more than a pile of rubble by this time tomorrow."

"That's what I heard." John looked at the big painted sign on the transport. "What does the TJ stand for?"

"Someone told me it stood for Trojan Horse or something like that."

"Doesn't that concern you?"

"It's just a name, John. Come on it'll be time to board soon." Ben watched the smiles on the happy faces of the Dewey Street residents as they climbed aboard. Some were in their Sunday best while others in t-shirts and blue jeans. The massive doors closed as the monster sized bus lifted slowly off the ground. The two watched the transport turn toward the west as they reflected back on happier times. They both fell silent as they watched it slowly disappear in the afternoon sun. Twenty minutes later John heard TJ Five preparing to land ready to pick up the remaining Dewey street residences. There was man in a police uniform keeping the residents away from the landing area. He looked over and as soon as he and John made eye contact John turned away.

"We're not going with you," John told Ben as he shook his head. "The van is loaded with as much groceries as she can carry and we're heading north," John paused, "to Canada." He turned his head away from Ben and looked at his family who were waiting and wondering what to do next. "I want to find out what this is all about." John turned back to Ben. "You're welcome to come with us. We could use a good cook in the family," John smiled.

"I don't know how Carol is going to respond to that comment," Ben said with a smile that quickly turned to a frown. "What do you think you'll find in Canada?"

"I have some friends there. They're part of the resistance."

"Terra Bulls?"

"Of course not. Like me they're concerned about what we are doing to our planet. You know with all the nuclear waste, GMO crops, killing our bees." John shook his head. "Something's gotta give my friend and I don't think being middle class is the answer."

"Perhaps not, but I have fewer years ahead of me than behind. I think I'll see what's over that next hill my friend," Ben's voice wavered. "I'm going to miss you, John."

In just that moment the sun's rays became partially blocked as TJ Five hovered over the landing site only meters from where they stood.

"I guess this is goodbye," John said. "Are you sure you don't want to come with us?"

Ben shook his head and they hugged their final goodbyes. John watched the old man climb into the transport and waved him a safe journey. He texted Carol and told her to stay out of sight until the last transport left. He went back into his little market and peeked out the window where he saw his policeman friend scanning the area for any last minute stragglers. Satisfied, the officer climbed on the final transport and John watched as it slowly moved through the sky. He walked down the aisles he had known so well mindlessly straightening some cans of beans on the shelves as he passed by and locked the doors for the last time.

"I think I'm going to miss this place," he said as a tear made its way down his cheek. He grabbed a couple of drinks and walked out the back door. He got in his van and drove around the corner to where his family waited. As he helped them with all their suitcases, he looked at Uncle Ben's Diner one last time as another pang of sadness overwhelmed him. Ben had always looked after John when he was young and his life would never be the same again. John and his little family of four stood beside the van all alone on a now big empty street. They stared up at the sky as they watched the final transport head off to somewhere middle class.

Ben looked out the window as the majestic bird rose into the sky and he waved goodbye to the Washingtons and his little diner. He reflected back to all the days and nights he spent cooking for his customers and friends. He thought about the kids that would come in for a soda and fries who were now bringing their kids in for energy drinks and such. "My how times have changed," he said out loud to himself. He wondered what was going to happen to John Washington. He had known John since he was just a kid. John's parents died soon after he was born and he tried to help him whenever he could. During summer vacations, he would let John work in the back doing odd jobs from cooking to cleaning and sometimes he would let John serve a meal or two. He had to be careful because John was technically too young to work, but those laws were made for the rich and not for the folks who struggled on Dewey Street.

The plane continued for hours on end as Ben sat in his seat and looked at the clouds below. His mind drifted back to the good times he had experienced and all the good friends he was going to miss back home.

"Please place your hands on your laps," ordered the voice over the loud speaker. "The transport will be landing soon."

Ben did as he was told and felt the warm vibrating force field as it enveloped him and held him rigid while the plane lightly touched the runway. The force field faded and Ben peeked out the window. "Oh my god, no!" He looked past the prairie land toward a fence that enclosed rows and rows of army barrack looking buildings.

As the passengers stepped off the transport they saw some buses heading directly toward them. On the runways next to the airplane was a man in uniform along with two other men with rifles slung over their shoulders.

The passengers deplaned and mingled as the buses waited twenty meters behind the man in uniform. "Welcome to your new homes," the officer said and smiled. A murmur quickly passed through the crowd.

One passenger in the back spoke first. "This ain't no middle class neighborhood. It looks like some kinda prison to me." The others intoned in agreement and the officer could see the anxiety growing within the crowd. He knew how to handle crowds like this and if things got edgy, he always had back up. His men's weapons were loaded.

"Of course it is. You just haven't seen the inside yet. We spent all the money on luxury furniture and beautiful paintings for you to enjoy on your time off," the officer paused. "But then, if you would have preferred us to have spent it all on the outside." The officer shook his head. "I think you would have been extremely disappointed sleeping on a cheap bed while watching a small Holovision at night." He waved the buses closer. "Surely you've heard of gated communities? That's where all the wealthy people live these days. I don't think you should make such a quick judgment on your brand new free homes. You're welcome to come and go as you please. The drivers are here to take you to your new homes and they will issue you your keys and the necessities are already inside waiting for you to enjoy. This is your big day. Shouldn't you see your new homes before you decide?" He looked around and saw that he was getting the usual nodding of heads. The officer glanced at his men and gave them a wink, then turned back to the new residents. "Good, now people with last names starting from A to C take bus number one and…"

The groups piled into the buses and waited to enjoy their first experience living in a gated community.

Middle Class Compound
Section B
Quadrant 16
Cedar Fort, Utah, U.S.A.
Saturday, July 4, 0015
1300 hours

The residents of Dewey Street departed the buses and were led to a small building where each was processed and assigned a living area. It was five o'clock when everyone had finally settled into their new homes. The first thing Ben noticed when he walked inside his new home was an enormous HV mounted on the far wall.

"I guess we'll be watching a lot of Holovision here," he said out loud when his eye caught a flashing yellow button on the remote sitting on a table beside the sofa with a sign below - *Please press*.

Ben pressed the button as the HV came to life. An attractive young lady with shoulder length brunette hair in her mid-thirties wearing a short white skirt with a tennis racket on her shoulder appeared with her fourteen-year-old daughter with long blonde hair, a son two years younger with a fishing pole by his side, and her husband, also in his thirties, wearing a classic wool blend tweed suit holding a briefcase all smiling and standing behind her.

"Hello, my name is Suzy. Welcome to Middle Class Section B. We hope you had a safe and restful flight. Congratulations to you for your long deserved promotion to becoming part of the prestigious middle class," she said sporting a big smile. She made a backhand swing with her racket hitting an imaginary ball.

"There are so many advantages being a middle class citizen. We hope you will love it as much as we love having you join our team!" She placed the racket on her shoulder and started to skip lightly down toward the barracks as the camera followed. Once past the barracks she turned left toward the dining hall and slowed to leisurely walk. "Here is dining hall one!" she said and rubbed her tummy. "You can order whatever you want!" She stopped as the doors to the dining hall opened. People began exiting the cafeteria talking and smiling to one another. A child was walking beside her parents and handed Suzy an ice cream sandwich. Suzy took a small bite of the dessert and handed it back to the little girl. "Yum yum! It makes you want to come down here and enjoy a late night dessert, doesn't it?" She handed off her tennis racket to a woman walking toward her in a similar dress.

"The Ana Asea Sevens have worked hard to fulfill your wishes of becoming a middle class citizen." The camera followed the announcer as she moved from the dining hall to another section of the compound. "You have seen where your restaurants are, however if you prefer to cook yourself, we have numerous grocery stores located throughout your town." She pointed to the supermarkets lining the road and continued her walk as the scene faded out and then faded back to where she was now standing at the entrance of the activities quadrant. The rest of her family had now been replaced by a man in his fifties wearing a golf shirt and holding a new golf bag. There was another girl dressed in a swimming suit with goggles along with people dressed in bowling shirts, Karate gis, and a lady in a long white wedding dress with her fiancé wearing a black tuxedo.

"There is a golf course and bowling alleys, along with swimming pools and a variety of entertainment facilities for you to enjoy," she said with a permanently fixed smile. "There is nothing to worry about living here, but I bet you figured that out pretty quickly. So, what else is there to do while you are here? I know we can count on you to help out when asked." Suzy waved goodbye as the scene faded to an office where a lady wearing a grey suit with short black hair and matching glasses sat behind a large dark walnut desk.

"Thank you, Susan. My name is Maria and it is my job to make sure things are running smoothly so you don't have to," she said with a slight smile.

"Guess you're now wondering how we pay for all these luxuries and I'm sure that you want to do your fair share. So we have assigned each of you duties based on your age and expertise. I know you will find your work enjoyable and rewarding as you spend your days at Section B. The best part is it is only a half-day job!" Maria smiled and she faded into the background as names started appearing on the screen.

"Please use the remote to scroll to your name and a duty roster will appear along with your supervisor's name and contact information. Have a wonderful time here at Section B. One last thing to remember, after 7 PM the gates will be closed and electrified for your own protection."

"I have lived my entire life without worrying about my protection," Ben said to himself. "Maybe I should have taken John's offer." Ben walked into his bedroom and opened the closet door. He gasped as he pulled out a bright orange and yellow coverall uniform with his name, a number along with a barcode printed underneath. A matching hat and two sets of black leather work-boots with his name etched on the back.

"This is middle class?" Ben angrily shouted and threw the uniform back into the closet as he watched it fall to the floor. A few minutes later he heard the three blasts of the horn signaling it was six o'clock, dinnertime. He started to walk toward the dining hall when his eye caught the rows of hedges two meters from the fence. He turned away from the dining hall and walked toward the open gate. "I wonder what kind of bushes grow like that?"

Ben was only ten meters from the gate when he heard the sound of a vehicle's motor and wheels getting closer and closer. He turned around and saw two armed guards coming his way. He stopped and waited for them.

"Good evening, sir," said the first guard.

"Hello," Ben replied. "A nice evening for a walk, wouldn't you say?"

"Didn't you hear the dinner bell?" the second guard asked.

"I'm not hungry so I decided to take a look around outside the fence for awhile. Maybe go for a nice walk."

"It's too dangerous past the fence line." The first guard moved closer to Ben.

Ben took a step back. "I think I can fend for myself if it is all the same to you."

"Sorry sir, but you'll have to come with us."

The officer moved even closer as Ben turned and took off toward the gate. He could hear the policemen yelling for him to stop. He picked up his pace when suddenly the green light resting on the entrance turned red as the gate slowly swung closed. He made it past the gate and watched as the doors swung back open as the officers gained on him. He ran through the tunnel lined with the hedges and seconds later he could see some light at its end until he felt a sting of electricity hit him in the back throwing him against the hedges.

Ben woke up two hours later in the infirmary where Sands and Chondra were standing next to his bed.

"What did you do?" Sands asked.

"I went for a..." Ben looked around to see if anyone else was in the room, "an unauthorized walk it seems."

"What?" Chondra said.

"Yeah, I decided to have a look around outside the compound and two guards showed up. They wanted to take me back so I ran. I made it past the gate and was halfway through the tunnel when they shot me with something that really stung! I fell against one of those bushes lining the tunnel and next thing I knew I am lying here talking to you."

"That's not what we were told. Seems you went off your medications again, got delirious and stumbled outside the gate into those bushes. Didn't you know those bushes have been genetically modified to keep us safe from intruders?" Chondra asked

"No."

"Well you missed those announcements at dinner tonight."

"I wasn't hungry."

Chondra looked at Sands and turned back to Ben. "You need to stay on your meds you know."

"But I don't take any..."

"Okay, okay. Just try to behave and do what you are told, alright?" Chondra bent down and gave him a kiss on the cheek as the two left.

Ben tried to turn on his side and found he couldn't move. "I can't move!"

A few minutes later a nurse entered the room. "Can I help you?"

"I can't move a muscle," Ben said.

"That should pass in a couple of days. The hedgerow you fell into has been genetically modified to inject a substance similar to a spider bite. It numbs its victims. Good thing your exposure was limited. We have lost a couple of residents that way."

"Don't you mean slaves?"

"Sir?"

"Never mind."

The workdays started at five in the morning and ended around five at night. The factories were all below ground. Section B was in charge of transport steering components. No one was really sure what it was they were making, but the orders were clear. Each member had a team leader who was in charge. It was hard work and when the horn sounded, most of them were so tired that they opted for the dining hall instead of cooking at home.

"This ain't no middle class. These hours are killing me," Chondra said between bites of a cheeseburger.

"It's more like a concentration camp," Sands replied. "And what's going on with all these pictures of faces painted on every building?"

"They are the head shots of each of our seven leaders," Chondra said. "Our barracks has Ana Asea Two on it. That way you don't go to the wrong building. You were required to watch HV on all this the other night."

"I forgot, but I do remember in school when they told us how the old communist dictators had their pictures placed everywhere, just like here. Why are there so many cameras?"

"Big Brother." Ben sat down beside them.

"Welcome back," Sands said. "Have you been taking your meds?"

"I don't take any…"

"Okay, okay." Chondra waved the discussion to an end. "Now who is this Big Brother you are talking about?"

"Don't you ever read?"

"No."

"George Orwell's book, *1984* on how the government took over the world. They fed the populace false information to keep them in line. It's how those in power stay in power."

"*1984?*"

"It was written in 1949 by George Orwell. He foretold, I guess is the right term, on how a few individuals rose to absolute power and kept it."

"How did they do that?"

"First of all, they took away our ability to defend ourselves, which violated our Second Amendment rights."

"We don't need guns, they kill people," Chondra said.

"That's exactly why dictators don't like them. Then they put cameras and recording equipment in our homes to listen to see if anyone was planning to overthrow them. Well, that was in the book," Ben stopped and stroked his beard. "Actually in reality we did it ourselves and we paid to have it done. Before the pursal we put listening devices all around our houses so we could order stuff we don't need from the internet."

"Why were they so scared of us?"

"Because they knew how badly they were treating us and figured someone or some people would finally get tired of it."

"Did they?"

"Yes. But not enough did. Everyone began watching HV and believed what the controlled media was telling them. We just drifted into a state of compliance, we became a nation of mindless drones."

"I don't believe all of that," Sands said. "No one controlled what *The Wolf* had to say. They told us so."

"And you believed them?"

"Yes!" Chondra agreed. "They told us all about middle class living and how we've been treated badly because we're..."

"Compare your life now with that on Dewey," Ben interrupted.

The tiny group remained silent for a few minutes.

"When they said a half day job, I didn't think they really meant twelve hours!" Chondra said.

"Didn't you see the conference last night on HV?" Sands asked.

"Yes I did," Chondra said. "So I guess things will get better."

"You see. Nothing has changed." Ben shook his head.

"Well, don't blame me if you're not happy about your situation, but I know that mine is going to get better. I just have to buckle down and work through this. They've promised a big bonus and time off once we're finished with the new transport parts."

"I hope you're right," Ben sighed.

The big bonuses and time-off never materialized and as soon as one project was finished, an even more pressing project was announced. It wasn't long before some of the Dewey Street residents became fed up with the long hours and false promises that they staged a protest outside the factory. The factory went idle for over two days until the guards showed up. After a few bloody noses, arrests, and promises that this was only temporary, did the protestors return to work. To ensure compliance, Sam Johnson, the director of Section B called a meeting. He was in his sixties wearing the traditional dark blue corporate suit with their Section B stitched over the vest pocket with the logo just underneath showing workers wearing yellow uniforms and hard hats. They all had shovels or picks looking up toward their beloved seven leaders.

"As you know we are having a major disruption going on with the workers. If this continues we will miss our deadlines and that is not going to happen, right?"

The members all nodded in agreement.

"What are we doing to get them back to work?"

Officer Moore stood up. "We've had some of them disciplined, some of the younger kids we beat up and we even revoked holovision privileges to a few, but nothing has worked." Officer Moore returned to his seat. "What do you suggest Mr. Johnson?"

"We need another plan of action," Sam said and thought for a minute "Violence didn't work like I had hoped. Hmmm...any suggestions?"

"How about we drug them?" Dr. Barnes suggested.

"Drug them?" Mr. Johnson asked

"Yes. There are some powerful narcotics out today. When I was in private practice the teachers always seemed to have a handful of kids that were always causing disruptions in their classrooms. We used to be able to punish them with a smack on the hand with a ruler, but that caused lawsuits from the parents. So we convinced the parents their kids were dysfunctional and needed medication."

"Really? They bought that?"

"At first they were skeptical, but they didn't discipline their kids at home. Once the meds calmed them down at home, it became a big hit with the parents and the teachers," Dr. Barnes replied.

"Order the meds," Mr. Johnson said.

Dr. Barnes pressed the intercom. "Holly?"

"Yes Dr. Barnes?"

"Place an ongoing order for Lithotriaxon."

"How many?"

"Enough for the entire Section B population."

"Yes sir, but what about the side effects?"

"Just do it." Dr. Barnes hung up.

"How are we going to get them to swallow those pills everyday?" Officer Moore asked.

"Don't worry about that. We will add it to the water supply. You have to drink water you know."

"Just like we used to do with fluoride. Excellent idea. When will the medication arrive?" Officer Moore asked.

"Shouldn't be more than a day."

"We will try to keep things contained until then."

"Just do your best Officer Moore. It won't be long until they quiet down."

"I will inform my men."

"Good. Now remember we do not drink the water. We use our own bottled water and I will take precautions that our homes and only those restaurants where we eat don't get the tainted water either."

Three days later the workers became more drone-like, less agitated. They went to work, came home, and watched holovision until bedtime without complaint.

"It reminds me of the days when I worked with the mentally ill," Sam told his secretary as he switched on the monitors. "Look at them. They're as docile as milking cows. These new attention deficit drugs work as good as the old lobotomies, maybe even better!" he laughed.

The Ana Asea Sevens had worked out the perfect world. They needed manual labor to build their empire on Earth as well as Mars and they found the perfect people to achieve those goals. They took a lot of their ideas from the early Roman Empire, except they didn't call their workers slaves.

Chapter 18

EARTH

Dewey Street
Saturday, July 4, 0015
1400 hours

It had been over an hour since the last transport left Dewey Street. John Washington looked around at the now vacant town where he had spent his whole life. He had figured he would probably die here, but not anymore. He was going to miss his friends, especially Ben. A deep sadness fell upon him as he gave his little grocery store one last look.

"Is everyone ready?" John Washington turned to see his little family standing by the van.

"Where did everyone go?" Suma asked.

"I don't know. Somewhere middle class we're told."

"Why didn't we go with them?" Ket asked.

"It's a long story," John replied forcing a half smile.

"We'll have plenty of time on the road to talk about it." Carol opened the van doors for her children. "Come on. Everybody inside. We have a long ways to go."

John sat down in the driver's seat. "Engine on."

"Destination please?"

came the computerized voice.

"Angry Squirrel Hotel - Canso, Nova Scotia."

"Mapping... Alert!...Alert!...Border Crossing Required."

"Override," John said to the computer.

"Proper clearance necessary to override."

stated their van's computer. John pulled out his passport and held it up to the dashboard's red-eye.

"Scanning...please wait...Entrance denied."

the computer responded. A red warning sign soon blinked across the windshield. The computer continued,

"John Washington and family requesting unapproved destination. New destination - Middle Class Location Section B Quadrant 16 as authorized by Clear-Vision mandate #44590. Please comply. Federal Authorities have been notified."

"What the hell?" John turned to Carol. "I knew these self-driving cars were a bad idea."

"What are we going to do?" Carol asked.

"We gotta get out of here," John said and before anyone could move, John grabbed the door handle. "It's locked. It won't open!" He tried to lower the windows. "Damn!"

"What are we going to do?" Carol asked.

"Ket! Grab me the hammer in the back."

"Here you go, Dad."

CRASH!

John reached through the broken driver side window and unlocked the van from the outside. He opened the door and kicked it with his left foot. "I can't get out of my seatbelt!"

"Security Alert! Please close passenger door and remain seated. Federal Authorities have been notified."

the van's computer continued.

"Non-compliance is a punishable crime under Federal Statue #07681. Please remain seated and close all doors and remain seated. Federal Authorities are on their way."

John's door began to automatically close but John wedged his hammer into the door's hinge creating an exit for his family. A loud buzzing sound filled the van as they all looked at the windshield.

"Please Close All Passenger Doors and Remain Seated."

"John?"

"Get the kids out! Hurry! Our van is going to take us to jail." John grabbed his seatbelt and pulled on the tab once again. "It won't unlock! Carol get my old army knife in the glove compartment."

Carol opened the glove compartment. "Here!"

John cut the webbing, jumped out of the van as it started to move forward. He quickly stabbed and flattened both front tires and the van came to an abrupt stop. "There." He handed the knife back to Carol through the half opened driver side door.

- WARNING! -

- TIRE FAILURE ALERT! –

flashed on the windshield followed by

- TIRE REPAIR COMMENCING -

"You've got five minutes at best. Now cut yourself and the kids out. We've got to get away from this van. Meet me at Ben's." John started sprinting towards Uncle Ben's Diner.

Carol quickly cut the seat belts and hurried the kids out the driver side door. They followed John as he ran down the street toward the diner. He grabbed a rock and threw it through the windowed door, reached through the broken glass, and unlocked the place. He walked to the backroom and kicked in the door to Ben's office. He opened the desk and grabbed the keys and said out loud, "Sorry Ben, but I remember how you talked about having rebuilt an old sports car years ago. I just hope it runs." John opened the security lock to Ben's garage and swung open the doors and there it was. It was painted bright red with white racing stripes running down each side. He noticed on the front grill was an emblem of a horse in full gallop. On the hood was a hand-sketched name of the car.

"Mustang?" John smiled and thought to himself, *Not a lot of room, but it's sure a cool looking car. I hope it doesn't rain though, it seems Ben forgot to put a roof on it.* John opened the door and sat down in the driver's seat.

"Engine on!"

Nothing happened.

"Start."

Still nothing.

"Damn! It's not working!"

"You have to put the key in the ignition, dear," Carol said.

"Where did you come from?" John turned abruptly. "What key are you talking about?"

"The one you place in that hole there." Carol pointed to the ignition switch to right of the steering wheel.

"I don't see a key."

"Check the sun visor." Carol pointed to the piece of cloth sitting on top of the windshield.

John lowered the visor when all at once two car keys fell into his lap held together by red keychain with the picture of a white Mustang.

"Which one do I use?" John asked.

"Try them both. One is for starting the car, the other is for locking the doors."

He inserted the first key and felt it slide effortlessly into the ignition. "Engine on!"

They waited but nothing happened.

"Damn!" It still won't start!" He pulled out the key as Carol grabbed his hand.

"It's the right key, honey," she said. "You have to turn the key, step on the clutch located on the far left and step on the gas pedal to your far right all at the same time."

John turned his head. "How do you know all this?"

After several failed attempts the motor started making a whirring sound.

"I was watching an old movie and that is how they started these car..."

"VarOOM!" came a rough sound from under the hood as the car started to shake.

"My god! This thing sure makes a lot of noise!" John yelled over the engine's clamor.

Carol sat in the passenger seat and instructed him on how to work a manual transmission and what to do if he wanted to raise the roof. She told him where the brakes were along with what the dials on the console meant.

"It's got a roof?"

"Yes. Before the driverless cars took over we were allowed to drive roofless cars. They were called convertibles."

"Must have been a good movie!" John smiled at Carol as she shrugged her shoulders.

"It was a documentary. The kids had to watch it for school."

"Oh."

"Now let's go get the kids," she said as John pulled the sports car slowly out of Ben's garage.

It wasn't long before Ben's restored Mustang was headed toward the cooler climates with the Washington family singing songs and passing the time.

"I hate the drive these days," John said as another truck whizzed by. "Those monsters practically blow you off the road."

"Where are we going?" Carol asked.

"Canada."

"I thought you said Nova Scotia."

"This changes things. We have to find gas now and figure a way to cross the border without detection."

"Doesn't your cousin, Mandon live in Ontario?"

"Yes he does and I've been talking to him. He doesn't like this Clear-Vision any more than I do. There's a group of people who have found an area north of Ontario that is so far, untouched by all this craziness. They even have some organic seeds to plant," John said.

"I thought that was illegal."

"It is, but it's the only thing we can do right now."

"Why did you turn off the megaway?"

"Harder to track us taking these side streets."

The potholes and over-brush made it difficult for the pony car to maneuver, but they continued. John and his family drove past deserted home after home on their way north.

"My pursal's GPS keeps wanting to go to the megaway," John exclaimed. "I have to keep re-entering the codes every half hour. I guess someone doesn't really like you off the grid so to speak."

"I know and that is concerning. John! I found something!" Carol said excitedly as she closed the glove compartment.

"What is it?"

"It says map of the United States. It has a bunch of lines going everywhere."

"Those are roads!" John said. "Atta boy Ben. You've saved our butts one more time." John threw his pursal out the window.

"Why did you do that?" Suma asked.

"It could alert the authorities to our location. The same reason I made you guys leave yours."

The hours passed by as they traveled through deserted small towns and factories.

"Where did all the people go, John?" Carol asked as they drove by the houses in disrepair. The yards were turning brown from the extreme summer heat. Some of the roofs had fallen and there were broken windows everywhere.

"Everyone moved to the city. We can't survive living in the country anymore."

"Why not? Surely country people aren't going to move into the city. It's just not natural for some. Lots of folks like wide open spaces."

"No power. Those power lines have been inoperable for years in favor of wireless."

"I've heard about Nanotech's kilo-powered energy platform. It was big news a few years ago."

"That's right. Nanotech built towers around the cities and with nano-technology they were able to power everything wirelessly, even our mass transportation systems were designed to pick up the qubits. If you lived outside the radius of the towers then you were out of luck."

"What about solar?" Carol asked.

"Good question. Didn't you see the panels?"

"Yes."

"They were used until the temperature rose another eight degrees and that was just enough to cause a constant cloud formation. It finally thickened enough to effectively block the sun's rays."

"They could still live off the land. They could use firewood to heat their homes, cook their food, and grow their own crops. Couldn't they?"

"No one needed to heat their homes anymore. What they needed was a way to cool them. As for the crops, remember reading about the Big Deal? Deal's new ways of genetically growing crops in this heat turned those crops into something I wouldn't want to eat."

"And you thought spraying crops with glyphosate was bad?"

"No thanks. Deal's stuff was intolerant to any types of poisons you could throw at it. I wouldn't touch that with a spoon. Heck, even if I went crazy and decided to plant a garden, I would have to buy the seeds from Biochore and pay a technology fee. This fee is what put the small farmers and anyone who wanted to grow their own food out of business. The key to controlling people is to control their food supply and Biochore knew that better than anybody else. Organics became a thing of the past. Biochore ran ad after ad showing how their genetically modified seeds had helped the poor and it worked. It was frowned upon to eat natural. Those that resisted their genetically engineered foods were labeled freaks and welfareons."

It was sundown by the time the little family crossed the border into Ontario. John called Mandon from an outdated telephone. "Hey I'm getting a dial tone!"

"I wanna hear!"

"Me too!"

"Okay guys, hurry." John looked up at Carol.

"Hello?"

"Mandon, this is John."

"What number is this and where are you? I almost didn't answer, I didn't think these things worked anymore."

"Well this one does. We just crossed the border."

"You drove?"

"Yes."

"How? I mean, no one is allowed border crossing these days. Did you know they are talking about putting up a wall between Canada and the U.S. like the one down in Mexico?"

"That's crazy."

"What isn't these days? Now it's the illegal Canadians wanting U.S. jobs."

"They can have them," John said.

"I didn't think the cars would let you cross? Even if they did, how did you get past the Border Patrol?"

"My van alerted the authorities when it found out I wasn't on the transport to one of their middle class concentration camps."

"On the run?"

"Yep. So I borrowed a friend's car. It's the old style with gas pedals and such. The stick shift took awhile to figure out, but here we are. We took some back roads across to Canada. No one is guarding them because they know self-driving cars won't take those roads anymore."

"Yeah. Everyone thought how cool it would be not to have to worry about driving. They said it was safer, but what they didn't say was how we've traded one more freedom for convenience."

"Speaking of convenience my tank's about empty. To find gas, we've had to break into abandoned homes along the way."

"Why not use your pursal?...Oh yeah. They can track your whereabouts with that."

"Unless you have a lot of silver it really makes it tough to keep off the grid. So far I've been pretty resourceful if you know what I mean," John smiled.

"I do. In fact, it seems that you're really getting good at this criminal thing," Mandon laughed. "Just give me your coordinates and I'll come and arrest you in a few hours."

John smiled and hung up the telephone while the little band of fugitives looked for a place to rest and wait.

It was midnight when they heard something resembling an old engine getting louder. The van stopped at the telephone booth and a lone figure stepped out and looked around.

"Mandon!" John yelled across the distance. The man turned toward the voice and walked over to the family. He wore an old yellow t-shirt with the words "Save our Planet" printed in green.

"John! How the hell have you been? I've missed you." Mandon gave him a big bear hug.

"God it's hot. Even up here," John replied and returned the embrace.

"The temperature keeps rising, John. Can you believe it? The radio and holovision news media guys are blaming all this on those welfareons."

John laughed and said, "I see some things stay the same in this old world."

"It's about the only thing," Mandon replied. "Come on, let's go before someone sees us."

"Did you bring some gas?"

"Right here." Mandon poured gas into John's Mustang.

"Where is everyone? This neighborhood looks deserted. Are the Landhelpers coming?"

"Landhelpers? Nah. They only destroy the towns where people had been promoted to middle class status."

"Why?"

"I guess it's to make sure the only homes they have now are those Gulags or what is called a gated community."

"Just in case someone decides he wants to leave?"

"Something like that I guess."

"So where did all the people around here go? Surely not to one of the Gulags?"

"No. They've moved into the cities. It's the only place that provides food, and power for you to live. I guess it's easier to keep an eye on your sheep when they are all gathered in one spot."

"You sound a little paranoid?"

"Yeah, well maybe I am. Doesn't matter anyway. The rest of the "Resistance," as the media has recently coined us, have gone ahead. They felt by portraying us as traitors to the grand scheme of their rule would scare others away from joining. So we do with what we can. No time to waste. We found a place northeast of here about a four day's drive and then a hike through the mountains. There is a stream with running water and the altitude is high enough for some crops to grow."

"Sounds like Nirvana," John said.

"As close as we can get these days," Mandon said.

Chapter 19

EARTH

Plaza de la Constitución
National Palace
Mexico City, Mexico
Thursday, July 9, 0015
1500 Hours

"Señor Dr. Maltido," Ana Asea Four said, "what good are these random numbers you have shown me?"

"It looks like one day soon we will be traveling toward the stars," Danny Maltido paused to see how the conversation was moving.

"Go on."

"I fear the radiation zones, along with the rumored climate changes are having a somewhat negative effect here. It may be wise to consider a major move...let's say, sooner than later?"

"What makes you think there is a problem?"

"Nothing that I know of. However, if there is a need to bring the *right* people on board should we decide to move up the timetable when it comes to space exploration." Danny waited for a moment. "I have created this unique algorithm to choose the best and brightest among us who would most benefit the project."

The Ana Asea Four leaned closer to Danny. "Dr. Maltido, I would like a little example of this...algorithm you think of so highly."

Danny unsnapped his pursal in *traveling* mode and watched as it grew into *texpanded* mode. He then inserted a jimmy.

"Where did you get that?"

"The jimmy?"

"It's illegal and must be confiscated and you arrested!"

"Illegal in the wrong hands, wouldn't you agree?"

"How did you get it?"

"I made it."

"I should have you executed immediately. You are too dangerous to be allowed to live. Guards!"

"Are you sure that is the best use of my talents?" Danny interjected, holding his hand up. "I could have more and have given them to friends with specific instructions in case should I say, have an accident?"

"Are you blackmailing me?"

The doors swung wide open and two guards raced into the Ana Asea's office and grabbed Danny. "What do want us to do with him, Most High?"

Ana Asea Four pondered the situation and finally waved them off. "Release him," Number Four said and looked at Danny. "For now."

The guards shoved Dr. Maltido to the side and walked out the door.

"I could've done much damage, but instead I am offering you my services," Danny said.

"Where did you get the plans to make additional keys?"

"I had an opportunity to look over the plans before they were destroyed."

"Had one or created one?"

"Does it matter at this point? As I see it, you have two choices. You can prosecute me and take your chances that I have not made any more or you can benefit from my knowledge."

"You are a very resourceful man."

"Thank you, sir."

"It was not intended as a compliment."

"Shall I continue?"

"An interesting quandary." Ana Asea Four stared at Dr. Maltido for what seemed like an eternity. Danny had once heard the first one to speak in situations like this would lose, so he held his tongue. Just then the jimmy's handle popped out. No one moved.

"Well?" the Ana Asea asked.

"Thank you, sir. Now once I turn the handle it will unlock the code, but we need to connect it to the grid in order to see what it can do," Danny rose from his seat and walked to the wall terminal.

"You need a two verification password and clearance to operate that one." Ana Asea Four opened a top portion of his desk exposing another terminal. He entered an array of encrypted numbers and passwords. "We have taken additional safeguards to protect sensitive information in case one of our keys," Ana Asea Four pointed his finger directly at Danny, "falls into the wrong hands."

"Your honor, I came to you with the best of inten…"

"ACCESS AVAILABLE"

came the computerized male voice as the terminal on the wall blinked.

Danny walked over to the terminal and inserted the jimmy. "It will take a minute or two to find the grid code and unlock the information."

"You do not look like others of your race and what is that accent of yours?"

"My mother is British and that is where I got my um, good looks," Danny smiled.

"Creo que estás mintiendo," Ana Asea Four remarked.

"Aren't we supposed to use only English from now on?" Danny replied with a smile. "And I am not lying."

"Perhaps not, but if you are I will find out."

"GRID ACCESS AVAILABLE"

came the computerized male voice.

- WAITING -

blinked the console monitor.

"What areas do you want me to search?" Danny asked.

"Mexico City. Your city as a matter of fact," Ana Asea Four replied. Danny knew that the Ana Asea wanted to see whose names would appear. He knew many qualified individuals from Mexico City, being a native of the town himself.

"Certainly, your honor," Danny said. "A wise choice." He connected his pursal to the terminal and turned on the jimmy and they waited. Two minutes later a list of two hundred names appeared.

"What? That is way too many!"

"It is not finished, sir. This is the parent list. Should you prefer to change to sub-level Alpha parameters of the search it will only use these names."

"Oh."

"Change the top level parameters and you will most likely get a new list."

"The list now dropped to fifty," the Ana Asea remarked as he scratched his chin as he looked over the list.

"Yes. This is the Big Brother list. These people are ranked from one to fifty. Should you decide to change the sub-level Beta parameters this list will rearrange those fifty, deleting or adding subjects due to the changing requirements."

Danny could see the Ana Asea's eyes light up. "And where is your name?"

"Right here." Danny pointed to his name hovering at the top of the list. He then pressed another button and a new list appeared. "This is the Little Sister list. This is the list you will probably find the most useful. Do you recognize any of these names?"

"There are some on here I would agree with," Number Four said and turned to Danny. "This can be very useful, Dr. Maltido. What do you want for it?"

Danny paused as his pursal *texpanded* and continued blinking and flashing.

"What is your pursal doing?"

"It is waiting for more input."

"Turn it off!"

"Yes sir."

Danny hoped his subroutine had finished its job as he slowly reached over and grabbed the jimmy's handle and slowly turned it.

"Now!" Ana Asea Four yelled and reached his right hand out with his fingers outstretched. "Dr. Maltido, let me see your pursal."

Danny slowly handed over his pursal.

"What did you press?"

"Press? Nothing sir."

"I saw you press something and you better tell me or I'll have you arrested on the spot."

"With all due respect, your most high. I honestly did nothing but what you asked."

The Ana Asea checked the history, downloads, and uploads confirming what Danny had said.

"What does the name Maltido stand for?"

"It is Spanish. I think it means little devil."

"The Damned One, I think is a more direct translation." The Ana Asea handed the pursal back to Danny. "What do you want for it?"

"The pursal is yours as my gift should you want it."

"I don't want your pursal. I want to know what you want for your code."

"It is yours for free. However, I heard through the grapevine there is some interest in colonizing Mars. If so, I would really like to work on that project. I am good with installing computer systems and should we colonize Mars then having a progressive computerized interactive grid system would be very beneficial don't you think?"

"We already have software and hardware engineers working out the plans."

So you are further down the road than I thought, Danny thought to himself. "Yes, but who is overseeing the entire project?"

"You?" the Ana Asea asked and laughed.

"The algorithm is yours," said Danny as he simultaneously pressed two keys and the pursal beamed the information to the Ana Asea's terminal.

"The data is sitting in the cloud right now waiting for you to access it. The code is not protected so I would download it as soon as possible."

"In that case I recommend you leave immediately and I will see what, if anything, can be done concerning your request."

"Thank you, Ana Asea Four. I eagerly await your decision."

Danny walked out of the office and checked his pursal. "That was close," he whispered under his breath and walked out of the building.

No sooner than the door closed shut did the Ana Asea turn to download the information. He then did an extensive search on the guy named Danny Maltido. Everything looked in order. He had gone to the right schools, majored in virtual algorithmic software and hardware engineering. He was an independent contractor for VR Systems Inc. and would be perfect for the Mars job. Almost too perfect and that concerned Ana Asea Four and he didn't like being concerned. He pressed the call button on his headset.

"Get me my Companion."

"Yes sir," his secretary replied.

"René here."

"I need you to snoop around town. Talk to people and get me all the information on a man named Maltido, Danny is his first name," Ana Asea Four said and hung up his pursal.

"I know he pressed some buttons and I want to find out why," Ana Asea Four said out loud to the now empty room.

Chapter 20

EARTH

**Angry Squirrel Hotel
Mahone Bay, Route 3
Canso, Nova Scotia
Friday, November 14, 0020
0530 Hours**

Five years had passed since the Washingtons had left Dewey Street. They had enjoyed planting their own organic crops and living off the land, but they always knew it soon would have to end. It was daybreak when John Washington, along with five others, left the Angry Squirrel Hotel overlooking the Atlantic Beach for a little recon. The rest stayed behind finishing up the details of the planned invasion.

"Water Shed Road is up ahead," Susan said reading from an old Canadian map.

"I see it," Mandon said.

"Turn left on Tower Road."

"Are you sure?"

"Yes I'm sure," Susan replied sternly.

"I don't like driving around in this car very long."

"Trust me. Did you see the plaque at the hotel?" Susan asked.

"No."

"It talked about the name."

"What name?"

"Angry Squirrel. It seemed there was this ship called the HMS Squirrel and it invaded Canso in the seventeen hundreds. They killed, pillaged, and burned the villages. This caused Canso to develop a stronger military. At least that's what I think. I really didn't have time to read the rest."

"So they're angry at the squirrel?"

"Something like that."

"That's nice but I think we need to concentrate on... dead end! Great! Now what?" Mandon asked.

"Keep going."

Mandon turned to Susan with a shocked look on his face. "You're kidding right? There's nothing ahead but grass, weeds, and a swamp or two."

"Keep going straight."

"What if we get stuck out here?"

"Quit whining and turn right at that distant maple tree and you'll see it," Susan said.

Mandon stared at Susan and then turned to the backseat. "John, any suggestions?"

"I know what I'm doing," Susan said and John just shrugged his shoulders.

"You better." Mandon pulled the van off the paved road onto the grassy meadow that seemed to ride like there was a road underneath. "This doesn't feel like grass to me."

"It's not."

Mandon slowly turned the van once they passed the majestic maple tree and there sat the Mars Transport Station. They took the van as close as they dared to the entrance.

"Welcome to Cree Air Force Base," Susan said as the troop exited the van.

"You're not going to find this place with a GPS I'm betting." John scanned the base through his binoculars.

"It seems they want to keep this place a secret," Mandon replied.

"Who was Cree?" John asked as they walked toward a clearing near the base.

Mandon replied, "Not a who. It was named after the Cree Indians. They were the largest group in North America. In Canada they are referred to as First Nations."

"Don't we call them tribes...Wow! Look at the size of this place!" Carol said as she stopped at the edge of the woods.

"Yep. The bigger the better." Mandon pulled out his binoculars and surveyed the complex. "More access points."

"Those are pretty tall fences and they look hot," Carol said.

"We brought gear to compensate for that," Mandon replied.

"This place is a military base for god sakes!" Carol exclaimed.

"Not to worry, we have been working on this plan for days now."

"Days?" Carol asked incredibly.

"Just kidding. We've been working on this for a long time," Mandon said.

"There are cameras everywhere!"

"I'll make sure they get my good side!" Mandon laughed. "Relax Carol. We just need to get in, do our jobs, and get out."

It was early evening when they finally return to the Squirrel.

"How did it go?" Jackson asked.

"We're all set. You guys?" Mandon asked.

"Just finishing up. I would say we have a go."

Carol looked around at everyone and put her hands on her hips. "Are you guys serious? Have you seen this place? It would be easier to break into Fort Knox. I don't know what you guys have planned unless it's to go to jail."

Saturday November 15, 0020
0015 Hours

"RISE AND SHINE!" Mandon screamed at the sleepy crew. "This isn't summer camp, let's go!" he continued as Gordon grabbed a large wooden spoon and started banging on a large skillet.

"Jesus Christ!" Curtis yelled out. "You're going to wake up everyone here!"

"That's the plan," Mandon said.

"I'm talking about our neighbors?" Curtis pointed to the adjacent wall. "Aren't we supposed to leave quietly?"

Gordon sheepishly stopped his banging as the sleepy crew gathered their belongings and set out to Cree.

Mandon made a right at the dead end and drove the van into the heavily wooded area just up ahead.

"That should do it. We are only a half a klick from the east fence." The other vans pulled up next to them as everyone got out.

"Did you notice the grass?" Curtis asked as he parked his van next to Mandon's.

"It felt strange," Julie the other driver said, "almost like…"

"There's a road beneath it," Mandon interrupted. "Susan happened upon it when she was checking out the compound the other day."

"Having trouble keeping your car on the road, Susan?" Curtis laughed.

"Screw you, Curtis," Susan shot back. "If you continue, the road will take you to the entrance."

"God it's cold up here!" Gordon said. "It must be seventy degrees!"

"A nice change isn't it?" Jimmy replied.

"Must be the offshore winds and I didn't bring a jacket or anything."

"Who has a jacket these days?"

The little troop slowly, quietly moved through the woods until they saw the lights streaking through the encampment.

"There it is!" came a voice from the back.

"Shhh! Quiet now," Mandon whispered.

The space ships sat on the tarmac docked and ready as Mandon and the rest slowly made their way toward the security fence.

"Those things are huge!" Gordon said.

"Quiet!" John held his hand up with a closed fist.

"Are you sure this is smart?" Carol asked. "If we get caught…?"

"If we don't get on those ships, we'll die here," John interrupted. "You don't think that the Ana Aseas are going to make room for us, do you?"

"How are we going to get there undetected?" Carol asked.

"Look at the size of those monsters? They're as big as an ocean freighter, big enough to carry 1500 people maybe more per trip," Gordon remarked.

"So what's the plan? Just hide in one them until they take off?"

"Of course not. All we have to do is break into the office of transports in the administration building over there to right," Mandon pointed to the lone brick building where two guards stood at the front door with rifles slung over their shoulders, "and add our names to the roster," Mandon replied in a hushed tone.

"How are you going to get past the guards?" Carol inquired.

"Don't you think I've thought about this?" Mandon said.

"It sounds like a good plan. Well, as long as it works." Danelle shrugged her shoulders.

Carol continued, "We are twenty strong and don't you think they won't notice an additional twenty people? Where are we going to sit? We'll need IDs, retina scans and papers. How are you going to do that Mr. Wizard?"

"That's why we need to get into the office tonight. I have to get the manifest and add our names, delete twenty others, and return the adjusted copy," Mandon replied.

"I don't like it. I mean who are you going to leave behind?" Carol asked.

"My research showed some Biochore folks will be onboard the Santa Maria, mostly middle management. They're going to have to wait for the next bus I'm afraid," John snickered. "If I know Biochore, those guys won't be missed."

"Can't argue with that." Mandon raised his hand for a high five.

John and Mandon zipped up their rubber suits and slipped on their gloves and footies. "How do I look?" Mandon asked.

"In one piece," Danelle said. "Let's try and keep it that way, okay?"

"Thanks for the pep talk."

"Good luck," she said and gave him a forced smile.

Mandon put on his headgear, gave them a thumbs up, scaled the fence, and carefully maneuvered over the barbed wire on top and quietly dropped to the other side, along with John.

All of a sudden one of the searchlights caught a low flying bat. It traced the bat for a second or two and then went back to cycling the compound.

"Oh no!" John said. "It has a motion sensor."

"No worries." Mandon took two devices out of his pocket and handed one to John.

"What is this?"

"A fogger. It snaps to your belt buckle. When you flip the switch it will emit smoke around you concealing your movements from the detectors."

"Did you know it could pick up motion?"

"Boy Scout training," Mandon said and smiled. "Now switch it on."

"Roger."

Soon both foggers began to spew out smoke all around them.

"I can't see where I'm going."

"Turn on your night vision goggles."

"Oh yeah."

A sick turtle could have beaten the two as they slowly crawled across the compound toward the administration building. Mandon finally arrived and hid behind the bushes lining the main building. He looked around for John, but he was nowhere to be seen. Twenty minutes later Mandon felt a tap on his shoulder.

"Aarrggh!"

"Shhh..."

"Where have you been?" Mandon asked.

"Charges."

"What?"

"A distraction. We're dead men if that searchlight catches us. How many foggers did you bring?"

Mandon held up two fingers.

"So much for always being prepared. My fogger's out," John said.

"I don't have enough smoke to cover the two of us back to the fence anyway. Those charges better work!"

"We probably won't know if they don't."

"Thanks for that pleasant thought," Mandon said and motioned it was time for them to go.

Hidden in the shadows the two slowly inched toward the two men in uniform guarding the entrance.

"I don know why all thee hurry up in geeting dis ship ready?" the first guard asked.

"Ya. Ist long journey. Eevry one seem en big hurry," the second replied.

"Many scared faces. I no like."

"Ya."

"I knew it!" John whispered.

"Shhh…They'll hear us."

John pulled out a remote, pressed the red button and watched it blink faster and faster until they heard a loud boom followed by streaks of light spewing out in all directions. Sirens began wailing and all four perimeter spotlights turned toward the east fence.

"Vas ist dat?" the first guard asked and pulled the AK-47 assault rifle off his shoulder.

"Eet came from ober de'er," the second guard replied. With an M-16 Carbine in hand they both ran toward the explosion and light show.

"Now," John whispered and the two ran up the stairs of the unguarded building.

"The door is locked!" Mandon pushed and pulled the handle.

"Keep an eye out for our officer friends." John pulled out a pencil looking device and inserted it into the lock.

"Roger." Mandon peered around the building's edge keeping the guards in sight.

As soon as the handle appeared, John turned the key and slowly opened the door. "Let's go!" The two scurried into the hallway closing and locking the door behind them.

The guards stopped at the east fence only to find some protestors chanting, "Save our planet…save our planet." They held signs and threw some firecrackers at the guards.

"Donn shoot Igor!" the second guard said. "Foolish Canadians! Go home! Es late you trespass! Go home or I have you arrested."

The little group said a few more words and turned away.

"You see. Ees nothing."

The two guards leisurely walked back to the front entrance. "Ees almost time for home."

"Ya."

"I found it!" Mandon whispered as he scanned the list with his pursal.

"All we have to do is add our names and remove... hey! Here are those Biochore names!"

Two hours later, the new manifest was placed back where it belonged with twenty new names added and twenty removed. "I would love to see the faces on those middle management worms when they find they don't have a seat," Mandon said.

"Yeah, they know what's going on with the earth. They should. They helped destroy it," John replied. "Talk about poetic justice." He looked at his watch. "Have you uploaded the retina scans yet?"

"Doing it now."

The new guards arrived and did a quick perimeter search of the building before returning to their post.

"Good night Igor, Hans."

"Good night. Protestors tonight. Throw firecrackers at Igor. Ha ha. They leave when we say arrest," Hans said and pointed to the east fence. Then they left for home.

"Protestors? This late?" Johnson asked.

"Nothing makes sense anymore these days. I mean, why are we guarding this entrance? I mean, there is nothing important here. Just some administrative crap."

"I dunno. I just do my job and collect my pay."

"John!" Mandon said.

"What?"

"I found something," Mandon said. "I was doing some data recon and came across this. He pulled his pursal out of the terminal. This was sent out today!"

"What does it say?"

"Shhh...not so loud. Let's see. Phase 1 – Mars habitant Dome sites completed. Stop. Martian area ready for transport. Stop. Phase 2 – constructed – Stop. Martian area ready for transport. Stop. Phase 3 – constructed – Stop . Martian area ready.... – John! This thing is a mile long! They've already built two entire cities on Mars. Those ships weren't weather regulators at all. They were used to transport supplies and materials to Mars and now they're ready to transport people."

"I thought you knew that already," John said.

"I thought we were going to have to build the cities with the supplies onboard. These guys knew Earth was toast years ago."

Chapter 21

MARS

Thornton Residence
Domette 64
Gemini - Sol Friday 6, 0012
1945 hours

"Oh my god!" Ken said as he slowly stopped in his tracks hoping not to catch the monster's eye. The Halkomelem had returned to the task at hand as he continued to rip the insulation out of their domette. Beside the Halk lay twisted metal and pulled insulation. The monster had penetrated the outer hull and was only inches from gaining access to the inside. The panels were bent and laid on the ground with a couple meters of insulation on top. Ken could see the hot wires as they danced and threw off high voltage sparks against the ferocious Martian wind. Now Ken knew why there wasn't any power. *The Halkomelem has shorted it, but how could that beast endure the electric shocks, not to mention the weather?* he thought to himself.

Ken bent down for a closer look at his father. "Dad?" Ken radioed his father as he lay against a pile of rocks.

"Pop? Are you okay?" Ken slowly moved closer to his dad.

Ken quietly picked up his dad and pulled his limp body behind a large rock, safely away from the Halkomelem and turned his spot laser to maximum. The spot laser hummed as the energy continued to build. He knew that the spot laser couldn't last very long at this level, but he had to stop that Halkomelem. Ken watched as the beast pulled and bent the wires carefully to the side. Ken watched as the monster used the sparks from the main voltage line to cut into the inner metal housing.

He's a smart one. I didn't know they were capable of reason, Ken thought.

Ken looked at the spot laser, which was vibrating to overload and started toward the Halkomelem. The Halkomelem turned, and leapt toward him in one single motion. The déjà vu experience of Ken's last encounter raised its ugly head.

His knees went weak as he felt his heart burst out of his chest, but he held firm. What seemed like minutes lasted mere seconds and the Halkomelem grabbed Ken's shoulders. The Halkomelem looked into Ken's eyes as Ken slammed the spot laser into the beast's chest. The Halkomelem screamed as its head jerked back, but Ken dug the laser deep into the monster's chest. He then pulled his knife out of the Halk and plunged the spot laser into the side of its neck hoping the beast's anatomy was similar to his own with a carotid artery. The monster screamed in pain waving its arms wildly, throwing Ken to the red Martian clay. Ken pulled himself off the ground and turned to watch as the Halkomelem reached for the blade buried deep within its neck. Ken could see he had hit the artery as the blood raced from the beast like a neglected faucet turned all the way up quickly fading into the Martian atmosphere. The pulsing laser knife continued pelting the beast with its liquid fire as the Halkomelem began to waver. The beast reached over and finally pulled the spot laser out of its neck and moved towards Ken. The monster dropped the knife to the ground as it tried to steady itself.

What does it take to kill this thing? Ken wondered as he slowly backed away from the approaching beast.

The Halkomelem quickly closed the distance between himself and Ken. Now within reach he pinned Ken against the domette when all of a sudden the beast felt a new burning sensation pierce into the carotid artery on the other side of its neck. The monster's grip on Ken loosened as he began waving the other arm wildly. Yeri dug the spot laser deeper into the its matted neck and held on for dear life. The spot laser continued pelting blue fire in the beast's neck making him kick and throw both arms from side to side as it screamed in pain. One arm caught Yeri's helmet throwing him down onto the red Martian dirt. No sooner than Yeri could get back on his feet did he see the monster reach over and pull the laser from his neck and throw it to the ground. Ken, trapped by the domette, tried to slide away from the monster but he was too close. The Halk quickly grabbed Ken by the helmet, gave out a roar, and fell to the ground bringing Ken down on the Martian soil with him.

Ken stared at the sky only to see his dad holding the bloody spot lasers in hand peering at the two of them.

"I think it's dead," Yeri said as he turned off the laser and brushed the red dust off his suit. "That damn thing scratched my helmet!"

"Are you going to just stand there?"

"Oh, I guess you want your laser back."

"Get this damn thing off of me!" Ken yelled into his microphone.

"Alright, alright," Yeri protested. "Come on big fella." Yeri grabbed an arm and pulled as hard as he could to one side. The beast finally rolled off of Ken.

"I hope you didn't hurt yourself," Ken said.

"No. I'm fine, thank you," Yeri smiled.

"Help me reconnect the power couplers so we can get back inside."

"So that's a Halk?"

"Come on. It's freezing out here and I don't know if Charlie here has a brother."

"Good point. I'll pick up the tool box."

"What shape is it in?" Ken asked still looking at the dead monster.

"The shape of something that died. What are you talking about?"

"The tool box."

"Oh."

"Where is the box?"

"I don't know," Yeri said.

"I guess you forgot where you put it, when you and Charlie were playing catch."

"He almost killed me!"

"You're too ornery to die," Ken said.

The power couplings looked like they had been chewed and then snapped in two. Ken tried to replace as much insulation as he could and then half welded the outer metal in a fashion to hold it until morning. It took another twenty minutes to reconnect the power couplings. Fortunately, this was what Ken did when he was at work. He grabbed a coupling sleeve and used it to connect the wires. The sleeve absorbed the energy and melded itself into the power lines. He worked quickly as the temperature continued to fall.

"How much more time?" Yeri asked.

"The grid is repaired. Now all I have to do is connect to the main and then make some cosmetic repairs and we're home free. At least until morning."

"Well, I'm going in. It's cold."

"Wait. I still need you."

Yeri turned up the hand and foot heating unit in his suit to maximum and surveyed the terrain for any more unwelcome guests.

"It's cold out here! How much longer is this going to take?"

"Shhh..." Ken said as he carefully reconnected the live wires to the circuit board.

POP!

"Yeow!"

"Ken?" Yeri asked.

"It's nothing."

"I saw sparks." Yeri moved closer to his son.

"Just hold the light steady. Okay?" Ken shook off the electric charge. He quickly moved his left hand back and forth. "That was fun."

A few minutes later, Ken had finished his band-aid repair job to the outer damage of the hull. It would need a lot more work in the morning, but tonight it would hold.

"How does it look?" Ken asked with a sense of pride.

"It's going to need a paint job."

"Yeah, but it should hold us through the night."

"My suit is losing heat. Let's get out of here," Yeri said.

"Okay." Ken bent down and grabbed the Halkomelem's arm.

"What are you doing?" Yeri asked with his PeeP shining on the beast.

"Help me get him inside."

"ARE YOU CRAZY?"

Ken bent down, grabbed a foot and waited for Yeri. "Probably."

Yeri looked at Ken as he held half the monster in his arms. "Jesus! Tima isn't going to like this at all. To tell you the truth, I'm not so sure I like it."

"Come on. It's late and I can't drag this guy back to the dome all by myself." Ken slowly dragged the Halkomelem toward the domette. "Do you want T-Minus crawling around here tomorrow?"

"I think it isn't going to matter at this point."

"Well, I for one want to know how Charlie can survive living on Mars without a spacesuit or anything. Don't you?"

Yeri sighed and grabbed the Halkomelem's other arm and leg. He grunted and they slowly moved the beast across the Martian desert. "You're crazy bringing this thing into the house and I must be crazy for helping you."

"Easy now, Dad. Don't you want to know what this thing is? I mean we never see them during the day and if there is a report about one being around, you know the drill. The authorities are all over the place. Something's going on and I want to know what."

"We shouldn't get involved. After all, we have a special task force that specifically handles these kind of things."

"That's what concerns me. Why is everything so hush-hush?"

"I don't know, but I do know that you're in violation of some pretty severe laws if you bring this thing in the house. The authorities should be notified."

"Yeah and then we'll never know what's going on."

The power, along with the lights, came on as Tima and Beth watched the compression numbers climb.

"They should be here in a minute or two," Tima said to Beth in a sigh of relief as they waited in front of the lift.

"Air Pressure – 1015 Millibars – Please Stand Back."

stated the computerized voice.

Ding! Dong!

The girls stood by the front door as the exhaust vented the air underneath the floor as the door slowly opened showing Ken and Yeri standing over the dead monster.

Chapter 22

EARTH

Cree Air Force Base
Canso, Nova Scotia
Saturday November 15, 0020
0400 Hours

POP! POP! POP!

It was just before dawn when the distant noise alerted the automated security system.

POP! POP! POP! POP! POP!

The sirens activated while the searchlights triangulated once again toward the noise and quickly lit up the area at the north fence this time.

"I guess our protestors are back," Johnson said as they jogged over to the fence. They could see the signs and sighed as they watched the people scream and throw more firecrackers.

"Save our Planet…Save our Planet!" came the shouts as they waved their homemade signs back and forth.

"Alright…alright…don't make me call this in or you'll all spend the rest of the night in jail. Now move along."

With the guards distracted by the protestors, the two amateur burglars quietly unlocked and opened the east side window, trying to make as little noise as possible as the guards threatened the picketing crowd outside the north fence.

"John?"

"What?"

"Those lasers are set to kill aren't they?"

"Just keep cool."

"Carol, we are out of the building making our way to the east fence. Over," John whispered into his antiquated walkie-talkie with one knee on the ground next to the bushes lining the building. "Where did you get these?" he turned to Mandon.

"What's that saying? Always be prepared?" Mandon said with a wink as John put the walkie-talkie back to his mouth.

"Carol?"

"Did you make the changes? Over."

"Roger. Over."

"Okay. Good luck and I love you." Carol turned off her walkie-talkie and walked up to the fence with the other protestors. "Let's go!" Carol said to the others. "They aren't going to help us."

"Listen to her and we'll forget the whole ordeal!" yelled the guard over the shuffling picketers.

The first couple of protestors dropped their signs and slowly backed away from the fence. The guards watched as the rest left one by one. When the last one was out of sight, the guards turned back toward the entrance. "What is this world coming to? It's fricken four in the morning."

"I'll do a walk around just to make sure."

"Okay, there'll be some fresh coffee for you when you get back."

BOOM!

came the explosion showering the field with flashes of light coming from the west side of the compound.

"What the hell?" The guards grabbed their weapons and rushed to where the spotlights were pointing.

"Now!" John whispered intensely releasing his grip from the outer building wall. They both ran with legs bent almost on all fours trying their best to avoid detection.

The fence was only twenty meters away when the searchlights caught them. John knew it wouldn't take long before the lasers got a lock on them.

"Hit the smoke!" John shouted to Mandon.

"Not yet," Mandon said.

John quickly reached into his pocket while they both zigged and zagged hoping to buy a few more precious seconds. John could see the beam hit the ground beside and in front of him as the searchlight continued to recalculate their positions in order to eliminate the threat. John knew it would be only a matter of seconds before the targeting system would be able to accurately predict their movements and failing that it would spray the area in machine gun mode. They continued to dodge back and forth hoping to make the fence but even if they did the climb would be their end. John reached into his pocket once again and grabbed the remote. He didn't see the light beam and assumed it was on his back. They finally reached the fence and with only a matter of nanoseconds until he would be dropped he pressed the switch, closed his eyes and stopped on a dime.

"Don't move!" he yelled to Mandon as he held down the firing pin. Mandon stopped within a centimeter of John and they waited not moving a muscle each preparing to be shot in the back.

BOOM!

came another explosion and light show from the north side of the compound once again. The computerized searchlights turned north as the blanket of darkness covered them.

"Hit it!" John shouted and pressed the red button one last time.

Mandon deployed the smoker and they both waited as the smoke enveloped the two along with the fence.

BOOM!

came the final explosion from the bushes lining the western section of the building sending the search lights moving all around the Administration Building as the two guards who were circling the compound ran toward the building. They met at the front steps and checked the door.

"Something's not right about all of this."

"Yeah. I know," Johnson replied. "Well, I don't see anything here, but I did notice the search light was over at the east fence for quite a long time."

"East fence?"

"Yeah the east fence. You know where the picketers were earlier. I think I'll check it out," Harman volunteered.

"Is something smoking over there?" Johnson asked.

"Fire?" Harmon looked over to the east fence.

"I don't see any flames. Intruders! Come on let's go!" The guards ran toward the smoking fence.

Mandon and John had just landed on the other side of the fence and started to run.

"Halt!" came a voice from behind them.

"Keep running," Mandon said. "They can't see us through the smoke."

"Good idea."

BAM! BAM! BAM!

"They're firing at us!" Mandon said.

"Don't stop!"

They ran through the woods all the way back to the van. When they got there the motor was running and the air conditioning was a welcome relief.

"You made it!" Carol said.

"The day I can't outsmart a couple of rent-a-cops is the day I..."

"Uh huh. I thought I heard gun shots," Carol interrupted.

"Gun shots? It was probably just your imagination," John countered.

"Well, my imagination almost got you killed."

"Did you find the list?" Danelle asked.

"Yep. You guys took a big chance throwing firecrackers at those guards you know," John said.

"We had to make it look real," Carol said.

"Well, it fooled them and fortunately it kept their attention long enough for us to sneak into the building." Mandon removed his gloves. "This suit really makes you sweat."

Chapter 23

MARS

Thornton Residence
Domette 64
Gemini - Sol Friday 6, 0012
2100 hours

"WHAT IS THAT?" Tima screamed as she watched Ken and Yeri drag the Halkomelem's lifeless body into the living room.

"It's a Halk or was a Halkomelem," Ken replied. "Help me move this big fella over to the lab."

"I will not! Don't you bring that thing in here," Tima said. "Little T, Togo. Go to your rooms."

"Ah Mom."

"NOW!" She turned and pointed toward the bedroom. Then she turned abruptly toward her husband. "You're not going to bring that thing in here. For god sakes! He's getting blood all over the place. Have you notified T-Minus?" Tima asked as she ran to the kitchen and searched for a towel. "There's blood and guts all over my nice clean floor. KEN!" She turned toward the beast. "Why in the world would T-Minus tell you to bring this thing in the house anyway? What is this world coming...?" Tima looked back at Ken with her eyes going wide. "Oh no. You didn't call, did you? If they find this thing in here? Ken...what were you thinking? Get this monster out of my house. NOW!"

"I am going to do no such thing!" Ken's head jerked up. "We're going to get to the bottom of this once and for all. I want to know what all the secrecy is about."

"You're going to end up at Herschel digging for ice!" Tima waved an angry finger and turned to Yeri. "Both of you!"

Yeri raised his hands and looked at Ken.

"They have to catch us, first," Ken said with a smile and a wink. "Now, do you want this guy to spend the night bleeding on our nice living room floor or in my lab?"

Resigned to the task at hand Tima grabbed an arm. "You owe me big time for this Mister," she said as the men stood still in shock as Tima pulled on the Halk. "Well? Let's go!"

Ken, Yeri, and Tima slowly dragged the three hundred pound beast back to Ken's lab while Beth wiped the blood soaked lift and floor as best she could. All four of them with Beth's help lifted the Halkomelem onto Ken's workbench and Ken began his examination.

"He has a familiar look to him, don't you think?"

"No!" Tima said still shaking from dealing with a dead monster in her house. "Look at this mess! Who is going to clean it up?"

Yeri turned and gave her a boyish smile.

"Oh no I'm not!" Tima said defiantly placing both fists on her hips. "You two brought that thing in here and you two boys are going to clean up after yourselves." Tima stormed out of the lab. "I need a drink," she said to Beth as Beth threw another blood soaked rag into the trash bin.

"Fix one for me too," Beth said with a sigh.

"His facial features look almost…human. See?" Ken placed his hand on the beast's chin and moved it side to side. "His jawbone and teeth. The scales are strange, but the hair looks to be… ape like."

"Now how would an ape get to Mars?" Yeri asked. "Ken, have you been dipping into Tima's sake again?"

"I'm not so sure. He has a carotid artery, which probably saved my life. Do you still have access to the lab?"

"You know I do," Yeri said absent-mindedly. "Hey, what are you thinking?"

Ken scraped a variety of scales, blood, hair and a fingernail. He cleaned it and carefully placed them on some slides. He held the slides to Yeri's face and said, "I need you to run a DNA sample."

"No."

"Please?'

"Can't do it. Too many guards."

"They know you," Ken replied.

"It's too late. My suit isn't recharged and..."

"Aren't you the least bit interested in finding out what could toss you the length of a football field?"

"It wasn't that far," Yeri said.

"Oh yeah? It looked to me like you scored three points tonight. As the football that is," Ken said and laughed.

Yeri stared at Ken for a few minutes, looked at the Halk and then turned back to Ken. "You want me to just walk into the lab tomorrow morning with some Halkomelem samples? I can see it now. Excuse me for a minute, but my son and I killed a Halkomelem last night and we're curious to what kind of DNA it has. You don't mind do you? I would be slapped in irons before I got the DNA part out."

"That's why we need to run it tonight. We can get there if we just modify our suits a little."

"Tonight? Do you know how cold it is out there? Let's just wait and go to jail tomorrow."

"Can't." Ken secured the slides inside his front zipper compartment on his spacesuit.

"Why?"

"Because someone will see the damage tomorrow and this place will be crawling with authorities. T-Minus will be called and they're going to know there was a struggle out here last night. Even if we hide this guy, we need fresh samples to run an accurate DNA. You know that. By the time they've finish with us, not to mention keeping a close eye on our whereabouts for a month or two, we'll never unravel this mystery."

"You're right. I hate it, but you're right," sighed Yeri. He and Ken suited up one more time and Ken took the lift to prepare Friggy for transport to the lab.

"Dad? Where are you going?" Tima asked with her arms crossed, as she tapped her foot on the floor like she did when her children were caught with their hand in the proverbial cookie jar. "And where is my husband?"

"In the bat cave."

"What? Oh no you're not. If you think you can just leave this monster in my house while you two go joy riding you have another thing coming," Tima said.

"We're going to the lab," Yeri said.

"The lab? This late? That rock your helmet hit must have shaken that thick skull of yours and when it did, it must have knocked something loose. Do you know how cold it is out there? You'll both freeze."

"Those new prototype suits Ken was talking about came in last week. Guaranteed one-hundred degrees plus below."

"Have you tried it out?"

"That's what Elotec claims," Yeri grimaced.

"Uh huh."

"Ken is already outside warming up Friggy."

"I see now where Ken got his insanity. You're crazy!"

The pressurized door opened and Ken walked back into the domette and removed his helmet. "Friggy is ready to roll," he said. "By the way honey, I have a favor to ask."

"Uh oh, here it comes," Yeri said under his breath.

"What?" Tima stared at Ken with her hands clinched tight on her hips.

"We need you to cut up Charlie here and put him in the bin before dawn."

"I'm calling a doctor. No, a psychiatrist, because you've both lost your..." She shook her head and looked at the ceiling. "I will do no such thing."

"Beth will help," Yeri interjected.

"Help?" Beth tried to clean more blood and guts off the floor. "It's staining the floor! It's never going to come out now," she said aloud and looked to Yeri.

"Sweetheart, it's important," Yeri said as he grabbed some R-40 refrigerant out of Ken's lab and his pursal off the table and stuffed them in his suit pocket. He picked up his helmet and examined it for cracks. "Ken? Do you have any Dioxathane canisters around here?" Yeri scanned the lab.

"Yeah. I keep a spare in the rover. Why?"

"Just wondering." Yeri turned to Beth. "You need to help Tima cut this thing up and get rid of it."

"And how are we going to do that?" Beth yelled a little louder than she meant.

"The trash bin. He should give us plenty of free energy for a few days." Ken tried to make it sound beneficial, but Beth and Tima were not having any of it.

"You've both been out in the cold too long. No. No way am I going to spend the rest of the night hacking away at this... this.... Thing! No!" Tima crossed her arms for effect.

"Look," Ken said as he held his helmet in his arms, "T-Minus will be here in the morning snooping around for any evidence of Charlie and if they find him..." Ken raised his shoulders.

"You gave it a name?" Tima asked incredulously.

"Just do it. We can't stay here and argue all night. Time is of the essence." Ken zipped his suit.

Tima looked at Beth and shook her head. "No, we will not be party to this insanity. You should've never dragged this whatever it... CHARLIE is in here. Beth and I are not going to..."

"Good. Then it's settled," Ken interrupted. He could see the fire of controlled rage in Tima's eyes. "Make sure this place is spic and span by first light."

"I didn't say I was going to do it," Tima said.

"I know," Ken replied and he walked to the lift and put on his helmet.

"Do you have any bleach?" Beth asked.

"In the kitchen, top shelf." Tima looked at the lift as the door closed and turned to Beth. "I hate living with that man."

Beth pulled an old meat cleaver out of the cabinet sharpened it and handed it Tima. "You get used to it." A tiny smile escaped her lips.

Coronae Laboratories
Coronae Scopulus
Hellas Planitia
Hellas Quadrangle, Mars
Gemini - Sol Saturday 7, 0012
0100 hours

It was one in the morning when the two walked up to the main entrance to the laboratory. The building was empty except for the guard sitting behind the desk reading the news. Yeri removed his helmet, looked into the retina scan, and waited for the secondary door to open. The guard looked up from his pursal and watched the two men amble up to his desk.

"Can I help you?"

"Hello Ryan. I'm Dr. Thornton, Yeri Thornton, and I have some soil samples that I need to run."

"Kind of late don't you think, Dr. Thornton?" Ryan stood up.

"Yeah, well, you know how it is. Us old folks can't sleep when we start thinking about something. Anyway, this project is so big it takes forever to compile during the day," Yeri said with his helmet resting on his arm.

Ken pulled his helmet off and placed it in the storage area named guest.

"Hmmm...Who's this?"

"My son, Ken Thornton. He's been helping me with the soil samples."

The guard held up a retina scan to Ken's eye. "You're not on the authorization list Mr. Thornton. I can't let you through."

"Perhaps you know my wife. Tima Thornton?"

"Sorry. I don't care if you're Jesus the Christ himself and walked on water to get here. My orders are no one is allowed back there after nine without proper clearance."

Yeri turned to Ken. "I'll walk you out." As soon as they were clear of the guard Yeri whispered to Ken, "Go around the building to Section-8 and find the escape hatch. It will automatically open in case of a structural breach."

"How are you going to open it without setting a bunch of alarms off?"

"You just let me worry about that. Now get over there and wait."

"Why don't I just wait in the Frigg until you're finished."

"And who is going to reprogram Dnet to run these samples?"

"I can walk you through it."

"And if something goes wrong?"

"You can explain it to me over the air."

"Over the pursal? That would be like having a Microsoft technician solving an Apple computer problem remotely."

"You're right. I read about those companies in history class. They had totally different operating systems. Did you know the pursal put them both out of business?"

"No."

"Years ago this high school kid named Dusty was working on some really leading edge quant…"

"Is this going to take long?" Yeri interrupted.

"Sorry," Ken apologized.

"Look, we don't have a lot of time here and if something goes wrong I'm going to need you to punch the right buttons. Now go."

Ken knew he needed to physically be there because they only had a small window to find out what was going on. This would be their one shot. So he waved to the guard and nonchalantly walked out into the freezing night air as if nothing happened.

This is fricken nuts and it's cold out here. Now where in God's name is section-8? He roamed around the yard until he found a wall with

Section-8 painted on the side and an escape hatch located next to the ground. Ken looked at the size. *I hope I don't get stuck in this thing.*

As soon as he thought that he heard alarms going off and lights came on all around him.

"Damn! I must've tripped something!" He looked around to see if anyone had seen him.

"Ken! Ken!" He heard his name being called as he saw a light shining out from the small whole in the building. He bent down to see the hatch had completely opened.

"Come on, come on! Let's go!" Yeri yelled.

"There's a lot of air rushing toward me!"

"It's to keep out the Martian atmosp... what do you care? Let's go."

Ken crawled into the hatch. Seconds later his head popped out the other side where Yeri grabbed his helmet and pulled him the rest of the way through. Ken got to his feet and pulled his helmet off. "This is your idea of sneaking me in?" Ken asked.

"Shhh...Here's a surgical mask. Act like you belong here. If someone comes up to you, tell 'em... tell 'em you're my new apprentice."

"What am I going to do with my helmet?"

"Just carry it with you."

"Why am I carrying it?"

"Just make up something. Now come on. Let's go before we get caught."

"Some plan."

"Shhh... Hurry."

The two sprinted down the yellow hallway toward a sign, flashing **Exit**. Yeri opened the door with Ken close behind. Yeri grabbed the railing and went downstairs taking two steps at a time. He stopped at a landing on SubTwo to catch his breath.

"How many more steps?" Ken asked but got no response. "Where are we going?"

"SubSix."

"That's four more floors down!"

"Shhh…hurry up and walk quieter. You're going to wake up everybody with all that stomping!"

"I'm not stomping."

The two continued down the stairs while the sirens were screaming as the warning lights swirled blue and red in the hallway.

Yeri held his hand up.

"Why are we stopping?"

"Shhh….To see if anyone is following."

"Why didn't we just take the lift?"

"Can't."

"Why?"

"Let's go. We only have three more floors," Yeri said.

"This helmet is getting heavy."

"Do you complain this much at home?"

The two continued down the stairs as the lights flashed along with a recorded audio now telling everyone to vacate the area.

"Why are we stopping again?"

"Quiet! We're here." Yeri pushed the green door labeled *SubSix* painted light blue directly above it. "Damn! It won't open."

"What's wrong?" Ken asked.

"Locked. It's never locked. They only lock down SubSeven and below." Yeri looked to the heavens. "Unless we're in a lockdown."

"Are we?"

"Didn't you see the blinking red lights and hear the warnings going off every ten seconds?"

"Yes but…"

"That's a lockdown and it's because of us, er me," Yeri interrupted.

"What are we, er you going to do?"

"You are going to have to burn through the lock. Do you have your spot laser?" Yeri asked.

"Yes."

"Get it out! No, wait…I hear footsteps. We have to go lower."

"Lower?" Ken questioned.

"We have to find another way to SubSix."

"The footsteps are getting louder!" Ken whispered.

"Someone's in the stairwell!" came a voice from above.

"Move!" Yeri whispered back.

Two more flights down left them bent over panting with their hands resting on their knees.

Ken turned his head to the red door and above it was etched SubEight painted red. "We're cornered," Ken whispered and put his helmet on the floor. "Is there a SubNine somewhere?"

"No."

The stairway creaked and shook as the footsteps from above continued. "They're getting closer."

"Give me your spot laser."

"Why?"

"You did bring it, didn't you?"

"I already told you. We're not going to break into SubEight, are we?" Ken reached into his pocket and pulled out the knife.

"You want to explain to security what you're doing here?"

Ken fired up the laser and moved the setting to ten and handed it to Yeri. "I don't know why I let you…" Ken mumbled to himself as he put his helmet back on. Yeri handed him back the laser and watched as the flame hissed and sparkled a deep blue flame eager to go to work. When Ken touched the metal lock with his liquid flame it screamed and hissed as the metal slowly gave way to the onslaught of blue fire. Sparks were shooting everywhere. The acrid smell of burnt metal along with wisps of smoke began to crawl up the stairwell.

"They're going to know something is wrong pretty soon when they get a whiff of this," Yeri said as Ken slowly cut through the metal.

The footsteps continued and it sounded like whoever it was had picked up speed.

"Come on, come on!" Ken yelled at the laser.

"Take it easy, Son," Yeri said.

"It's too slow."

"Stay on task."

"Who's down there? Show yourself!" came the distant voice echoing through the stairwell.

"There. It's done!" Ken hit the door with his shoulder. The door complained with a loud creak as it reluctantly gave way and opened into the hallway.

"Stop!" came the voice from above. "I have a weapon." The footsteps that clanked down the stairway quickly turned from a walk to a run.

Yeri and Ken entered SubEight and quickly looked around for a place to hide.

"Where to Dad?"

"I don't know."

"It was your idea to come down here and then what? Wait until security greets us? Haven't you been down here before?"

"Can't get clearance for SubEight. We should be able to get to SubSix from here," as soon as the words left Yeri's mouth they heard someone shout.

"What's that smell? Intruder in the stairwell possibly on SubEight," came the voice calling for backup.

"They're closing in. We gotta hide," Ken said as he took off on a sprint with Yeri close behind as they dashed down the hallway of SubEight. Ken stopped and grabbed the handle of one of the doors halfway down the hallway. "Try some doors."

"Don't be ridiculous. Everything is retina scanned around here."

"Then what do we do?"

The blue and red lights and sirens continued, followed by a mechanic voice,

"Intruder Alert...Intruder Alert...Intruder Alert..."

"The bathrooms...quick!" Yeri pointed at the bathroom sign across the hall. They both broke out into a run that would have made the legendary race horse Secretariat proud.

Ken grabbed the men's door handle.

"Don't be stupid," Yeri said as he grabbed Ken by the sleeve and pulled him into the ladies room.

"I hear footsteps," Ken said.

"Get in the far stall and stand on the toilet. Try to keep out of sight."

"The toilet?"

"Yes and shut the door."

Ken climbed on the toilet and squatted keeping out of sight. "Great plan," he whispered.

"Shhh…" Yeri said louder than he wanted. He sat on the toilet with his feet pressed against the door.

The door to the women's room opened and two security guards walked in. Ken and Yeri could hear the doors to the stalls open and close. The guard who had just closed the stall next to Yeri stopped and turned to the second guard.

"I'll finish up here. You go up to Six and I'll check Seven," the first guard said.

"Roger," the second guard replied and walked out of the ladies room.

The first guard grabbed the handle of Yeri's stall door and…

BAM!

In a flash the door slammed into his face knocking him off his feet as his head careened into the sink counter behind him.

Yeri and Ken looked at the unconscious guard.

"Is he dead?"

"No. But he's going to have one hell of a headache when he wakes up."

"Now what?" Ken asked.

"Well, Sleeping Beauty ain't going anywhere for a while," Yeri said as Ken ran toward the door. "Where are you going?" Ken stopped in his tracks.

"I don't know," Ken replied.

"Get back here. We've got work to do," Yeri said.

"We gotta get out of here."

"And go where?"

"SubSix?"

"No. At least not yet. Now help me pick this guy up," Yeri said in a hurried tone. Ken grabbed one arm and with Yeri holding on to the other they walked to the bathroom door, opened it as Yeri stuck his head in the corridor and looked both ways.

"Where are we taking him?"

"It's all clear. Let's go!" Yeri said.

The unconscious guard's foot was caught on the closing door so Ken and Yeri gave it a good yank freeing the officer and continued to drag him behind them down the hallway.

Ken stopped for a second "Where are we going?"

"Quit stalling."

"I'm not…" Ken sighed out of frustration. "I just want to know…"

Yeri stopped in front of office 802. "We're here. Now help me prop up Officer," Yeri looked at his name badge, "Sam so he can look at the monitor."

"Why 802?"

"I have my reasons. Come on."

"He's heavy."

"Quit complaining," Yeri said as he held the officer's head to the scanner. "Open his eyes."

Ken gently placed two fingers on the officer's eyelids and slowly pulled them back.

"He'll be awake before we finish if you don't speed it up."

"Would you like to try?" Ken asked.

Officer – Sam O'Riley – approved.

Yeri heard the familiar click and pushed open the door. "Hand me your spot laser."

"The door's already unlocked. We don't have to burn it off," Ken said with a surprised look on his face.

"Just hand it to me!" Yeri said in a demanding voice.

"Okay!" Ken, somewhat irritated, handed Yeri the spot laser.

Yeri quickly grabbed the tool and wedged the spot laser between the door and wall. "Okay, now let's get Sleeping Beauty back to the ladies room."

"Back in the ladies room?" Ken questioned. "Why not just leave him here. We gotta go."

"Not so fast. We have to cover our tracks and the best way to do that is to keep them confused."

"Well it's working. I'm confused."

"Nothing new there," Yeri smiled. "Come on. Turn him around and let's go."

*****

"This guy stinks!" Tima yelled out as she walked back into the lab with plastic garbage bag.

"Isn't there something we can do to mask that smell?" Beth placed a black matted hairy hand into the bag. "I've got to sharpen the blade again. Charlie is full of bone and gristle."

Tima walked over and opened the incinerator door. She tossed another bag of bones and fur into the open maw as the flame engulfed the remains of Charlie. She went into the kitchen to once again clean and sharpen her own knife and then she walked back into the lab to relieve Beth for a few minutes to clean and sharpen hers.

"Well, the good news is you'll have some free energy for a few days," Beth laughed as she walked to open the lab door. "What are you going to do with that butcher knife once we are finished?"

"I'm going to use it to kill two men who left me here to spend all night cutting this monster into bits." Tima lifted the cleaver high in the air and then plunged the knife deep into another limb and turned her head as more blood spurted in every direction. "We have to hurry Beth, Charlie has to disappear before dawn."

The sun was slowly creeping over the city of Mars when the domebell rang.

"We're going to need more bleach," Beth said, still cleaning the rest of the blood and hair off the floor of the lab. Tima walked over to the lift. She pressed the button and there appeared a group of men in special spacesuits marked "T-" on their helmets. Tima yelled out to Beth. "It's T-Minus!"

Chapter 24

EARTH

"Good evening my fellow Earthlings. It is a great honor to speak to you today. We, the Ana Aseas, have ruled your planet for twenty years as of today. It has not been without its challenges." Ana Asea One looked across the crowds and smiled. "I want you to know we have not turned a deaf ear to your concerns. The temperature is getting hotter with each passing year. The BuffaPrime shortage has caused record increases in the cost of beef. Our oceans are now too toxic to swim in and the air is slowly becoming unbreathable." Ana Asea One shook his head and paused. "Many of you have already undergone recoding and have easily adapted to the changing environment, but there are still many of those who are unable to enjoy those benefits. The middle class and the newly promoted middle class have found the procedure financially out of their reach and of course the waiting list is long. However, I have great news. There has recently been a major discovery that will allow us to repair our world. Our cows will continue to multiply at a much more rapid rate lowering the cost of beef. The oceans and air will soon return to their once pristine state. I am sure each and everyone of you wants to know about this major discovery and I have beside me our top scientist who will explain his wonderful discovery." Ana Asea One extended a hand to the scientist leading him to the microphone.

"I would like to introduce a warm," One gave a slight grin, "welcome to the man who will save us. Dr. Wiseman!" The Anna Asea led the clapping as Dr. Wiseman walked over to the podium.

"Hello my fellow Earthlings. My name is Dr. Wiseman and I have good news for you. We have discovered a cure for our sick world. I, along with some of my most trusted and intelligent scientists, have uncovered a bacterial strain found in the Allen Hills meteorite which smashed in the Antarctica over thirteen thousand years ago," Dr. Wiseman paused and then raised both hands with his fingers pointing out toward the heavens and shouted into the microphone. "This bacteria is the KEY that will restore our plankton to its once healthy state."

The signs above the cameras displayed

APPLAUSE...APPLAUSE...APPLAUSE....

The audience clapped along with the music coming from the speakers set on the stage. A few minutes passed when the music slowly subsided as Ana Asea One swayed back and forth to the rhythm like he was enjoying the festivities.

"Yes, today is a time for celebration," Ana Asea One said into his own microphone and then turned toward the doctor. "It is a time to reflect on how Mother Nature's attempt to destroy us has failed. Fortunately, all of her efforts have been overcome with good old human ingenuity. The human race has fought a long hard battle against Mother Nature," the Ana Asea paused, "and we... have...WON!"

The signs above the cameras blinked

CHEER...CHEER...CHEER...

The audience waved their hands and shouted with enthusiasm as they watched the signs blink telling them what to do.

"What is so wonderful about this meteorite is it came from Mars," Dr. Wiseman said. "On this monumental occasion I, along with the Ana Asea Sevens, have chosen to be the first ones to bring back the Mars bacteria to Earth. Our ships are ready for transport as we speak.

This bacteria will allow us the ability to create multiple strains at such a pace I would venture to say will heal our world in record time."

Ana Asea One turned to Dr. Wisemen, "Let's give a big applause to our new Savior of the World!"

The displays blinked

APPLAUSE...CHEER...APPLAUSE...CHEER...

The crowd erupted in a euphoria of screams and clapping. A man beside the sign waved his arms enticing even greater audience participation, Ana Asea One walked over to the podium where Dr. Wiseman stood. Dr. Wiseman turned and walked away.

"As we ready our venture into space in order to save our planet I want you to know that I will be leaving my most trusted servants to lead in my stead. General Sanchez, as you know, has been awarded the World Medal of Honor for his heroism in Africa. He will lead, along with the other Ana Aseas' Companions, while we travel to Mars to gather more bacteria in order to save our world. Please give these men the respect and obedience you have graciously given us." Ana Asea One turned to Sanchez. "General? Would you like to say a few words?"

Sanchez caught unaware of all of this looked around only to feel the guards nudging him toward the podium. He walked up to the microphone met by a round of cheers and applause. He leaned into the microphone. "Did this news surprise you as much as it did me?"

The audience clapped and cheered.

"I just hope for our sake that when our leaders leave for Mars they don't forget to come back," General Sanchez smiled and looked to Ana Asea One as nervous laughter passed through the crowd. "But then if they couldn't find any more of this rare bacteria I doubt they would want to, wouldn't you agree?"

Silence filled the crowd.

"But we know in our hearts that the Ana Asea Sevens would never leave us to die on this planet. These are the ones we chose to lead us and we know their decisions have been instrumental in shaping the world as it is today," Sanchez said.

"He is enjoying this too much I fear," Ana Asea Two whispered to One.

"We need to get him off the stage," Ana Asea Three whispered to the rest.

"Agreed," Ana Asea One said and walked back to the podium.

"After all," continued the General, "do we really know if that rock they found actually contains..."

"Thank you General for your ongoing wit and wisdom," One quickly interrupted the General and turned to the audience with a smile. "He is a joker at times and there are times when his humor does seem to get a little dark. I believe it is his dark side that was necessary for him to be able to accomplish all of these heroic feats," Ana Asea One said as he motioned Carlos offstage and paused like he was deep in thought. He raised his head and stared at the audience. "To be fair, the General was only stating the fears that would eventually arise from news organizations and such behind our backs...to instill fear and uncertainty. But we want you to know those fears are unfounded. But you say, how can we be sure?" Ana Asea One asked. "First off, we ourselves have undergone hybridization and only feed on raw meat. We have loaded only enough to last us only a few weeks. We have to return to Earth, that is, if we want to eat." The One gave a big smile. "And I have a big appetite!" He rubbed his stomach and smiled.

The crowd giggled at his response. Ana Asea One gave them all a big grin.

"When we do return we will be launching an ongoing mission not only to Mars, but also to venture out further and further to other planets, other worlds. But who will pilot these ships? We can't nor can anyone who has become a Crosser, at least not yet. But there will come a time when a suitable planet is found to sustain livestock. I know there are many out there waiting to be discovered. It is time that mankind spread her wings and fly to the stars." The clapping resumed along with some shouts and hoorays, but not quite the fervor as before.

"As you know it is just not feasible to transport animals into outer space. So, only those who have not had DNA recoding will be allowed access to our space program. The really tough part about all of this is finding enough vegetarians who want to fly!" the Ana Asea chuckled along with the audience.

"But who would want to leave now that our planet is healing? Trust me when I tell you that there is nothing to fear. We have won and I would like to also inform you that the price of DNA recoding has now been reduced by almost ninety percent! Now everyone can join the ranks of being called a Crosser. You can enjoy fine dining at Tartars and other restaurants of like. Yes, today is a day of change. A day of hope and a day of conquest!"

The crowd burst into a roar of excitement.

Ana Asea One held up his hands to quiet the crowd. "In the near future, we will be exploring the outer reaches of our galaxy in order to find new worlds to conquer." The Ana Asea waved a hand. "So there is no need to worry. We have heroes among us, one being General Sanchez. He will help lead us into this new area of Earth renewal. Thank you and I hope to see you all watch as we take to the stars in the coming weeks," Ana Asea One said and turned over the microphone to Frank, his public relations man.

"Let's hear it for our thoughtful and benevolent leaders who would rather risk their lives for our world than task others to risk theirs," Frank stated with a grin from ear to ear. "Yes, our modern day Saviors are willing to take a big sacrifice flying to Mars." Frank turned toward the Ana Aseas and then back to the audience and whispered, "Better them than me, don't you think?" The crowd applauded and cheered. "Now who wants to become a Crosser? Steaks every night? No more spinach? Are you as excited as I am?" The crowd cheered. "We are in the process of building new hybrid stations in every city. All we ask is for your patience. If you want to join the growing ranks of Crossers all you have to do is contact Hybrid Central and you will be given a number and location. Unless of course, you want to sign up for our space exploration program, then you need to call..."

The leaders left the stage and were walking together down the stairs.

"When is the next transport ship to Mars scheduled?" Ana Asea One whispered to the other leaders.

"In two weeks," Ana Asea Five replied in a hushed voice.

"What's taking so long?" Ana Asea One asked.

"What's the hurry? Getting a little nervous down here?" came a voice from behind.

Ana Asea One stopped in his tracks. "Sanchez? What are you doing here?"

"Just wondering what you guys are up to and why I was chosen to keep the peace while you guys are gone?" Carlos asked.

"You are a hero in the eyes of your fellow men. I thought it would be an honor for you to run the planet until we return."

"It's the return I'm worried about."

"Oh Carlos, you are the cautious type, aren't you?" Number Two asked.

"Yes and it is a trait that has kept me alive," Sanchez retorted and walked away.

"I just can't wait to get off this dying rock," Ana Asea Four whispered to the others as he watched Sanchez disappear into the crowd.

"What do you think they will do when they find out we aren't coming back?" Number One asked.

"Who cares? Those idiots will more than likely create more destruction to the world than global warming could ever do I am betting," Ana Asea Three intoned.

"I don't trust Sanchez," Ana Asea One stated aloud to the rest of the Ana Aseas.

"I thought he was one of your most trusted servants outside of your Companion," replied Ana Asea Five.

"He's a little too ambitious I fear," Ana Asea One said. "Remember that transport accident off of Ireland a few years ago?"

"Yes. Wasn't it due to pilot error?" Ana Asea Seven asked.

"I'm not so sure."

Chapter 25

EARTH

Kangerlussuaq World Office
Nuuk, Greenland
Monday, January 5, 0021

(Two Days Later)

"Ana Asea One?" his secretary beeped. "General Sanchez is here," she said as she pulled some documents from the desk as she held the receiver on her shoulder. "No sir...He didn't say..." She put her hand over the mouthpiece and looked at the General. "The Ana Asea wants to know why are you here."

"It's urgent that I talk to him. It's a matter of world security."

She relayed the message. "Sir? Yes sir...I will tell him."

"Wait here," she said.

Four hours later the intercom buzzed. "Yes sir," she said and turned to General Sanchez. "He will see you now."

Carlos Sanchez hated to wait, even if it was for the Ana Asea. He opened the door and walked over the Meshkabad rug with his dirty boots toward the already standing Ana Asea. "What's the meaning of making me wait over four hours?"

"I was unaware we had an appointment today, Mr. Sanchez," One said as he looked down at the mud tracked all over his beautiful oriental rug.

"GEN...um...we didn't," the General said. He suddenly realized what a mistake this could be if his temper got the best of him. "I am just concerned that the safety of the Ana Aseas could be in danger." General Sanchez sat down uninvited.

"Have a seat."

"Thank you, your highness."

The Ana Asea sat in his lambskin leather rubbed chair. He rubbed the arm as he talked. "This chair is made from the finest lambskin available."

"I'm sure you will miss it, Herr Ana Asea," the General smirked as he watched for any telltale signs.

The Ana Asea squirmed for a second and then quickly recomposed himself. "What on earth do you mean?"

"You know exactly what I mean. That speech Saturday night."

"What about the speech?" the Ana Asea paused. "Oh, I see you are upset that I didn't inform you about your promotion earlier. I thought it would please you more to hear about it with the rest of the world."

"Let's cut to the chase. You know damn well the Earth is toast. We got twenty years at best before this planet ends up looking like Venus, hot and dead. I'm not interested in keeping the peace on a planet full of tombstones."

"I don't know what you're..."

The General interrupted the Ana Asea and he knew it could cost him dearly, but he didn't care anymore. "Don't piss on my back and tell me it's raining. Your space exploration program is your ticket to Mars. You guys are heading out of Dodge before someone figures all this out and the riots start. I'm not going to keep the peace so you guys can sneak out the back door. Only a fool fights in a burning house and this place is really starting to smoke."

"I see," Ana Asea One said. He stared at the General who stared back. The minutes passed and still, no one said a word. "You're right, Carlos." The Ana Asea sat back and relaxed into his chair. "I will miss this leather chair," he paused. "The transports will be ready to go in less than two weeks. If you keep this news to yourself, I will add you to the Pinta."

"Which one are you on?"

"The Niña."

"I want to be on that one," the General said.

"The Niña is only for the hand picked."

"Then I guess I just joined your little gated community," Carlos said.

The Ana Asea turned his head away from Carlos and looked out the window. "You win, General." The Ana Asea smiled. "I will make room on the Niña for one more. Just keep this under your hat until then. Okay?"

"Well, I guess I can keep a low profile for the next few weeks," the General smiled and arose from his chair.

The Ana Asea stared at General Sanchez as he walked out of his office.

"I knew it. I've given my best years to further their cause and this is how I'm treated?" Carlos said aloud as he got into the rental. "Once we get to Mars, I am going to get a little payback from those guys." The General sat in traffic with the air conditioner on high. "They made a mess of Earth and I'm not going to let them screw up Mars too!"

Two hours had passed since the General left Ana Asea One's office. One waited for the lights to dim and he watched as the curtain parted showing a wall with six separate viewing screens.

"Is everyone here?" the Ana Asea One asked as he scanned the view screens. "Good."

"What's this about? We are busy preparing for the trip," Ana Asea Three said.

"General Carlos Sanchez came by for a visit today. He has uncovered our plans and has threatened to expose us if we don't let him board."

"What are your plans?" Ana Asea Seven asked.

"Sanchez is dangerous and a ruthless killer. I could always count on him when it came to doing...what was necessary to maintain world order, but we have no need for his type on the new world."

"What do you want from us?" Ana Asea Two asked.

The Ana Asea One was silent for a moment as he recalled earlier when General Sanchez stormed into his office with mud on his boots. The mud stained Meshkabad had to be removed and the thought of losing his precious rug still enraged the Ana Asea One. *That son of a bitch will pay for his actions.* Number One looked to the monitor and said, "I need someone."

Chapter 26

EARTH

Federal Building
Suite 303
New York, New York U.S.A.
Friday, January 9, 0021

(Four Days Later)

Carlos was back in his office located in the New York Federal Building. His calendar had been cleared except for one last appointment. He marked the launch day on his calendar with a big red X. "A few more days and I'll be off this stinking rock. Those bastards aren't going to get away with leaving me here," Carlos said when he heard footsteps coming down the hall. The clock on the wall showed it was five minutes until four o'clock when there was a knock on the General's door.

"Enter." The General stood up and placed one hand on his 40-caliber resting in his holster strapped to his side. Carlos watched the doorknob as it slowly turned and a man dressed in a dark blue suit strolled nonchalantly into his office.

"Quitting a little early today, Mr. Sanchez?" the man said smiling on the other side of the dark stained oak desk. He looked down to see Carlos' hand on his side-arm. "Expecting some trouble?"

"Just being careful," Carlos replied. "Can I help you?"

"My name is Special Agent Wilson and I came by today to congratulate you. I hear you will be our next leader."

"Thank you," Sanchez said. "But as you can see I'm a little busy right now."

"Perhaps right now, but you'll have plenty of time when I'm through with you," Agent Wilson grinned. "This isn't a social call Mr. Sanchez."

"It's General and if you don't leave now. I'll have to call the authorities."

Agent Wilson placed both hands on the desk and leaned in toward Carlos in a threatening manner. "I know you're dirty and I am going to take you down. I know what happened in Luanshya."

"I saved that village from a group of terrorists. Don't you ever watch the news? Now get out of here. I don't have time for this."

"When I'm finished with you," the Agent smiled, "you're going to have nothing but time. You see Mr. Sanchez, I just want you to know that I finally received permission to investigate the Luanshya invasion."

"Why tell me now? Why not just indict me when you have something?"

"Because I want to see you squirm. I want to see you sweat. I want the world to see the kind of man you really are. I want to watch as they remove your medals, awards, and strip of you of being a general. I hear prison meals these days consist of mostly dead mice and cockroaches for people like you."

"Agent Wilson. You won't live to see the day."

"That's Special Agent Wilson to you," the man said and smiled. "Oh yeah? I have a meeting in a few minutes with the attorney general. Her office is just down the hall if you want to sit in, but I got a feeling that a coward like you doesn't have the stomach for it. I am also going to be on *Rat Catchers* tonight and I think you may find the topic very interesting," Agent Wilson gloated.

"Get out of my office, Wilson!" Sanchez stood with his right hand holding a tight grip on his gun.

"Oh I'll go, but I just want you to know I'll be around, kind of like a cat playing with a mouse. You're going down Mr. Sanchez. You are going down hard." As Special Agent Kevin Wilson shut the door behind him, Sanchez threw a paperweight and watched it slam against the door and fall to the ground.

Carlos was fuming. He grabbed his pursal and left his office seconds later. He took the elevator to the underground parking lot and walked toward his personal spot. When his black SUV came into sight, he took out a special pair of glasses and pulled out a spray can, something he did religiously. The General had made a number of enemies throughout his career and he was not one to take chances, especially on his life. He sprayed his door – nothing; then the passenger side door – no new fingerprints or residue. He sprayed the front hood and still nothing. The General was about to get into his car and then remembered the look in the Ana Asea One's eyes when he exposed their little plot and that made him feel a little uneasy. So he took his hand off the door handle and decided to be a little extra precautious tonight, so he crawled under the car with a flashlight in hand. He shined the light into the engine compartment and saw a small charge of C4 wired to the ignition and to the hood latch. "I guess they decided they didn't have room for me after all." He carefully removed the wired C4 from his car. Then an idea came to him. "Those guys want to see a big bang. I think I'll just give them one. In fact, I may just be able to kill two birds with this stone," he said as he stared at the C4 in his hand.

The General rushed back to his office, unlocked his metal storage cabinet, and picked up twenty pounds of C4. He inserted blasting caps into each one and placed them in a large black leather briefcase. He walked down the stairway to the first floor of the garage. He walked toward his car like he did before but this time he casually walked up to Agent Wilson's car. He stopped to tie his shoe and as he knelt down he carefully slid the briefcase full of explosives under Agent Wilson's black SUV. He then slid underneath Wilson's car and connected the explosives to the ignition wire. "We'll see who makes the news tonight," the General said and slowly walked out of the garage undetected.

"I guess that just about sums it up," Agent Wilson said to the attorney general.

"I believe we have enough for an indictment," she said. "By the way who are your sources?"

"All I can tell you is I have a guy who has been eavesdropping on the General's conversations."

"How? Those lines are secure. Only Big Ben has full access."

"He said he's familiar with code breaking technology."

"Can he be trusted?"

"With the information he has already provided, I believe so."

"But that won't hold up in court."

"It will under the Patriot Act."

"I don't think this counts as an act of terrorism."

"It will be with what I have. It's some pretty damning evidence," Agent Wilson replied and rose from his seat.

"Okay. You know I'm going out on a limb for you."

"I'll send you what I have so far. You're going to be a hero when we're finished with General Sanchez." Agent Wilson opened the office door to the hallway.

The attorney general grabbed her purse. "Sounds good. I'll walk you to your car?"

"Thank you. We can talk more on the way."

"Executive level?"

"I'm ready when you are."

Minutes later, Agent Wilson bid the attorney general goodbye as he sat inside his car and watched her walk away. He then closed the door. "Ignition on."

KA-BOOM!

The intense explosion echoed throughout the garage followed by flames shooting out from the main entrance. The entire Federal Building sitting directly above the parking garage shook in response. Flames blanketed the cracked ceiling and the smoke belched out from the underground parking lot. A crowd of curious onlookers gathered to see what had caused such an event. The fire department arrived within minutes of the onslaught and pulled as close to the fractured building as they dared. They pointed their hoses toward the inferno and unsuccessfully tried to squelch the intense flames.

"We're going to have to let this one burn itself out," one fireman said to his partner.

"Keep the hoses straight. We have to make it look good," the other fireman replied and looked over to see the holovision cameras and crew had arrived.

Two more engines showed up along with a half dozen police cars. Firemen and officers ran helter-skelter through the crowds toward the Federal Building.

"Reminds me of Oklahoma," Officer Tom said.

"What happened there?" Officer Dan asked.

"A crackpot terrorist dynamited it with fertilizer."

"Fertilizer?"

"Yep. Read about in history class. This looks like the same M.O."

Both officers arrived at the entrance and stopped. "Did they catch the guy?"

"Yep. He and his accomplice drove a truck underneath the building, very similar to this."

"Can't these guys be a little more creative?"

Cracks ran up and down the Federal Building as a result of the attack. The missing and shattered windowpanes decorated the first six floors above the building. The people surrounding the building watched the entire structure waver in response.

"Jesus. This is one of the worst I have seen!"

"Let's just hope the Feds built this thing sturdy," replied the second fireman.

"Government workers built this? Oh man! We are so screwed."

"Cut the jokes," came the captain's voice through their headphones. The captain sent his men to the other side of the building where another fire was emerging. Suddenly the entire structure collapsed within itself.

On the garage entrance laid those unfortunate souls covered with glass and burnt to the bone. They were just leaving to go home and got caught in the middle of the blast and fire. Some were burnt so badly that one couldn't identify if they were male or female.

The helicopters swirled around the smoke and debris as Channel H-2 floated their remote cameras in the air as they filmed the live footage of the aftermath. The news media speculated that the Terra Bulls were responsible for the attack on the federal building.

"Well, well," the General said as he drove his rental down the interstate. "I see the Ana Asea Sevens wanted to play hardball." Carlos Sanchez turned off the main road on to a partially hidden dirt road that led to his special hideaway.

General Sanchez watched the news the next day in his cabin in Mount Taurus near Cold Springs on the Hudson River an hour or so drive outside of the Big Apple. He used this little getaway for times when he thought he may be in the crosshairs of some dissident whose family member he may have had to relocate or erase. He knew he would be safe for the time being and he needed a plan to even the score when it came to the Ana Aseas. He continued to watch the holovision when the announcer told him exactly what to do.

"The man responsible for this terrorist act is a lone wolf named Yusef Mohabajinagin." A picture of a man with sandals, wearing a dirty white turban and beard was shown standing with a rifle over his shoulder. "Yusef Mohabajinagin was captured early this morning shouting the slogans of the Terra Bulls. He is in custody and no longer a threat to the world."

"Thank you, Jason," Courtney replied. "It is rumored that the Ana Aseas in their fight for world peace will stand in judgment of the crimes against Mr. Mohabajinagin. And now in the news, The Terrorist's Red Alert has been activated for the next two days worldwide. Please stay inside and take all necessary precautio..." Sanchez turned off the holovision.

The Ana Aseas are going to stand in judgment of Yusef? hmmm... Carlos thought to himself. "Looking to cover your tracks, Señor One? We'll see about that." The General turned the holovision back on.

"...Steven Carpenter just broke the three minute mile today by nine point five seconds and that takes care of the sports world. The Ana Aseas have gathered today in New York City painfully near the attack on the Federal Building. They have assured us the world is a safe place and these attacks are the results of a few remaining fugitives who will soon be captured. Now, to leave on a positive note, the Ana Aseas will be boarding the Niña next Saturday morning from their new launch site on Chappaquiddick Island at sunrise. Stay tuned for live coverage of this monumental event!"

"It should be a real blast to see our leaders embrace space exploration with such vigor," Courtney said.

The General had heard enough. He picked up the telephone.

"Hello."

"This is General Sanchez, let me speak to Brian Donager."

"One moment please."

Brian Donager came on the line. "Mr. Sanchez! I thought you were dead?"

"General Sanchez thank you."

"I am sorry General. What can I do to be of assistance?"

"I need you to help me out just one more time?"

"Of course General. What can I do?"

"Do you still have friends at Brotherly Love?"

"The Maximum Security Prison?"

"Yes. I need an inmate released."

"Free Yusef? Are you crazy? What've you been drinking?" came the voice from the other end of the line. "The man just admitted to the world what he did. He has more guards around him than the Pentagon."

"Well, he is..um.. innocent. As you know I don't like anyone getting a raw deal."

"But the papers say…"

"Let me explain," General Sanchez said. "It was me that Yusef tried to kill."

"And you want to give him another shot at it?" Brian asked.

"Yusef was hired by the Ana Aseas to have me killed and as you now know he didn't. So they're about to double cross him."

"What are you talking about? Yusef is a terrorist. He even admitted it!"

"Of course he did. He was told to because the explosion had to be explained."

"He destroyed the entire Federal Building along with practically everyone in it!" Brian replied.

"You don't know the whole story," Sanchez replied with a smile.

"What do you want?"

"Turn on your pursal scrambler to frequency one."

"Frequency one? Okay. Done."

"Good. Now I want you to do exactly what I tell you."

Kangerlussuaq World Office
Nuuk, Greenland

"I think you all know why I have summoned you," Ana Asea One said.

"We do, however…" Ana Asea Two paused, "this could backlash on us if we are found to be responsible."

Before Ana Asea One could answer, Ana Asea Four remarked, "When I agreed to have the General, uh silenced, I assumed it would have been done a little more…discreetly?"

"I understand your concerns my fellow Ana Aseas. I too was surprised at the magnitude of this undertaking. I promise to find out why my directives were so poorly carried out."

"You better. We don't want anything to go wrong at this juncture," Ana Asea Five said.

"I assure you, the man I hired will have a lot to answer for his... let's say intemperance?"

"What do you plan to do?" Ana Asea Two asked.

"Well, now that the General isn't an issue anymore, we've no need for Yusaf. Agreed?" Ana Asea One asked as he waited for the nods from the other leaders before continuing. "Yusef was picked up yesterday morning by the local police. He was beaten and tortured until he confessed on HV to being a rogue Terra Bull. His confession was aired last night on the evening news."

"I saw it," Ana Asea Two remarked. "I also heard make-up was having a hard time covering and hiding the beatings inflicted on him earlier that day."

"You could see some swelling, but that can easily be explained. I did like his confession and I was pretty comfortable with the believability that Yusef portrayed himself as the lone terrorist. Once we have him executed that should ensure this problem goes away permanently," Ana Asea One said to the other Ana Aseas as he sipped a glass of his favorite Richeborg Pinot Noir wine. "A toast to our success and to Mars." Ana Asea One raised his glass along with the other six. He then downed the red elixir and sighed, "Only seven hundred bottles were produced and it's a shame we cannot bring all of them with us."

"Ever since I became a Crosser, fermented grapes in wine make me sick. However this one doesn't?" Ana Asea Seven looked to Asea One.

"Yes, I had all these genetically modified so I could add blood to the mix."

"Ahhh...Smart thinking. Now then, how are you going to execute Yusef?"

"Didn't you offer him immunity if he confessed?" Ana Asea Six asked. "Execution isn't what I would call immunity."

"Oh? Did I say I would grant him immunity *before* we executed him?" Ana Asea One asked and laughed.

Chapter 27

Cape Kopechne
Chappaquiddick Island, Massachusetts
Saturday, January 17, 0021
0800 Hours

(Eight Days Later)

There was a huge crowd forming around the Niña. Eager faces appeared out of nowhere in hopes to catch a glimpse of the seven Ana Aseas. The media coverage blanketed the planet. The day was declared a national holiday so everyone could proudly see that the world was back and space exploration would become the next frontier of hope. Security was especially tight in the days leading up to the launch. Only the top officials, scientists, and technicians were allowed close to the Niña.

Chris Rice looked around the transport as he waited for the Ana Asea Sevens to appear. Ever since he had gotten the call from Sanchez he had had a lot of trouble sleeping. He remembered how he had sent in the Hueys to attack those poor African people. He still felt guilty about what he had done in order to get money for his wife's surgery. Unfortunately she had died before getting to the operating table.

Now he was put in charge of guarding the Niña so he had complete access to her. Chris grabbed a backpack from the storage folded it up and place it inside a very large leather bound briefcase as he entered the spaceship.

"Excuse me! No one is allowed in the engine compart…. Oh sorry, General Rice." The guard immediately straightened to attention and saluted, eyes staring forward.

Chris returned the salute. "At ease Private. Has anyone been in here lately?"

"No sir," the Private spoke still standing erect.

The General could see the fear in his eyes. "Your name?"

"Bailey, sir."

"Private Bailey has anything unusual been going on around here?"

The Private relaxed and placed his hands behind his back. "Besides the animals, nothing really."

"Animals?"

"Yes sir! They gutted half the ship to make room for chickens and some roosters."

"Chickens?"

"Must be a thousand of 'em, sir!"

"Where are they?"

"I don't know, sir."

"Well go find out and report back to me. I want to know why there are chickens in here and who authorized them."

"I have orders to guard this station."

"Well, Private looks like you have new orders. Now get going!"

"Yes sir!" The Private saluted and hurriedly walked away from the engine room.

"Chickens?" Chris repeated a couple of times to himself. He felt like a caged animal himself. If he didn't go through with Sanchez's plan then Carlos would expose his dealings in Africa. Carlos had covered his tracks well. He had wired all the WDG Luanshyan money into an offshore account under General Rice's name instead of his own. Carlos then had the Krugers transferred out of Chris' account to other offshore holdings leaving Chris the original agreed-upon amount. Chris didn't think anything of it until he got the call last week. Carlos, it seemed, was holding all the cards. Do his bidding or face a military court-martial for his role in stealing the Shyans money in order to get his wife medical treatment. All nice and neatly wrapped. Especially since everyone thought that Carlos had died in the Federal Building explosion.

Chris looked around to see if anyone else was around. Once he was sure he was alone he opened his briefcase and went to work.

Two hours later General Rice was leaving the engine room when he saw Private Bailey back at his original station.

"The chickens are roosting on deck three." The Private saluted noticing the General's backpack.

"Deck three? That's for passengers."

"I guess some people are getting bumped off the flight, sir."

"For chickens?"

"Seems that way, sir," the Private said still eyeing the backpack.

"At ease. Is this yours?" General Rice asked pushing the backpack into the Private's face.

"No sir!" Bailey said. "Never seen it before, sir."

"Well, someone left it in...THE ENGINE ROOM!" General Rice screamed. "Have you seen anyone entering or leaving the engine room?"

"Only you sir."

"Then how did this empty backpack get in here?"

"I don't know, sir."

"Then who should I ask?" General Rice was only inches from the Private's face.

"I don't know, sir."

"Is that all you can say, Private?"

"Yes sir, I mean, no sir."

"How long have you been at this post, Private?"

"Since 0400 sir."

"Did you sweep the area after your replacement?"

"Yes sir and I did not see the backpack, sir."

"It was hidden in the back. I almost missed it myself. Who did you replace?"

"Lawson, sir."

"It looks like Private Lawson is going to have a visitor."

"Yes sir."

"I expect you to make a more thorough sweep of any room you have been ordered to protect from now on."

"Yes sir. It won't happen again, sir."

Chris could see and almost smell the fear emanating from the Private. He nodded and placed his hand on the Private's shoulder and looked at him straight in the eyes.

"Good. Now make sure no one enters without proper authorization. The engine room is secure and I am going to report that through your recklessness you allowed unauthorized contraband on board. Do you know what that can do to one's record?"

"Yes sir. I'm sorry sir. I...I don't know what to say."

The General stared at him and sighed. "Do you understand that lives of our leaders are in your hands?"

"Yes sir. I am proud to serve the Sevens."

"If I overlook this incident, will I regret my decision?"

"No sir!" the Private yelled.

"I want you to get rid of this backpack immediately. Do... you... understand Private?" General Rice threw the backpack at him.

"Yes sir."

"Good. This ship is due for take off at noon which is in a little over two hours. If something goes wrong you may find yourself clasped in irons for the rest of your long life. Do you understand?"

"Yes sir. Nothing to worry about sir. I will make a final inspection before I leave the ship."

The General stared at Private Bailey for a minute and then finally spoke. "I will consider this matter settled. Now don't make me regret my decision." General Rice turned and walked down the hall toward the transport exits.

It was ten in the morning when the first Ana Asea walked out to the platform in front of the Niña. The other six Ana Aseas walked behind him to the platform and waved to the crowds and camera. Ana Asea One leaned into the microphone connected to the podium with a sign in front with bright green letters, which spelled NEW HOPE against a sky blue background with sunflowers, wisteria vines, poppies, and paintings of happy bees flying around them.

"Thank you," he said and waited for the crowd to calm. "Thank you." Ana Asea One waved again and watched the crowd hoot and holler. He waited another minute and tapped the microphone and the crowd calmed. "It brings me great joy to see all of you here to witness the next step in Man's evolution." The crowd clapped and some hoots started again, but the Ana Asea waved them into silence. "We have walked the precipice of human disaster and it has been a perilous journey for all. Today..." the Ana Asea looked around and spread his hands to the sky, "today is the first...the beginning...the new evolution of man's quest. And you ask what that quest shall be? It is the mark of our intelligence and determination to thwart all obstacles in our way. We've conquered our global warming concerns. The plankton has survived and the fish are returning to our seas in abundance. The animals and plants on our mother are returning, growing, and bringing about Earth's NEW HOPE."

The crowd shouted, "New Hope...New Hope...New Hope!"

The Ana Asea allowed it for a few more minutes before he continued, "The New Hope is the hope that we've learned. We've learned many lessons as we stared into the abyss. We know...we know...no matter what nature can throw at us, we can overcome and mankind will continue. We will continue our right to exist in whatever way we choose."

The crowd fired up again with more hoots and chants. The Sevens looked at the faces in the crowd and returned their smiles. *I hope they all rot in hell* Ana Asea One thought to himself. *I've sacrificed so much to help them and they've repaid me by polluting my earth.*

"To show our beloved world and all its inhabitants that we care so much for her, we the Sevens will be the first to step foot on Mars. When we pass the moon, remember that we are the pioneers of this New and Improved Age. We'll soon return with enough bacteria to continue in helping heal our beloved Earth. This new bacteria will allow us to create a world where there is no smog, no pollution. A planet where we can once again play and enjoy being outside like our ancestors once did. Today will live in infamy!"

General Sanchez was watching the big event from his cabin. "He better come through on his promises or I'll have his hide. Those lying bastard Ana Aseas, leaving us here to die while they fly off into the sunset. We'll just see about that," General Sanchez said to the holovision.

The Ana Aseas Seven pointed toward the wall facing the rocket engines. "Here is our terrorist, Yusef, who has been strapped to the launch pad. His face is covered as requested and he will die for killing all those innocent people at the Federal Building. This is how he has chosen to die today as penitence for his evil deeds. As we leave this earth aboard the Niña, Yusef will also leave this world from the flames of our ship's engines. It will be instantaneous and he asked to receive his punishment in this manner to show others what's in store for those who terrorize others. You are watching history being made as mankind spreads his seeds to the stars and the journey has now begun!"

The Ana Aseas turned in unison and walked to the transport followed by the CEOs of Biochore and Humanochore along with their families and handpicked officers while the crowd clapped and cheered. The onlookers wished them Godspeed while others kneeled and prayed for their safe return. The transport's engines began to glow and as fast as a cheetah could chase its prey the rockets glowed from red to violet and the entire audience felt the ground shake. Like a jet plane, the Niña traveled down the runway and flew off into the distance.

"Nice little farewell speech," Ana Asea Seven said as the flight attendant brought them all drinks.

"Even though our first coup failed I think everything has worked out just fine," Number Two said. "The People's Coalition was a good idea and it would have worked except for..."

"Okay, okay," Ana Asea Three interrupted. "So launching a nuclear attack was a bad idea. How did I know the winds would change that much?"

"Not to worry. It's all behind us now. Way behind us!" Ana Asea Five laughed.

"You know? Those fools actually believed that a computer randomly picked the world leaders," Ana Asea Six remarked.

"It's harder for me to think they believe we're coming back!" Ana Asea Four chuckled.

"Farewell Earthlings, you bunch of suckers." Number One raised his glass to a toast and everyone joined in.

"Are the colonies finished?" Number Four asked.

"All but a few. We had to cut back on the original number of people scheduled for Mars," Number One said.

"Why?" Number Three asked.

"Dinner of course," Number One said. "Remember the chickens?"

"Of course. Can't we get a BuffaPrime or two?" Number Five spoke up.

"Once we restructure some of the domettes from living quarters to feedlots, I don't see a problem. But we have to keep it a secret from the rest of those vegetarians," Number One said in a condescending tone.

"I think we may have a problem on Mars." Number Four hung up his pursal.

"What's the matter?" Number One asked.

"Danny Maltido."

"Who?"

"I just received a call from my Companion, René, and it seems that we may have a little problem to deal with when we arrive."

Ding

"This is your captain speaking. We are approaching lunar orbit and in thirty minutes we will enter a Hohmann Transfer Orbit. Once we are locked in position over Huygens Mons which, by the way, happens to be slightly taller than Mt. Everest on Earth, a thirty-second laser burst will hit our wind sails propelling us to a speed where we will be able to reach Mars in less than three days. The cabin lights are green for now, but when it turns red make sure you have buckled yourselves securely in your seats. Seconds before Laser Burst Impact you will first feel a bag of air expand in front and behind you to soften the sudden acceleration. There is no need to panic as long as you are in your seats. Thank you for flying, PanStar."

Ding

"I'm getting a little hungry," Ana Asea Two said. "Anything I can get you guys before the big bang?"

"Bring us a couple of birds," Number Four said.

Number Two returned with two de-feathered dead chickens. He took out his knife and sliced them up as they each grabbed their favorite parts.

"Nothing better than chicken tartar don't you agree?" Ana Asea Six asked as he bit into the chicken's neck.

"Yep. Ever since I became a Crosser, the idea of cooked meat just turns me off," said Ana Asea Seven as the others nodded in agreement when the intercom came alive once again.

Ding...Ding

"This is the captain speaking and we are now closing in on the moon. Please return to your seats and prepare for Laser Burst Impact in five minutes."

Ding...Ding

"So what's the problem with Mr. Maltido?" Ana Asea One asked.

BANG!

"What was that?" Ana Asea Two asked as they all looked at one another.

"The engines have stopped!" Ana Asea Three answered.

"I don't think it's anything to worry about. They're probably just positioning us for the Big Bang," Ana Asea Five said when suddenly everyone felt a rumbling throughout the ship and the lights started to flicker.

The inflight hologram automatically turned on. Everyone stopped what they were doing and looked at the screen.

Ding...Ding...Ding

"This is the captain and for some reason our engines have gone offline. There is no reason for concern." The captain's speech began to unravel. "We are in a stabl:e o.rb'i"t a.n"d ..." Fuzzy lines began to interrupt the captain's appearance as his image wavered and disappeared only to be replaced by a familiar face to the Sevens.

"Good evening Ana Asea Sevens."

Number One looked up and gasped. "What's Sanchez doing on our screen? I thought Yusef had taken care of him."

"I guess you are wondering what I am doing here and I know you are all relieved to see that I am alive and well. I am afraid I may not have as good of news for you."

A worried look came over the entire group.

"Ah, my cameras are showing there looks to be a little concern coming over your faces as well as it should." Sanchez stopped and smiled. "My intel has confirmed a small explosive has just detonated and that is why your engines have stopped. I know you will be able to maintain lunar orbit until a rescue ship can reach you, but unfortunately I have some even more bad news. My sources have informed me that a small nuclear device has been planted on your transport and is set to go off in," Sanchez stopped, looked at his watch and returned to the camera, "Wow! Not very long so I guess I will hurry. As a trusted servant to Ana Asea One I felt it was my sworn duty to tell you of these dire circumstances as soon as I became apprised of this unfortunate situation. There is only one problem." Sanchez bowed his head showing a small frown. "It seems I'm too late to help you out of your little predicament. I can't tell you where the bomb is and even if I knew it probably wouldn't matter because to disarm this little nuclear firecracker would take at least ten minutes. I know because before I contacted you I tried to figure out some way to save you all." Sanchez sported a bigger grin. "To show my un-dying, oops that's probably not the word I should use right now. To show my, um, continuing loyalty to you all for your countless generosities I felt it would be the least I could do is to let you see the uh final countdown? Good luck and have a happy rest of your, um premature shortened existence. I hope you spend the rest of your time thinking well of me as I of you." Sanchez smiled into the camera as the monitor flashed

Countdown

And the numbers began to scroll across the middle of the screen.

5:00...4:59...4:58...

"I thought you had him killed?" Ana Asea Three asked.

"That Son of a Bitch! I knew he couldn't be trusted," Ana Asea One exclaimed.

"What are we going to do?" Ana Asea Two interrupted.

"He's lying. No way he could get through our security," Ana Asea Six said.

"I agree. It's just a joke. Well, the joke's on him. Ha ha," Ana Asea Four said as they watched in silence as the countdown continued.

00:59...00:30...00:15...00:10...

The screen suddenly went blank and then reappeared as a fat pink pig burst through the middle of the screen sticking his middle finger out at them from his white-gloved hand saying,

"Th..th..th..That's All Suckers!"

The crowd, along with the holovision cameras, watched in awe as the Niña passed the moon's outpost. All of a sudden a bright light appeared and the moon showed an eerie looking halo.

"The ship exploded!" came a shout from the onlookers.

"How could this have happened?" shouted another over the gasping crowd.

- Tragedy in Space -

appeared on the holovision screens across the world.

"The Niña carrying our world leaders, the Ana Asea Sevens, exploded just seconds ago near our moon today. We fear there are no survivors."

The cameras showed a close-up of the explosion from one of the moon's orbiting satellites.

"A sad day for all of us. Details to follow. This is Courtney Hughes with *The Wolf.*"

"Did you see feathers?" Harry turned to his wife as the two senior citizens stared at the screen.

"Of course not! Dear, aren't you due for an eye exam next week?"

"My eyes are fine. I know I saw some feathers."

"Well, you certainly have an imagination don't you?"

"Fine. Don't believe me."

Private Bailey was standing in the crowd as his knees weakened and his faced turned white as a sheet with fear at what he saw. The Private made his way through the crowd. He got in his car and drove north toward Canada never to look back.

All of a sudden Brian heard his ringtone go off as the pursal squawked, "Carlos Sanchez." He pulled his pursal from his belt and watched as it grew into a handset. "I never get tired of watching that," he said as he put the pursal to his ear. "Carlos! I've been waiting for your call," Brian said. "Did you like the burning at the stake?"

"I'm not sure."

"Well I am," Yusef replied over the pursal. "Why did you spare me when I tried to kill you?"

"I needed a favor. Now put Brian back on the line."

A moment later, Sanchez continued, "Good work, Brian. Your tickets have been processed and you will be boarding on the Santa Maria. Chris and I will be on the Pinta next Sunday at 0700 hours. That's if you can make it."

"No worries. I'll see you on the Red Planet," Brian replied and hung up.

"Chris Rice," Sanchez said to his pursal as it was still in celling mode.

"Dialing," the pursal voice replied.

"Carlos?" Chris Rice answered with a hint of anxiety.

"Are you ready?"

"I just have a few loose ends to tie up."

"Then I'll see you next Sunday at 0600," Carlos replied.

"Copy and by the way, would you like to know how I blew it up?" Chris asked.

"Blew what up?" Carlos asked.

"Oh sorry. I forgot about Big Ben."

*****

Sunday morning at 0600 found Carlos, Chris, and Yusef standing close together in the parking lot near the launch site.

"Who took Yusef's spot?" Carlos asked.

"There was this irate middle manager from Biochore who was demanding access to the flight. He said that he and nineteen others were supposed to fly out on the Santa Maria in two weeks, but they all have been bumped. He came down here and threatened to expose the Ana Asea's plan to Mars and stop the mission if he, his family, and the others weren't allowed to leave the planet," Chris said.

"How did he get bumped?"

"Who cares? I just couldn't risk him blowing my chances at getting off of this round oven."

"And so you obliged him?"

"Not the way he wanted, I'll wager," Chris said and laughed.

Carlos quickly glanced at his pursal. "It's about time for us to board." Carlos then turned to Chris. "Are you sure you want to come?"

"I've got nothing to keep me here." Chris shook his head.

"I heard about Julie," Carlos said. "What happened?"

"Julie was on a vent and all prepped for surgery when a power outage occurred. No problem, right? But then the back-up generators failed and no one could explain what or how it all happened."

Carlos turned his head and smiled. Chris noticed Carlos had turned away, but continued. "By the time power was restored," a tear came to Chris' eye, "Julie was dead."

"Well, you did all you could Chris," Carlos said as a slight grin crossed his face. "And at least you can now go with us to Mars."

"Yeah," Chris replied in a subtle tone of defeat.

Carlos slapped Chris on the back. "Now, now, we've given up much to get here. You know Julie would have wanted this for you." Chris nodded. "Okay, let's get going," Carlos said and grabbed his carry-on and stared at Yusef for a minute before he spoke. "Yusef, do you know what to do?"

"Why do you want us to wait six months before my men blow the nuclear power plants?" Yusef asked.

"I want to make sure I don't have to return to this dead rock and if I have to, I want to live a few more years. If Mars works out like I think, then I don't want a bunch of DNA recoded pigs following me."

"They've been told that they can't come," Yusef said.

"They've been told that the earth is healing. What do you think they're going to do when they find out that they've been lied to? Here's some real cash," the General said and handed Yusef a suitcase.

Yusef opened it and saw rows and rows of silver and gold coins. "This is a lot of money. Why are you giving it to me?"

"I have no use for it on Mars. Anyway, it will help you pay the men you're going to need to pull this off. I have a friend on Mars who can reverse the DNA recoding, but he charges a lot. So you and your men will also be able to live on Mars. Dr. Feingold will do the operation once you arrive on our little Red Planet. Here are the coordinates where the Lusitania will be," the General handed Yusef a document that stated where to pick up the explosives, which power plants were to be destroyed, and the rendezvous point. "You have one day to board the ship once the nuclear power plants have exploded. Do you still have your pilot's license? I mean, can you fly something this big?" the General asked.

"Yes sir, Herr General. I know the test pilot for the Niña prototype. I am sure he will be glad when he hears the news."

"Good, then you'll have no problems. Just remember, once I get word that all the power plants have been destroyed, Chris here will send you the launch authorization codes. All you have to do is punch the numbers into the keypad, which will unlock the flight controls. Once the controls are unlocked you have only ten minutes to launch. Do you understand?"

"Yes sir. Thank you sir. I will contact my men and we will do good work for you."

"Good," the General said. "I will see you and your men on Mars in a little over six months." They shook hands and Yusef left.

"Dr. Feingold?" Brian asked. "He's figured out how to reverse the hybridization process?"

"No."

"Then who is this Dr. Feingold?"

Sanchez just smiled.

"He doesn't exist? Then why did you tell him there was...?"

"Do you think he and his men are going to blow up their planet if they think there is no way to get off it?" Carlos interrupted.

"True, but the Lusitania? Isn't it a little risky naming the ship after one that was sunk by a torpedo fired from a German sub during the First World War?"

The General laughed. "Fitting isn't it? I mean who says history doesn't repeat itself? I wonder if they'll figure out the name before she blows." Sanchez turned to Chris. "Now, I hope you've taken care of our little luxury liner."

"Yes sir," Chris said. "Once Yusef enters the combination, all the doors will automatically shut and lock. A quick video will come on telling them that Dr. Feingold has died and so they can't come to Mars. Then a short documentary will appear on the screen above them where I begin to tell them a quick history of how a German torpedo hit and destroyed the passenger ship Lusitania, in 1917. I tell them that, as passengers on this Lusitania, they will have the unexpected honor of reliving this memorable event from World War I. As they watch the real torpedo heading for the ill-fated ship on the screen, they will get the same thrill of an explosion and perish like those did. Seconds after they see the torpedo hit and destroy the real Lusitania, the C4s will light up their ship like a New Year's Eve fireworks display."

"Outstanding!" Carlos exclaimed. "Think he can try to kill me and get away with it."

Chapter 28

MARS

Coronae Laboratories
Coronae Scopulus
Gemini - Sol Saturday 7, 0012
0300 hours

Back at the laboratory Ken watched as his father placed some of the officer's blood on the counter by the sink. He opened the stall directly facing the counter and sat Officer O'Riley on the commode pulling his pants to his ankles.

BAM!

O'Riley's head hit the side of the stall as he slumped over falling to the cold tile.

"He fell off the commode again! Should we put him back on it?" Ken inquired.

"No, but that should keep them stumped for a while," Yeri replied.

"But he saw us," Ken said.

"I don't know that and neither do you. Anyway, do you have any better ideas?"

"He's going to have a doozy of a headache when he wakes up."

Yeri and Ken returned to lab 802 and slowly closed the door.

"What are we doing in here?" Ken asked.

"This room has been off limits even to those who have clearance on this floor. I wanted to know why and I needed time to think."

"Don't take too much..." Ken flipped on the light switch. "...What in the world?" Ken looked around the room and saw desks and cryptanalysis machines humming in the background.

"Is that a crypta...?"

"Turn that damn light off!" Yeri yelled.

Click.

"Why do we have code breaking machines?" Ken asked as he turned on his PeeP.

"They're online too," Yeri said as he stroked his beard.

"Look over there!" Ken said as his PeeP casted a narrow beam to a white machine lined with symbols Ken could not readily make out. "I think these are the new CR-1000s. I remember reading about the CR-900s back on Earth. Those were the most advanced Cryptas ever made based on the old asymmetric cryptography. They used integer factorizations instead of just pure math. It was considered cutting edge back then, but these!" Ken shook his head. "These are CR-1000s and they use Shor's Algorithm."

"Shor's what?" Yeri asked.

"We're talking about using quantum physics here. Shor's Algorithm uses quantum integer factorizations to break coded messages! This is heavy stuff, Dad! The Crypta CR-900s use nine qubits, but this one is a full ten qubits," Ken said and looked around as he moved the beam of light around the room. "The Minister of Defense has taken a lot of care to keep all this hidden," Ken said under his breath.

"The Minister of Defense? What does he have to do with anything?" Yeri asked.

"Well, his name is all over the place. All these documents have his signature and here's a set of numbers pinned to the wall. It looks like a combination to a lock or something…"

"That's nice, but we've got to get to SubSix. Let's go."

"Now?"

"Yes. The guard has probably had time to sweep seven and six. He's most likely going to five as we speak. It's not going to be long before he wonders why his buddy hasn't checked in."

"Okay but give me a minute or two to look over these numbers."

"You've got thirty seconds," Yeri said and peeked out the door.

A minute later Yeri and Ken had walked over to the lift where Yeri pressed the button on the panel. The door opened and they both stepped inside.

"I thought we couldn't use the lift?"

"That's going down. The lower you go, the higher the authorizations," Yeri replied as the lift abruptly stopped and the familiar voice returned,

"SubSix"

Yeri walked over to lab 621 and pressed a number of buttons and looked directly into the retina scan.

Yeri Thornton – approved.

"What's the matter with you?" Ken asked.

"What do mean?"

"We're supposed to be evacuating and they think there's an intruder. Why couldn't you access the lift down to SubSix with your retina scanner?"

"You cannot use the lift to go down when the building is in shutdown."

"Okay. That makes sense. Well then, what are they going to do when they find out that we...uh you aren't evacuating?"

Yeri looked over his shoulder at Ken. "Nothing."

"Nothing? We aren't going to do anything? Won't they call you after seeing that you entered a lab and ignored the warnings?"

"No," Yeri said and shook his head.

"Why not?"

"Because I'm waiting for Ryan to get back to his post. Then I'm going to call and give him hell about all this ruckus he's caused. How I almost lost the soil sample I was running and he'd better have a good explanation why I can't work in peace and quiet at two o'clock in the morning."

"How am I going to get out of here?" Ken asked.

"You worry a lot, don't you?"

Ken shook his head and watched as Yeri placed a small sample on one of the slides. "By the way, how did you breach the building?"

Yeri lifted the first slide to the light. He squinted as he looked for anything unusual. "I didn't breach the building. I just made the computer think there was a breach." Yeri placed the first slide into the microscope.

"How?"

"I borrowed some of your R-40," Yeri said and flipped on the microscope's light switch.

"Yeah, I saw you put it in your pocket. What does R-40 have to do with opening the hatch?"

"A structural breach can occur in many ways. The quickest way to locate a crack is when the temperature outside invades the temperature inside." Yeri perused the slide.

"Yeah?"

"Each building has its own inner and outer temperature sensing devices. If there is a sudden twenty degree drop or rise between the two then it signals a possible breach."

"And that's where the refrigerant comes in?" Ken asked.

"You're not as dumb as your mom said." Yeri pulled the slide out from the microscope.

"Mom thinks I'm pretty smart, thank you."

"What are you doing?" Yeri asked.

"Looking for the ON button," Ken said.

"It's the big green one in front of you marked ON."

"Oh." Ken pressed and held the green button until Dnet came to life. After two minutes of cycling through code and after checking its memory the display finally showed READY.

"You know, the only reason we are in this mess is because you know more about programming Dnet to run DNA samples than I do," Yeri remarked.

"So…you need me because I'm smarter than you," Ken said with a smile.

"Don't push it!" Yeri grinned. "And don't screw it up. I don't know how much time we have left."

Ken looked down at the flashing screen. "What's the password?"

"OdinGodOfAsgaard."

"Sounds like a song I heard years ago."

"A song?"

"Yeah. It went something like... Odin agotta da vee uh...we're in!" Ken said as the main screen came online.

"It's *In a gotta da vida*," Yeri corrected.

"No Odin?"

"No," Yeri replied.

"What the hell does *in a gotta* mean then?"

"It's in a garden of Eden, the guy was drunk and slurred his..." Dnet groaned suddenly as its start page appeared asking for input. "Yes!" Yeri interrupted and clapped his hands.

"Calm down, Odin, I'm only in. I'm going to need a few seconds to figure this out." Ken pulled up menu after menu, entering and changing code as Yeri sat helplessly watching the show.

"Dad, hand me slide number one." Tray one popped out. Yeri put the first slide containing the Halk's blood in the tray.

"Warning - unrecognizable entity in tray one."

"I know, I know," Ken said aloud to the machine as he continued to type and scan through documents entering additional lines of code.

"Tray one - Processing."

"There." Ken turned to Yeri. "Hand me the other three samples."

"Is it ready?

"No. I'm just hungry."

"Funny man." Yeri carefully picked up the pressed glass and handed them to Ken. He placed the cells in tray number two and the fingernail sample in tray three. He opened tray four and placed the hair he had retrieved from the Halk.

"Okay, here we go." Ken hit enter and watched as the trays slowly slid out of sight.

"Now what?" Yeri asked as he stared down at the machine.

"We wait." Ken manipulated dials and entered additional code trying to keep one step ahead of Dnet. Once satisfied that everything was running cleanly he looked at Yeri. "So how did you get the sensors to think there was a structural breach when there wasn't one?"

"30 seconds...60 seconds...90 seconds..."

came a male's voice from Dnet.

"Just a minute," Ken said and punched a line of code into Dnet. "Now it will alert us every five minutes."

"Thanks."

"Yeah well, how did you fool…"

"…the sensors? I applied the R-40 refrigerant to an outer wall in the kitchen near the freezer. I left the freezer door slightly open and placed a fan close to it. The fan was on its side to make it look like an accident. The monitor will show the breach next to the freezer. When the guards and the rest of the patrol walk in the kitchen, they'll assume it was a freak temperature error caused by someone who forgot to completely shut the freezer door."

"But the freezer isn't enough to change the temperature twenty degrees."

"No, not like the R-40, but we've had false alarms before and this will be chalked up to another one."

"What about the intruder?"

"I'm still working on that one. Any ideas?"

"No."

"Just what I thought," Yeri winked at his son. He watched the machine lights blink on and off. "I don't know how you got me into this," he said with a sigh.

"Come on. You're just as curious as I am. You know we're not going to get a straight answer from the government."

Yeri picked up the intercom.

"Who are you calling?"

Yeri looked directly at Ken. "Don't say a word."

"Front desk."

"What in the hell is going on around here? Is this Ryan?"

Ken strained to hear the conversation on the other side, but Dnet was making too much noise.

"Breach? Intruder? No, I must have gone to the bathroom when you came by. Yes I heard the sirens… Of course not! Did you expect me to roam the halls looking for some terrorists?… I didn't think so. Are you drinking again?…No, I didn't see any guards…. I'm in the middle of a run and I can't leave now. ... A guard down? ... In the ladies stall? What's he doing in the women's bathroom? Never mind, I don't want to know. Have you caught the intruder? ... No? Are you sure there is an intruder? I mean have you seen anyone?... No? Are you sure you haven't been drinking? ... Look! Now put the goddamn bottle away and find that intruder if there even is one... Secure? Of course the door's secure... Yes I will call if I see anyone." Yeri replaced the receiver. "Jesus!" Yeri turned to Ken. "Stay here."

"Where are you off to? You told the guard you weren't going anywhere," Ken said.

"I know what I told the guard. Do you want to see your actions played back for us in court tomorrow?" Yeri asked.

"I didn't think about that," Ken said.

"I know." Yeri walked out of the door and into the lift. An hour later, Yeri walked back in and went directly to Dnet. "Anything?"

"No. What were you doing?" Ken asked.

"Saving your ass," Yeri said as he concentrated on the computer read-outs. "Nothing so far?"

"Your ass is in the fire too you know. So what did you do?" Ken continued.

"I fixed the problem."

"How?"

"Doesn't matter."

"It does to me."

"You're not going let go of this bone, are you?" Yeri asked.

"Nope. I want to know."

"Okay, well I hurried over to the janitor's closet and picked up some ammonia, bleach and then went over to Tima's lab and found some fresh fertilizer. I set a timer and now we wait. Oh yeah, I grabbed your spare Dioxathane canisters you were carrying in Friggy. I hope you don't mind."

"You d-d-didn't!" Ken stammered. "Do you know how much explosive power is in one of those containers?"

"No."

"You've got to stop it, before it's too…"

KA-BOOM!

"…late."

The entire building shook as the Plexiglas windows blew out devastating the entire second and third floors above ground as the cold Martian air rushed inside the building. Trays of vials jumped off the counters and slammed into the floor leaving shattered glass everywhere. They both grabbed the shaking walls as cracks ran down top to bottom as the floor beneath them shook so violently it caused Dnet to dance to its tune while the chairs fell all around them.

"This building is about to collapse!" Ken shouted above the rumbling. "What were you thinking?"

"I had to make sure those tapes were destroyed."

"Along with us too?"

"Emergency Lights On!"

came the computerized voice as Dnet sat a foot from away from its original position as it ground to a halt.

"Great job, Dad," Ken said. "Without power we'll never find out what this thing is."

"Yes we will."

"Oh yeah? Did you bring a pack of batteries too?" Ken tried to control his anger as best he could.

"Just be patient Son. I know what I'm doing." Yeri flinched as the words came out.

Ken shook his head. "Yeah. I can see."

"Emergency Power Back-up Initiated!"

came the voice from the room's speaker.

"Please standby."

A few minutes later the emergency power backup generator kicked in and Dnet continued humming along. It was 0500 when the machine beeped that it had finished. Yeri looked at Ken who was monitoring and adjusting the readouts.

Beep!

the machine sounded out once again reminding everyone the results were in.

"Ken?" Yeri asked.

"What?"

"Dnet's finished."

Ken slowly removed the cell samples from their trays and handed them to Yeri. "Here you go."

Yeri looked over the slides with one hand and stroked his beard with the other. "Hmmm…"

"What is it?" Ken asked as he stared at the blank screen waiting for the readout.

"These samples have been changed!"

"Yes, I had to increase Dnet's ability from analyzing just plant DNA to uh monster DNA?" Ken scratched his head and turned to Yeri. "I had it search its database on all additional non-plant life organisms."

"What parameters did you use?"

"The ones available. Why?"

"This doesn't make any sense," Yeri said and put the slide under his microscope sitting on the table beside him for a closer look. He turned on the lamp and stared at the specimens for a few minutes more.

"What's wrong?" Ken asked.

"These slides. They look more like…no, it can't be." Yeri shook his head and impulsively adjusted the lenses.

"What can't it be?" Ken asked.

Yeri looked into the microscope once again. "These stains are definitely purple! But only plants have cell walls."

"Dad, what attacked us last night was not a tree!"

"Are you sure these are the right slides?"

"Oh my!" Ken placed a mocking hand to his mouth. "I think some of the chives I had for dinner must have found their way onto our slides. I knew I shouldn't have been eating when I was slicing up Charlie." Ken stared at Yeri. "Of course these are the cell slides."

"Yeah I know. If I am reading this right, Charlie here has a..." Yeri paused, "...cell wall!" Yeri exclaimed. "The cells should be showing pink, but they are... purple."

Dnet's tray opened with its readout for the second sample. Ken carefully picked the blood sample slide out of the tray and placed it under his microscope. "Hmmm...Looks to me like Charlie is... I mean, was sick."

"He seemed pretty healthy a few hours ago," Yeri said.

"Well, his blood is showing signs of a viral infection."

"So you're saying old Charlie here is nothing more than a sick plant?" Yeri asked.

"Seems like you pretty much got thrown across the yard by an ailing bush."

"Yeah right. Well, that bush of yours scratched my new helmet." Yeri turned to Ken. "What stain did you use?"

"Negative. Why?"

Yeri sat down at Dnet's terminal and stared at the readout on the screen. "Did you see this?"

"See what?" Ken asked as he looked up from his microscope.

"Dnet just confirmed that Charlie here has a cell wall," Yeri said.

"I am glad we are all in agreement. So what does that mean?" Ken asked.

"Well for one thing, it means that his cell wall is why old Charlie here could survive this Martian atmosphere. Cell walls are thicker and consist of two layers to protect the host from a hostile environment."

"But animals don't have cell walls."

"No they don't, but Dnet's report says Charlie's cellular matrix has a triple cell wall which isn't like any plant cells or any cells we have ever encountered. Dnet's data base is registering this as a new cell," Yeri said as he watched the screen as the cursor blinked waiting for input.

"Want to name it?" Ken asked. "How about Yeri?"

"A monster's cell wall with my name? I don't think so."

"A triple cell wall at that! Where did Charlie come from?" Ken asked.

"Your guess is as good as mine."

Ken looked at Dnet's screen. "Cell walls? Infections? These readings. They're all wrong. Dnet can't even find a matching blood type. It's registering a new one!"

"We can name that one Ken."

"No thanks," Ken said.

Beep!

"The scales and hair are ready," Yeri said. Ken and Yeri pulled out the slides and examined them through their microscopes. "Nothing like this has ever existed on Earth and I seriously doubt he is indigenous to Mars."

"So what is he and where did he come from and where's his spaceship?" Ken asked.

"It's got to be the machine." Yeri turned to Ken. "Are you sure you knew how to reprogram this thing?"

Ken looked at Yeri and shook his head. "Except for Dnet dancing around the floor shaking itself to bits from your earlier fireworks display? I don't know. You tell me."

"Are you telling me the truth? I need to know," Yeri pressed.

"I'm not a kid, Dad and I didn't screw up your precious computer. Even if I did, I don't think I could mess it up even though you gave it a good shot. This thing looks pretty failsafe."

"Well something is screwed up. These readings have got to be wrong," Yeri said and checked the calibration and then he ran a complete diagnostics. *Everything checks out, but it doesn't make any sense. The readings have got to be wrong, but...* He shook his head and looked at Dnet questioningly.

"What's the problem?" Ken asked as he noticed his father deep in thought. "DAD?" He pulled the hair slide from the microscope. "Fifty cell strands instead of the usual twenty on the hair. Nothing makes sense with this guy," Ken said and handed the slide to Yeri.

"Of course nothing makes sense. He can survive without a spacesuit on Mars. Think about it," Yeri said as he placed the hair follicles under his microscope.

"Anything?" Ken impatiently asked.

"Shhh… I want to check this." Yeri walked over to Dnet and pulled the readout of the hair sample.

"You're on to something, aren't you?" Ken paused as Yeri went back to his microscope.

"Something's wrong about Charlie's hair."

"Yeah, so Charlie here needs a haircut? So what? Everything is wrong with this guy. At least when it comes to any living organism we have ever encountered!"

Yeri pulled the hair slide and inserted the slide with the scales and examined the samples. "These aren't scales!"

"Then what are they?"

"It's called a microbial mat."

"A what?"

"A microbial mat is a multilayered sheet of microorganisms. It looks like they have created a protective shell around Charlie here. These biological organisms form a colony what we call mats. They prefer a moist atmosphere but they also do well in desert regions."

"Like a barrier between something moist and something extremely dry?"

"Exactly and they can weather high and low temperatures."

Ken peeked at Dnet. "Dnet confirms that it is a microbial mat, but it can't identify the organisms."

"Let me guess, it wants a name?"

"How about Beth?"

"No!"

"Then what does all of this mean?"

"It means we got a problem."

"Charlie needs a bath and a haircut?"

"No. But I think I know what Charlie is now," Yeri said.

"Well? What is he?"

Chapter 29

MARS

Ding! Dong!

"T-Minus wants in!" Tima said.

"Oh crap!" Beth replied.

"What do you want me to do?"

Ding! Dong!

"Not ready yet. Hold them off." Beth poured the last of the bleach in an effort to clean the blood off the floor.

"How?"

"I don't know but you better think of something quick."

Tima pressed the intercom. "This is Mrs. Thornton. Can I help you?"

"T-Minus here and we have a report of a Halk sighting."

"I haven't seen any Halks around here."

"There appears to be some damage to your dome."

"Probably the kids playing outside yesterday."

"Uh huh. May we enter?"

"Now's not a good time. The house is a mess. Perhaps this after…"

"I was not asking Mrs. Thornton. This is a police matter and you are directed to obey my orders or possibly face criminal charges. Do you understand?"

"Oh my gosh." Tima acted as innocent as she could and perhaps a little dumb. "Okay, now Ken showed me how to operate this thingy the other day. You see we just upgraded the lift and the controls are a little confus…"

"NOW Mrs. Thornton!"

"Okay, okay. You're making me nervous!" Tima turned and shouted as she held down the intercom button. "Beth! Can you help me open the lift door for T-Minus."

"Just a minute," Beth said in the distance as she finished throwing the last blood soaked rag into the trash bin.

"Mrs. Thornton!"

"I'm sorry, but I have a friend staying with me and she knows more about how to operate this thing better than I do. You see she was here when they were doing the up..."

"Mrs. Thornton! You are trying my patience and if this lift does not open in ten seconds I will have you arrested for obstruction of justice."

"Hello? This is Beth. Can I help you?"

"Open the goddamn door!"

"Of course, sir. I am always willing to help the authorities." Beth looked at Tima as she nodded and smiled.

Tima watched as the band of T-Minus officials entered the dome. The first one to enter took his helmet off and looked menacingly at Tima.

"Good morning, Mrs. Thornton. It looks like you've had quite a night," the Minister of Defense said.

"I don't know what you're talk... oh the power outage. Yes, it was a fright, but fortunately nothing of any consequence," she replied. "Neither of us got much sleep as you can tell."

"Ah yes. Power outages can be trying. Is your husband here?" the Minister asked.

"My husband?"

"Yes. Ken Thornton? Our records indicate he lives here with you. Is that correct?"

Tima nodded.

"I don't see him anywhere around. Perhaps you could tell me where he is?"

"I don't know," Tima replied.

"You... don't know?"

"No. He's an important man and I assumed he was out early this morning on a site call," Tima offered.

"There have been no site calls recorded. Are you sure you don't know where your husband is, Mrs. Thornton?" The Minister pressed as he moved closer to her. "Who is this?" the Minister asked as Beth entered the living room from the kitchen.

"Just a friend," Tima said.

"A very good friend to stay with you all night when your husband is not around. I think this could be… Beth Thornton?" he asked and she nodded. "I see." The Minister of Defense paced around the room and looked over the place with a casual but critical eye. "You keep a very, very clean home. Do you not, Mrs. Thornton?"

"I try. Do you have a problem with that?" she asked.

"Oh no. It's just with all this Martian dirt and dust, most homes have a little bit here and there."

"Well, we like to keep ours clean," Tima replied.

"What's that smell?"

"Smell?"

"Yes. It's odd for a home as clean as yours to have such an awful smell."

Tima looked at Beth.

"Oh that! It's from the chemicals I used when I permed my hair last night," Beth said. "Do you like it?" She forced a weak smile.

"Uh huh," the Minister grunted. "And where is your husband, may I ask?"

"I left him at home. Why?" Beth asked.

"Did you know there was an intruder in your husband's lab last night and an explosion occurred earlier this morning?"

Beth held her hands to her face. "Is he alright?"

"I thought you left him at home?"

"He must have gone in while I was here."

"Yes. I'm sure that's what happened. So tell me again why you left him alone to come over here in the middle of the night last night?"

"The power outage," Beth quickly replied. "Tima asked me over to watch the children while she checked the breakers."

"She couldn't do this with the kids around?"

"Ken usually watches them but he was gone last night," Tima said.

"Didn't you say he left early this morning?"

"Did I say that?"

The Minister nodded.

"Well, early morning, late last night. It's really all the same you know."

"I see. Mrs. Thornton I am only going to ask you one more time. Where is your husband?"

"I don't know, probably repairing a down ReDS or something."

"You don't know?"

"No."

The Minister of Defense had his hands clasped behind his back and turned to his men. "I want you to survey the area around this dome. Anything unusual is to be reported to me immediately. Do you understand?"

"Yes sir," came the reply and as his men went to the lift, the Minister stayed behind. "Do you mind if I have a look around?"

"I don't usually like to have strangers poking around in my things without my husband here," Tima said. She tried to stop him but he muscled his way past her.

"I'm sure your husband will not mind," he said as he strolled into the lab.

Tima looked at Beth and they both sat down and waited.

"Sir! Donager here reporting in. We have finished the perimeter sweep," came the voice on his pursal *celling* mode.

"Anything unusual to report?"

"Yes sir. A Halkomelem was here, definitely his footprints. It also looks like something was dragged from where the dome was damaged to the front entrance."

"Thank you, Donager. Good work. Let me know if you find anything else."

"Yes, sir. Oh and there was…a rock that looked like it sustained some fresh impact marks, from a suit or something, maybe a helmet?"

"Okay," the Minister said and walked back into the living room.

"Have you two told me everything?" The Minister stared at Tima and glanced at Beth.

"As far as I can remember, why?" Tima said and casually sipped her coffee.

"It's awfully hot in here. Why is your incinerator still on?"

"I just filled it before you arrived."

"With what?"

"What most people normally fill their incinerators with, why do you ask?"

"Mrs. Thornton, if I find out that you lied to me." The Minister shook his head. "I am going to personally see to it that you will be digging ice at Herschel for the rest of your life."

It was time for Tima to put her hands to her mouth.

"Are you sure you've told me everything?" he asked again with his hands behind his back as he leaned closer to Tima with a raised an eyebrow.

"What do you want me to say?" Tima felt the threat clear to her bones and that caused an equal amount of anger to well up inside. "Okay, you want the truth? A Halkomelem dropped by for a visit last night. We got tired of him banging on the door, so Ken went outside and killed it. He then dragged him inside and we cut up old Charlie here for some extra fuel. Ken left early this morning to the office to brag to his employees about what happened and I called Beth over so we could sit and enjoy the warmth thanks to that monster cooking in the oven. There, anything else?" she said and glared into his eyes.

The Minster returned her stare for what Tima felt as a painfully long five seconds. "No ma'am. Please have your husband give me a call when you see him. Thank you," he said and spoke into his pursal.

"Donager?"

"Yes sir."

"Let's go by the lab and have a talk with Yeri..." the Minister paused a moment and looked at Tima, "...and Ken," he hung up and walked out.

"Tima! What if he believed you?" Beth asked.

"I don't know if I believe it myself." Tima sat down and this time added some potato vodka to her cold coffee.

Chapter 30

MARS

Coronae Laboratories
Coronae Scopulus
Gemini - Sol Saturday 7, 0012
0530 hours

"Human? Charlie?" Ken asked.

CRASH!

"The samples!" Yeri yelled.

"Sorry," Ken said and bent over to clean the mess off the floor. "You're crazy. No human could live out here in this hostile environment. We're barely holding on ourselves." Ken shook his head.

"Remember the flock of seagulls?"

"What do birds have to do with this?"

"When those Humanochore scientists genetically engineered humans back on Earth they didn't stop to think about any unintended consequences."

"What?"

"Let's say you dump radioactive waste and trash into the ocean. The fish in the ocean die or become toxic. You have fish for dinner and then you end up with cancer from eating some poisoned sushi. Life is like a game of chess. You make a move and then you have to figure out if that move will place you at an advantage or disadvantage depending on what your opponent does."

"We all know that."

"But it doesn't stop there. You have to look deeper and deeper into the game. The deeper you look is how you figure out if this will be of long-term benefit or peril to you.

Well, it seems that curing cancer and turning humans into carnivores wasn't the only thing that was happening. They saw the two transformations and figured that was it, but it wasn't. I remembered reading a report about how some of the genetically modified humans had survived when others had died in situations of drowning and smoke inhalation."

"What do you mean?"

"Like those seagulls, they had adapted to their environment."

"But isn't that a good thing?"

"So did their minds and that part was kept out of the media."

"Hmmm…"

"Yeah. I had read reports where some of the BuffaPrimes went missing and were found eaten raw and there were no other animals left to take them down, if you know what I mean. A lot of weird incidences started occurring after we launched the procedures worldwide. Dogs and cats, and even humans started disappearing which became a huge concern, but it was all kept from the masses."

"Why?"

"Money and power."

"I remember now! It was just like what the Yersinia Pestis virus did to the seagulls? The Crossers adapted to their new environment," Ken said.

"Exactly. It was rumored that the Ebola virus had genetically manipulated itself in ways that could alter the bodies DNA at will, enabling us to adapt to conditions that would otherwise kill normal people. I thought it was just a lot of bunk, but now I'm not so sure," Yeri said.

"You mean that these Halks are really Crossers and their DNA adapted to the Martian atmosphere in order to survive?"

"As far fetched as it sounds there is no denying the results."

"That explains all the government cover-ups then."

"Do you know what's more concerning than this?" Yeri asked.

"You mean besides the fact that Earth may not be dead?"

"Earth may become our worst nightmare! We left those people on Earth to die. If they genetically altered themselves in order to survive Earth's toxic environment, well, they not only could have adapted to the radiation and global warming, but they may also have the technology to launch an attack on Mars if they so choose."

"But these half-humans don't appear to have our intelligence."

"That's another problem my father was concerned about." Yeri picked his pursal and dialed. "Viruses, by nature, mutate. That's why we can't cure the common cold. We don't know which strand it will mutate into next."

"So when we gave these viruses a chance to mutate our DNA, even if they do it correctly the first time, it could change without notice. Is that what you're trying to say?" Ken threw the rest of the compromised slides in the trash and sat down.

"You damn well better believe it. Their DNA changed to what it considered important for survival and that could mean changing brain patterns if necessary. These new Earth people could easily be coming here to find out what we've been doing all these years. The problem could be that no one is reporting back to Earth so they continued to send more. They may have concluded that we're killing them and if so we don't know what they might do next. These new Earth people may be unaware of the problem. After they've been here for only a short while their DNA changed to accommodate to their new environment. Their bodies adapted and it also changed their brainwave patterns turning them into the type of beast that we killed last night," Yeri remarked.

"They would have protection from the Martian atmosphere," Ken countered. "I mean, it is just common sense to use a spacesuit when venturing out to another planet. Especially when the planet like Mars can't support life. It kind of blows a big hole in your theory don't you think?"

"Good point. But something is happening to them when they arrive," Yeri shrugged his shoulders. "I just don't know what."

"So you're saying those Crossers who adapted to the deadly atmosphere on Earth did so not only from a physical aspect, but it is very likely a mental change too!" Ken pondered. "They may not be anything like what we think of as humans."

"That is highly probable given what we have seen here," Yeri agreed.

"So what do we do now?" Ken asked.

Yeri shook his head in disbelief.

"Well, well, well," Ken continued. "Isn't this a fine mess? Let me get this straight. We leave all those poor souls to die on Earth and they adapt. Now they are sending emissaries here. Somehow they end up changing into half-human half-monster when they get here and then we kill them?"

"We need to warn the Ministry of Defense," Yeri said.

Ken shook his head. "No we don't."

"What are you talking about?"

"Remember SubEight?"

"What about it?" Yeri asked.

"The ten qubit cryptas! It's what the military uses to listen in or capture enemy transmissions. In fact, I'm betting that the Earthlings think they are talking to the Minister of Travel and Planet Security when they are actually talking to the Minister of Defense."

"So the Minister of Defense knows they are trying to contact us or maybe he is contacting them? I don't know, Ken. Why would the Minister of Defense care?"

"The question is why are code breaking machines secretly locked away in his office? You can't even get clearance to go to level eight."

"It does seem like our friendly Minister is doing something a little mischievous," Yeri said.

"Okay, let's assume the Earthlings are still alive then why haven't we heard of or met any of Earth's ambassadors?"

"I don't know. Nothing makes sense, but then perhaps we don't have all the pieces to this puzzle yet."

Chapter 31

MARS

Washington Residence
Domette 23
Dao Vallis, Hellas Planitia
Hellas Quadrangle, Mars
Gemini - Sol Saturday 7, 0012
0530 hours

John Washington woke up and quickly changed out of his long johns. He bent over to give his wife a kiss, but before his lips touched her cheek she awoke.

"Where are you going, honey?" Carol asked, her eyes half open as she tried to shake sleep's command over her.

"To work," John replied and gave her a quick kiss.

"Aren't you doing the seven to sevens this week?" She was awake now and pulled the covers close to her as she sat up pulling her knees to her chest. She turned and looked at the clock. "It's five thirty! Can't it wait? You were up pretty late last night after that phone call."

"It's important that I get to the lab as quickly as I can." John started toward the door.

"Something's wrong, isn't it?" Carol climbed out of bed. "At least let me fix you some breakfast."

"It can't wait. Lives are at stake here. I gotta go."

"It was that call you got last night, wasn't it?" she asked. John didn't reply. "Who was it, John? … John? … I need to know if something goes wrong," she pleaded.

John shook his head and then he finally acquiesced. "Remember our friend on the transport?"

"The one who talked the Minister out of sending us back to Earth?" John nodded his head. "If he needs your help… I love you," Carol said.

John kissed her passionately on the lips. So passionately that it made her wonder if she would ever see him again.

John suited up and made his way through the cold Martian atmosphere toward the lab.

Coronae Laboratories
0600 hours

Minutes, which seemed like hours, passed until John saw Ryan, the guard, through the Plexiglas window. He entered the airlock and waited. The inner door opened and John pulled off his helmet and walked up to the guard. "What the hell happened here last night? Have you seen second and third?"

"I think we've been attacked!"

"Attacked? From who?"

"I don't know. I think there are some terrorists in the buil...what are you doing here? It's only six. Aren't we on the sevens this week? Never mind, I'm glad you're here. There was a structural breach warning last night. It was in the kitchen, but it turned out to be a false alarm. An intruder is somewhere on site. SubEight's stairwell lock was burned off and this scientist, Thornton, has been screaming at me all night!" Ryan said in exasperation.

"Where's O'Riley?"

"Unconscious. He suffered a severe blow to the head."

"Where?"

"SubEight. In the ladies bathroom. It looked like he fell off the toilet."

"What was he doing? Never mind, I mean did you leave him there?"

"I put him on the couch in the ladies room."

"SubEight?"

"Yes! Someone's down there. Like I said, they burnt the lock off the door. We've searched the entire building and we can't find the intruder. Now, why are you here?"

"Steve called me to come in early."

"Why did he call you? Oh yeah, the explosion."

"He said T-Minus is on their way."

"T-Minus? Oh crap. I hope I don't lose my job over this," Ryan said.

"You're in the clear, however, Steve said he wants you to go home and get some rest. We're going to need you in a few hours and he wants you refreshed."

"But I'm still on the clock."

John stared at Ryan. "You're free to stay, but Steve was pretty adamant about you getting some rest. If you overlook something now, he's going to blame it on you for not following his orders. I mean it's up to you if you want to take that chance."

John went over to the desk and cycled through the monitors.

"I think I'll stay and ask him," Ryan said.

"Sure. Whatever," John said. "Not my funeral."

Ryan walked around the desk and started to fiddle with another monitor. "Still snowy."

"If you're going to stay, at least be quiet," John said as he quietly tried to remain patient.

A few minutes passed and Ryan turned to John. "You may be right. I might be needed later and I would probably be a little more help if I caught a catnap. Is the cot available?"

"I just sealed off the hallway in SubOne. Sorry," John said. "You can share the couch in the ladies room with O'Riley down in SubEight," John smiled.

"I'm not going down there alone again. Not without T-Minus and some guards."

"Then why don't you go on home? There's nothing else you can do. I'm just going to sit here and wait for Steve and the guards. I'll keep the monitor watch," John said.

"Okay. I'm out of here. By the way, that explosion took out the recording devices along with the upper floors. We got nothing, John," Ryan said as he looked back at the snowy monitor. "See you later."

"Ryan?"

"What?"

"Is Yeri still here?"

"Who?"

"Mr. Thornton."

"I haven't seen him leave. I wouldn't bother him if I were you. He is sealed in and he thinks the explosion released some toxic fumes in the hallways. He said he couldn't open the door."

"Are containment procedures in place?"

"Yes. Everything below is completely sealed off."

"Get outta here, Ryan. You've earned your pay."

Ryan threw John the headset, suited up and left. "Good luck."

"I'll tell Steve!" John shouted back as he watched Ryan exit the building.

Ring … Ring…"John here."

"John? This is Steve. Where is Ryan?"

"He's um, feeling sick and went home. He called me to come in."

"Sick? Why didn't he call me? That's protocol."

"Sir, he's not thinking straight. There was an explosion, which took out the upper floors and released some toxins into the ventilation system. When I got here Ryan was staggering and slurring his words. Could be the toxins so I sent him home."

"Smart thinking, John. How are you doing?"

"No problems, sir. By the time I arrived most of the toxins had been filtered out except for the levels below ground. SubOne and below have been sealed off."

"I just got a call from the Minister. He is on his way. Anything else I need to know?"

"That's all I got. In fact, I just arrived here a few minutes ago. I was just about to make my rounds when…"

"No! You are to stay where you are. I need you to greet the Minister when he shows up."

"Yes sir. Are you coming?"

"I'll be there within the hour. Now don't move from that desk. Do you understand?"

"Yes sir. You can count on me."

"Good." Click.

Ring...Ring... Yeri pulled out his pursal.

"John, what took you so long?" Yeri asked as a smile crossed his face.

"I was on the cell with the boss. The Minister is on his way. Ryan's gone now. By the way what happened to O'Riley?"

"His face hit the bathroom stall door."

"What?"

"Well, to be honest the door hit him in the face and knocked him out."

"Why?"

"Had no choice. Do you know there are CR-1000s in 802?" Yeri asked.

"Cryptas? Aren't those for code breaking?"

"Yep. And the room is lined with them."

"You broke into 802? Even the guards have to have written authorization from the Minister to enter that room," John said.

"We didn't really break into the room. We had a little help."

"What?"

"Never mind. So, how's O'Riley doing?" Yeri asked.

"Ryan put him on the couch in the ladies room," John replied.

"Let's hope he stays there."

"Roger. Have you called Danny yet?"

"Yes, he will meet us at the landing site at 0800."

"There's a landing site?"

"I told you I would always have your back."

"Is he bringing the key?" Yeri asked.

"He didn't say," John replied.

"What's going on?" Ken asked.

"Shhh..." Yeri waved his hand. "I see. The Minister himself? When? No. I can't. You're going to have to disable the containment... Yes... We're fine... Hurry."

Yeri hung up his pursal. "That was John, the guard upstairs."

"Who is John? I thought you've been talking to Ryan all night," Ken asked.

Yeri shook his head. "How many times have I talked on my pursal tonight?"

"Twice, the first time was on our way to the lab and now. You've been using the lab intercom the rest of the time. Why the pursal, now?"

"Privacy," Yeri said as he pulled the rest of the specimens out of Dnet. "At least you didn't drop any of these."

"Why do you care about these specimens now? We're toast and there's no way out."

"We have John."

"That guy you just talked to?"

"Uh huh."

"I gather from your conversation with John that the Minister is on his way."

"That's right. He is and time is critical."

"How does John fit in to all this?" Ken asked.

"John and his nineteen friends arrived here on the Santa Maria. He had changed the manifest documents to include them. Soon after we departed, the Niña exploded as it passed the Earth's moon."

"I remember seeing it on the news. What happened?"

"No one knows, but the names on the roster included the Ana Asea Sevens and the rest of the world's most influential government leaders along with Biochore, Humanochore, and Nanotech officials to name a few."

"What does that have to do with anything?"

"Sabotage was suspected and the records were ordered to be closely scrutinized when all transports arrived. Any unauthorized passengers were to be returned to Earth."

"What does that have to do with…?"

"John?"

"Yes. How does he fit in this crazy scheme of yours?"

"John and his nineteen friends boarded illegally."

"You helped a bunch of stowaways?"

"John and I sat beside each other on the Santa Maria. I figured something was wrong when he told me he was a scientist. He didn't look much like a scientist. Don't ask. He just didn't. I've seen my share. I knew some of the Biochore middle managers from my days working at the CDC in Atlanta. I knew they would be on the transport, but no one showed. So I checked the onboard manifest and compared them with the boarding roster and uncovered the discrepancy. John's group didn't know there was a separate onboard manifest. They got clearance on the ship, but it could easily be counterchecked while en route. I exposed their little plot and that's when John came clean."

The lights came and the familiar computer voice sounded,

"SubSix Containment Seal – 75%"

"Atta boy, John," Yeri said. "Anyway, when John told me the whole story, I was duly impressed. I knew that a man like John Washington could better serve us here on Mars than a bunch of spineless Biochore middle managers. So I told him that unless he changed the onboard manifest, his group would be found out and summarily deported. They usually don't even check the onboard and if they do, they just about always wait until the transports land. After the Niña blew up I told him there could be changes in security protocols so I recommended him being proactive, no use taking any chances. Unfortunately, security caught him before he got all the names changed. His was the only one left so they bound him and returned him to his seat beside me. I was instructed not to talk to him. It seemed there had been changes in security protocols. Every transport was now required to check all passengers en route."

"I figured they would have interrogated him on the ship," Ken said.

"No room. As you know every ounce of space is precious so his seat was the only place he could sit. Anyway, they didn't have the expertise when it comes to interrogation techniques. He figured he was dead meat and told me he was going to sacrifice himself in order to secure his family and friends a chance to stay on Mars. I told him to keep quiet and I would see what I could do. When we landed he was greeted by the Minister of Defense and his gang. John was arrested and interrogated for hours. John maintained his silence through the whole ordeal and believe me, the Minister can be very persuasive when he wants. John wouldn't expose the others even if it meant his life."

"How did you get him free of the Minister?" Ken asked.

"SubSix Containment Seal – 50%"

"Not long now," Yeri said. "I had some influential friends at the WDG. An Australian fellow named Brian Donager worked with the Minister on one of the imminent domain issues in Africa. I met Brian when I was working for the CDC and we struck up a friendship. Right after the tragedy in Luanshya I went down there to access the damages and make sure there were no viral outbreaks. I met some of the villagers who returned to Luanshya to pick up the rest of their belongings. Most had left to live with relatives in neighboring cities after Sanchez's invasion of Luanshya. I asked one of the locals, Jocarah, why he wasn't at the compound, I mean gated community. He said no one was. Everyone left Luanshya after the invasion. I called Donager and he confirmed no one showed up when the transports arrived. Probably for the best if you ask me. I hung up with Brian and turned back to Jocarah. I asked him about the money the World Development Group had promised. He had no idea what I was talking about. He said they were asked to sign a piece of paper and then take two retina scans and the money would be theirs in a couple of weeks, but they never saw it. I told him the WDG would never have them do two scans. Jocarah said it was this general named Sanchez who ordered the scans and bought the land from them. Jocarah told me when he accessed his account he found a huge amount of money was deposited and a microsecond later it was transferred out. His wasn't the only one. It seemed all the other accounts experienced the same thing. No one knew what happened to it all so like the money they just disappeared. All of that pain and devastation and they never saw a Kruger.

"Where did all the Krugers go?"

"It all went into an off-shore account. I contacted a friend of mine while we still lived on Earth, Danny Over…uh something or another."

"Who was he?"

"A guy I met at this bar in Germany. We got a little too drunk that night and he mentioned something about working with cryptas. So I called in a favor."

"To find the funds?"

"Yes. Funny you know I saw him at the mall yesterday morning and he said his name was Danny Maltido. Now I know I had a lot to drink that night, but I could have sworn it was..." Yeri looked to the ceiling for a minute trying to gather his thoughts. "Well, anyway he used his jimmy to trace the funds. Danny found the accounts and we were able to trace the money back to a guy named Christopher Rice and finally to General Carlos Sanchez. They basically stole the relocation money from the Shyans."

"Oh my god!"

"God had nothing to do with this."

"You still haven't told me how you freed John."

"I knew I needed a friend to help me clear him so I walked around the ship to see if I knew anyone. I saw Brian Donager way in the back and I thought why not? So I went over and talked to Brian and asked for his help. He was a little reluctant at first to help a bunch of stowaways. The Minister of Defense had recently promoted Brian to lead T-Minus. He said this position allowed him a lot of latitude when it came to Martian policy."

"I bet," Ken said.

"I told him about Sanchez and how he had used Brian to funnel the funds into his own personal accounts."

"Wow. What happened?"

"Brian was livid. He asked what was the name on the off-shore account and I told him the funds were rerouted to a company called Kraals Inc."

"You've never mentioned Brian before."

"No need. Anyway, Brian agreed to help me clear John when we landed. Brian and I met with the Minister of Travel and they released John a few hours later."

"I thought the Minister of Defense was after John?"

"He was but it was the Minister of Travel's jurisdiction and since the Defense Department lacked any evidence and you can't prosecute someone because you suspect wrongdoing so they had no choice but to free John Washington."

"What did you say to get the Minister of Travel to overturn the arrest?"

"We informed him that John Washington was an undercover agent for the Ana Asea Sevens. There was at least one on every transport. We said it was a mistake on the manifest. John's identity had been accidentally revealed and he was trying to change it when he was caught."

"Didn't they want to know why John didn't tell them this before?" Ken asked.

"Very good old boy. The Minister of Defense was furious when he heard that John was an agent. He complained about all of this wasting his precious time. Brian told the Minister that it was not John's job to make those decisions. I then told him John was not allowed to identify himself to anyone according to strict orders of the Ana Aseas."

"What was his response?" Ken asked.

"He said that John should've ignored that directive when the Ana Aseas were killed. I countered that argument saying that John was well versed in disinformation and he didn't believe the news until he had proof. In the end they had no choice but to let him go."

"And that's why John just happened to end up being a security guard in the same lab where you work?"

Yeri smiled as his pursal rang.

"SubSix Containment Seal – 25%"

"Yeri, John here. You guys better be ready to move. T-Minus is here."

"Thanks John," Yeri said.

"SubSix Containment Seal – 0%"

"Time to go!" Yeri said and slowly opened the door. He poked his head into the hallway and he saw the elevator doors open.

"John!" Yeri said as John stopped halfway out of the elevator.

"Come on, let's go!" John motioned them to the elevator. Yeri and Ken ran to the door just as it closed them inside.

"Where are we going?" Ken asked.

"Down," John replied.

"We can't go down. The halls will be crawling with T-Minus in no time."

"Not where we're going."

"What?" Ken exclaimed.

John pulled out a passkey and inserted it in a small panel next to the elevator buttons. He waited ten seconds and turned the key. The panel opened up displaying two new buttons.

"I didn't know there were more floors?" Yeri stared at the panel.

"SubNine and SubTen."

"Which one are we taking?" Yeri asked.

"SubTen," John said.

"Why not Nine?" Ken asked.

"Because we can't get out of here from Nine!" John looked at Ken with frustration in his voice. "Does he always talk this much?"

"Just asking," Ken said sheepishly.

Yeri spotted the camera as it was recording them on the elevator monitor. "Oh boy. I guess they have us now."

"Hold on," John said and he reached into his pocket and pulled out a remote control looking device. He pressed the red button and the monitor went dark. "There."

The elevator continued its descent until it came to a full stop as the computerized voice announced SubTen. The doors opened presenting a long hallway in front of the trio. The red and blue warning lights were still rotating when John pulled out a small mirror and looked both ways.

"We're clear," John said.

Ken moved past Yeri and as his foot touched the hallway he felt a hand on his collar and was jerked back inside.

"What are you doing?" John asked.

"I don't know."

"Look, do you want to explain why you are on this highly restricted level to a Court of Inquiry tomorrow?"

"I thought Dad blew up the tapes!"

"We're not stupid. We have back up systems in case someone tries to do what you guys did. Fortunately, for you guys I just disabled the secondary, but the tertiary recording is another matter."

"Tertiary?"

"Yes. We have redundancy security systems built into these buildings. The third and fourth systems don't start to record until the second system fails."

"And when the elevator monitor went blank?" Yeri asked.

"Is when I blew it up with this." John showed them the remote detonator.

"Good thinking," Yeri said.

"We're not out of the woods yet." John pulled out two wrapped sticks the size each a half a meter long. He threw one to the left and the other to the right in the hallway. White smoke began to billow up filling the hallway.

"Time to go," John said and stepped into the hall. "Yeri, grab my shirt and have Ken grab yours."

"Ready."

"Okay we are going to have to run. This smoke won't last very long."

So the three turned left and ran blindly down the smoke filled corridor until John hit the wall followed by the other two.

"Ouch!" Ken said.

"Shhh…" John replied.

"Which way?" Yeri asked.

"Hold on," John said and pulled out his pursal. "Danny?"

Nothing.

"Damn," John lit up another smoker and threw it down the hall leading to the stairs. "Danny, come in." John turned to the other two. "He's not answering. I guess we are just going to have to try and get out of here ourselves." John waited a few seconds as the white smoke swirled around the hall. "Okay come on. They can't see us now," John turned right and quickly moved down the hallway followed by Yeri and Ken.

They continued down the hallway until...

BANG!

"OUCH!" John's shin caught something hard and he fell to the floor. Yeri fell into John and Ken ran into Yeri.

"What's going on? I can't see a thing," Ken said.

"Stairs. We have to climb out of here."

"How many?" Yeri asked.

"You don't want to know," John replied. "I hope you guys are in shape because we have to go back up to the surface."

"That sounds like a hundred steps or so," Yeri said with dread in his voice.

"You can do it, Dad," Ken said trying to rouse Yeri's spirits.

Coronae Laboratories
Main Floor
0730 hours

"Mr. Washington!" the intercom rang through out the entire building. "MISTER...WASH..ING...TON...! Where the hell are you and why aren't you here to greet me?" The Minister turned to his men. "Something's wrong here. I knew that worm was a stowaway. Where is Yeri Thornton's lab?"

"I don't know, sir," Brian Donager said.

"Well? Get behind the desk and pull up the employee list."

"It's going to take a minute. The computer isn't responding."

"Check the drawers!" the Minister yelled.

"Yes sir!" Brian opened the drawer on the right side of the desk. He quickly thumbed through the folders looking for the list. He closed the drawer and opened the one on the left side.

"What's taking so damn long?"

"I'm going as fast as I can sir."

"Well go faster, you idiot."

"Yes sir." Brian Donager fumed as he ever so slowly found and pulled the file containing the employee list and placed it on the desk. "I think I have it sir."

"Think? Do you or don't you?"

"Give me a minute."

"We don't have a minute."

"Yeri Thornton's lab?" Brian asked and blankly stared at the list testing the Minister's patience.

"Jesus!" The Minster shouted and turned to Chris Rice. "Chris get over there and help Donager find Thornton's lab!"

"Here it is, sir. Lab 621," Brian said.

"Give me that." The Minister held out his hand for the list. Donager slowly handed him the file. "Are you always this slow?"

"Didn't get much sleep last night, sir. The baby kept us up."

"You stay here and try to keep awake while my men take care of the important stuff. Understand?"

"Yes sir," Brian said.

"Sanders."

"Yes sir?"

"Keep an eye on Mr. Donager."

"Yes sir."

"Okay men," the Minister turned and sneered at Brian. "Let's go."

"Yes sir," came the replies.

The Minister and his men took the stairway down to SubSix. The Minister opened the door to the hallway and looked around. "Where is Dr. Thornton's lab?"

"Two doors on your left sir!" Chris said.

The Minister raced over to the door and looked into the retina scan. "Administrative override," came the voice from the intercom as the door unlatched itself.

"Let me know if you find anything unusual," the Minister said. He walked in and switched on Dnet. The screen lit up blue and he entered his password. Dnet activated itself as the cursor blinked waiting for more input. The Minister selected all previous transactions from the last 48 hours.

"Nothing? Something is going on here and I am going to find out what," he said and ran a log diagnostic program that showed the last few runs had been deleted. "What have you been doing Dr. Thornton?" he whispered to himself as he saw some smashed slides in the wastebasket.

"What's that?" Sanders asked as he stared at the monitor.

"Looks like smoke?" Donager replied.

"Are you going to call it in?"

Beep! "Brian Donager calling." The Minister placed his pursal *cellular* to his ear.

"What is it?"

"Brian here. The monitors finally came back on and they are showing a lot of white smoke. I can't see anything."

"White smoke?" he thought for a minute and asked, "Where?"

"SubTen."

"SubTen! Damn it!" The Minister turned to the other agents roaming around the room. "Greenfield, your team is in charge of SubTwo, Three, and Four. Hallmann, send your team to SubFive and Six. Peterson your team to SubSeven and Eight. Everyone else? We are going to SubTen – STAT."

John and Ken stopped for another rest break. Ken looked at John and then for Yeri, who was nowhere to be seen. "Where's Dad?" Ken asked.

"I thought he was behind you," John said.

"You go ahead. I'll wait," Ken said.

"Don't wait too long." John said. "I'll see you guys at the top. Let me know if you need any help."

Ken nodded as John ran the rest of the way up the stairs.

"Dad?" Ken called out.

"It's dark down here. I can't see a thing," came the distance voice.

"Turn on your PeeP."

"My PeeP?"

"Yes. Just shake it like Tima said."

"I know how to turn the damn thing on thank you very much."

"I'll be down in a minute," Ken said as he ambled down the stairwell.

"You guys go ahead!" Yeri yelled back. "I'll catch up."

"We don't have time for you to catch up," Ken said as he slowed his decent upon hearing familiar footsteps growing louder. Suddenly a beam of light appeared around the corner as Ken ran down the rest of the way to help his dad.

"What are you doing?" Yeri asked.

"Helping an old man cross the road," Ken replied.

"I said I would be there Mr. Boy Scout. You know," Yeri smiled, "I'm not too old to take you on."

"Then I'll race you to the top?" Ken asked.

"Uh, well, let's say we save that one for another day." Yeri held out his hand for Ken to grab. Ken and Yeri hand-in-hand ran up the rest of the way as quickly as possible. "This is a lot of work you know," Yeri said as they turned another corner, "and it's all your fault, Son."

"Mine?"

"Yes and my legs are starting to cramp."

"Do you always complain this much?" Ken asked mockingly. Yeri smiled at him. "Not much further, Dad."

"That's what you said a hundred steps ago." They reached another platform and turned a corner only to be met by another winding staircase. "You gotta be kidding me!" Yeri huffed.

"Last one. I promise," Ken said.

"How do you know that?"

"I don't but I don't think you want me to tell you anything else right now." Yeri grabbed Ken's hand tighter as they both stumbled wearily up the remaining stairs. They reached the top of the stairwell only to be met by a long corridor that twisted and turned for a couple of kilometers. They moved as quickly as their tired legs could move until they came to a wall of Plexiglas with a door blocking their escape.

"What took you so long?" John asked as Ken and Yeri almost ran into him.

"Ken was having some trouble keeping up," Yeri sighed with his hands on his knees.

"Uh huh," John replied.

"It's dark in here," Ken said. "Is that a door over there?"

"I thought I was in better shape," Yeri muttered under his breath and turned his head. Ken walked over to the door.

"Be careful," John admonished.

"Did you hear something?" Yeri asked aloud.

"Voices!" Ken replied in a nervous tone.

"I figured the smoke would have tipped them off." John shrugged his shoulders. "Couldn't be helped."

Ken grabbed the door handle. It wouldn't turn, so he yanked on it anyway. "Damn. The door is stuck." Ken looked at Yeri. "What do we do now?"

"We have to get this thing open," Yeri said.

"I have my spot laser," Ken said and pulled the knife out and tossed it to John.

"No good. This can't be burned off. At least not in the time we have left."

Ken took a closer look at the door. "A keypad? I haven't seen one of these in years. What's the code?"

"I don't have the code," John replied.

"No code?" Ken exclaimed. "What are we going to do?"

"We better think of something quick," Yeri said as he anxiously looked down the hallway.

"Even if we open the door what then?" Ken said exasperated. "We'll be caught as soon as we leave the building. I don't know about you, but running around outside in spacesuits is not the best way to avoid capture, not to mention I lost my helmet."

"I guess you're gonna have to hold your breath then." Yeri shook his head.

"Danny? Come in!" John yelled into his communicator. "Where can he be?"

"It doesn't matter where he is if we can't open this lock," Yeri said.

"No worries. I saw this lock years ago and I figured I could just ask Danny to hack into the main frame and get us the combination, but I can't reach him."

All at once John's pursal popped into *celling* mode. "Danny Maltido calling."

"John, this is Danny. I am on my way."

"Danny I need the combination to landing bay door #1178. We can't get to the landing site."

"No can do. Too much security. That is why I am late. I've been monitoring the military bands. Everyone is looking for you. I'm five minutes out. Good luck."

"Damn!" John exclaimed out loud.

"What?" Yeri asked.

"Danny can't get the combination to the lock."

"Try your jimmy."

"I tried. I set my jimmy down on the lock when a bolt of electricity hit it so hard it burned it out and almost electrocuted me!"

"What?" Ken asked.

"The whole damn gate is electrified except for the keypad. I guess it's a failsafe mechanism in case someone like me wants to break in so don't touch it!" John said.

"We gotta get out of here before the Minister's men find us and time is running out," Yeri said in exasperation.

"Well, I think if we explain why we are here it won't be so bad," Ken said.

"Oh yes it will," John replied. "If his men catch us, we will disappear and it will be blamed on Yeri's explosion."

"So all we need to do is enter the correct sequence of numbers and we're home free. Let's see, that's about one in ten billion? The odds are kind of against us," Yeri said and looked over at Ken.

"It's actually more like one in three hundred and sixty for a four digit code," Ken said. "But we don't know if it is only a four digit code." Ken looked at the keypad deep in thought.

"So what do we do?" Yeri asked. "Start punching in numbers and hope?"

"No, that we take too much time and given that we don't even know how many numbers and the order it would be more like one in ten billion."

"Isn't that what I said earlier?" Yeri exclaimed. "And why are we talking about what can't work?"

Ken turned to Yeri with his eyebrows lowered. "Remember the Cryptas in Room 802?"

"Yeah, what does that have to do with anything?" Yeri said.

"I saw some numbers on one of the documents pinned to the wall and I told you it looked like numbers to a combination or something. Remember?" Ken asked.

"No," Yeri said and turned toward John.

John punched in a combination of numbers and tried the handle. "Nothing," he said and just shrugged his shoulders.

"I think those were the numbers to this lock. I can see the numbers, but I can't quite remember the sequence," Ken said.

John went over to Ken. "We got nothing else. Give it a try."

Ken walked over to the keypad. "Let's see if this works."

8...1...4...2...9...3

He pulled the handle and nothing. "Damn."

"Try again," John shouted over his shoulder as he stared down the hallway.

3...8...1...4...9...2

He pulled the handle and again, nothing happened.

"We're running out of time!" Yeri sang. "I can hear footsteps."

"I know."

1...4...9...2...3...8

"Wait a minute," Yeri said. "I know those numbers."

"You do?" Ken asked.

"Remember your history? The Mayflower? Columbus?"

"Of course. We came to Mars on the Niña, Pinta, and Santa Maria. What does that have to do with anything?"

"What year?" Yeri asked.

"January 17, 0021."

"No, no, no! Not us...Them!"

"Them?"

"Columbus!"

"Oh, them them. That's easy. 1492. Everyone knows that."

"One would think," Yeri smiled at his son.

"That's it!" Ken said. "August third 1492, Columbus sailed the ocean blue! That's gotta be it!"

"Shhh...." Yeri said. "Quit talking and punch in those numbers!"

"Okay, okay." Ken turned to the keypad and pressed the numbers:

8...3...1...4...9...2

Then they heard the bolt unlock. Ken turned the handle. "Let's go!"

The three walked through the door and into the empty chamber. The room had a desk, a chair and a sofa. There was another Plexiglas door on the other side of the room.

"What are you doing?" Ken asked. "You need to close that door!"

"Just give me a minute," John said with his pursal *texpanded* facing the door. He pulled out a small connector from his pursal and inserted it into the lock.

"We don't have a minute," Ken countered as he watched John fiddling with his pursal. "John!"

"Just a minute!" John said as he continued entering numbers into his pursal.

"John!"

"Quiet!" John said after another minute passed. "There. That should do it," John said and shut the door. He gave Ken a look of irritation and then put his pursal to his face. "Call Danny."

"Calling Danny Maltido."

"Is that the landing pad?" Ken asked as he looked through the other Plexiglas door. "It looks like it opens from the top!"

"That's right," John said as he hung up the pursal. The green light above the door turned red.

"Danny's here!" John said.

"Atmosphere Venting Please Standby."

came the computerized voice over the monitor. They could hear a loud rush of air as the landing bay side wall vents opened in order to fill the tanks with oxygen.

"Atmospheric Pressure 0 Millibars. Do Not Enter."

The room started to shake as the roof opened up.

"Here he comes now," John said as the transport descended onto the platform.

"Atmospheric Pressurize 150 Millibars. Please wait."

The three men stood helplessly waiting for the landing bay to repressurize when they heard a loud noise from behind.

BANG! BANG! BANG!

"They're hee'rree," Yeri sang.

"We're too late," Ken exclaimed in exasperation.

"Atmospheric Pressure 500 Millibars. Please Wait."

The Minister smiled as he walked to the door bent down and he punched in the code to the combination lock. He grabbed the handle and turned it, but the lock wouldn't budge. "What the hell?" He reentered the code and still nothing. "Damn it! It's not working!"

"I changed the code," John said into the intercom.

"You?" the Minister screamed. He pulled out his pursal *cellular*. "Donager! Are you still at the front desk?"

"Yes sir."

"Shut up and listen! My office is on the left, there is a jimmy in the wall safe. The code is four then wait exactly two seconds. Then press eight and wait exactly four seconds next press zero one one. Got it!"

"Yes sir!"

"Listen to me. There is a power switch on the wall. Switch it to the OFF position."

Brian grinned as he looked at the switch still in the ON position and said, "Done!"

"Then why am I still talking to you?" the Minister screamed in his pursal.

"Sorry sir!"

The Minister turned and pressed the intercom, "You guys have nowhere to run."

"Atmospheric Pressure - 800 Millibars - Please Wait."

"By the time you figure out how to override or break in we'll be long gone," John said.

"My men are right now getting me my jimmy to unlock this door and you all will be tried for treason," the Minister grinned. "That's if you make it to trial."

Ten minutes had passed when the Minister pulled up his cellular. "Donager! Where are you?"

"On my way, sir," came the response.

"He should've been here by now," the Minister growled.

The door to the Minister's safe opened without a hitch as Brian reached in and grabbed the jimmy. He also grabbed the Minister's code breaking book along with all the notes he had concerning the Halkomelems. He quickly glanced through the information and stuffed it all in a suitcase by the desk. "Let's see the Minister get out of this one!" Brian smiled as he walked out of the Minister's office and suited up. He pulled out his pursal and sent a text. "Got it." He then took one last look around and then opened the front door.

"Another couple of minutes and we're outta here," Dennis said as he looked at the screen showing 900 millibars.

Ken turned to Yeri and sighed. "I'm beginning to miss my little domette."

"Why don't you click your heels together Dorothy and say there is no place like dome," Yeri smiled.

"I forgot my ruby slippers," Ken countered.

"Atmospheric Pressure - 1015 Millibars."

came the computerized voice as the light above the door turned green as they heard the Plexiglas door click.

"He got it!" Danny grinned as he returned his pursal to his belt and quickly exited the transport. The door automatically opened as Danny walked into the waiting area to greet the trio. He saw the Minister and smiled as he took off his helmet and walked over to the Plexiglas door separating him from the Minister and his men.

"Overman?" the Minister looked like he'd seen a ghost. "I thought you died with your men when I blew, I mean when your transport blew up over Ireland!"

"Overman! Dennis Overman!" Yeri turned to Ken. "I knew Danny Maltido didn't sound right."

"The only thing that died that day was my name, Carlos." Dennis Overman smiled. "Mr. Sanchez, when I get finished with you you're going to be wanted for murder both here and back on Earth."

"General! I mean Minister to you, Captain Overman!" Carlos Sanchez yelled. "I don't care what you have on me and since everyone thinks you're already dead, I won't have a problem proving them right. When I open this door Overman you won't be able to escape my wrath," the Minister gave him a sly grin.

"I would love to stand here and talk about old times General but I have your transport to pilot and tomorrow I have an appointment with the Martian High Council. Guess who I'm going to be talking about?"

"I don't think you're going to be around that long. My men will have my jimmy here any minute and we'll see who is going win."

"In that case I guess I should go. I'll see you in court," Dennis said in his all too familiar British accent, smiled and waved goodbye to Carlos.

"Overman! I'm not through with you!" Minister Sanchez yelled into the intercom as the four exited the waiting room and closed and locked the Plexiglas landing door behind them.

"Where is my key? Donager?" Sanchez yelled into his pursal. The Minister turned to his men. "He should have been here by now and we could have stopped them."

"Don...a...ger?! Where are you?" Sanchez once again screamed into his pursal.

"He suited up and left, sir," Sanders said.

"What?"

Then all of a sudden they felt the ground beneath them shake. "NO!!!" Sanchez screamed out loud. "Damn it!" he yelled at the Plexiglas barrier. "I am going to hunt them down and when I catch them," the Minister of Defense turned toward his men and flared, "I'm going to roast them like a pig at a barbecue!"

The ship's engines now at full power ascended through the skylight as the crew flew out into the early morning Martian sky.

"There are suits in the rear and I suggest you put them on if necessary," Dennis said.

"Isn't this the Minister of Defense's private ship?" Ken asked.

"It's like a mini transport," Yeri said.

"How did you get it?" Ken asked as he examined one of the helmets for a fit.

"A jimmy is a nice thing to have around. Wouldn't you agree?" Dennis replied.

"But didn't you give me your jimmy?" Yeri asked.

Dennis nodded. "Brian lent me his."

"How do they work?" Ken asked from the back of the transport.

"Magic," Dennis smiled.

"When did you change your name?" Yeri asked.

"I wanted to go to Mars and I knew the name Overman would raise some flags. When I met with Ana Asea Four in Mexico, I changed my name to Danny Maltido."

"Wouldn't he do a background check?" Ken interrupted.

"I inserted a subroutine to build a persona named Danny Maltido while my pursal was connected to the Ana Asea's grid."

"What if you had gotten caught?" Ken asked.

"I almost did! The Ana Asea noticed that I pressed the button launching the subroutine."

"What did he do then?"

"He thoroughly checked my pursal and found nothing. Fortunately once the subroutine finished I programmed it to erase itself. When it blinked twice I knew I was safe."

"You took a big chance, Dennis," Yeri said.

"It was the only way I could get to Mars."

"I see Carlos has kept his Lander well maintained," Yeri said as the Lander continued floating across the rooftops into the red Martian sky as the men suited up.

The lander passed over the plains of Zea Dorsa located southwest of the city with the four men lost in thought.

"So…those Halks are really humans, eh?" John asked.

"Yeah. Pretty pissed humans if you ask me. The problem I keep running into is how they got here. I haven't seen any ships or heard of any transportation devices."

That was when Ken spoke up. "How many rovers have we uncovered on Mars so far?"

"I don't know. At least a couple dozen or so," Yeri said.

"Thirty-six to be exact," John said.

"Thirty-seven," Ken corrected. "I found another one. We called it *Pat* because that was the name on it."

"*Pat?* Well you found an original. I think the one you found was lost years ago named, Pathfinder?"

"That makes sense. We called it *Pat* because the rest of the name was stripped off from being outside too long. Well, until Tiga named it Friggy."

"Friggy?" Dennis asked.

"Yeah, she said it was something about a Queen of Asgard and Friday," Ken said.

"Well then, perhaps we should call our little transport here Alsvior. That was the name of the chariot that pulled the sun and the moon across the sky," Dennis said as he maneuvered the ship toward Hellas Quadrangle. "Not long now."

"Tiga said we should call Minister of Defense Sanchez, Loki since he is so mischievous." Ken laughed. "I wondered how General Sanchez ever became our Minister of Defense here on Mars."

"He was elected. Remember?" Dennis Overman asked.

"Wait a minute," Yeri remarked. "Sanchez the Minister of Defense is the same as General Sanchez back on Earth?"

"One and the same," Dennis said.

"But he's a Crosser. How did he survive? We don't eat meat here," Yeri said.

"I don't know. I just want to go home," Ken interrupted.

"I'm right there with you Dorothy," Yeri laughed as he put his hand on Ken's shoulder. "It's been a long night."

"Yes it has been, Scarecrow." Ken smiled at Yeri.

"Does that make me the Great and Powerful Oz?" Dennis Overman asked. "After all I'm the one flying you home."

"I've heard you're more like the Cowardly Lion." Yeri laughed.

"What are you talking about?"

"Something about giving cowards medals."

"That's what Sanchez told me on Earth. Where did you hear that?"

"Kim knows Beth from work and she told Beth the story, but she didn't mention it was you. Carlos always had her listening in on his conversations."

"That was his first mistake."

"He never figured on Kim and you getting together, I guess," Ken said.

"Like Ken, I did wonder why we kept finding so many rovers," Dennis remarked.

"I know why. Brian just sent me a text. He has the notes and code book," Yeri said.

"I didn't know Brian was part of all this?" Ken stated.

"Yep. I guess Sanchez figured Donager would never find out how he used him to steal all the WDG's Krugers. I told Brian what we were doing here and he said he had a plan to take down the Minister once and for all and sure enough he knew what he was doing. When Sanchez gave him the combination to the safe, he thought he could trust Donager not to go through his files."

"Oops!"

"Yeah a big mistake. It seems that T-Minus has been eavesdropping on the Earth ships' communication links and when they landed, Sanchez would send his men out to kill the crew, dismantle the ships, and build rovers along with some transport ships like this one," Yeri remarked.

"Except one or two now and again would get away?" Ken asked.

"Like Charlie?" Yeri asked

"Who?" John asked as the transport prepared for descent.

"A Halk that made an unscheduled visit last night and started all this ruckus."

"Be careful on your way to the courthouse tomorrow. I think Minister Sanchez is going to be on a rampage and there's no telling what he might do in order to try and stop us," Dennis said. The transport landed and Dennis dropped off John.

On the way to Ken's dome Ken looked at Dennis. "How did you avoid Sanchez for all of this time? You were one of the guys I would have thought Sanchez would have kept a keen eye on."

Overman showed Ken his thick-rimmed glasses, "I don't need these and I grew a beard, dyed my hair jet black and I always wore a hoody when I worked. Sanchez's ego was so big he never considered a bunch of computer geeks much of a threat, so he really never paid any attention to us." Dennis pulled out a picture of him in disguise and showed it to the group.

"You took a big chance showing Carlos your real self," Yeri said.

"I just wanted to see the look on his face."

Yeri laughed. "It was like he saw the devil."

"He did!" Dennis smiled.

The transport stopped by Ken and Tima's. Ken and Yeri boarded the lift and waited.

"If this was my lift we would be inside already," Yeri said giving Ken a wink.

"I'm not in that much of a hurry," Ken replied as the door opened while the exhaust vented beneath the floor.

"It's about time you two got back," Beth said and she ran and gave Yeri a big hug. "Oh Yeri, I was so scared. That Minister of Defense Sanchez was over here this morning."

"I know, honey. Tomorrow we'll all be meeting with the Martian High Council about Carlos Sanchez." Yeri turned to Ken and Tima. "We gotta go. We have a big day tomorrow you know."

With that Yeri and Beth entered the lift as Yeri looked at Ken. "I'm proud of you, Son, and I'll see you tomorrow."

Ken smiled back as the lift closed.

Yeri and Beth boarded the transport with Dennis waiting at the helm.

"Dennis? Kim told me Sanchez tried to kill you?" Beth asked.

"Sanchez was my superior in the military and he hated me for changing the launch codes during the One Day War. When we were both privates I made it so he couldn't launch the missiles. He blamed me for making him look bad and said my efforts hurt his promotional chances. It was years later when I was instructed to work under him from the Secretary of Defense on Earth. When I found out Sanchez had it in for me I figured he would try to upstage me in arresting a Terra Bull cell I had uncovered. So I gave him some disinformation about where the Terra Bulls were to see if I was right. My team caught the Terra Bulls in Germany while Sanchez's men were roaming around in a cockroach-infested warehouse in England. When he found out what happened, he decided to give us, er, me some payback. Once the prisoners were secured for transport he instructed me to drive my men to London to go on another mission and we had to leave that night. Now Berlin to London is a long ways and I found it interesting he didn't fly us to London. I mean how effective can one be if you had been riding in a military jeep for twelve plus hours? We were also ordered not to talk to anyone. I had requested a few days off, but he refused. He said when we arrived he would explain everything. The problem was when we got there he was very evasive about the mission. That concerned me especially since his raid in London blew up in his face."

"Speaking of blowing up. I read about you guys. That was when Sanchez was promoted from being a colonel all the way to a general. How did you survive the explosion?"

"Once everyone was aboard the airplane, I left the airfield. I contacted an old friend of mine who had a jet on a nearby runway to take me to Greenland. He could get me there in half the time of that old transport. This would give me some time to find out what was going on. Why all the secrecy? I wanted to meet this contact of Sanchez's before my team arrived. If necessary I was going to speak to the Ana Aseas myself. I didn't want to put my team in unnecessary danger, even if it meant a court martial."

"What did you find out?"

"There was no contact. Sanchez orchestrated the whole thing so he could take the credit for arresting the Terra Bulls."

"Jesus! He killed his own men for a promotion?"

"Sure did. Sanchez thought he killed me along with the others and his secret would be safe. I let him think that and so I simply went off the grid. I changed my name from Dennis Overman to Danny Maltido. Maltido meaning *little devil*."

"Well that was appropriate."

"Back on Earth I had some contacts in the field of Cryptography and so I called in some favors. We spent months working on advanced algorithms along with a couple of Crypto-machines I bugged. They were the new CR-900s. Kim, his secretary, provided me with Sanchez's transmission codes. So any receiving and decoding transmissions he got came to me a millisecond before Sanchez received it."

"So you knew what Sanchez was doing when he called Brian Donager at the WDG?"

"I knew everything. Even the snipers he sent in to kill the villagers and they even killed some of his own men in Luanshya."

"Why didn't you tell someone?"

"I did. I contacted a friend of mine Kevin Wilson. He had gotten promoted to Special Agent and I knew he would love to get his hands on Sanchez, but he was killed in the Federal Building explosion."

"The one in New York?"

"That's the one. After that I laid low. You don't live long going after a man like Sanchez unless you are prepared to withstand his retaliation. Sanchez was too smart, too powerful to get his hand caught in the cookie jar. Anyway, without legal concrete evidence, no one would believe me over the word of a hero. In fact, he could have just as easily blamed me for the transport explosion. He could have easily accused me of killing my own men. I mean why else would I have not been on that transport? I was also under investigation for the failed Terra Bull raid on Summerhill Ranch thanks to Sanchez."

"Good point."

"I didn't think it really mattered at the time because I had overheard all I needed about Sanchez and his communications to the Ana Asea Sevens. I knew Earth was toast so I gained an audience with Ana Asea Four in Mexico and made a compelling case to why my team was needed on Mars."

"But Mars had the CR-1000s now."

"And who do you think programmed them?" Dennis smiled. "I created a subroutine that would copy and send me any information that the CR-1000s captured concerning any transmissions coming in or going out."

"So you knew all the time what was going on with the Halkomelems? Why didn't you expose him back then?"

"Like I said, you don't live long crossing Sanchez. Again he could have said I fabricated the transmissions and where is the evidence? And don't forget. I would have had to expose my true identity and I was a wanted man back on Earth. The idea of serving time in Hershel was not appealing either and I wasn't about to take that chance."

"So how did you evade Sanchez for so long?"

"I had been dating his secretary, Kim, for quite a while and we decided to make it a more permanent relationship. Sanchez brought her to Mars with him and so all she had to do was keep me aware of his schedule. He wasn't interested in a bunch of computer geeks anyway, but he would show up now and again just to instill a little fear in case we tried anything underhanded."

"Didn't he wonder why you were never there when he passed through?"

"Nah. He considered us weak and worthless, and he had other pressing matters than to keep up tabs on my whereabouts. In fact, as long as he had his guards watching us, he didn't think there would be anything to really worry about."

The transport touched down at Yeri and Beth's. Yeri bid Dennis goodbye and entered the lift. As the lift descended Yeri said out loud, "It's nice to be home."

Thornton Residence
Domette 64
Gemini - Sol Saturday 7, 0012
1500 hours

"Ken?" Tima shook him once again. "Wake up."

"Huh? What time is it? We have a meeting with the Council."

"It's three in the afternoon. Yeri called an hour ago and he said the meeting with the High Council had to be rescheduled at nine tomorrow morning."

"Oh god. We have to be careful that Sanchez doesn't try anything."

"I don't think he'll be doing much. Mr. Sanchez has been charged for treason."

"Who turned him in?" Ken asked.

"One of his own. Yeri said it was Brian Donager."

"Brian? He's the one Dad was telling me about. Brian was in charge of the World Development Group back on Earth," Ken said.

"Yeah, well it seems Sanchez had double-crossed Brian concerning a relocation situation in Africa. Yeri told Brian what Sanchez did to him on their way to Mars and Brian vowed to get some payback. I guess he finally did. This morning he showed the Council the code books and documents he took from the Minister's safe earlier this morning. He also told them about the Cryptographic Recorders in room 802. They have the police guarding 802 right now in case Sanchez shows up. At ten this morning the Council agreed there was enough hard evidence to bring charges."

"Has Sanchez been arrested?" Ken asked.

"Nope. He seems to have disappeared for now," Tima said.

"I guess he figured it out when he saw everything missing from his safe."

"There is talk that he is heading for Hershel."

"The prison? I wonder why?" Ken asked.

"I don't know but that's what Yeri thinks," Tima said.

"Oops," Ken saw his spacesuit hanging in the closet. "Forgot to recharge it again." Ken walked over to a socket and plugged it in.

"Are you hungry?" Tima asked.

"I need to go into my lab for awhile. I have a dozen of those worthless Elotec actuators in need of repair," Ken said. "Can you bring breakfast in here when it's ready?"

She looked at Ken and said, "Sure. Breakfast or dinner. Whatever you want to call it will be ready in an hour."

"Thanks."

"I hear it's going to be a beautiful night for star gazing."

Ken smiled. "Tomorrow is going to be a big day for us and all of Mars..."

Chapter 32

MARS

Thornton Residence
Domette 64
Gemini - Sol Saturday 7, 0012
1945 hours

KA-BOOM!

A flurry of fire and explosion rocked the colonies once again. People were dying and there was nowhere to run for safety except to Sanctuary if you had time to get there.

KA-BOOM!

Ken grabbed the escape hatch once more and pulled as hard as he could. "It's still stuck! We have to get out of here before those shockwaves hit."

As soon as the words left Ken's tongue another fireball flashed by their dome as the lights from hell's arrows brightened the room with an eerie glow of death. Soon came another resounding boom as the Thorntons felt their domette shake as the plaster from the roof and walls fell all around them. Their house was dying and if they couldn't get out it would soon take them with it.

"Damn it! They're getting closer," Ken said and brushed off more debris from the handle. "Ouch!" He moved his other hand quickly away from the floor.

"What's wrong Hon?" Tima asked as her eyesight began to clear. Everything looked hazy, but she was glad to be able to see, even if it lasted only a short time. "Is there something wrong with your arm?"

"I'm bleeding. There's glass everywhere," Ken sighed and then they felt a rumbling from the other side of the house. They all looked across to the bedrooms as they heard a large crashing sound.

"Oh my god! What was that?" Tima asked.

"The bedrooms have collapsed. We're running out of time!" Ken shouted.

"Did you secure the hallway door?" Tima asked.

"We wouldn't be alive if I didn't," Ken said and looked at Tima. *We might not be alive much longer even if I did,* Ken thought to himself. As another flash passed through the domette, Ken quickly looked down and saw a keyhole. "What in the..." In an instant he knew exactly why the hatch wouldn't budge.

"Locked? It's locked... The hatch is locked!" Ken screamed and beat the hatch door with his fist. He looked at Tima and saw the tears. "How can it be locked?"

"I did it!" Togo said.

Ken looked in disbelief at his son. "What?"

"With Grandpa's jimmy. He gave it to me for my birthday present and it works too!"

"Why did you lock the hatch?" Ken tried to calm his nerves as the walls all around them continued to crack throwing even more pieces of paint and plaster toward the floor. The bedrooms were gone and he knew it was only a matter of minutes before the skylight, along with the whole domette would cave in.

"So no one would sneak in our house and steal my key. Grandpa said there was an evil man after it."

"Can I see your key?"

"Grandpa told me to keep it hidden."

"Where did you hide it?" Ken asked.

"In my bedroom under my pillow," Togo said.

Just then another flash appeared in the distance and Ken knew if he didn't do something soon, those shockwaves would be the final blow to their now fragile little house.

"The hallway has been sealed off!" Tima said. "The bedrooms have collapsed. What are we going to do?"

Ken looked around the wreckage they once called home. "Maybe a pry bar will work. I got to find something to break this lock or..."

"...but I guess you can see it," Togo interrupted.

"Don't interrupt your ....What did you say?" Tima asked.

"Do you want to see it?" Togo asked.

"I thought it was under your pillow," Ken said.

"Only when I am sleeping. I have it on a chain around my neck the rest of the time," Togo said and with that he pulled out a necklace with the jimmy dangling in the fading light.

Ken pulled the key from Togo's neck and inserted the jimmy into the lock, turned it and pulled. He tried the handle and nothing happened. "It's still locked." Ken had a perplexed look on his face as he stared at the hatch.

"It works Daddy. I promise."

Ken tried again and still nothing. "No it doesn't."

Togo gently pushed Ken aside. "Let me try, Daddy."

Ken looked at his wife and she shrugged. "If we can't open the hatch…" she said and just looked away.

"Might as well. Okay little guy – here," Ken handed Togo the key and watched as his son placed the key into the lock. Ken bent over to turn the key like before, but Togo grabbed his hand. "No, Daddy. You have to wait until you see the handle."

"What handle?" Ken asked.

"You know, the handle that comes out when the key's ready. It will tell you," Togo said and waited. All of a sudden a squared handle grew out from the rounded shaft of the jimmy. "There it is," Togo said.

Ken shook his head in disbelief as Togo turned the key and this time they heard the tumblers click. He grabbed the hatch and it easily lifted with the help of the hydraulics underneath it. "Let's go!" Ken said as a grin appeared on his worn face.

Tima watched as Ken crawled on hands and knees into the narrow passage way. "You're next, Togo." Tima said.

"Daddy has my key."

"He'll give it back to you on the other side."

"What's on the other side?"

"Just go!" Tima said in exasperation. Togo slowly crawled into the tunnel. "Okay Tiga, your turn."

"I want to go with you," Tiga said as her grip tightened on Tima's sleeve.

"You have to follow your brother. I'll be right behind you. Now hurry!" Tima said as the house made another rumbling sound.

"Okay," Tiga released her death grip on Tima. As Tima surveyed the tunnel she noticed there was only one way to close the hatch. She backed into the tunnel closed and secured the metal door. "The hatch is secure, but I can't turn around!" Tima exclaimed.

"I don't know what to tell you," Ken said.

"In other words, I have to do this crawling backwards!" she said out loud.

"I guess they didn't think we would ever have to use these things," Ken said.

"I bet you don't have to crawl backwards using Yeri's DTs."

"I'm sure there's an upgrade we haven't heard about," Ken replied. "But if I know Dad, he'll surely tell me all about it next time I see him."

A few minutes had passed as they struggled down the passageway when they all heard a thundering sound pelting down on the closed hatch.

"Whew," Ken said, "that was just too close."

"I wonder how many made it to Sanctuary?" Tima asked.

"We'll find out when we get there," Ken said as he turned on the air vents. "Come on Tiga, Togo keep crawling. I don't know how long our hatch can keep that Martian atmosphere out."

An hour passed while the little family continued crawling in darkness on hands and knees.

"I'm tired," Togo said.

"Okay everyone take a break. I know it is a long tunnel, but no one thought we would ever have to use it."

"Good thing we have it," Tima said as sweat fell from her brow. "It's hot in here."

"Well, we are underground in close quarters. I haven't been this warm in a long time. Feels kind of good to tell you the truth."

"How much further?" Tiga asked. "I gotta go potty."

"Just hold it, we're halfway there."

"God, I hope so," Tima said.

Two hours total had elapsed when Ken's head hit a wall.

BANG!

"Ouch! I guess we're here." He pulled out his PeeP and shook it one more time. The light glowed as he found the handle and turned it. "I hope there still is a Sanctuary on the other side!" He said a little prayer as he slowly turned the handle. The hydraulics kicked in as the hatch popped open. Ken stuck his head into the room.

"Ken! You made it!" came a familiar voice.

"Did you ever doubt?" Ken said as he climbed out of the tube.

"What took you so long?"

"We had a few hiccups on the way, and not to mention," Ken shook his head, "it's a long crawl!"

"You know they have a new upgrade for the DTs now. You can get a roller slide. Instead of crawling you can just get on the slide and it will…"

"…get you to Sanctuary in half the time?" Ken interrupted his dad as they both laughed.

Chapter 33

MARS

Sanctuary
Dome 1
Dao Vallis, Hellas Planitia
Hellas Quadrangle, Mars
Gemini - Sol Sunday 8, 0012
0700 hours

The following morning was quiet. The Sanctuary satellite monitors showed how many buildings had been destroyed. The infrared cameras focused on the burning plasma meteors as they smoldered throwing off their deadly heat in all directions.

"What in the hell happened last night?" Syrtis Major's Governor Philips asked.

Ken stepped forward. "We've been attacked."

"I know we've been attacked," the Governor said. "I just don't know why and from whom?"

Brian moved closer to the Governor. "I know," Brian said and then whispered in his ear, "and you're not going to like what you're about to hear."

Brian along with Yeri, Dennis, John, and Ken told the Governor about how the Minister of Defense, Carlos Sanchez, was a Crosser and since he could only eat meat, the only food available were the dead prisoners at Herschel.

"Haven't you ever wondered why so many prisoners died in their first year at Hershel?" Ken asked.

They then explained how Earth had been sending emissaries to Mars to find out what had happened to them. The only problem was that none of them reported back to Earth. It seemed Sanchez found this to be an additional food source so he and some of his T-Minus team who were also Crossers captured those who came from Earth. The Earth Crossers had brought their own food knowing there was nothing for them to eat on Mars. Sanchez intercepted their communications to the Minister of Travel and told them he was the liaison between Earth and Mars. He instructed them where to land in what was usually a remote area near the colder regions of Mars, and then he killed them and ate their food. He destroyed and rebuilt their ships into rovers and then killed the rest of the Crossers to feed himself and his men. He kept the dead ones they didn't eat in an ice crater near Hershel. It was much like keeping some steaks in the freezer.

Once in awhile when he captured a ship he would release one or two of the Earth Crossers without spacesuits near one of the cities on Mars exposing them to this harsh Martian climate. Without protection their DNA quickly adapted to its new environment and they became what we referred to as a Halkomelem. The Halks were nothing more than Crossers. When they were suddenly exposed to the Martian atmosphere their body and brain quickly adapted to their new environment. Their bodies and ability to reason were replaced with more of a cold-blooded reptilian type of being in order to survive this hostile planet's atmosphere.

"I think the reason Sanchez did this was to create fear and it definitely kept his job secure as Minister of Defense. This allowed him a lot freedom since the Martian people were being randomly killed and some simply disappeared because of the Halks. Haven't you noticed how hush-hush it became when one was captured?" Yeri asked.

"I figured T-Minus was doing a good job controlling these Halk things. I never realized Sanchez was the one creating this mess," the Governor said nervously. "We should have seen this coming."

"We can never predict what can happen when we mindlessly dabble with DNA and genetics. It was like playing a game of chess with Mother Nature. She just responded to the moves we made and unless you can see what moves you opened up for her to make you may find yourself playing a game you can't win," Ken said.

"You see, Mr. Sanchez always had a violent side to him and when he became a Crosser it enhanced that aggression. A human carnivore must kill and eat whatever it can find to survive and that can mean us if necessary. It's disgusting, but in his world, it was his only option," Yeri added.

The Governor turned to Yeri. "We can't keep him and his men here, because we can't feed them. And as citizens of Mars we can't send them back to Earth." The Governor shook his head. "So what do we do?"

"First I think we need to open the lines of communications with Earth," Brian said.

It was late afternoon when the Governor called a meeting with all the heads of the different provinces and a special message was sent to Earth: A proposal for peace. They now understood why Mars had been attacked and they promised that those responsible for destroying and killing the emissaries from Earth would be punished. The letter also warned that those who had undergone any hybridization procedures would be better served to remain on Earth. The conditions on Mars could and did cause undesirable traits to quickly emerge if a Crosser became exposed.

The Council of Elders on Earth responded within hours of receiving the messages from the Governor of Mars. The Council sent their own message apologizing for the destruction they inflicted on the Red Planet. They, being Crossers themselves, realized their tendencies were more toward the violent side and in haste they chose war over communication. They then offered to send a prisoner transport for those responsible along with some ships supplied with materials in an effort help rebuild Mars.

After the meeting Governor Philips walked over to where Ken, Yeri, and the rest were standing and smiled.

"What's the verdict?" Yeri asked.

"Earth agreed to send some ships supplied with materials in an effort to help us rebuild our cities and towns."

"That's nice, but what about Sanchez and his crew?" Ken asked.

"A prisoner transport is already in route as we speak," the Governor replied.

"A prisoner transport?" Ken asked.

"It will be here in less than a week."

"But I thought being a citizen of Mars means Sanchez and his men cannot be extradited to Earth," Brian said.

"I thought so too, but it has been brought to my attention that in our Articles of Citizenship Section V in the Martian Constitution of the People states that no one who had undergone hybridization or requires meat to survive shall be allowed citizenship."

"So can we send them back?" Brian asked.

"As soon as the prisoner transport arrives he and his men will return to answer for their crimes against humanity."

"What do you think they will do with Sanchez and his men?" Ken asked.

"They will probably live out their extended lives of almost immortality in prison."

"That is truly a fate worse than death if you ask me. Living hundreds and hundreds of years without a possibility of parole," Tima said. "I almost feel sorry for him."

"What?" Ken asked.

"I said almost," Tima said as a slight grin crossed her face.

Ken, Tima, Yeri, Beth, and Brian all walked with the Governor over to the window and gazed out at their cold, Martian world. In the distance there appeared a blue and white ball happily turning and floating free and easy. Ken sighed, remembering from where they had come. He turned and looked at his fellow Martians. On their faces, he could see the sadness and loneliness each felt being so far from their real mother. They missed the warmth and nurturing Earth had once provided. Now it was just a distant neighbor slowly turning in its own carefree manner.

A tear found its way down the face of Governor Philips as he remembered happier times. Ken, standing next to him, placed a hand on the Governor's shoulder in an attempt to comfort him and said, "Now the rebuilding can begin and hopefully one day we can find a way to return to our real home... Earth."

Epilogue

This book was written hopefully as a fictional account of what our future holds, or at least it is one account of what our future could hold. The chemical and pharmaceutical corporations are genetically altering our food without disclosing this information to the consumers. If what they are doing is safe, then why all of the secrecy? More and more of our crops are being altered in the name of helping man, or is it really helping the bottom line? Have you ever asked yourself why so many allergies have appeared so suddenly? Gluten? Peanuts? Fish? Where were they before GMOs and seed oils?

We didn't learn about the unintended consequences when we turned the friendly honeybee into a vicious killer and no one knows how to right this wrong. We now have to live with these aggressive and dangerous creatures that until now had never roamed our planet.

The pharmaceutical and chemical companies may see their bottom lines increase from selling DNA-altered seeds to our farmers, but who is going to pay the bill? Man has been given everything he needs to survive on this earth. Do we really need to eat genetically altered foods? Do we know the long-term effects and if we could peer into tomorrow would it be a better world? Can man in just a few short years improve upon what nature has provided us for thousands and thousands of years? If I were a betting man, I would put my chips on the side of nature. Since we've altered our eating habits it is no coincidence that we are experiencing a dramatic rise in cancer, heart attacks, diabetes, and gout, just to name a few.

The advent of air warning systems in some of our cities is an anathema to nature. Instead of addressing the problems of air pollution, we simply put out a sign?

Regardless of what we think about fossil fuels, there are two things we know. One is that they pollute our air, which is the most important element for human survival and secondly, fossil fuels are nonrenewable. As our planet becomes more and more advanced, energy is becoming more and more in demand. There is no way around it, but there is a way through it.

You have more choices about helping your planet than you realize. You can choose more Earth-friendly energy sources or not. Ask yourself do my needs really justify buying that big gas guzzling SUV or would a hybrid SUV be sufficient? Your purchases drive what is produced and not the other way around. If we want to help our planet, then it is up to us to spend our money in an intelligent and thoughtful way always asking, "will buying this help or hurt my world?"

All change, good and bad, comes from knowledge. The most effective way to bring about change in the world today is through the dollars we spend every day. If we quit buying products that contain vegetable oils and preservatives and/or come from genetically altered seeds, those companies will have to discontinue adding those ingredients to their products or go out of business. If we opt for more fuel-efficient vehicles, the car companies will make fuel-efficient vehicles. If we pull our support away from the politicians who promote the wasteful uses of our planet's resources then there will arise politicians who are more earth friendly.

If you think, *what difference can I make when there are millions of others that continue to support those that pollute our planet,* take heart. As you change your habits and beliefs you will begin to impact others. We are already seeing more organic vegetables and dairy in our grocery stores. You can even buy grass-fed beef. These changes are not random events, but based on a growing consumer base who wants to eat natural foods instead of those laced with chemicals and altered DNA strands. If we refuse to eat products with questionable chemicals, the manufacturer will quit adding them. After all, how can BHA and BHT keep something "fresh?" How can a chemical keep it fresh? It can't, it just changes the molecular structure of the food so it can sit on the grocery store shelf longer. Without adding those chemicals the food will naturally decay and stink. The nasty smell is a warning not to eat that food. But then if you don't eat it, the manufacturer will have it eat into his profits. That is why he laces his food with chemicals so it can last longer without smelling and he is hoping you will buy it and consume it.

Where does change begin? The journey to help our planet begins with you.

Mars is a pretty planet to observe on those clear nights, but I don't want to live there and I don't want my children or my children's children to have to make that choice either. Our tomorrows are built on our choices today.

Glossary

ANA ASEA Sevens

A - Asia
N - North America
A - Africa

A - Australia
S - South America
E - Europe
A - Antarctica

Hush Little Baby

Hush, little Baby, don't say a word,
Mama's gonna buy you a Mockingbird.

And if that mockingbird don't sing,
Mama's gonna buy you a diamond ring.

And if that diamond ring turns brass,
Mama's gonna buy you a looking glass.

And if that looking glass gets broke,
Mama's gonna buy you a billy goat,

And if that billy goat won't pull,
Mama's gonna buy you a cart and a bull.

And if that cart and bull turn over,
Mama's gonna buy you a dog named Rover.

And if that dog named Rover won't bark,
Mama's gonna buy you a horse and a cart.

And if that horse and cart fall down,
You'll still be the sweetest little baby in town.

About the Author

Barry Brown plays golf and chess in his spare time and also enjoys shooting pool. He loves vacationing in Myrtle Beach every year with his family. When he's not writing, he can be found working in his vegetable garden growing organic crops. He lives with his wife, two sons, one cat, and two dogs near Charlottesville, Virginia.

www.ingramcontent.com/pod-product-compliance
Lightning Source LLC
Chambersburg PA
CBHW070042120726
47909CB00002B/275